WHISPERING THREADS

WHISPERING THREADS

A Virginia Davies Quilt Mystery
Book Four

By
David Ciambrone

Names, characters, businesses, places, events, and incidents are either the products of the author's imagination or used in a fictitious manner. Any resemblance to actual persons, living or dead, or actual events, is purely coincidental.

No part of this publication may be reproduced, stored in a retrieval system, or transmitted in any form or by any means, electronic, mechanical, photocopying, recording, or otherwise, without the written permission of the publisher.

Text Copyright © 2022 David Ciambrone

All rights reserved.
Published 2022 by Progressive Rising Phoenix Press, LLC
www.progressiverisingphoenix.com

ISBN: 978-1-958640-13-5

Printed in the U.S.A.

Book and Cover design by William Speir
Visit: http://www.williamspeir.com

This title was originally published by
White Bird Publications
ISBN: 978-1-63363-327-8
LCCN: 2018950387

ACKNOWLEDGMENTS

Writing is a solitary affair, but, any author will also tell you their writing depends on a host of others who have provided needed information, ideas, inspiration, critiques, just plain support when we needed it and someone to listen when things go array. To this end, I'd like to thank the following people and groups for their support bringing this book to life.

The Williamson County Coroners for their sound critiques and support.

My publisher, Amanda M. Thrasher, at Progressive Rising Phoenix Press.

My wife Kathy for her support, and wonderful ideas for the story.

Now retired, Supervisory Deputy U.S. Marshal Hector Gomez

CHAPTER 1

With a large black backpack slung over her shoulder, Virginia Davies Clark hurried down the main corridor of the Orange County John Wayne airport toward the escalator to baggage claim. She brushed a strand of blonde hair from her face as she rode down toward the baggage claim carousels. After a quick glance at the people below, she spotted her old friend, and sometimes co-conspirator, Donna Bolette. Virginia reached the bottom level and hurried to Donna.

With shoulder-length dark-brown hair, large brown eyes, and an olive complexion, Donna had the men that were standing around waiting for their bags watching her. She hugged Virginia when she reached the luggage carousel. "Well, Virginia, we're going to Rancho Mirage to a quilt retreat?" She looked at the carousel as it started to turn. "I'm packed and ready. We can take my car, so cancel your rental."

Virginia looked at Donna. "You're going? What about your travel agency... your clients?"

"That's what staff is for, my dear. It's a perk of being the owner. Anyway, my husband is out of town on business, so I figured my bikini and a little sun and pool time in the desert would be good for me. And we haven't been able to get together for some time."

Virginia pointed, "There are my bags. Oh, that red box with the straps is mine, too. I'm glad you're coming. While we're there, I want you to meet a lady who is a great quilter and a desert rat. She owns eleven square miles of desert and mountains out there. From a hill near her house, you can see the Salton Sea."

"Sounds like fun." Donna helped Virginia yank her bags and box from the carousel and extend the handles. "My car is this way." She walked toward the large glass doors with Virginia catching up. "I got us reservations at the hotel where the retreat is. That way you got a discount. Where does your friend live?"

"South of Palm Desert, in the middle of nowhere. She has a large southwestern designed ranch house. She has quilts, rocks, gems, minerals, and old maps. She's got legends about the old days in the Coachella Valley and the area around there, too. Her quilt room is the size of my living room. I'll call her after we check into the hotel."

"Okay," Donna said. "Here is my car. Let's load up and head out before traffic gets heavier."

Virginia walked up to the white Infiniti QX80. "Nice. An SUV? Where do you go off-roading, the mall?"

"Very funny." Donna touched the door handle and the doors unlocked. "It's got four-wheel drive and a four-hundred horsepower engine and leather seats. It also gets shitty gas mileage. But the air conditioning is to die for, and we'll need it where we're going."

They loaded Virginia's suitcases and box next to Donna's three bags.

Donna closed the tailgate. "I was going to ask, what's in the box?"

"My travel sewing machine."

Donna turned and gave Virginia a blank look. "A traveling sewing machine? You serious?"

"Yeah. I wasn't going to bring my Bernina to the retreat, so I got a rugged one, and Andy's grad students made a special case for it. That thing can take a five-foot drop on concrete and not have any damage. It's got my machine and all its accessories in it, and it doesn't weigh that much."

Donna slid into the driver's seat and buckled up as Virginia got in the front passenger side. Donna started the car and glanced at Virginia. "I bet TSA had a ball with that."

"Oh yeah. I had to tell them about it and show it to the airline counter lady. The security locks the students put on it would stop locksmiths, TSA, and Houdini from getting in without the key."

Donna frowned. "Why the special locks?"

"Well, I mentioned I didn't want it easily opened, so Andy's graduate students went a little overboard in the design. They were quite proud of their security mechanisms."

As they drove through the traffic on the freeways, Virginia kept eagerly twisting and turning, looking out the windows at the landscape where she had once lived. "Things have gotten even more crowded since Andy and I moved to Texas a few years ago. But I still miss southern California. How many places can you have breakfast on the beach, play in the snow in the mountains, have dinner in the desert, and then go home at the end of the day?"

"In this country, none that I know of, but here. So, this friend of yours we're going to see, what does she do for a living?"

"She has a boatload of money and doesn't really work. She minds her property, does quilting, and belongs to multiple quilt guilds. She's also into rocks, gems, and mineral hunting, and I think she has a mine or two on her land. Trust me; she'll show them to us. Her husband died a few years ago.

He left her a rich widow. He had just banked a ton of cash by selling his software or computer type business he had started. He didn't need to work for the rest of his life. Only it ended too soon."

"What did he die of?"

"I'm not sure."

"How do you know her?"

"Well, she's a quilter and teaches classes all over the west. I had her for some classes, and we hit it off. She donated some items to my museum in Texas, the San Gabriel Museum, and the one I worked for in Orange County, the Southbrook Museum. Her husband and Andy had become friends, too."

"What's her name?"

"Carol Jean Putman. And she's sixty, thin, attractive, and can run circles around both of us. She's got a lot of energy."

"I like her already."

Virginia settled back and watched the scenery start to turn more desert-like as they drove east on Interstate 10. "She's anxious to see us. She wants to tell us about her newest quest. It's something about a ship, or ships, of the desert, a treasure, and some strange rocks."

CHAPTER 2

Virginia and Donna followed the bellhop to their adjoining rooms, on the second floor overlooking the golf course, at the Omni Rancho Las Palmas Resort in the Rancho Mirage. After tipping him, they opened the connecting door and unpacked. Virginia looked in on Donna. "I'm heading down to the lobby to find out about registration for the quilt retreat. What are you going to do?"

Donna held up her fire engine red, string bikini. "I'm going to the pool, get some sun, and have a drink. Find me when you're done." She looked out the sliding glass door at the view of bright green fairways, tall palm trees, and a sparkling pool. "By the way, when does this quilt shindig of yours actually start?"

"Tomorrow morning."

"Don't wake me."

"I'll be back shortly. I'm just getting my credentials, tote bag, schedule, and whatever other stuff they have. No meetings today. While I'm checking-in to the retreat, I'll call Carol Putman. I'll ask her if she'd like to have dinner with us here tonight."

"Okay, sounds like a plan. Come get me by the pool when you're finished."

Sometime later, Virginia, in her bright blue bikini and floppy straw hat and carrying a towel, strolled to the pool, and reclined on a chaise lounge next to Donna. She looked at her friend. "I see you've had a few colorful drinks and haven't gotten wet yet."

Donna removed her sunglasses and turned toward Virginia. "Yeah, four to be precise. I only paid for one. Those two nice gentlemen by the pool bar have been very attentive. And cute."

"I'm surprised they aren't sitting around you vying for your attention."

"They were. I told them to keep cool until my friend came. Then the odds would be better."

Virginia removed her hat and fluffed her hair. "You didn't."

Donna glanced at the two men. "Yep. Now, they'll be trying to buy you drinks, too, and get us to play in the pool with them."

Virginia spread her towel on the chaise lounge and laid back. "Play in the pool and elsewhere. You do remember we're married, don't you?"

"Yes. But it's fun to flirt. And I'm a little over a hundred miles from home, and you're about fifteen hundred. So, what happens in the desert stays in the desert."

"You honestly believe that?"

Donna pointed at the huge, rocky, barren, mountain with green tree on top. "Isn't that Mt. San Jacinto? That thing seems to have just sprouted from the desert straight up to what—11,000 feet?"

"Yes, that's the mountain. And stop changing the subject."

Donna chuckled. "Okay. Not really. But it's fun to fantasize." Donna put her sunglasses back on. "Don't look now, but here they come."

Virginia watched as the two men walked toward them. They stopped. A man with black wavy hair, in a bright Hawaiian fabric and surfer style bathing suit, sat next to Donna, while the other brown-haired man with a tank top and surfer style bathing suit, sat next to Virginia. They engaged in small talk, had a couple of drinks, and Virginia and Donna took a dip in the pool with them. About four o'clock, the men asked if Virginia and Donna would like to have dinner with them.

Virginia gave them her sad face and said, "We'd love to. But I'm terribly sorry, fellas, we already have dinner plans tonight. We're dinning with a rancher." Her face brightened. "How about tomorrow, say seven?"

The men smiled. The taller of the two said, "Tomorrow would be great. We'll see you in the lobby at seven tomorrow night."

Donna touched one of the men's legs. "That sounds great. Sorry about tonight." She watched them move away. She turned to Virginia. "We have dinner plans tonight? You called Mrs. Putman?"

"Yes. She's expecting us at six at her place. I got directions. She's excited to see us."

Donna looked in the direction the men had taken, then back at Virginia. "So, let me get this straight. We're spending the evening with this eccentric friend of yours instead of being wined and dined and flirted with by two young and handsome businessmen, probably with expense accounts, who would love to seduce us?"

"They're reps of some type for some mining company, aren't they?"

Donna scowled. "Your point?"

"It would get boring."

"Your guy, the one sitting next to you, James, is an engineer. You like engineers. Your husband is an engineer."

"He's not my guy." Virginia looked where the men had gone. "He is? An engineer? Nuts."

"Told ya."

Virginia frowned at Donna. "How do you know he's an engineer?"

"He told me. He's a mining engineer." Donna took a breath. "They both told me what they do, who they worked for, and what they're doing here."

"Oh. So the one who was drooling over you? What's his name?"

"Paul. You have a poor memory. Probably from being married so long. And he has a degree in geology."

"Okay, Miss Marple," Virginia said. "What are they doing here?"

"They are searching for an exotic mineral near here, even on or near your friend's ranch. They'll be here for a week or so. My guess is we'll be seeing more of them." Donna sighed. "I hope."

"I bet you're right." Virginia looked at the clock on the side of the pool bar. "We should be getting ready."

Donna took the last sip of her drink and stood. "Okay, let's go see your friend. If she's got all the interests you said she has; this could be intriguing. Oh, since you know where we're going, you drive tonight."

At six that evening, after driving past a seemingly endless series of expensive houses, pristine shopping arcades, and lush green golf courses, all interspersed by tall palm trees and other desert plants. They pulled off the main road and onto a dirt side path.

Donna leaned forward and looked at the path. "I'm glad this car has 4-wheel drive and high ground clearance. And thank God, and because it's so hot, I also thank Infiniti, for the great air conditioning."

"I agree. Now, it seems to be a great investment." Virginia drove another two miles over the dusty, rut-filled road, past various, but sparsely populated, desert cacti, aloe, Ocotillo, creosote-bush scrub, Joshua trees, California fan palms, and various colored and textured rocks. She stopped at a rusting iron gate held in place by two stone columns. The sand had piled on the south sides driven by the relentless, slow-moving, winds.

Donna glanced around. "Hot and desolate. The gate's closed. Now what?"

Virginia bent forward, then pointed. "There's a camera." She lowered the side window and looked at a small black metal box set into the stone column. She heard a voice. "Virginia?"

"Yes, Carol. It's Virginia and Donna."

"Good. I'm opening the gate. Drive through and follow the road about a mile up the hill."

"Okay." Virginia raised the window. When the gate swung open, she drove up the incline to a large, stuccoed, ranch house, with a red tile roof. Two satellite dishes were mounted on the lower side of the roof over the four-car garage. Three other buildings were off to the side. One structure was about six stories tall. Virginia swung the car under the front portico and parked. She and Donna slipped out of the SUV and started for the ornately carved and stained, wooden front doors when they flew open. Carol Putman stepped out.

Virginia looked at Carol's five foot five, slim figure. Her graying, black hair was shoulder length and turned up at the collar of her western styled shirt. She wore jeans and cowboy boots. She had a turquoise and silver necklace with matching bracelets. "Carol, nice to see you again." Virginia hugged her. Turning, she motioned toward Donna. "Carol, this is my old friend, Donna Bolette."

Carol gave Donna a hug and welcomed her. "Let's go inside where it's cooler. She stepped aside, and Virginia and Donna entered. Carol closed the big doors and led them into the living room. It looked to be the size of a hotel lobby and was decorated like a Spanish hacienda.

Donna stopped and took in the size of the room. "This is even more spectacular than Virginia described. It's beautiful."

"Thank you. It's comfortable. Don't get to spend a lot of time in here. Got a large piece of dessert to manage." Carol motioned to a couple of overstuffed leather chairs near a huge stone fireplace with an opening large enough to roast a whole pig. They all sat.

Donna looked out the large glass sliding doors onto a covered patio with outdoor kitchen and another stone fireplace. Beyond was a spectacular view of the colorful desert at sunset. "How big is your ranch?"

"Not really a ranch, honey. More like a vast expanse of rock and dirt that is colorful in both beauty and history. My spread is about eleven square miles. Got a lot of natural critters, a couple mines, mineral deposits, and a mix of flora and fauna. I've got a few geothermal springs here, too. They're related to the San Andreas fault that runs not too far from here."

"I'd love to see some of it sometime. Do you get many visitors?"

"I'd be happy to show you around while you two are in town. Normally things are pretty quiet around here. Most of my guests are snakes, coyotes, birds, and other creatures. I don't bother them, and they reciprocate. But lately, I've been looking into some strange goings-on."

Virginia sat closer to the edge of her chair. "Like what?"

"Well, a while back, I found some strange rocks I couldn't identify." Carol's expression changed to serious. "Also, there's something funny about one of my old mines. Then, there are the ships of the desert I mentioned to you, Virginia."

Donna frowned. "Strange rocks? Mine problems, and a ship in the desert?"

"Yeah. I know it sounds funny, but they're all real. After dinner, I'll show you the samples of rocks. Maybe, when you have time, I'll try to show you where I saw the ships."

Donna's eyes widened. "Did you say ships? More than one?"

"Yes. Old, eighteenth century, Spanish three-masted sailing ships. Spanish galleons actually."

"Oh."

"That's intriguing." Virginia looked at a glass and wood display case. Behind the doors sat a collection of various gems, rocks, and minerals. "Is the strange rock you mentioned in there."

"Yes, a small sample anyway. Let me show you. It's strange to me, but I've found ancient Indian relics made from it. Legends say they have magical powers. Damn heavy, too." Carol rose. "Let me get a sample of the rock and a figurine, and you can see for yourselves." She walked to the cabinet, opened it, and took out some samples. Carol returned and handed them to Virginia and Donna. "Take a look."

Virginia hefted the rock and then carefully examined it. "I think this is ataxite. I've seen this before in museums, even my museum. We have a statue made from the stuff."

Carol tilted her head. "What's ataxite?"

Virginia held the rock and sat back. "One of the geologists at my museum in Texas told me about it. He said, through the ages, mankind has been fascinated with the heavens. For thousands of years, we have been gazing upon the stars and marveling at rocks falling from the sky. In historic times, meteorites that were observed descending from the heavens were often regarded as messages from God. Depending upon the local culture and the current social environment at the time, these objects were considered as either good or bad omens."

Carol raised an eyebrow. "That chunk of rock is from outer space? Really? A special type of meteor?"

"Yes." Virginia turned the rock in her hands. "If I'm right, this rock is older than the earth. It's a meteorite and a very special one. It is mainly iron and a lot of nickel and a trace of iridium and a few other elements. Iridium is an element that is scarce on Earth, usually found in higher concentrations in meteors. Like I said, appears to be ataxite. Ataxites are the most nickel-rich meteorites known; they usually contain over eighteen percent nickel. This one may have more, maybe about twenty percent to thirty percent nickel. And they are extremely rare. This sample is most likely part of a really big one."

Carol's eyes widened. "Valuable?"

"Very." She handed the rock to Donna in exchange for the artifact. It was a dagger. Virginia scraped some corrosion from the surface. "This meteorite knife is old. And before you ask, yes, it is very valuable, too. The local peoples must have had a reverence for it. You can see where they managed to put what looks like the crude images of what looked like a god and some sort of sailing vessel on it. It may have been a ceremonial knife of some kind."

Donna looked surprised. "Sailboat? How did ancient people, living in the desert, see a sailboat?"

Carol shrugged. "Haven't a clue."

Donna looked at the cabinet. "Anything else strange in there?"

Carol motioned toward the cabinet. "More of the same. Plus, there are some uranium, copper, gold, lead, and silver samples, and believe it or not, turquoise. They're all from my eleven square miles of dirt. Oh, I own the mineral rights all the way to China, too. Got water wells too, thank goodness."

"Where did you get this rock, exactly?"

"On the section of my property that is south of here, in the direction of the Salton Sea. That's where a couple of my old mines are. They're old gold mines. I had thought they were played out years ago. Turns out they ain't. There's another one closer to here. That's the one with the turquoise. There was once a uranium mine, but no one has mined it in decades."

Donna set the rock on the coffee table. "Has anything else unusual, besides the ships in the desert and the meteor, been happening around there lately?"

"Come to think about it, yes."

Virginia turned as a Hispanic woman entered. "Miss Carol, dinner is ready in the dining room."

"Thank you, Liana. We'll be right there." She rose and motioned for Virginia and Donna to follow her. "Let's make a quick side trip to my quilt studio. I'll show you something that will blow your minds."

They followed Carol down a beautifully decorated, tile-floored hallway to a huge quilting studio. They stepped into the room onto brightly colored floor tiles. Massive quilts hung on the walls. Others were folded over shorter quilt racks. Cabinets for fabric and supplies lined one wall. A design board with various quilt blocks adhered to it covered another wall. A large, waist-high cutting table sat away from a wall to provide access from all sides. A custom-made sewing machine table sat to one side with a large area around the machine to hold fabric. Carol closed the door and switched off the lights. They stood in the dark, staring at the far wall. One of the quilts glowed in the dark. Two others also glowed but started to fade out "Is that strange enough?"

CHAPTER 3

Virginia and Donna stood staring at the glowing quilts. "How'd you do that?" asked Donna.

Carol switched on the lights. "I think it's something in the fabric dyes. I made the dyes for those quilts myself from native materials I gathered from around my land."

Virginia stepped close to the quilt and felt the fabric. "Maybe it's radioactive." She turned toward Carol and Donna. "You said there is uranium on your land, didn't you?"

Carol nodded. "Yeah, that and other stuff."

Donna's eyes widened. "Should you be touching that if it's radioactive?"

"I'm not sure if it is. But it's probably like the old watches we wore that glowed in the dark. The radiation couldn't go far in air or through stuff, so as long as I don't eat or breathe it, it should be okay. I think." Virginia looked closer at the fabric. "When did you make these?"

"Over the past four years."

"Did you get the clays and stuff from the same place?"

"Well, the same general area, yeah. Some came from closer to the Salton Sea."

"Do you still have the dyes you made?"

"No." Carol shook her head. "I used them all. The little bit that was left, I threw away. I can always make more."

"How do you feel?" Donna asked. "I mean, has anything changed health wise since you made the dyes, colored the fabric, and made the quilts?"

Carol turned and started out the door. "Liana is waiting to serve dinner." She led Virginia and Donna to the dining room.

On the way, Donna leaned close to Virginia and whispered, "She didn't answer my question."

"I noticed," Virginia said. "I noticed her long-sleeved shirt, and she coughs a lot."

She looked at the architecture as they walked. "This place is bigger than I thought." They turned and entered a huge room. Virginia almost gasped at the size of the room. "Looks like we're here." The dining room looked like it was straight out of an old California Spanish hacienda. A dark green china cabinet stood against one wall. In the center of the room sat a polished, rustic, wooden table. She thought the table had to be well over ten feet long and about four to five feet wide. Foods and place settings were arranged at one end. Twelve straight-backed chairs were positioned around the table.

Carol held her hand out in a welcoming gesture. "Take a seat, ladies, and let's eat."

They took places around the table and ate a meal of steak, vegetables, salad, and mashed potatoes. Liana cleared the table and then brought coffee and chocolate cake. After dinner, they returned to the living room and sat around the stone fireplace.

Carol looked at Virginia. "What's your schedule at the conference?"

"I've got a number of classes scheduled for the next couple days. But I left a lot of free time to spend with Donna, and for shopping, and exploring."

Carol smiled. "Good. I'd love to take you two around my place and show you the beauty of the desert. Maybe we will get to see the ghost ships of the desert."

Donna leaned forward. "I'd like to see your mines and where you got the dirt you made the glowing dyes from."

"Can do." Carol took a breath. "Virginia, when are you and Donna free tomorrow?"

Virginia and Donna glanced at each other. Donna shrugged. Virginia checked the calendar on her iPhone. "I'll be free about two. Donna's got most of the day."

Donna eagerly nodded. "Yeah. I'm free all day. But tomorrow evening we may have dinner dates."

Carol leaned back. "Great! Donna, why don't you come about nine? I'll send a car for Virginia at two so she can join us."

"I like it when a plan comes together," said Donna. She turned toward Virginia. "You okay with this?"

"Yes. I'll be waiting at two in the lobby." Virginia looked at her watch. "It's getting late. We should be heading back to the hotel. We'll see you tomorrow."

Carol beamed. "Wonderful. Be sure to wear comfortable clothes and bring sunglasses, sunscreen, good hiking shoes, and hats."

Virginia rose to her feet. "We can do that."

Whispering Threads

After parking the car at the hotel, they went to their rooms and sat on Virginia's balcony. Virginia took a drink from a plastic water bottle. "What did you think of Carol's place?"

"It's a one-floor castle." Donna put her feet up on the iron railing. "That place is huge. You could feed an army in that dining room. I liked her. But she's not telling us everything."

"I know. But she knows there's something strange happening on her land and around it. She asked for help. Maybe we can assist her while we're here."

"She wasn't too forthcoming about what she suspected."

"I know." Virginia shrugged her shoulder. "Maybe the glowing quilts have something to do with it. Or, maybe it's the ships in the desert she mentioned. We need to find out."

"You just can't let a mystery go by without getting involved, can you?"

"I guess not." Virginia took another drink. "How bad could it be?"

"With you and me involved, pretty bad. In case the fertilizer hits the ventilator, did you bring your Smithsonian Central Security Service badge and credentials? How about a gun?"

"Yes. I brought my Walther .9mm, three magazines, and an extra fifty round box of ammunition."

Donna chuckled. "Oh. I bet TSA just loved you."

"You could say that. The SCSS helped."

"Good. Running around on eleven square miles of desert could get dangerous, especially if there are strange things going on." Donna lowered her feet and looked out at the golf course. "Ms. Putman did say eleven square miles, didn't she?"

"Yep. That's a lot of desert."

Donna cracked a smile. "Oh, I've got my husband's .38 special, too."

Virginia gave her a skeptical look. "I thought California frowned on armed, honest citizens. Just the bad guys are allowed firearms."

"Yeah, you're right. No sense of humor. You can't get a permit around here unless you're a friend of the sheriff. So, it's just the cops, the crooks, and gangs that carry guns. But we'll be on Carol's land, and that's private property. And I brought it here with me in accordance with the law."

"Nice to know."

"Glad you approve." Donna set her drink on the little glass covered patio table between them. "Did you happen to notice we're being watched?"

"From the eleventh tee area? The flashlight was a dead giveaway. Amateurs."

"Yes. Why is someone watching us? We're fully clothed. No string bikinis, not topless or naked. Why spy on two out of hundreds of women here for that quilt thing?"

"I don't know. Maybe it's because we're some of the youngest. Let's go inside so whoever is out there can go to bed." Virginia got up, picked up her water bottle, and entered her room through the sliding doors. Donna followed, closed the door, and locked it. Virginia drew the curtains.

Donna leaned on the dresser. "I'm going to Carol's place at nine tomorrow. She's sending someone to pick you up at two. That's her plan, what's ours?"

Virginia hopped onto the bed, fluffed up a pillow, and leaned against the headboard. "Here's what I was thinking, you can chime in any time."

Donna sat on the small couch and put her feet up on the coffee table. "Go ahead."

"Well, I think you should try and get her to show you where she obtained the meteor fragment and the mine or pit that she got the materials for the glowing dyes. If she can point out where she's seen the ships of the desert, that would be great. I'd like to know where on her land those places are and if they're connected somehow. If that's too much before I get there, we can see more when I arrive."

"I think I should take my pistol. It is the wild desert out there."

"I agree."

Donna rose, opened the small refrigerator, took out a bottle of water, and offered it to Virginia. Virginia shook her head. Donna took her seat again and sipped some water. "I'll keep an eye on her for any signs of illness. Her skin looked thin and pale, and I noticed some thinning of her hair. She evaded the question earlier. I'm wondering about radiation poisoning."

Virginia nodded. "Good idea. She's spunky and doesn't want to let anything get her down, even something serious. Let me know if you see anything."

"Donna looked at her watch. "Better hit the hay. Long day tomorrow." She climbed to her feet and headed for the connecting doorway. "Good night."

Virginia woke with a start in the dark at the sound of the phone ringing. She glanced at the glowing dial of the alarm clock. *Three A.M. Who's calling at this hour? Andy?* Her heart raced. *Is he okay?* She sat up, reached for the phone, and answered, "Hello?" She straightened her twisted, oversized, University of California at Irvine T-shirt.

"Is this Mrs. Virginia Davies Clark?" said a male voice she didn't recognize.

"Yes. Who are you?"

"I'm Detective Ferguson, Riverside County Sheriff's office."

Virginia frowned. "What can I do for you at this hour, Deputy?"

"You're a friend of Mrs. Carol Jean Putman. Is that correct?"

"Yeah." *Abrupt. Where is he going with this?*

"Well, I hate to inform you, ma'am, but she is dead. You are named in her will as the executor of her estate and the new owner of the B bar P ranch. That's the miles and miles of desert she has... er had. She must have thought a lot of you."

"I am? I guess so." *What the hell is going on?*

"You didn't know?"

"That she died? No. That I inherited her ranch? No. That's a big surprise. How did she die?"

"She was murdered." His voice sounded tense. "We are starting an investigation and would like to talk to you."

"Okay." She rubbed her eyes. "When?"

"How about five this morning in the coffee shop of your resort?" Ferguson asked.

Virginia brushed the hair from her face. "Are you joking?"

"No. We like to get things going as fast as possible in homicide cases."

"Am I a suspect?"

Ferguson chuckled. "No. We found that you were at your hotel at the approximate time of the homicide. And we ran a background check and discovered you are a federal special agent with the Smithsonian Central Security Service. And like I said, you... well you kind of own her ranch right now."

"Doesn't my inheriting her ranch make me a suspect? It does on TV cop shows."

"It normally would. But under these circumstances, no."

"If you know I wasn't at the ranch when she died, why do you need to talk to me?"

"Mrs. Clark. We'd like your help. We tried talking briefly to her staff. They were shaken up and reluctant to say much. They're afraid of the police. I guess you get that way if you're from their homelands. The Smithsonian Central Security Service has agreed to you assisting us. In case they haven't called you yet, and I'm guessing they haven't, you're assigned to this case. I'm your new best friend."

Virginia looked at the phone receiver in her hand, and then said, "You called the Smithsonian Central Security Service in Washington, D.C. at this hour and actually got to talk to someone? That's better than I can do."

"Yes. Don't forget they are three hours ahead of us."

"Still... They assigned me to the case? Who'd you talk to?"

"The sheriff and I talked to the director of the SCSS."

"Oh boy." Virginia rubbed her forehead. "The director?" *Heaven help me.*

"Yes. He thinks a lot of you."

"Good to know. Wait 'till Donna hears this."

"Would that be Mrs. Donna Bolette?" Ferguson asked.

How'd he know? "Yes. She is here with me. Just so you know, after I spring this news on her, she *will* be helping me. Neither you nor I can stop her."

"When we told the director of the Smithsonian Central Security Service that she was with you, he said you'd say that. Your agency's director said they have deputized her in the past to help you. He's doing it again. She's now, and I quote, 'back in the service of the Smithsonian Central Security Service as an armed, federal special agent with his agency with full investigative and arrest powers.' Your director also said to give you two plenty of room, and don't ask you a lot of questions about your methods. Not if we want this case solved."

Virginia chuckled. "Good for him. He'll stay on my Christmas card list for that. Deputy Ferguson, Donna will contribute more than most of your officers. We've done this before. And if she's been deputized by him, you can't stop her from working with me on the case."

In an exasperated voice, he said, "Yeah, so I was informed. See you at five?"

"Yes, and I'm bringing Donna. You buying?"

"I didn't think I'd have a choice. I'm looking forward to meeting you two."

"Oh, just one more question, you said Carol was murdered. How?"

"She was stabbed with what looks like an ancient stone knife near a mine. That's why your director authorized you to work the case. One of her ranch hands found her. He went looking for her when she didn't return about eleven last night. He was lucky to find her. That ranch is huge. He said she was glowing."

Glowing? "Did you see her body out there?"

"No. The deputies who responded, a detective, and the coroner's deputies did. I arrived as the coroner was removing her body. They said she had some material on her that was glowing."

"I see."

"Does that glowing thing have any meaning to you?"

"Yes." Virginia swallowed. "When is an autopsy going to be done?"

"The Coroner is going to do the autopsy first thing this morning. What did the glow–"

"Okay. Thanks, Detective. See you shortly." She abruptly hung up and sat staring into the darkness.

Virginia jerked at the sound of Donna's voice. "I take it that wasn't good news?" The lights came on, and Donna, in an extra-large, baggy, Mighty Ducks hockey team T-shirt, walked to the end of the bed and sat.

"Autopsy? Who died?"

Virginia stared at Donna for a second and then said, "Carol Jean Putman was murdered last night on her ranch. She was stabbed with a stone knife similar to the one she showed us. She was reported to be glowing in the dark, too."

"That's terrible. I'm sorry."

"That's not all."

Donna's large brown eyes widened. "Being dead and glowing isn't bad enough? It gets worse?"

"Oh yeah. Carol wasn't glowing, something on her was. And I'm the executor of her estate and the new owner of her rather large piece of the desert."

"Oh boy."

"It gets even better. The Smithsonian has assigned us to help the Sheriff investigate. We are meeting a Deputy Detective Ferguson at five this morning in the hotel's coffee shop for breakfast."

Donna's eyes widened. Her face brightened. "Us, like you and me?"

"Yes. The director of the SCSS has deputized you. It seems the director likes us. You're back in the saddle."

"At this hour? He likes us?"

"Yes. Let's see if the SCSS sent me a notice." Virginia picked up her laptop computer from the side table and turned it on. She logged into her e-mail and found a message from the director of the SCSS and opened it. She nodded. "Yep. You and I are on active duty as of an hour ago. He's sending your credentials and a badge by special courier to the hotel. They moved extremely fast. Kinda makes you wonder, doesn't it?"

"Yeah. But it looks like the band is back together. We'll need to go to her place right after breakfast."

"I agree."

"When do we tell our husbands?"

Virginia pushed the covers off her and swung her legs off the bed. "Once we get a handle on things."

Donna stared at the floor, then looked at Virginia. "Who'd want to kill her, and why?"

"That is what we're going to find out. Whoever did this is going to pay and pay dearly. Don't forget your gun."

CHAPTER 4

At five in the morning, it was still dark outside as Virginia and Donna strolled into the resort coffee shop.

Businessmen going over documents and sipping coffee occupied two tables by the back. At booth sat a young man and a short, dark-haired woman, both dressed in plaid shirts and jeans, looking at a map. Closer to the entrance, in a corner booth, sat a wavy, dark-haired man with a tan complexion, wearing a white shirt, bolo tie, and jeans. A gold sheriff's star and a semiautomatic were attached to his belt. He waved them over. Two folders and a cup of steaming coffee rested on the table in front of him.

Virginia and Donna, both wearing jeans and polo shirts, moved to the booth. Virginia set her backpack on the floor next to the booth and looked at the badge. "Detective Ferguson?"

"Yes." He opened the folder and glanced at pictures of Virginia and Donna. "Have a seat, ladies. You might like to order before we start."

After breakfast, Ferguson slid a blue folder to Virginia. "Here are the pictures from the crime scene. The CSU is going back at first light to make sure they didn't overlook anything last night. I'll keep you posted on anything else they find. As soon as I have any lab and autopsy results, you'll get copies." Donna studied the pictures then examined the folder.

"Why is this blue?"

"Nothing important or sinister about the color. It was the only extra one I had."

Virginia kept staring at the photograph of the knife. "Looks like another ataxite knife."

Donna nodded. "Sure does."

Ferguson frowned, took the picture from Virginia and looked at it. "What do you mean this is another ataxite knife?"

"Carol had a different one in a display case last night. It's ancient." Virginia took the picture back. "We examined it."

"Another knife?" He rubbed his head. "What's ataxite?"

"It's a meteor. And yes, it is valuable." Virginia's cell phone rang.

Whispering Threads

She pulled it from her backpack and answered. "Hello?"

"*Señora* Clark," sobbed Liana, "I'm sorry, *Señora* Carol is dead. The *policia* said you are the person who controls the estate now, and... and will be the new *Doña*. Will you be coming here soon? What do I tell the others who work here? We have no place else to go. Because of where some are from, they fear the *policia*."

Virginia looked at the phone. "Liana, how'd you get my number?"

"*Señora* Putman had it in her phonebook."

"I see." Virginia sighed. "I am sorry about Carol's death, too. I'm with the sheriff right now. Donna is here with me. You remember her don't you, Liana?"

"*Sí*. I like *Señora* Donna."

"Good. She and I will be out there about nine or so this morning. Can you tell me the gate code so we can get in?"

"*Sí*." Liana sniffled. "The code is 3579. I will have coffee and some... some biscuits for you when you come."

"Thank you, Liana. Oh, tell the other staff people not to worry. They will continue to have a home there on the B bar P ranch."

"*Gracias, Señora* Clark." Liana's voice cracked. "I will tell them."

"One more thing. Can you please find the gentleman who found Ms. Putman, and have him at the house when we get there?"

"*Sí*. Emilio will be here. I get him."

"Okay. We'll be there at nine. Good-bye." Virginia hung up. She looked at Ferguson. "You heard?"

Ferguson nodded. "Yes. Maybe I should be there, too."

"No. They're scared. No police. Donna and I will take care of things at the ranch. We'll keep you in the loop." She noticed a slight frown, and twitch of his right index finger. "That's how it's going to work, Detective. Remember, I'm the new *Doña* out there, and we're assigned to this case by Washington."

"Okay." Ferguson shrugged. "Just keep me posted on any new developments."

Donna glanced at her watch. "Better start getting things ready. It's almost six-thirty, and I, for one, would like to drive around a little out there in the daylight before confronting the scared ranch help."

"Good idea." Virginia pulled the map from the blue folder and opened it. She pointed at the area on it where the ranch was located. "Detective, can you mark where Ms. Putman was found?"

Ferguson looked at the map, pulled a pen from his shirt pocket, and made an X. "Right about there. When you get close, you'll see some sheriff's vehicles and maybe a couple CSU vans. I'll let them know who you are and that you will be there early this morning."

"Thank you." She used her cell phone to photograph the map, then folded it and returned it to the folder. She slid out of the booth.

Donna followed. "Thanks for breakfast. We'll be in touch." They walked to the coffee shop entrance and left. Donna watched out of the corner of her eye as Ferguson slid his folder into a battered briefcase and exited the coffee shop. He walked toward the front hotel doors. As they strolled out the rear of the lobby, Donna glanced around the pool area ahead of them. "Well, lookie there. Our new friends, Paul and James. Shall we see if they still want to take us to dinner tonight?"

Virginia looked at Donna. "You're concerned about dinner? We've got a murderer to find."

"Yeah, but a girl's got to eat, and charming, male company, who'll likely pay for it, should be encouraged. All work and no fun makes this girl grumpy. Besides, you wanted to pump them for information, didn't you? This way they'll be relaxed, and their guard won't be up."

"You're hopeless. Hopeless, but right. Okay, let's go talk to them." They hurried across the walkway, entered the pool area and walked up to the two men. Virginia smiled. "Hello, guys. Remember us?"

James turned and grinned. "Yes. I sure do. Are you two lovely ladies still interested in dinner with us tonight?"

Virginia nodded. "Yes.

"Good. How about we meet you two in the lobby at seven tonight?"

"Okay."

Donna smiled at Paul. "Looks like you guys are dressed for field work. Where are you off to?"

"We're checking some possible sites between here and the Salton Sea."

Donna tilted her head and touched his sleeve with her finger. "Isn't that close to the B bar P ranch?"

"Yeah." Paul nodded. "We're going to need to look at some locations on the ranch. The old gal who owns it is being difficult. She's limiting our access. But we're confident things will change." He looked at his watch. "We need to be heading out. See you, two ladies, tonight." They headed toward the side of the building and far parking lot.

Virginia chuckled. "Donna, you charmer. Looks like the boys are going to either try again to get permission to go on the ranch, or trespass. I wonder when they were there before?" Donna started toward the rear doors leading to a swimming pool, the golf course, and the building where their rooms were. "Wait until they find out who the new *Doña* of the ranch is."

At seven, Donna drove her Infiniti QX80 out of the parking lot and to California Highway 111. She turned south and drove toward the ranch past the same expensive houses, pristine shopping arcades and lush green golf courses as the night before. At a little before eight, she punched the gate code into the control box. The gate swung open. She drove through the gate and pulled to the side of the dirt road. Donna watched the gate close in her rear-view mirror. She glanced at Virginia.

Virginia held the crude map of the ranch that Carol had given her and stared at it. She referenced the map Ferguson had marked. "Okay, go about a hundred yards. There should be a trail off to the left. Follow that. We should see emergency vehicles after we get over that ridge."

Donna looked out the front window. "Maybe I should engage the four-wheel drive. Haven't used it yet. Most of my off-roading is at a shopping mall. This may be fun."

"We're going to a murder scene."

"I know. But we need to get there first." Donna pulled out and followed Virginia's directions. As they topped the ridge, she spotted two CSU vans and two sheriff's jeeps parked about a half mile below them near what looked like a cave opening. "There they are."

"Wait." Virginia looked through her binoculars. "There is a vehicle on that far hill. Someone is watching the sheriff's folks below. And they're trespassing."

Donna squinted. "Shall we go see who's there?"

"You bring your gun?"

"Oh, yeah."

"Okay, head that way."

Donna accelerated down the slope and across the desert, trying to avoid large rocks and sturdy looking vegetation. She carefully maneuvered across a dry arroyo and started up the hill. As she reached the crest, the jeep, about two hundred yards away sped off in a cloud of dust.

Virginia snapped pictures with her digital camera and telescopic lens. "Looked like there were two men."

Donna stopped the SUV. "Did you get the license?"

"Not too clearly. Too much dust. Maybe the sheriff can do some enhancements like they do on NCIS."

"You do remember that's just a TV show, and fiction?"

"Yeah." Virginia looked at the picture on the camera's screen. "But some of it is true. We'll see what Ferguson can do with it, later."

"Want to give chase?"

"No. Let's go see what the cops are doing and take a look at the site."

Donna turned the SUV around, and carefully drove to the crime scene. She parked next to a CSU truck. Donna slid out of the car and hurried next to Virginia as a deputy approached.

Virginia slung her backpack over her shoulder and held up her gold SCSS badge. "Special Agents Virginia Davies Clark and Donna Boletti."

The deputy stopped and smiled. "Yes, ma'am. Detective Ferguson said you'd be coming."

Virginia looked at the deputy. "Find anything new?"

"Yes. The lab folks found tire prints and a geologist's hammer near that cave entrance. The hammer is fairly new compared to the other rusty stuff around. We'll see what we can get off it." He pointed. "The tire prints are in a wetter area over there."

Donna started to walk toward the cave. "Where'd the water come from?"

"Inside the cave. There's seepage from the rocks that make a little stream. Goes about a hundred and fifty feet out, and then disappears into the sand. That's why there're a few palm trees, a couple creosote bushes, and brush over there."

Virginia started to follow Donna and said, "Mind if we look around?"

"No. We're done here. The CSU guys are finishing packing up. You'll have the whole place to yourself in a few minutes."

Virginia took out her camera and displayed the picture of the jeep to the deputy. "Can I send this to you and see if you can ID the owner? It was on the ranch watching you work."

The deputy nodded. "Sure. I'll see what I can do with it." He gave Virginia his e-mail address. She sent it to him.

"Thanks. Let me know what you find out, if anything."

Virginia caught up with Donna at the cave. "I wonder what's inside?"

"I don't know." Donna wet her lips. "But what do you say we look around out here for now." She adjusted her baseball cap. "We can go caving later."

Virginia looked at the mouth of the cave and the trickle of water coming out. She turned and looked around the area. "What's bothering you?"

"A couple things."

"Like what?"

"Liana said the police told her you were the executrix of Carol's will, and you are now the owner of the ranch. The new *Doña*. How'd they know? They had to have seen the will last night. And they moved pretty fast to get us involved instead of asking us to leave town like usual."

Virginia rubbed her forehead. "You're right. I hadn't thought about it."

"Did you see anything important or interesting in the crime scene materials the detective gave you?"

"No, not really except that they made a mess of the crime scene. It was dark when they got here and accidentally drove over anything that may have been visible in the dirt. Obviously, they tried to stay clear of the actual murder location, but who knows what else may have been here. The photographs of the knife and the stab wounds were clear." Virginia gripped the camera strap. "You see anything?"

"I think the jeep has returned."

"Yeah, I see it. And we've got company coming from the ranch road." They watched as a green pickup truck, with B bar P printed on the doors drove into the clearing and stopped. An older man hopped out and hurried to Virginia and Donna. "¡*Señoras*! *Por favor,* follow me back to *la casa del rancho*... ahh... house. It is not safe out here."

Virginia looked at the old man. "It's daylight. Why isn't it safe? Animals? Snakes?"

"No." He rubbed his hands together and looked around, fear in his eyes. "The men in the jeep up on the hill... they have been around a lot and are back. *Señora* Putman is dead. The men, they disturbed the *el ánimo*... the spirits. The *naves del fantasma, er...* ghost ships, they return. Not safe. We must go. *Nas vamos ahora*."

Donna looked at Virginia. "He wants us to go to the house with haste. He's scared."

CHAPTER 5

Virginia quickly climbed into the front passenger seat of the Infiniti as Donna hopped into the driver's seat. Donna started the SUV and followed the ranch truck out of the little canyon at a slight distance to avoid the dust the truck kicked up.

Virginia gripped her seatbelt as they bounced along. She glanced at Donna. "I was thinking—"

"Now we're in trouble." Donna stared out the front window at what passed for a trail.

"As I said, I was thinking about what you said about the police, and what's going on around here. The sooner we get to the house, the sooner we may have some answers."

"I agree. The sighting of the mysterious jeep puts another wrinkle on things. You don't think the two men in the jeep are Paul and James, do you?" Donna pointed. "There's the house."

"I don't know, but I had given it some thought. They did say they had been around here. Maybe we will get some answers at the house from Liana, and tonight at dinner."

They pulled up in front of the big hacienda and stopped. They hopped out and hurried inside.

Liana met them at the door. "Welcome back, *Señoras*. I have coffee and some fruit and pastries in the dining room. Will you follow me, *por favor?*" She led them to the dining room. A large silver coffee urn sat on a side credenza with cups and saucers, around it. Next to the urn rested a tray of various pastries. Virginia and Donna took some pastries and cups of coffee and sat at the table.

Virginia took a sip of coffee, set the cup down and looked at Liana. "Liana, I have a couple questions for you, and I'm sure you have some for me. But let me go first. Why was the gentleman who came to get us so nervous?"

"The spirit ships are back." Liana's face tightened. "That means trouble or danger. And *Señora* Putman was murdered last night." Liana made the sign of the cross. "The desert spirits are angry."

Virginia nodded. "I see. Who told you about Mrs. Putman's will and that I was the... the *Doña* of the ranch, and when?" She looked at the short Hispanic woman, standing nervously near the credenza. "Please, Liana, get some coffee, take a seat, and relax. This is not an inquisition. Donna and I want to find out what's been going on around here and find Mrs. Putman's killer."

Liana smiled weakly, poured some coffee, and wiped a strand of black hair from her face. She pulled out a chair and took a seat across from Virginia and Donna. "*Gracias.*" She sipped her coffee. "The police said you were the person who would... would *ejecute*... execute Ms. Carol's will. You were the overseer of the ranch, and you were a federal officer, and we needed to be careful around you. I think he wanted to scare us because ICE is also federal."

Virginia shared a glance with Donna, then Virginia turned back to Liana. "When was this?"

"Early this morning. Very early."

"Which deputy told you?"

Liana reached into a pocket of her apron, pulled out a business card and handed it to Virginia. "This man."

Virginia took the card and looked at the name. *Deputy Detective Ferguson, Riverside County Sheriff.* "Interesting." She handed the card to Donna. "Liana, do you know where a copy of Mrs. Putman's will is and who her lawyer is?"

"*Sí.* The will is on top of Ms. Carol's desk in her office. Her lawyer's name, and address, and his telephone number, are on the cover. The office is locked. I have the keys for everything, and a set for you." Liana took a key ring from another pocket in her apron and pushed it across the table to Virginia. "Each key has what it is for on it."

"Thank you." Virginia took the keys as she watched Liana clenching and unclenching her hands and wetting her lips. "Liana, why are you so nervous?"

Liana looked like she was ready to cry. "*Señora* Clark. The police said you and *Señora* Bolette are *federalizes... policía federal*. There are a few who work here who..."

Virginia smiled. "Liana, Donna and I are not with the immigration department. We do not care about that. We are special agents with the Smithsonian Central Security Service. We are like archeologists with badges and guns. You know what an archeologist is, don't you?"

Liana nodded. "*Sí.*"

"Good. Your, or anyone else's, immigration status is not our concern. Okay? Tell the others who we are and that we will not be giving anyone up to the immigration authorities, or to anyone else. We will protect you as best we can."

Liana nodded and smiled. "*Gracias*. Would you like me to call Emilio now? He is the man who found *Señora* Putman. He is nervous. The police were... bad to him. They mentioned ICE if he didn't cooperate."

Virginia finished her pastry and coffee. "Yes. Please send him in. If you think it will help in calming him, I'd like you to stay while we discuss what he saw last night. And assure him we are not ICE."

Liana rose and walked out of the room. A couple of minutes later she entered ahead of a short Hispanic man of indeterminate age. His skin was like tanned leather with wrinkles on his face. He had thinning, salt and pepper hair, dressed in jeans with a bright western style shirt. His cowboy boots were dusty. Liana took him to a chair across from Virginia and Donna and sat next to him. Liana touched his hand to reassure him, then looked at Virginia. "*Señora* Clark, this is Emilio."

His eyes darted around the room, and then, he looked at Virginia and Donna. He spoke in a low voice. "*Buenos dias. ¿Cómo puedo ayudarle?*"

Virginia sat staring. Donna translated. "He wants to know how he can help you."

Virginia smiled. "*¿Hablas Inglés?*"

"*Sí.* A little."

"Good. Emilio, My name is Virginia Davies Clark." She motioned towards Donna. "This lady is Donna Boletti."

He nodded. "*Sí.* I know."

"Good. I want you to tell me exactly what you saw last night when you found Mrs. Putman."

Emilio swallowed. "The *inspector de Policía*... he said—"

Virginia nodded slightly. "The detective threatened you with ICE?"

"*Sí.* And he said not to tell you about all that I saw."

Donna chuckled. "Something smells and it ain't the fish. So much for interagency cooperation."

"Right." Virginia frowned. "I need you to tell me everything. There will be no reprisals. You are safe here."

"The *policía*?"

"Since Carol's death involves ancient artifacts, and things that could be important to the government, this is now a federal matter. We are the official federal officers involved. That means, my friend here, and I are the ones in charge. I'll handle the sheriff's detective. You will not be implicated or harassed. If necessary, I'll place you, and anyone else who needs protection, in federal protective custody here at the ranch so the local police and sheriff can't touch you. Other federal agencies wouldn't be able to touch you either."

"*Gracias*." Emilio took a deep breath and slowly let it out. "We all liked *Señora* Putman. She has been good to us. She did not come back to the *casa* last night, so I went looking for her. She has not been well. Her sickness is getting worse. I was... worried about her. She said earlier she was going to look for the spirit ships. I went to the spot where she usually goes, but she was not there. I went to the old gold mine on my way back. When I got close and saw her body, I saw a small glow. When I got there, it was Mrs. Putman who was glowing."

"She was glowing in the dark? Her body?"

"No. Not her body. It was parts of her blouse, her hat, and spots on the legs of her pants. Her hands had... had... spots that were glowing soft. Her hair... it sparkled a little."

Virginia leaned forward. "Her hair sparkled?"

"*Sí*. Like a halo."

"A halo?" Donna leaned forward. "Are you sure that was a gold mine?"

"I think so." He looked at Liana, then back at Donna. "There are a few old mines. It is hard to remember which ones were what. *Señora* Putman knew."

"How did she get there?"

"She took a horse. I brought it back to the barn before the *policía* arrived."

"Was anything glowing on the horse?"

"*Sí*. The saddlebags had some spots on them. There were spots on the saddle and the horse's hoofs. I washed everything down, so they no show."

Virginia shifted in her chair. "Do the police know about the horse?"

Emilio grinned. "No. *La policía* did not ask. The officer was mean, so I did not tell him."

Donna chuckled. "Good for you."

Virginia frowned at Donna, and then gave Emilio a smile. "How'd they miss it? Weren't there any hoof prints at the site?"

"The cars and trucks they brought destroyed them. It was dark when they came. I do not think they saw the hoof prints."

"I thought so." Virginia chuckled. "Now, what didn't they want you to tell me?"

"The desert spirit ships. They were there at the back of the valley that is toward the Salton Sea."

"You saw them?"

"*Sí*. All most everyone here has seen the spirit ships. They were out on the desert last night. Very bad."

"Did the police see the ships?"

"No. The ghost winds came up. The ships were fading away when *la policía* came. I didn't point them out to *la policía*."

"Okay. Anything else?"

"The knife. It is sacred. It is from the ancient ones. It had glow spots."

Donna rubbed her finger in a circle on the smooth table surface. "So, the police saw the knife glowing?"

"*Sí.*"

Virginia leaned forward. "Anything else you saw or heard?"

"No."

"Thank you, Emilio. You've been very helpful. And don't worry about the police. I'll handle them."

Emilio stood, bowed slightly, "*Gracias, Doña Virginia.*"

He walked out of the room.

Virginia looked at Liana. "What does he do around here?"

"He is the grounds caretaker, minds the horses, and is our...handyman."

"Wow, that's a lot. I take it he is good at what he does."

"*Sí.* He is a good man. Would you like to read *Señora* Putman's will?"

"Yes. I'd like to know what else is involved. One more question, how did the sheriff know about me being the executor? Did the police officer see Mrs. Putman's will last night?"

Liana shook her head. "I don't think so. But it was in an unlocked file cabinet. They could have searched the files. I took it out this morning so that you could see it." She rose from her chair. "If you will follow me, I'll show you to the office." Liana led Virginia and Donna down a hallway to a large ornately carved, wooden door. She unlocked it, stepped in and turned on the overhead lights. She walked to the windows and opened the heavy drapes. Bright sunlight streamed into the room.

Donna switched off the light as she entered. "Don't need them right now."

Liana pointed at the large wooden desk. "Everything is there." She pointed to a door. "The ranch files are in the file room in there. They are also on the computer. The password is Murrieta." Liana strolled to the entrance. "If there is nothing else, I'll leave you to reading. Oh, will you be moving here from the hotel?"

Virginia stepped to the desk and picked up the will. "Not sure yet. We have a dinner engagement tonight. We'll see about what to do after that."

"Okay." Liana left the room.

Donna turned to Virginia. "I have an idea. Why don't you get comfortable and read all that legal mumbo-jumbo, and I'll go take a look around. It's still light, so whatever spooked Emile probably isn't around now."

"Good idea. See if Liana knows if there are any two-way radios around. Not too sure about cell reception out there."

"I'll do that." Donna left the room.

Funny, Carol's password is the name of a famous California bandit Joaquin Murrieta. He was like a California Robin Hood. Murrieta was the inspiration for the character of Zorro. Virginia sat on a soft leather sofa and started to read the document when she noticed a painting on the far wall. It was an oil painting of the desert from the viewpoint of the house. In the back of the painting, situated against the mountains were two Spanish galleons seemingly floating on the desert floor. She looked at the signature, but couldn't decipher it. The date on it was seventeen seventy-five. Virginia returned to the sofa and read the will. Finished, she set it next to her. *Shit. According to this, I'm the executor of Carol's estate and now the owner of the ranch. And unless I want to sell it, it belongs to me. That's strange. If I'm going to find Carol's killer and do something with this ranch, I'll need to figure out the legend of the ghost ships of the desert. Maybe I should call her lawyer to make sure this is legit.*

Liana softly knocked on the door and entered. She handed Virginia a handheld radio. "*Señora* Boletti is using channel 24." She turned and headed for the door then turned. "Will there be anything else?"

"Yes, just a quick question. Why is everyone so spooked about the ghost ships?"

"They only come when there is big trouble, or someone is disturbing sacred grounds. Sometimes they warn of earthquakes… or death."

"I have another question. Do you have any ideas about who would gain by Carol's death?"

Liana thought. "Not really. The band of Native Americans that have part of their reservation neighboring the ranch could try to claim the ranch. There are some mining companies who want to do things here. But I don't know why they would want her dead. There are treasure hunters that are around too that don't like her. Is there anything else?"

"I see. Thank you. I do want to see the quilt room again, but I know where it is."

Liana smiled and left the room.

Virginia put the will in her backpack and picked up the handheld radio. She stood and started for the door when the radio squawked. "Donna to Virginia."

Virginia pressed the talk button. "Virginia here. Go ahead."

"This place is huge. Emilio gave me a better map. I'm at a site that the map says is mud pots. They're like little mud volcanoes. They bubble mud. Another place has steam vents and yellow stuff around. I found the turquoise mine, too. Got some samples."

"Sounds like you're having fun."

"Yeah. But it's damn hot out here. Found something else. And I'm also being watched."

"Are you close to the border of the ranch?"

"Not right now. That's the point. Want me to shoot them?"

Virginia's hand tightened around the radio. "You serious? Them? More than one?"

"Yes. Two."

"Tempting as it is, don't shoot anyone quite… yet. What else did you find?"

Donna cleared her throat. "I found where Mrs. Putman got her stuff to make the glowing dyes. I think it is anyway."

"Okay. Let's discuss our findings later."

"On my way back. Watch your six. The ghost ships aren't the only strange things here."

CHAPTER 6

Virginia was sitting on a barstool at the kitchen island sipping iced tea when Donna walked in.

Donna set her walkie-talkie on the granite counter top next to Virginia's. She removed her baseball cap, rested her messenger bag on the floor, and sat next to Virginia. Liana gave her a glass of iced tea. Donna took a sip and set the glass down. "Liana, do you know where Carol mixed the pigments for her dyes?"

Liana thought for a second, and then pointed out the window. "*Sí*. She used the small red shed out back. She mixed her dyes and colored some of her fabrics there."

"Is the building locked?"

"*Sí*."

Donna rubbed the cool glass against her forehead. "That feels good. Did the sheriff's people go out there?"

Liana shook her head "No."

Virginia looked at Donna's troubled face. "Where are you going with this? What's wrong?"

"I'll bet the cops searched the house, but not the outbuildings."

Liana nodded. "They looked around the house, but not very well. They did not go to the other buildings."

"I took another look at the site of the homicide." Donna paused to drink some more tea. "The emergency vehicles, and the cops themselves, messed up any earlier tracks or signs in the dirt. I can understand that to a point. It was very dark. But they went into the mine and took samples."

Virginia frowned. "How do you know?"

"Someone forgot an evidence bag with fresh chips of the rock from the walls." Donna pulled a small plastic baggie from her messenger bag and set it on the island. "Why would they be interested in the rocks and dirt inside the mine?"

Virginia shook her head. "I don't know."

Donna finished her tea. "I followed some of their tracks into the desert.

They didn't go far. But the tracks I followed met another set out there. Someone else was there besides the police and whoever it was talked to them. Well, maybe more cops, but they came from a different direction. I also found some hoof prints a ways from the site the cops hadn't messed up. I saw the tracks where Emilio took the horse away. I'm guessing that was Emilio. It was obvious the police didn't know about the horse, and for some reason, never asked how Carol got to the mine. Maybe they thought she walked. But at night? It's quite a distance away, and I know I wouldn't want to walk out there, and that far, at night. Too many things that go bump in the night."

Virginia drank her tea. "You said on the radio you found some mud pots or mud volcanoes?"

"Yeah. They are interesting. You need to see them sometime."

Virginia looked at her watch. "It's almost noon. We should head into Palm Springs. I'd like to talk to Carol's lawyer and think about what we've got so far. Later, we need to get ready for dinner."

"Good idea. On the way, let me show you the mud volcanoes. They are something."

Virginia looked at Liana. "Have you seen them?"

"*Sí*. They are strange. The mud boils. *El Diablo*. They have some near Morelia, in Michoacán, my home in Mexico."

Donna rose and picked up her messenger bag. She brushed her dark brown hair back and pulled on her hat. "Get your stuff. I'll meet you at the car."

"Okay." Virginia slipped off the stool and hurried out of the kitchen.

Donna looked at Liana. "In the past few months, has anyone been asking Mrs. Putman to sell her estate?"

"*Sí*. A mining company," said Liana.

"Anyone else interested in her land?"

"*Sí*. Some people who said they were environmentalists. *Señora* Putman said they were snakes in the grass." Liana frowned. "*Señora* Putman said there were some spirit hunters around, too. She ran them off. Also, someone from the government has been around asking her questions."

"Which agency?"

"I do not know."

"Do you know which mining company it was that wanted the ranch?"

"No. Maybe the name is in the files."

"Virginia and I will take a look later. Thank you." Donna headed for the door, stopped and turned. "One more question. Is there an Indian reservation close to here?"

"*Sí*. Part of it borders this ranch. Someone from the tribe talked to her, but I don't know what they wanted."

Donna looked out the window at Virginia heading toward the SUV.

"Got to go. Thank you for your help. If anyone calls, or comes here and asks for information, or wants to look around the ranch, tell them to leave. Then call Virginia right away. You and the others are not to speak to anyone without Virginia, me, or Mrs. Putman's lawyer present. Be sure to tell the others who work here. Oh… tell everyone to stay *on* the ranch."

"The *policía*?"

"Especially the police. And do not tell anyone what you've told us. Okay?"

Liana straightened, smiled, and nodded. "*Sí*." Donna hurried out to her car.

Donna pulled the SUV to a stop near a smooth boulder. "The mud pots are just over that rise. We walk from here." She hopped out of the car and joined Virginia in front. They hiked up the slope to the ridge and looked down across the shimmering desert floor. Dust devils swirled in the distance. Near a stand of desert plants, including aloe, Mexican ocotillo, and palms, bubbled brownish blue mud. "Want to have a closer look?"

"Sure, we're here, why not? This is fascinating." Virginia carefully walked down the hill and stood a short distance from the mud pots. "Geothermal activity. We're almost on top of the San Andreas Fault. It's what made the Salton sink."

"I know. But this is cool. Oh, there's a steam vent about a half mile from here, and a couple of cinder cones." Donna chuckled. "The cinder cones are all over the place. The map Emilio gave me shows where the ancient meteor knife came from. The notation on the map says strange star rocks."

Virginia gazed at the surrounding scene. "I'd like to see the cinder cones, and the meteor crater later." She looked to the west. The desert continued to naked ridges and peaks stripped of most vegetation by wind and erosion. Virginia pushed her sunglasses up on her head and squinted, then pointed to the southwest at a green area. "What's over there?"

"It's a cluster of bushy palms surrounding the oasis pond."

"An oasis?"

"Yeah. There are a number of them on the ranch." Donna looked around.

"You know this, how?"

"I saw some, like that one, and others are noted on Emilio's map. There are a lot of Joshua Trees and Desert Tortoise around, too."

"You sound like a travel agent."

"If you recall, I own a travel agency in Newport Beach."

Virginia pulled her sunglasses back down and slowly turned around studying the area. "Where were the people that were watching you?"

Donna pointed. "Down there." She turned and started for the SUV. "Want to see the gold mine and the turquoise mine, too? Got some samples in the back of the car."

"Not now. We can look at the turquoise at the hotel. You said you found where Carol got her minerals for the dyes. Is it close?"

"I found it, but no, it isn't close. It's a couple miles because of the route you have to take a car or off-road vehicle. A horse, on the other hand, can get there quicker. It's in the mountains on the west side of the ranch. I think they are the Santa Rosa Mountains, or part of them."

"We can make a trip there later." Virginia looked at her watch. "We'd better be heading to Palm Springs. I'll call Carol's lawyer from my cell on the way. Maybe we can see him today. And it's hot. I can't wait for the air conditioning in the car."

Donna led the way back to the SUV. She turned the car around and carefully navigated out of the desert onto a dirt road. After following it for a few miles, she hit the paved highway. They drove another mile to State Route 86 north.

Virginia called Carol's lawyer and made an appointment for two in the afternoon. They stopped for lunch in Palm Desert and then continued to Palm Springs.

Virginia and Donna strolled into the office building on Palm Canyon Drive in Palm Springs. The difference in temperature from the dry, hot outside to the cool inside was jarring. They located the office of Brian Anderson, Attorney at Law. They opened the door and stepped inside. The reception area was decorated in the usual California desert motif.

A young, attractive female receptionist smiled and greeted them. "Hello. How may I assist you?"

Virginia stepped to the counter. "I'm Virginia Davies Clark, and we have an appointment at two with Mr. Anderson."

The woman looked at her computer screen. "Yes. If you'll have a seat, Mr. Anderson will be right with you."

Virginia and Donna sat in comfortable, overstuffed chairs with desert designs. They paged through some local magazines set out on the table. They looked up as the door to the office area opened, and a man stormed out. He turned slightly and yelled, "You better do something about that damn will, or else." He stomped out of the office.

A tall, thin, man wearing a western shirt, bolo tie, and pressed jeans stepped into the waiting area. "Mrs. Clark?"

Virginia rose. "I'm Virginia Davies Clark, and this is my associate Donna Boletti."

Anderson smiled. "I'm very pleased to meet you. I was going to try to call you. Will you follow me?" He led them down a brightly lit corridor to his office. They sat on a sofa with Mr. Anderson sitting across from them in a chair. "You mentioned on the phone something about Carol Putman's will? You've seen it?"

"Yes. Did you write it for her?"

"Yes." He frowned. "Is there a problem?"

"No. At least I don't think so. I just wanted to make sure the copy I have is her actual will. You do know she died."

"I heard about it early this morning. That's why I was going to contact you. The police said the autopsy should be done today, and I can get the death certificate about ten tomorrow from the coroner. Now, may I see the copy of the will you have?"

Virginia pulled the copy of the will she took from the ranch out of her backpack and handed it to Anderson. "This is it."

He took the document and examined it. "Yes. This is the latest one. It is registered with the county, and it is valid. You are the executor of the estate and the sole beneficiary. That is somewhat unusual but perfectly legal in California."

Virginia's eyes widened. "I really own the whole shebang?"

"Yep. If you would like me to, I'll do the paperwork for the county, the bank, and get the deed changed and registered."

"Yes. Please do."

"Okay. I will need you to go to the bank tomorrow with me to settle things there and sign some documents."

Virginia nodded. "Fine. What time?"

"How about three in the afternoon?"

"Which bank?"

"Wells Fargo. It's on South Palm Canyon Drive."

"Okay." Virginia stood. "Thank you for seeing us on such short notice. I'll see you tomorrow."

Donna climbed to her feet. "That man who stormed out of here as we came in, I hope he wasn't upset about this will."

"That is exactly what he's upset about. He is with some group that wants part of the ranch and thought they should get it."

"Why?"

"I think they're a nonprofit of some type that's been active in the mining industry And for some reason, he thinks they deserve part of Mrs. Putman's ranch. He is a bully and not very nice. I told him the will is iron-clad, and the company will have to deal with the new owner. Watch out. He and some of his friends don't like being thwarted. They can get rough."

Donna frowned. "What's his name, and what's the organization called?"

"He's Frank Coombs. He has a criminal record for assault and battery and weapons charges. The organization's called Agua Caliente Mar Management."

Virginia shook his hand. "Thanks for the information, and the warning. We'll watch out for them. See you at three tomorrow at the bank."

Virginia sat staring out the window as Donna drove down California 111 toward Rancho Mirage and the Omni Rancho Las Palmas Resort. Virginia sighed. "What the hell am I going to do with eleven square miles of desert?"

Donna chuckled. "First, we find a murderer. Second, we see what the ranch does to make money and how much it's worth. Then figure out what to do with it. Nice second home. But you also need to consider the people who work there."

"I know. For now, we find the killer, and then figure out what to do with the ranch. For suspects, there are the Indian neighbors who'd like the ranch, some mining companies, like our two dinner dates, a few treasure hunters and an environmental group or two. There could be some more we don't know about yet. Maybe Andy will have some ideas." Virginia laughed. "He'll want to keep it."

"Okay. We're almost to the hotel. Now that that's settled, we need to get ready for tonight."

"Funny, we're having dinner with two guys who may be behind some of the trouble at the ranch, or maybe murderers."

Donna nodded. "True. But they may not. You wanted to interrogate them. We can be charming and sexy and try to weasel information from them, and see if they are the rancho's *banditos,* or not. What are you wearing?"

Virginia ran her hands through her blonde hair. "Something to entice, but not too sexy."

"Not too sexy? Trying to be a prude?" Donna quickly glanced at Virginia. "Is this the Virginia I use to know and love? Not sexy? "You? How else are we going to quickly make two men reveal their darkest secrets?"

"Right. But remember my dear, we're both married, and they may be killers. And we need someplace on us to hide our guns and badges."

CHAPTER 7

Donna parked her car in a spot near the building with their rooms. Grabbing her messenger bag, the evidence baggie, and her box of turquoise, she followed Virginia to the stairs and up to their rooms. After tossing her belongings on her bed, she noticed the red bulb on the phone blinking. After checking her messages, she hurried to the connecting door to Virginia's room, knocked, then opened it. "Guess what's here."

"Your credentials and badge?"

"Yep. Got a message from the lobby. A U.S. Park Service Law Enforcement Ranger delivered a special package for me and requested they give it to me ASAP. I'm going to run over to the lobby and get it. Want to come?"

"No. I think I'd better call Andy and apprise him of the developments. If I know him, he'll want to come and help."

Donna smiled. "He's teaching."

"I know. That's what I need to remind him. You going to call your hubby?"

"Later, after I get my badge. Can I carry my gun now?"

"Yep, and I advise that you do. This case is getting weird."

"Okay." Donna hurried to the lobby and returned in a few minutes. She set the package on the desk and opened the box. Inside rested a case holding her SCSS credentials and her gold badge. She took them out and set them on the desk. *They look just like Virginia's. Only this time I get to keep them instead of them being temporary and giving them back. Hot dog!* She looked up as Virginia walked into the room.

Virginia grinned. "Looks like you're good to go. We are officially a team. Congratulations. The director likes you, and he likes us working together. We get results. Did you get a note telling you we're on the clock, so we get paid, and our expenses are covered?"

"Yeah, I noticed that, too."

"Now we have to figure out what we can wear tonight that is both sexy and practical."

Donna plopped onto the bed. "I didn't bring anything like that. I wasn't planning on having to dress sexy. Practical yes, sexy, not so much."

"You're the one who, a while ago wanted to dress sexy, remember?" Virginia looked at her watch then smiled. "We've got a little time, let's go shopping. Bring your new creds and your gun." She turned and went into her room.

At six, Virginia and Donna returned to their rooms from shopping. They proceeded to get ready for the evening.

At seven they strolled into the lobby and turned most men's heads. Virginia adjusted her low cut, blue dress, with a matching handbag. Donna wore a tight-fitting white blouse with a black pencil skirt slit down the back to make walking easier. Her black handbag was similar to Virginia's. They spotted Paul and James across the room and walked toward them.

The two men quickly rose from their seats and smiled. James cleared his throat. "Wow. You two look beautiful."

Virginia gave a slight bow and said, "Thank you, sir. Where did you two plan on taking us for dinner?"

Paul looked at Donna with yearning in his eyes. "We were hoping you like Italian."

Donna nodded. "It's a food group. We love it."

"Good. We made reservations at Miro's."

"Sound's great." Donna took his arm. "Shall we go?"

Donna slipped into the rear seat of a dark blue BMW next to Paul. Virginia rode in the front next to James. They headed up Palm Canyon Drive toward Palm Springs and the restaurant.

Miro's was a typical southern California-Spanish-desert motif. They were escorted to the patio area for quiet, outside dining.

Seated, Virginia looked around the area. "Very nice. I bet the food is as good as the atmosphere."

James and Paul exchanged quick glances. Paul looked at Donna. "We thought you'd approve. Shall we get some wine before we order?"

Donna chuckled. "Yeah. A little libation can't hurt." She noted Paul's happy expression.

After dinner, they sat sipping the remainder of the second bottle of wine.

Virginia leaned back in her chair. "I'm sure work is the last thing on your minds right now. But I was wondering about what you said when we met."

James gave her a curious look. "What was that?"

"You said you were trying to get on the B bar P Ranch to do some… prospecting, or looking around, or whatever it is you do. You said the owner wouldn't let you on the ranch. Did you go back, yet? What are you looking for?"

James and Paul tensed, then relaxed. "Yeah, we went back to see if we could get the old gal to let us look around. When we got to the gate, the woman on the speaker said the old lady had died suddenly, and we'd have to get permission from the new..." He looked at Paul. "What did she say?"

"She said from the new *Doña.*" Paul shrugged.

"Whatever, or whomever, that is."

Virginia set her glass down. "The term *Doña* is equivalent to the term *Don*. It's an honorarium for the owner or head of a large rancho or community. It's like an English Lord or Laird in Scotland."

James waved his hand dismissively. "Nice to know."

"So, what are you going to do? Wait and see the new *Doña?*"

"Well, we called the county. They said the deed and final filing of the other documents for the property transfer were going to be completed tomorrow, and we could probably get the information then. The woman on the phone said we could call the woman's attorney directly, but that probably wouldn't help us until the title transfer. I guess after the paperwork is finished, we'll contact the new owner, or the new *Doña.*"

Donna snickered under her breath. "This ought to be good."

Virginia gently kicked her under the table as she leaned forward giving James a view of her ample cleavage. She gave him a warm smile. "What are you looking for out there?"

James swallowed. "We're looking for possible locations with certain minerals, and also for possible geothermal sites."

"I see. What kind of minerals?"

"I'm afraid that's confidential."

Donna steepled her fingers, put her hands under her chin, and gave Paul a dreamy look. "Confidential?"

"Yes." Paul cleared his throat. "In our business, we try to find minerals, or certain ore locations with good potential yields. We want to keep it from the competition until we have the mineral rights sewn up."

Donna leaned closer to Paul and took a deep breath. "I bet your work can be dangerous."

His eyes widened. "At times. Sometimes, we accidentally trespass, and that's always hazardous. Then, there are people who are after what we are. Because we're usually a long way from civilization, things can get... treacherous."

She put her hand on his arm. "How about snakes and things?"

"Ye... yes. Especially sidewinders. But in the daytime, if we keep our eyes on what we're doing, and are careful, they tend to leave us alone."

Donna asked in a soft voice, "Have you ever heard of the ghost ships of the desert, or seen them?"

Paul gave a quick look at James and then sat back. "Yes. Everyone who's spent time near the Salton Sea has heard the stories. We've never seen the ghost ships. Some of the local folks, the indigenous populations, and the older Hispanic people, tell of them. They're superstitious. They think the ghost ships are forbearers of doom or some such nonsense. The story the tourists hear says the ships supposedly have vast treasures of pearls, or gold, or something on them, and are lost in the desert."

Donna smiled. "A romantic mystery. That's folklore at its best, isn't it?"

"Yeah. Right. That's all it is. Folklore." Paul glanced at his watch, and then looked into Donna's big, brown eyes. "I know a nice nightclub near downtown. We thought a little dancing would be fun. Are you ladies game?"

Virginia and Donna looked at each other and then nodded. Virginia slid her chair back. "I need to use the ladies room. If we're going dancing, I need to powder my nose as they say."

Donna pushed her chair back. "Me, too. I'll go with you. We'll be right back." She stood and went with Virginia to the restroom.

Inside the restroom, Donna leaned against the wall. "So far, so good. The boys have been on their best behavior. They aren't too forthcoming about what they are looking for. Their explanation of the ghost ships jives with what I learned from Liana, and the Internet."

Virginia nodded. "Yes. And Paul is having trouble keeping his eyes off you. You're laying it on pretty thick, girl. Dancing will be fun, and by the time we head back to the hotel they may be more informative about their work."

Donna moved to the sink area and applied some lipstick. "By then they'll be expressing their desires for the rest of the night, too."

"True. But we will have some time at the club to try and get more information."

They entered Zelda's nightclub. James and Paul had reservations. Virginia spotted shot girls selling boozed up fruit juice in test tubes for four dollars. By the size of the crowd, she figured Zelda's nightclub was a happening place. The music was top forty and hip-hop. The crowd was twenty to thirty-years-old. The dance floor wasn't big, but enough to get a groove on. There was a two-pole stage to dance on if you wanted more elbow room. She noted that the majority of the customers were out-of-towners just wanting a great time.

James led them to a reserved table near the edge of the dance floor and ordered drinks. For the next two and a half hours they drank, ate, and

Whispering Threads

danced. By one in the morning, they headed back to Rancho Las Palmas. At the hotel, Virginia and Donna stood by the pool off the main lobby.

Paul, his arm around Donna, looked at her longingly. "Anyone for a swim?"

Donna looked into his eyes. "It's late. Don't you have work to do tomorrow?"

"It already is tomorrow." He laughed. "But what time we start isn't as important as having fun with you now."

He's laying it on pretty think. Wants to score tonight. Not happening. Donna noticed a sly grin on Virginia's face. "What are you thinking?"

Virginia took a breath. "The pool near our building is usually empty at this time; it's away from the lobby and most foot traffic, so how about a little skinny dipping?"

What's she up to? Donna giggled. "Sounds like fun. Want to meet us there in ten minutes? Remember, if you have bathing suits on when we get there, we won't join you." *We won't anyway.*

James looked at Paul, then at Virginia. "We'll be waiting. Hurry."

Virginia turned. "Okay, see you there. If we're going to do this, we'd better go." She and Donna scurried toward their building.

On the way, Donna gave Virginia a quizzical look, and asked, "Are you nuts? Skinny-dipping with two horny, intoxicated men?"

Virginia started up the stairs to their room. "We can see the pool from our rooms. We'll watch, and when we see the guys slip in the water, we'll call security. When the officers arrive and find two naked men in the pool, they can handle them, and we'll get off scott free."

"Oh, I have an idea to add to make this even better. We want to keep the communication open with these guys for the investigation, right?"

"Yeah." Virginia tilted her head. "What is going through that devious mind of yours?" She opened the door to her room. They entered the room, went to the glass sliding doors, and scanned the pool.

Donna grinned. "Right after, or when, security arrives, so do we, but we're wrapped in these nice, fluffy, resort bathrobes. I like the bathrobes. As security officers are plucking the embarrassingly naked guys from the pool, we show up, so they can see us looking tantalizing and innocent. But we don't have to go naked in the water with them or worry about later. This should keep their interest, and they won't think we called security."

Virginia smiled. "I like how you think. Okay, let's get ready. As soon as we see them go into the pool, I'll call security."

Donna started for the connecting doors to her room. She stopped and turned. "Did you happen to note the writing on the side of their company work jeep and their truck as we walked by it in the parking lot?"

"Yeah. They said Litio Products." Virginia shrugged. "Funny name for a mining company."

"Must mean something to someone. Let's look it up quick before we do our little show for the boys and send them to the resort jail."

"Okay. We just need to slip off our shoes and put on the robes for when we go to the pool. We'll do this computer search quick." Virginia booted up her computer and did a quick Google search. "Well, look at this. Litio is Portuguese for lithium. It's an element that's got a lot of uses, including batteries." She did another search. "Here it is, Litio Products. The company is creating systems to extract lithium from the brine of the geothermal generating plants, and doing their own super-heated water extractions and separations in the Salton Sea and neighboring desert areas of California. Doesn't go into the ownership of the company. There are geothermal springs on the B bar P Ranch. So, maybe that's what the minerals they are looking for."

"Maybe. But they said minerals *and* geothermal stuff. That covers a lot of things." Donna looked at the screen, then at Virginia. "Wasn't that guy who was mad at Carol's lawyer from a company or some organization called Agua Caliente Mar Management? That means hot water sea management in Spanish. Coincidence? Competitor?"

"I don't know. We need to look them up, too. They're both interested in hot water, and Carol's… my ranch. But are they interested enough to kill?"

CHAPTER 8

Virginia did a quick Internet search for Agua Caliente Mar Management. The company was fairly new, dating from 2015. Their focus was to preserve the desert, especially the Salton Sea. They were also into environmentally friendly mining of precious metals and precious and semiprecious stones and minerals. *Gold and what?* Virginia glanced over her shoulder at Donna, standing by the sliding glass door. "Not really clear what they do, or who owns them." Virginia turned off her computer.

"Not surprising." Donna pointed out the glass door. "The guys just slipped into the pool. I'll call security. Time to put on our act."

Virginia and Donna hurriedly threw on the white, fluffy robes over their clothes and strolled across the parking lot to the pool. They stood just outside the fence and watched as the men were led away by three, hulking security officers. They turned and hurried back into Virginia's hotel room.

Virginia flopped onto the bed as Donna sat on the desk chair. She chuckled. "Well, we did it. The guys waved as they were being removed from the pool. I bet our little charade worked, and they don't think we called security."

"I think you're right." Donna pointed at the phone on the desk. "That flashing light means you got a message while we were flimflamming the guys. Want me to answer it?"

Virginia waved her hand. "Sure, let's see who left the message at this hour, then we'd better get some sleep."

Donna listened to the voice message, and then hung up. She sighed and looked at Virginia. "It was Detective Ferguson. Why does he call in the middle of the night? Doesn't he sleep?"

Virginia shrugged. "I guess not. What'd he want?"

"He had the autopsy results. He said Carol was stabbed to death by a double-sided, ancient, stone knife about eight-inches long. The knife was thrust up from under her sternum up into her heart. The autopsy also showed she was dying prior to her stabbing. She had cancer of the throat and lungs. He is waiting for more information on the material at the scene that was glowing. He'll touch base with you at our hotel, at breakfast at nine thirtyish."

"You guessed she was sick, but she was dying? That's a shock. Breakfast?" Virginia asked.

"That's what he said. Nine thirtyish. If you recall, I didn't think she looked okay, but I had just met her. She did have a dry cough, and her voice seemed a little raspy. However, I never met her before, so I had nothing to compare to. I figured she might have smoked in the past."

"She didn't smoke. The cancer may have been from her using radioactive materials to dye some of her fabric. That is, if the dyes are radioactive. We need to get a Geiger counter and test her glowing quilts. We still need to look at the shed where she dyed some of her fabrics."

"I agree." Donna yawned. "I need some sleep." She rose and headed for the connecting door. "See you in the morning—well, later this morning."

At nine-thirty in the morning, Virginia and Donna, both dressed in shorts and T-shirts, strolled into the hotel coffee shop. They had just started to look at their menus when Detective Ferguson arrived. He slid into the booth next to Virginia and signaled the waiter to bring him coffee.

Donna peered at him over the top of the menu. "Good morning, Detective. Glad you could make it for breakfast. You seem to like to call us in the middle of the night. Don't you ever sleep?"

"Sometimes I don't think so." He grunted. "It was a long night."

"That it was." Virginia set her menu down and glanced over at him. "The stabbing confirmed your suspicion, but the cancer was a new twist. Donna suspected something wasn't right about Carol's health. It could have waited until this morning, you know."

The waiter brought coffee.

Ferguson added sugar, then sipped. "Just what I need. Yeah, it could. But I wanted you to get the information quickly. You could have just listened to the message when you got up. You don't seem surprised about the cancer. Why not?"

"Like I said, Donna suspected she was ill." Virginia shook her head. "At the time, we didn't exactly expect cancer. We discussed it, but without more information, we weren't sure. Donna thought Carol could have had problems from smoking, but I knew she didn't smoke. Also, a few of her quilts glow in the dark."

"They glow in the dark?"

"Yeah." Donna drank some coffee. "She made a few of the dyes she used on the fabrics from some mineral deposits and plant extracts on her ranch. Some of what she used may be radioactive. If it is, we'll have to

Whispering Threads

figure out what it is and where it came from. She may have used some calcite, too."

Ferguson took another drink then set his cup down. "No shit? Radioactive stuff?"

Virginia nodded. "Yeah. We're going to check."

"She's got uranium on her ranch?"

"Uranium? I didn't say uranium, just radioactive. I don't think uranium glows. It's probably something else." Virginia glanced at her menu. "Donna thinks she knows exactly where it came from. We're going to look into it."

"Interesting. Anything else?"

"Yes, I'd like you to check on some people, and a couple of companies."

"Okay." Ferguson pulled out a spiral notebook and a pen. "Who's on your list?"

"A company called Litio Products, and another one called Agua Caliente Mar Management. The people are, Paul Blackman and James Kincaid. They both work for Litio Products. And Frank Coombs, he's with the Agua Caliente Mar group. Carol's lawyer said he has some prior arrests and he could be violent."

Ferguson took down the names. "What are their ties to Mrs. Putman?"

"They all want something on Carol's ranch. The Coombs fellow seems highly aggravated that his group didn't get part of the ranch in Carol's will. He was seriously pissed at Carol's lawyer. Why they want it is something we need to determine."

Donna waved the waiter over. "Shall we order?"

Donna drove her SUV to the ranch and parked in what looked like a barn. It held an old jeep, a Toyota Land Cruiser, a pickup truck, a flatbed truck, an ATV, a big trailer, and a large green tractor. She pulled in next to the tractor. "Looks like we have an assortment of vehicles to choose from for desert exploring."

Virginia hopped out of the car and looked around. She pointed to the far side. "Over there are some large pieces of equipment that look like they belong at a mine or a chemical processing plant. We'll have to check them out later. Let's go see Liana and find out if there've been any new developments."

They entered the large house and went to the living room. Liana was there talking to Emilio. They stopped talking when Virginia and Donna entered.

Liana turned and faced Virginia. "*Buenos días, Doña. Buenos días,*

Señora Bolette."

"Good morning, Liana." Virginia nodded at Emilio. "Good morning."

Emilio grinned. *"Buenos días, Doña."*

Virginia went to the large picture window in the back overlooking the desert and set her backpack on the floor. She turned and looked at Liana. "Liana, anything new, or important, happen while we were gone?"

"Sí. Un hombre enojado… angry man called. He yells a lot. He is from Agua Caliente Mar Management. He wants to talk to Miss Virginia right away."

"That figures. Anyone else?"

"Sí. A man from another company. He has called before. It is a company called Litio. He insisted on talking to the new *Doña.* I told him to call this afternoon. He said he would call back."

"Did he leave a name?"

"No."

"Okay. We'll handle them." Virginia said. "I have a question. Are there any Geiger counters around here?"

"Sí. We have many. I will get you one of the new portable ones we just bought. The batteries are fully charged."

"Thank you, Liana, and you too, Emilio. Please bring us one right away."

Liana nodded. "Okay. I'll get one, and then we will get back to work." She led Emilio out of the room.

Donna joined Virginia and pointed out the window. "The area I think she got the radioactive stuff that glows is that way. Want to take a look before anyone calls or arrives?"

"Sure." Virginia nodded. "I can't wait until our two friends from last night arrive and find out I'm the *Doña.* But we'd better wait on our excursion until we get the Geiger counter. We can see what it says about Carol's glowing quilts first, and then take it into the field."

A few minutes later, Liana gave them the Geiger counter and showed them how to use it. Virginia switched it on. The counter clicked sporadically.

Donna looked at the dial on the instrument. "Is all that clicking bad?"

"No. It's background radiation from the concrete slab the house is on and some of the building materials, especially the adobe. There seems to be a little more than I would expect in a house, but no telling what is in the dirt around here. Nothing to be concerned about."

"You know this… how?"

"I remember what one of my old boyfriends in college said when I went to his radiochemistry lab. He was a grad student doing some sort of research about separation of radioactive elements from spent nuclear reactor cores or something. He told me about it. Since it was a radiochemistry lab, they had radiation monitors all over the place."

Donna frowned. "Radio chemistry? Chemistry has a radio station in Orange County?"

"No, silly. Nuclear chemistry. Radioactive isotopes. Interesting stuff. I understood the basics of what he said, but not everything."

"What did you do in college, just date nerds?"

"I guess so. I did date a number of science and engineering majors, posed as the centerfold for the school of engineering's monthly magazine a number of times, and I married an engineering professor. Let's go see what happens when we take this thing into the quilt room."

Donna laughed. "Change the subject. Nice save."

Virginia went to the quilt room with Donna following behind. As they walked into the room, Virginia switched on the Geiger counter and moved it from side to side. The needle on the dial fluctuated back and forth while the instrument slowly clicked. As they stepped closer to the large, bright, red and orange quilt hanging on the far wall, the clicking became more rapid. "Looks like it's hot. The question is, from what? Uranium doesn't glow in the dark."

"I don't know." Donna pointed to another one. "Try that one."

Virginia approached the second big quilt and pointed the detector head at it. The Geiger counter responded with a low count rate. "This one isn't radioactive." She moved the Geiger counter around the surface. At two edges, on the binding, the instrument clicked faster. "It's hot here, here and over here, almost all around it. Maybe from a secondary source, like someone touching it, or maybe something in the binding."

"How about that smaller one."

Virginia walked up to the quilt. The machine didn't change. "It's got a low count rate, too. Not hot."

Donna went to the door and closed it, then turned off the lights. All three quilts glowed. The second one they tested, except for the radioactive spots on the binding that Virginia found, and the smaller one, started to fade. Donna switched the lights back on. "Okay. Those two are phosphorescent. Maybe the second one was touched and contaminated by something causing the hot spots to stay glowing. But they seem regularly spaced, so something is in the binding fabric."

"Meaning?"

"The two that faded after a while probably have some mineral that glows after exposure to ultraviolet light, like from the fluorescent lights in the room, and not from radioactivity. That big one on the other hand and the spots on the second, are—"

"Hot. Now, who's the nerd?"

"Okay, I dated a couple nerds, too. And I like to watch some of the science stuff on TV." Donna switched the lights back on. "Now, what do we do?"

Virginia sat on the chair next to the sewing machine and set the Geiger counter down. "Well, we've got something that glows, and it's radioactive. We've also got dyes that glow after being under UV light. That's probably from the fluorescent lights. Did Carol dye them out of something else? Where did the materials for those dyes come from? We are pretty sure uranium isn't radio-luminescent, so what's making these two quilts glow then fade?"

Donna started opening cabinets and looking inside. "Lots of fabric, thread, and other things in here. You're the quilt expert. You'll need to go through all this. Maybe some of this stuff also glows and is radioactive, or it's UV sensitive."

"You're right." Virginia picked up the Geiger counter and tested the boxes. "Carol's had radioactive stuff in here, and some may still be here. This will need careful handling."

Donna nodded. "I agree."

"We need to take a look at the outbuilding Carol used to dye her cloth. We were going to do that and got sidetracked." Donna looked past Virginia out the window. "Maybe there's more to this than her just using stuff from the desert to dye her fabrics. And you need to see the mines, steam vents, cinder cones, and geysers."

"Add them to the list," said Virginia. "Don't forget the meteor site. We also need to find the ghost ships of the desert, and solve Carol's murder, too."

"So much for your quilt retreat and show."

Liana entered the room. "There is a man on the phone who wants to talk to the *Doña.*"

Virginia raised an eyebrow. "Did he give a name?"

"*Sí.* His name is James Kincaid; he said he is a mining engineer with Litio Products." She pointed at a wall phone next to the sewing machine table. "There is a phone over there. Line two."

"Thank you, Liana." Virginia picked up the receiver, pushed the blinking button, and spoke. "Hello?"

She heard a man clear his voice. "Hello. My name is James Kincaid. I'm a field engineer with the Litio Products Company. I understand you are the new owner of the B bar P Ranch. Is this true?"

"Yes."

"Good. I'd like to arrange a meeting with you to discuss something important to both you and to my firm."

Virginia stifled a laugh. "Fine, when would you like to come?"

"Would this afternoon be okay?"

"Will you be coming alone or will Mr. Paul Blackman, the geologist, be joining you?"

"Huh? How'd you... yes, he'll be joining me, if you have no objection."

"Sure. Come at one."

"Great. One it is. Thank you. We'll be there."

"Oh, one more thing. Be prepared to tell me exactly what you want and why. I may have a lot of questions for you."

She heard him swallow. "Ahh... okay. We'll be there at one o'clock. Thank you." He hung up.

Donna leaned on the cabinet. "Did he recognize your voice?"

"I don't think so. He wasn't expecting me to be on the phone. He was shocked that I asked if Paul was coming."

"What are we going to do when they get here?"

"Find out what their real reason is to be snooping around here."

Liana entered the room, her face tense. "*Señora* Virginia, Señor Frank Coombs is at the gate. He sounds *muy* angry. He is the same man who called earlier from Agua Caliente Mar Management."

Virginia and Donna exchanged glances. "Oh boy. Well, he's here now, so open the gate, and let's see what he wants." Virginia sighed. "I guess the meteor will have to wait a few minutes."

Donna bit her lower lip. "We'd better have our guns ready, just in case."

CHAPTER 9

Virginia led Donna into the large living room. They sat near the huge stone fireplace and waited. A couple of minutes later Liana brought Frank Coombs into the room. He walked with a stride that suggested not so much brawn, but more like his hemorrhoids were killing him.

Liana stood to one side and waved her hand toward Virginia. "*Señora* Clark is the new *Doña* of the B bar P Ranch." Then she gestured toward Donna. "*Señora* Boletti is her friend. *Doña*, this is *Señor* Frank Coombs. He wishes an audience."

Virginia arched a speculative eyebrow. "Thank you, Liana. Mr. Coombs, take a seat."

Coombs, with black hair and bronze skin, dressed in a white shirt with a turquoise bolo tie and pressed jeans, frowned. He slowly sat in the chair indicated. "So you are the new *Doña*."

"Yes." Virginia leaned forward. "What is it exactly that you want or think you need from me?"

"Direct, I like that."

"I'm happy for you. Now, answer my question."

Coombs stiffened. "Look, lady. All we want is what should be ours."

Donna chuckled. "Who's we? Oh, and what exactly does the Agua Caliente Mar Management company do? The website is a little vague."

Coombs gave her an intimidating stare. When he realized it didn't work, he relaxed. "Okay. You're right. Being an ass isn't going to win me any points. It didn't work before on the old lady who owned this ranch either. I'm sorry. Can I start again?"

Virginia looked at Donna, then said, "Sure. Go ahead."

"The company is owned by the federally recognized Agua Caliente Band of Cahuilla Indians. The company was established to benefit the tribe, help preserve the earth, the Cahuilla valley, and the Salton Sea. It hasn't been easy. I am here to represent the company and the tribe." He handed Virginia a business card.

"You were pretty upset with the past owner's lawyer," said Virginia.

"Yeah. Not my best moment. I was upset. The past owner, Ms. Putman, was a cantankerous old gal, which was… well, frustrating. But she was honest and fair."

"I'm sure your attitude didn't help." Donna tilted her head. "So you're not into geothermal power generation?"

"No." He shook his head. "Definitely not."

"Your website says something about mining."

"Yes, but we're trying to do it, so we don't destroy everything around here. Mining gold and other precious, and semiprecious, metals and stones can be environmentally hazardous. Very hazardous. We're trying to do it in a manner that won't have an impact on the desert. We have a couple small mines in the mountains we're digging. We're using new methods developed by the Department of the Interior."

"Interesting." Virginia's expression grew guarded. "What is it you want from me?"

"We want part of the ranch. At one time, a long time ago, it was ours. But it now belongs to you. We're not allowed on the ranch. We would like to buy part of the property. Or, if you don't want to sell, maybe lease part of it or arrange for a fee type relationship based on the output of our planned operation."

"So, you want me to lease or sell you part of my ranch, or, if not that; let you mine part of it and split the profits. Is that correct?"

Coombs nodded. "That pretty well sums it up."

"Have you or some of your people been trespassing and watching us from a jeep?"

He jerked upright. "No. We don't do things like that. We respect what is ours and what is yours. We respect the land. That is why I'm here. We have not spied on you and have not trespassed. We would not do any harm to your land or you."

Virginia sat back. "Okay. Thank you. I understand what you want. What part of the ranch do you want to mine? And just gold? The mines are mostly played out."

"It's an area by the mountains to the southeast. If you like, I can bring you a map showing the locations and detailing our plans. We have ideas about a new location and reopening a couple old mines. The price of gold has gone up since they were closed. If you give us permission to prospect and mine the gold, I'm sure we can arrange a reasonable sharing agreement."

"Is gold the only thing you are interested in mining?"

"We are considering some other minerals like the turquoise you have and some of the meteor fragments."

"Turquoise and meteor fragments?" Virginia shrugged. "Okay. I can't promise anything at this point. I'm still getting used to the death of my friend and owning this ranch. I will take a look at the map and anything else you'd like to share. I promise to give it serious consideration. And we will keep anything you give us strictly confidential."

Coombs stood. "That's all I could ask. Thank you for seeing me. I apologize again for the way I came on earlier. Demanding to see you was not our tribe's normal custom. I can get excited."

"So I noticed. You have a criminal record, don't you?"

He glanced at the floor, then back at Virginia. "Yes. But that's in the past. I hope that doesn't upset your willingness to consider my tribe's plans."

"No. You've been honest. I will keep my word. Next time call for an appointment, okay? Is there anything else?"

He grimaced, as he stood then smiled. "No, ma'am. Thank you for giving me the time to present our request."

Virginia rose and extended her hand. He took it and shook hands. "Mr. Coombs, I look forward to receiving the information. Let me show you out."

As they walked toward the front doors, Donna asked, "Do you know anything about the ships of the desert?"

He stopped, turned and grinned. "Yes, of course. But what I know is probably exactly what you already know. Just the usual stuff, folklore really, about old treasure, gold and pearls, and spooky ghost ships. The tourists like the stories. If you get lucky, you may see them toward the Salton Sea."

"So they exist?"

"Yes. I've seen them."

"Okay. How about white gold?"

Coombs frowned and thought. His face brightened with realization. "Do you mean lithium stripping from the geothermal springs?"

Donna nodded. "Yes."

"Sure. I know about it, but we don't have anything to do with it. Others do it. We are not happy with the geothermal generators and the lithium stripping. They are causing more earthquakes, and we sit on the San Andreas Fault. Not good."

"How right you are." Virginia opened the door. "Thank you for coming, Mr. Coombs. I look forward to seeing your map and the other things you mentioned."

He smiled. "Thank you for seeing me and... well... being so courteous in spite of my behavior earlier." He then walked to his car.

Virginia closed the door. "That went better than I thought it would. He's frustrated. I feel sorry for the Cahuilla Indians. Maybe we can do something for them." She looked at her watch. "It's lunchtime, and the boys will be here at one. Better grab something fast. Gold, turquoise, and meteor fragments? That's an odd mix."

Liana came around the corner of the hall and stopped. "Don't forget your appointment at the bank in Palm Springs at three today."

"Thanks for the reminder. Liana, will you call the hotel and tell them we will be checking out tomorrow morning?"

"*Sí*. Will you be moving to the ranch?"

"Yes. Donna and I will move here tomorrow. It's too late to check out today and not be charged."

Liana beamed. "I will call the hotel immediately and get your rooms here ready." She hurried away.

"That sure made her happy," said Donna. She followed Virginia into the kitchen and helped make sandwiches. They went out on the spacious, covered patio with a massive stone fireplace at the end. Misters cooled the area. They ate their food looking out at the shimmering desert landscape.

The women returned to the living room as Liana escorted Paul and James into the room. James stopped and stared at Virginia and Donna. He frowned. "What are you two doing here?"

Paul looked confused as Donna chuckled.

Virginia pointed at two leather chairs. "Have a seat, gentlemen. I'm the new *Doña*, or owner, of the B bar P Ranch. I'm the one you need to talk to."

The men exchanged glances. Paul swallowed. "You two knew this all along and didn't say anything?"

Donna grinned. "It was difficult. We didn't know you all that well, and we wondered what you were up to."

James sighed. "I thought… well, I… I guess it's all business now."

Virginia gave them a quizzical look. "Just curious, what happened last night? When we came to the pool, the hotel fuzz was removing you. You guys end up in the resort jail?" James laughed. "No jail, but we are now at another hotel. The management had no sense of humor. I guess we upset the sensibilities of some uptight, prudish, self-righteous female guest."

"I see."

"Yeah. I'm glad you two weren't there yet. We saw you coming, but by then, someone had blown the whistle."

Virginia cleared her throat. "Okay, preliminaries are over. What can we do for you gentlemen?"

James sat back. "Our firm is looking for new geothermal areas to use to generate power."

"And remove lithium from the hot water?"

His expression grew guarded. "Ahh… yes."

Virginia leaned forward. "When we were all together last night, you mentioned mining and minerals. I suppose you want to dig up part of this ranch, too."

Paul spoke. "Well, we are interested in acquiring the mineral rights to a section."

"What minerals? Gold?"

"Hmm." Paul shifted in his chair. "Yes, gold and some other minerals."

Virginia looked at Paul with suspicion. "Some other minerals? Seriously? What other minerals?"

"In one spot you have some special... well, it's from the meteor crater."

"From the meteor crater? What the hell would you want from that?" asked Virginia.

Paul cleared his throat. "It's technical. You may not understand it all."

"Try me."

"The meteorite you have is one of the most nickel-rich meteorites in existence on earth. It also has a lot more than a trace of iridium. What you have is now in more demand. I'm sure we can work out some sort of deal."

"You mean it's ataxite?"

"Yes. You know about ataxite? I'm surprised." Paul said in a condescending voice. "The nature of ataxite is quite... well, you and Donna aren't scientists and probably wouldn't understand. For now, let's just say they are special." Virginia stared. *He's talking like we're children. And to think we went to dinner and went dancing with these guys. They either think because they're engineers and geologists they're superior to us, or they don't want to give up what they think is their advantage.*

"How do you know about my meteor?"

"We've obtained samples from the Native Americans in the area."

"Hmm... I see." Virginia got to her feet and stepped to the fireplace. "You are the second group today that wants to do some mining on my land."

James' eyes widened. "Others? What were they interested in?"

"Yep, you have competition. I'm not at liberty to disclose their request. But I'll tell you what I told the others. Send me a detailed description of what you want, why, and how you plan on doing whatever it is you want to do. Also, include how much you're willing to pay me to do it. I'll take a look at the information and let you know what I decide."

Paul looked at Donna. "We were hoping to get a little more commitment."

"Why?" Donna asked. "You haven't told us who owns your company, why you want Virginia's meteor, or exactly how you are going to get it and the gold without polluting the ranch. You also want to do geothermal extraction and then inject the water back into the ground on a major earthquake fault." Donna pushed a strand of black hair from her face. "Also, we want more on the lithium stripping process. We can't have you causing earthquakes or messing up the landscape for centuries to come. Give us the details."

Paul took a breath and slowly let it out. "James, I think the ladies have

Whispering Threads

made themselves clear. We have work to do." He looked at Virginia. "We'll be in touch. Thank you for seeing us." He rose and shook hands with Virginia. Donna led them out.

Donna watched the men leave then closed the door. She turned toward Virginia who was looking out the front window. "We sort of know what they want, but not why."

"They didn't tell us everything. They didn't answer your question about who owns the company as well." Virginia continued to watch the men drive down the driveway. "Two outfits want to do mining on my land, and they came the same day. And they came right after Carol died. There's something else going on. We need to find out what it is."

"Would Liana know anything about it?"

"I don't know. Let's ask her." Virginia headed for the rear of the house. They found Liana finishing making up a bedroom. "Liana, I have a question about the ranch."

Liana looked up from her work. "What would you like to know?"

Donna sat on an upholstered wing chair. Virginia plopped on the bed. "How does the ranch make money? We haven't seen any crops growing nor any cattle, sheep, or goats."

Liana sat on the edge of the bed. "We make money from the sale of gold, copper, lead, zinc, and silver. We sometimes sell calcite, celestite, colemanite, and fluorite. We also sell meteor samples, some antiquities, the unique turquoise we have, and... and... we use to sell some type of special material that glows," her face brightened, "and other stuff. We make most of our money from the copper, turquoise, meteor samples, and gold. The little bit of special glowing material we still sell, helps though. Many years ago there was a uranium mine. It played out years ago. Part of it collapsed. It is closed."

"How did you happen to know all about it?"

Liana looked down, then back at Virginia. "Besides being *Señora* Putman's housekeeper, I was her assistant and secretary."

"Oh. Well, you're my assistant and secretary now, too."

"Thank you."

Virginia's eyes widened as she realized what Liana had said. "Wait. There's a uranium mine here, too?"

"It is old. And like I said, part of it collapsed. It is no good anymore. No one has mined it in many years."

"Okay." Virginia nodded. "Tell me more about the ghost ships."

"Huh?" Liana looked confused. "They have nothing to do with the mine."

"I'm sorry. I know they don't. You said the mine is dead. Now I want to know more about the ghost ships. They keep coming up, and seem to scare Emilio."

Liana sat and thought for a moment, then spoke. "The ships have been sighted for a few centuries by the local people. They believe they forewarn of trouble. Bad omens. The legends say they are old treasure ships from the early sixteen-hundreds that got stuck here when the passage to the Gulf of California dried up. The stories claimed that they were loaded with pearls, a fortune's worth, millions of dollars' worth of exquisite pearls. The stories claim that the Spanish ships sailed into the Salton Sea area to find the legendary Straits of Anian, an all-water route from the Gulf of California to the Gulf of Mexico. Some stories claim that the Salton Sea and the Colorado River were higher and filled with water at the time. Supposedly, this was during an unusual flooding season. Some stories claim that after the ships had sailed from the Gulf of California and into the Salton Sea, an earthquake happened, closing off what remained of the Salton Sea from the ocean. Regardless, when the Spanish ships had sailed into the Salton Sea, turned around to try and head back home, they found that it was closed off. With the outlet to the ocean blocked, the water their ships were in was rapidly evaporating. The water slowly receded, and eventually, the ship was beached on the California desert, many, many, miles from the ocean."

"Pearls?" Virginia asked. "A treasure made up of pearls?"

"Yes," Liana said. "But there is more."

"Continue."

"Other versions of the tale involve a pirate ship loaded down with almost a million doubloons. Another tale puts a Spanish galleon on Lake Cahuilla, another name for the large inland sea that eventually became the Salton Sea. Lake Cahuilla existed in the 16th century and had a tribe of Native Americans living in the area at the time. Knowing that the Spanish were coming to take their treasures and probably hurt the tribe, the Cahuilla Indians instead ambushed the Spanish party that came ashore from the ship. Then the tribe mounted a full attack on the galleon and after a fierce battle, annihilated all the crew on board, claiming the ship for the tribe. The Cahuillas began looting the ship of the clothes, foods, and exotic items that the Spanish had brought with them, but they could not move nor break into the heavy large iron chests that were in the hold. While they were debating what to do with the treasure chests, a storm brewed up and began attacking the galleon. The Cahuillas were forced to desert the ship, which broke from its anchor, drifted off into the storm, overturned and soon sunk into the sea taking its precious cargo with it. By the time the lake supposedly dried up, the ship had been long buried under tons of dirt, sand, and silt. They say the ships are haunted and warn others of disaster."

Donna swallowed. "That was one hell of a story. People believe it?"

Liana smiled. "There are treasure hunters who come and search for the ships and the treasure. The Native Americans and Hispanic folks around here believe the stories, too. Most people who live here for a while see the ghost ships. Yes, people believe. Some believe the meteor had something to do with the ships being sighted, too."

"Anyone come close to actually finding the ships or the treasure?"

"There are stories, but none of them proven. But Mrs. Putman believed them and hinted that she had found either the ships or the treasure."

Donna relaxed the grip she had on the chair's arm. "Could that be the cause of Carol's murder?"

CHAPTER 10

"I don't know." Virginia shook her head. "Liana, besides the metals, you mentioned Carol sold some of the materials that glow in the dark?"

Liana nodded. "*Sí*. She sold the materials from the land and some dyes she made for cloth."

"She actually made the glowing dye here on site?"

"*Sí*. She had some that would glow if the sun or the big lights were on it first. But they fade out. *Señora* Carol and a couple of the ranch hands did mix them. But her arthritis got worse. And she and the men were getting sick, so they mostly stopped. We did it carefully."

"What kind of illness did she and the men get?"

"Trouble breathing, sore throats, loss of hair, sores in their mouths... they were tired a lot."

"Liana." Virginia wrung her hands. "Did Carol say what exactly they were using or how she found the materials?"

Liana shook her head "No. I don't think so." Her face grew clouded, and she frowned. "Mrs. Putman did say what it was, but I don't remember. It think it started with an R."

"Did Carol mention the white gold or geothermal operations in the area?

"*Sí*. She didn't approve of the geothermal power generation and putting the water back into the ground. We are on a big earthquake fault. She mentioned white gold too. She said it was lithium. She said some company was trying to get her to lease or sell some of her ranch for them to get the white gold. She said no."

Virginia rubbed her hands together. "I have a sneaky feeling the Litio Company and the tribe are interested in more than what they said."

Donna leaned against the doorframe. "Anyone interested enough to kill for it?"

Virginia looked at Donna and Liana. "Kill for it? Maybe. We've got the ghost ships of the desert, a possible treasure, the meteor, the artifacts, the turquoise, silver and gold mines. How do they fit into this puzzle? Then

Whispering Threads

there is the knife that killed Carol, and the one like it we have. They sound like artifacts from an Indiana Jones film. What part do they play in all this?" Virginia pushed herself off the bed. "We have a lot to think about. I'm going to call Andy, then get ready to see the lawyer."

"Want me to come along to see the lawyer?" asked Donna.

"You can if you like, but I think you can do more good here. If you would, go through the maps and ranch papers and see what you can find out about the ghost ships, mines, and what that stuff is that was glowing. Didn't Emilio say Carol's hair was glowing like a faint halo?"

Donna nodded. "Yeah."

"Call Detective Ferguson and see if the lab reports are done yet."

"Okay. I'll get on it." Donna looked at Liana hopefully. "I'm going to need your help."

"Okay," said Liana.

Virginia headed for the office. She plopped in the leather desk chair and dialed Andy's office.

The phone was answered on the third ring. "Dr. Clark's office. This is Sandy. How may I help you?"

"Sandy, this is Virginia, is my husband there?"

"Yes, Mrs. Clark, he's preparing for a lab. I'll tell him you're on the phone." She put Virginia on hold.

A second later Andy answered. "Hi, Tiger, how are things in the desert? Making progress on the investigation?"

"I've got more questions than answers. Things are definitely unusual out here."

"More unusual than ghost ships, glowing quilts, ancient artifacts, and investigating a murder?"

"Yeah. I'm going to the lawyer and will be back soon. After I'm done, I'll own a whole lot of desert."

"That's great. But from the sound of your voice, that's not the problem, is it?"

"No. I've got a lot of desert to go over and some strange outfits wanting to mine or do something with it."

She heard him inhale, then say. "How do they relate to the murder of your friend?"

"Don't know yet."

"Any developments on the glowing quilts?"

Virginia's voice cracked. "Not really. Carol made the dyes from materials here on the ranch. It made her, and the men who helped her, sick. I don't know what it is or where to look for it."

Andy cleared his throat. "The glowing stuff is probably a mix of Radium and a zinc salt, like a sulfide. The alpha particles from the Radium affect the zinc sulfide crystals, and they glow. It was used on watch crystals to make the numerals glow years ago. I remember a chemistry instructor told us about it when I was an undergrad."

Virginia leaned back in her chair. "That explains the ones that continually glow. But we've got a couple that glow, then fade."

Andy chuckled. "They're phosphorescent. Made from crystals of calcite, celestite, or other such minerals."

"You know this... how? That chemistry instructor?"

"No. I took a geology class, too."

"I didn't know that. But now I've got to finalize some things with the lawyer. Then, Donna and I have some more investigating to do. Thanks for the information."

"Virginia, be careful. Maybe I should come."

"We'll be careful. You need to stay at the university in Texas and teach. Donna and I will be fine. We're just going to do a little investigating."

"That's what worries me. But keep me posted on progress."

"I will. Thanks, Andy. Got to get ready to see the lawyer. Love you." She hung up.

Liana stood in the doorway. "*Señora* Clark?"

Virginia looked up at her. "What is it, Liana?"

"I am sorry. I said I didn't recall where the material Mrs. Putman used to make the glow in the dark quilts came from."

"I remember."

Liana smiled. "I just recalled where she got it. Part of it comes from near the meteor hole."

"Good. Thank you, Liana. Please inform Donna about it, too. Now, I've got to get to the lawyer's office and bank."

At four-thirty Virginia left the bank. She had produced her IDs, opened a bank account and signed all the notarized documents. She strolled out of the cool bank into what felt like a dry oven and hurried to her ranch car. She started it, switched on the air conditioning, sat back and closed her eyes. *That feels good. Now that I'm the owner of eleven square miles of southeastern California desert, and a lot of trouble, what am I going to do?* Virginia shook her head and drove out onto California 111. Deep in thought, she turned south and drove through Cathedral City, Palm Desert, La Quinta, and Indio. As she reached a more desolate area, she noticed an old, dilapidated, wind-scoured, advertising sign near the side of the road. The faded ad had a drawing of a comet, a desert community at the Salton Sea, and boats. *The old cities at the Salton Sea went bust years ago. Just a reminder of days gone by.* She continued to drive as the late afternoon shadows

Whispering Threads

moved slowly across the sand. *Wait, that sign just reminded me, the quilt that glows depicts a representation of the ghost Spanish Galleon and a comet or meteor. Only the ship glows brighter than the comet. There are some other features on it I didn't really study. And that seventeen seventy-five painting in the office of the galleons. Better look when I get back to the ranch.* She drove past some small businesses, a couple date palm groves and finally to the turnoff to her ranch. As she drove up the incline she spotted the mysterious jeep on a rise with two people watching her. She stepped on the gas and sped up the dirt road, leaving a dust cloud behind her. Her cell phone rang. *Now what?*

Virginia slowed, yanked her phone from her backpack, and answered. "Hello?"

"Virginia, Ferguson here. I've got something preliminary lab results from Carol's murder."

"Good. Is it about the stuff that glows?"

"Yes. The stuff that was glowing on the knife and Ms. Putman's hair samples contained a radium salt and zinc sulfide. The question is where'd it come from?"

A radium salt and zinc sulfide, huh? Andy was right. Virginia felt her heart skip a beat. "Good question, maybe E-bay."

"Seriously? E-bay??"

Virginia smiled. "Just kidding. My husband thought that would be what the lab would find. We think the source is somewhere on the ranch. Carol mixed the materials to make a dye for her fabrics. Donna and I may have an idea about where they came from. I'll talk to you later, hopefully with more information." She shifted her phone to her other ear. "I just spotted that mysterious jeep trespassing and watching me again. Any luck with the pictures of it I gave you the other day?"

"No. Well… the jeep is a World War II vintage. I'll send a deputy to see if he can find it and run them off."

"Good luck. It'll probably be gone. Wouldn't the jeep in the photograph be valuable?"

"Not in southern California. The movie people use them a lot, so they're everywhere."

"Oh. Okay. No luck there. Just so you know, I'm on my way to the ranch, and I'm now the official owner of the B bar P Ranch."

"Be careful, Virginia. Remember, the last owner was murdered, and we don't know why."

CHAPTER 11

At the ranch, Virginia parked the car in the barn and headed for the house. When she got inside, she dropped into an upholstered chair in the living room and sighed. She looked up as Donna walked in.

Donna stared with curiosity at Virginia, then sat on a chair across from her. "Everything go okay at the lawyer's and the bank?"

"Yes. But on the way back here, I saw an old, faded sign. It showed a comet, and the Salton Sea, an old seaside development, and a boat."

"What about the old sign?" Donna asked. "A comet and a boat? You okay? Were you out in the sun too long?"

Virginia chuckled. "I'm fine. I just think, since it is still light outside, we should go see that meteor crater and what's around it. Oh yeah, I talked to Detective Ferguson. I told him our mysterious jeep is back."

Donna raised an eyebrow. "Did you chase it?"

"No."

"What did Ferguson say?"

"He's sending a deputy to look for it. I asked about that picture you took of it the other day and gave him. All they could tell was the jeep was from around World War II."

Donna rubbed her chin. "Did he have any news from the lab about what was at the crime scene?"

"Yeah. Preliminary report says the stuff that was glowing and made Carol's hair look like a halo is a radium salt and zinc sulfide. Liana said the materials came from somewhere near the meteor crater."

"Maybe there is something else going on, and it isn't the gold or the uranium mines. Maybe it has to do with white gold or geothermal energy. But how does the meteor play into all this? And we still have the ghost ships to consider."

"Or maybe we're just paranoid."

"Someone did murder Carol, so I think we can rule paranoid out," Virginia said.

"You're right."

"You know, white gold and geothermal energy may be related to the murder, but there is more to this, much more. I think we need to go see that crater, like now."

"Do you know what time it is?"

"No." Virginia looked at her watch. "It's six-thirty."

Donna smiled. "What are we doing for dinner tonight? I don't think our two friends from Litio Products are going to be inviting us anymore."

Virginia tilted her head and frowned. "Where did that come from? After all this, you're worried about food?"

Donna grinned. "A girl has to eat."

Virginia stood and stretched. "Okay. Let's head back to the hotel. I need to find Liana and have her lock up, just in case. Maybe we can see the crater on the way to the hotel."

Virginia went to the kitchen and found Liana going through a cookbook. "Liana, we're going to see the meteor crater and then going to the hotel. We'll be back in the morning."

Liana's placed the book on the granite countertop. "Okay. Do you want anything to eat before you go?

"No. We'll get something on the way to the hotel, or there. But on the way here, I saw the jeep again on a rise not far from here. I'm concerned about the ranch. How secure can we make it at night?"

Liana grinned. "We can make it very secure and quickly. I can lock the gate from here. I can also lock the house. The walls are actually two feet thick and made of steel reinforced concrete. The outside is made to look like stucco. The windows are five inches thick and made of both hurricane resistant and bulletproof materials. There are roll down steel shutters, too. *Señora* Putman was concerned about safety. She said this *casa* could take a category five hurricane or a large EF5 tornado. We have held up very well to a big earthquake, too. I think it was a 6.5 or 7.5. The doors look like wood but are armored steel with big bolts for locking. You could hit them with a ram and not move them. They are like a safe's door. From here, I can also lock the barn and all the sheds. Emilio can lock up his cabin, and the boys can secure their bunkhouse, or I can do it from here. They are all built like this house. I can monitor them from here and also lock them. I will tell the men. They have alarms and weapons there, too."

Virginia stood staring. "Wow. Things must have gotten really bad for all that security."

"*Sí*. About six years ago we had a house invasion; I think that's what the sheriff called it. We are far out from other people. The robbers burst in and robbed *Señora* Putman and hurt her. They destroyed part of her home. She built this for us to live in."

"Wow. I'm glad you told me. Carol never mentioned that. Do you have alarms?"

"*Sí.* We have sensors, cameras, and alarms for anyone coming through the gate, moving around the outside of the house, barn and sheds, and the other buildings where the men are. If someone tries to break in, more alarms will go off. We can stop them. I have many guns and pepper spray in here. We can also shoot outside from the inside of the buildings. I will know if anyone is trying to move around outside or tries breaking in before he knows he's been detected. We have backup generators, water supply, and communications. All secure. We have an automated firefighting system and ninety thousand gallons of water for the firefighting system stored in underground tanks."

Virginia's eyes widened. "This isn't a house… it's a damn fort."

"*Sí.* It is a fort. *Señora* Putman was very proud of her fort. She would call it Cordone's Fort and would laugh. When you leave, I will tell the men. We will lock up, and we will set all the alarms. You will be coming back and moving in tomorrow, yes?"

"Yes." Virginia pulled out a piece of paper and wrote her and Donna's cell numbers on it. "I know you have my number, but… well, in case of trouble, call us immediately and call Detective Ferguson."

Liana took the paper and nodded. "I will." She smiled at Virginia, "I'll hold the fort tonight. *Por favor*, be safe."

Virginia led Donna toward the front door. *Who the hell is Cordone?* Virginia thought.

Sipping coffee after dinner, Virginia and Donna sat at a table in the hotel dining room overlooking the pool. Virginia looked at her watch. "It's eight, and we haven't heard from Liana. And I wish I hadn't let you talk me out of seeing that crater tonight."

Donna swallowed the last of her chocolate ice cream she had ordered for dessert and looked at Virginia. "Were you expecting a call from her? Why would she be calling? She said she would lock up."

"I know. But I still thought someone would try something after we left."

"Again, why? No one has bothered us so far. We didn't see anyone around the ranch that didn't belong there when we left. The two groups who want to do stuff on the ranch have been there, and we talked to them already."

Virginia shrugged. "I know. Guess this case is getting to me. We have a lot to do, and we're being watched. It's… well, unsettling. Anything could still happen."

"Boy, you're a barrel of laughs. For your information, that crater needs a four-wheel drive vehicle or a horse to get to it. There are some other

Whispering Threads

things close to it I want you to see as well. We wouldn't have time tonight. I don't like driving off road at night either."

"Okay. After we get back to the ranch tomorrow, we're off to see the crater. I was curious about something Liana said. She mentioned Cordone's Fort and that Carol laughed at the name."

"So?"

"Who was Cordone? Why name the ranch house Cordone's Fort?"

"I don't know. All good questions. From the way Liana told us about it, she didn't know why Carol named it that either." Donna looked outside. "It's still light, and the view is great. The mountains are gorgeous. I love the way they look at sunset. They seem to change as the shadows roll across them. Want to take a walk? Maybe that will relax you."

Virginia stretched. "I could use a walk to unwind. Let's pay the bill and go. There's a strip mall just down the street." She waved the waitress over to get the bill.

After paying, they strolled out the front of the hotel and started walking down Bob Hope Drive toward California 111 and the strip mall. Virginia looked toward the mountain in front of them. "That thing is sure big. It's got to be a few thousand feet high. We haven't got anything like that in the Texas Hill Country. I miss the mountains, the ocean being so close, and of course the desert. When we lived here, we could eat breakfast in Laguna Beach, overlooking the ocean. Then, we'd drive up to the mountains and play in the snow and have dinner here in Palm Springs. After all that, we'd go home to Mission Viejo. Same day. Can't do that anywhere else in the country."

Donna nodded. "You're right about that. But it is very expensive here, and it is extremely crowded, too. Then there's the traffic."

"You sure know how to spoil a dream."

"If you want to move back, I have just the place for you and will tell you all the great things about SoCal."

Virginia chuckled. "Real estate agents."

"Broker, dear… I'm a broker. Real estate agents work for me." As they turned into the mall, Donna pointed at a little dress shop that was still open. "Let's see what we can find in there."

"Okay." Virginia followed Donna into the shop.

As they browsed, Donna looked out the storefront window. "Why would three men be sitting in a vehicle staring at a dress shop? We're the only two in here."

Virginia glanced casually out the window. "One of them has binoculars. We can't be that interesting."

"Let's go and see if they follow us."

"I could just call Detective Ferguson and have him send a sheriff's cruiser to investigate. Might be a lot safer."

"Yeah, but not as much fun," Donna said. "Let's leave and see if they follow. If they do, then we call the cops."

"Okay." They headed out of the shop. Virginia hustled them to a sidewalk vendor with a pushcart, and they bought two small ice cream cones. "We need these like a hole in the head, but at least we can have an excuse to look their way. So far they're still in the car watching us. Let's stroll back to the hotel."

They walked slowly eating their ice cream when the suspicious car slowly drove past. Virginia's heart skipped a beat. *There're only two men inside now. Where's number three?* She looked over her shoulder. "We've got company behind us, and their car just turned into the resort front parking area. It's headed for this side of the lot. Maybe they think they'll use a pincer move on us." They finished their ice cream as they approached the parking lot.

"I see them. What are they up to?"

"We'll find out soon enough." Virginia pulled her cell out of her leather backpack, and speed dialed Ferguson and told him their situation. She put the phone back and slipped her pistol out. She held it by her leg as they walked. She noted Donna had her gun out, too. "They'll make their move when we turn into the parking lot. Be ready."

CHAPTER 12

Donna slowly took in her surroundings. "Okay. Do you want to confront them now?"

"No. Let them make the first move. We'll see what's up, and then do something appropriate."

"I have a feeling Ferguson won't like it." Donna stepped into the parking lot and moved a few feet away from Virginia. "Here they come."

The car stopped in front of them. The doors opened, and two men hopped out. Their open sport coats revealed glimpses of side arms. Virginia watched them as she held her gun in two hands in front of her. Donna swung around and faced the man behind them, gun at the ready.

Virginia spoke. "Hold it right there. Keep your hands where I can see them. Who are you, and what do you want?" One of the men from the car cleared his throat. "I'm Special Agent Norman Baker. We are with the U.S. Department of the Interior, Bureau of Land Management. We need to talk. My credentials are in my jacket pocket. May I get them?"

Virginia nodded. "Yeah, but go real slow."

"Okay." He carefully withdrew his credentials from his shirt pocket and displayed them for Virginia and Donna.

Donna waved her pistol at the man behind them. "You, move over there with the others."

"Okay." With his hands held away from his side, he slowly walked to the other men by the vehicle.

Baker removed his credentials case and tossed it to Virginia.

Virginia studied the credentials and badge. "You could have just called us on the phone and made an appointment."

Donna frowned. "What does the Bureau of Land management want with us?"

Baker shifted on his feet. "If you will lower your weapons, we'll be happy to tell you."

Donna glanced at Virginia. "Can I shoot them now and get it over with, or do we hear them out, and then I shoot them."

Virginia chuckled at the sight of the men's shocked faces. "She's kidding, I hope. No telling with her. She hasn't shot anyone in a while. Keep that in mind, gentlemen. What do you want?"

Baker tensed. "Are you serious? Is she serious?"

"Try something stupid and see."

"Okay, okay. I believe you." Baker held up his hands with palms toward the women. "Relax. You two are special agents with the Smithsonian Central Security Service, aren't you?"

"Yes."

Baker continued. "You now own the B bar P Ranch, correct?"

"Yes. Why does the BLM care?"

"You own something we need to investigate and secure. There are others who covet what you have."

"What do you, and the others, whoever they are, think we have, an A bomb?"

"Not exactly. But you have something from out of this world."

Virginia stiffened. *What does a meteor have to do with anything? Is it the meteor he's talking about?* Her hand tightened on her pistol. "What's on my ranch belongs to me. The federal government can ask for permission to come on my land. If I catch anyone, even your people, trespassing or prowling around, they're liable to get arrested, if they're lucky. They'll more likely get hurt or worse. I may even let my friend here shoot the trespasser. The ranch is a huge slice of very hot, dry, desert. Lots of not-so-nice critters live there, too. Then there are old dilapidated mines with deep shafts where you could have a serious, or fatal, accident. Understand?" *If they are who they say they are, I just threatened federal officers.*

Baker's jaw clenched. "Yes. We get the message."

"Good."

"It's pretty hot out here. Would you ladies care to go into the hotel bar and discuss this in a cooler environment?"

Donna lowered her weapon. "You buying?"

Baker sighed. "Yes. If it will make you happy, I'm buying."

She looked at Virginia with raised eyebrows, who nodded. Donna smiled. "Okay. Let's move out of the sun. We'll meet you in the bar."

They watched as the men climbed into the vehicle and drove toward the front of the resort. Donna looked at the shadows from the mountains as she and Virginia walked across the parking lot. "They could've offered us a ride."

"Would you have gone with them?"

"Probably not." Donna put her gun back in her purse.

Virginia slid her weapon into her backpack and watched the men enter the front of the lobby. Virginia slowed. "Are they what they claim to be? Something tells me they're not. Why all the theatrics? Why not just call

Whispering Threads

like the others did?"

Donna shook her head. "I don't know. It's awfully suspicious. Maybe Bureau of Land Management special agents don't have a lot of clandestine stuff to do around here, so they watch too many cop shows on TV."

"I'll call the SCSS and have them checked out." She pulled out her cell phone and talked to Washington, then Detective Ferguson, as they walked. "They're running them and will call back. Ferguson's sending backup."

They entered the hotel and proceeded across the lobby to the bar. The three agents had procured two tables and pushed them together toward the back and waved. Virginia and Donna skirted small round tables with other bar patrons and took two chairs at one of the tables.

Agent Baker sat back and smiled. "This is better. I'm sure you ladies have a ton of questions. But first, what will you have?"

After their drinks arrived, Virginia and Donna studied the three men. Virginia shifted in her seat to get easier access to her backpack and gun. "Why are there three of you? Why didn't you call me for an appointment? All this cloak and dagger stuff is a little over the top."

Donna set her drink down. "What makes you think we have…" she made air quotes, "…a not exactly A-bomb?"

"Okay. Fair questions." Baker took a sip of his drink. "We've been watching the ranch for a while now. We know you don't have an A-bomb or anything that can produce fissionable material. That would be the Department of Energy or Department of Defense's jurisdiction anyway. We are more interested in part of your ranch that is near the mountains in the southern section. Near the meteor crater. As to why we didn't call you, that was because we saw who was visiting you, and that you've been under someone's surveillance since you inherited the ranch. We think it was one of the groups who sent people to see you."

Why is everyone now so interested in that damn meteorite? Ataxite is rare and valuable, but give me a break. What's so damn important or unusual about it that the BLM wants it? We'll have to check it out… later. Virginia sipped more of her drink. "So you play big, nasty, armed, secret agent men, in a black SUV with dark windows, and spy on us, too. We spotted you, and we did see someone on my ranch watching us from a jeep, too. Oh, the intimidation crap doesn't work on us."

"Mrs. Clark. We believe they may be people from one of the groups. They may well be dangerous."

Virginia slammed her drink on the table. "You knew they were there and didn't tell me? Where were you hiding to be able to see our spies? Were you trespassing, too? Now you want me to trust you?"

Before they could react, Virginia's cell phone rang. She yanked it out of her backpack and looked at the screen. She glared at the men. "I need to take this." She pushed her chair back, rose, then hurried to the entrance of the restaurant and answered the phone. She listened, then hung up. *No such person as* Bureau of Land Management *Special Agent Norman Baker. BLM has no special agents in this area at this time. Who are these guys? Better let Donna know.* She texted Donna with the information and added that the SCSS was sending the closest federal agents, maybe Park Service rangers, Bureau of Indian Affairs or real BLM rangers, to apprehend them and for her and Donna to be careful. *Where the hell are the sheriff's deputies, Ferguson said he would send when I talked to him?* Virginia stuck the phone in her pocket and walked back, to the tables. "Sorry about that. Big ranch. Lots to take care of. Eleven square miles is a lot of dirt and sand."

Baker nodded. "We understand. It will take time to get up to speed on running it."

"Yeah." Virginia glared at Baker. "Now what exactly does the BLM want from me?"

Baker cleared his throat. "We need to examine the meteorite you have, the land to the south-east of it toward the Salton Sea, and take possession of them."

Virginia's jaw dropped. "What? Are you crazy? And you want me to play nice, just say yes, and hand all that over to the Bureau of Land Management?"

Baker smiled. "Yes. It would be easier for all parties concerned if you cooperated."

Donna raised an eyebrow. "The desert to the southeast of the crater?"

"Yes." Baker nodded. "And the meteorite."

Virginia settled back. "I'll think about it. I'll contact my lawyer and let you know. Don't call me, I'll call you."

"Mrs. Clark." Baker's face darkened. He pulled documents from his inside jacket pocket. "*We* have the authorization papers with us. *You* need to sign the documents *now.* You don't need your lawyer. The fewer people involved, the better. National security. I'm sure you understand."

"National security and the Bureau of Land Management? Yeah, right. Give me a break." Virginia noticed four uniformed U.S. Park Rangers and two men in sport coats enter the hotel and head for the restaurant. She nudged Donna and indicated the rangers to her with a nod. While Baker talked, Virginia and Donna carefully slid their pistols out and held them under the table.

CHAPTER 13

Virginia watched the Park Rangers go to the restaurant, and the two men in sport coats enter the bar. They sat in a booth behind the men at Virginia's table and seemed to be discussing some business deal. Then she saw the rangers reappear, one by the bar's kitchen entrance, one was standing in the hall to the restrooms. The other two were now at the bar's entrance. All the exits were covered.

She leaned toward Baker. "I'll do as I darn well please with my land—national security or not. And I do not think my land has anything to do with national security. I don't own an ICBM. This intimidation crap doesn't work with me."

Baker frowned. "Look… we don't need to make a scene, but *you* have *no* choice. Sign the papers or…" One of the men with him started to pull a semiautomatic from under his coat. Donna swung her gun up and aimed it at him. Virginia followed. "Leave it! Drawing a weapon to scare us wasn't too smart. And what was the rest of that sentence, 'sign the papers, or we'll kill you?'"

Virginia looked up. The two men in sport coats moved in a flash standing on both sides of the tables.

The man next to Baker displayed a badge case holding a sheriff's six-pointed gold star.

"Riverside County Sheriff. You three are under arrest. Do as the ladies and I say, or I'll let them shoot you."

Baker puffed up. "We are BLM special agents. This is a federal matter. Your assistance is not required or requested." The deputy smiled and nodded at Virginia and Donna. "Special Agents Clark and Bolette called for our assistance. Now carefully remove your side arms and place them on the table. Do it nice and slow. These ladies can't miss from where they're sitting. Then stand up slowly, one at a time."

The rangers hurried to the table and took the three men into custody and handcuffed them. The lead ranger read the men their rights. "You are charged with impersonating federal officers and suspicion of fraud. I'm sure the U.S. Attorney will think of more charges after conferring with these ladies. The county DA will probably have some impersonation, firearms, fraud, and other charges as well."

Virginia stood and slid her gun into her backpack and glanced at the lead ranger. "Sir, can I have the documents he wanted me to sign?"

"Sure." The ranger pointed at the documents on the table. "Go ahead and take them. The county DA, or the U.S. Attorney, will want them, so, you know, follow the chain of evidence procedures, Agent Clark. Is there anything else we can do for you?" He handed her two chain of custody bags and forms.

"Yeah." She stepped toward Baker and shot him an icy look. "Who do you really work for? Why are you trying to defraud me?"

Baker shook his head. "I know my rights. I don't have to talk to you."

Virginia motioned for the lead ranger to move away from Baker and the other men, but close enough for the prisoners to hear. "Ranger, can we talk to them first? Maybe let my friend and I question them out in the desert while you guys get some coffee?"

"He's been arrested, Agent Clark. They've invoked their right to remain silent and get a lawyer." The ranger realized what she was doing and smiled. "But I guess you could try to talk to them out in the heat. It's one hundred and eight in the shade right now. But you can't exactly torture them."

"Torture?" She put her hand on her heart. "Heavens no. We would never *exactly* torture them. Just some questions under less than ideal conditions, at least for them. Maybe we'd provide a little unconventional encouragement. You know, enhanced questioning. You guys thought waterboarding was effective but bad. You should see what my friend and I could do in the desert with hot sand and local flora and fauna. Trust me; we can be very encouraging."

She noticed Baker fidgeting. Beads of perspiration formed on his forehead. *Good. Made him squirm.*

Baker stammered, "No! Keep those women away from us. We have rights."

Donna turned toward Baker and shook her head. "Well... well... the big bad man is afraid of two women? What a wimp."

The ranger laughed and moved Virginia out of Baker's earshot. "Just so you know, they'll be tied up in paperwork for hours. No phone calls during the processing time. And it's late. Maybe we'll have to finish the processing sometime late tomorrow. In the meantime, they'll be held without bail. Tonight and tomorrow we'll have them in holding cells in an un-air-conditioned part of the station. Not much air circulation either. You know, it's supposed to be a hundred and thirteen tomorrow. And while we do the paperwork, we'll remind them that in the event they can post bond, you and your friend are out there somewhere waiting for them."

"Ranger, I like how you think. You guys and the sheriff have been a big help. Thank you."

"Any time. Just call. I'm sure the U.S. Attorney will be in touch as well as the DA." With people in the lobby watching, the rangers and deputies escorted their prisoners out of the resort.

Virginia grabbed the papers off the table and turned to Donna. "Let's go finish packing and take a look at these documents. Maybe we'll figure out who they actually work for."

Donna nodded. "Good idea." They headed for their rooms.

Once inside Virginia's room, Virginia set the papers on the desk, sat, and examined them. "It says the organization that is listed as the recipient of the land is the National Marine Management Agency or NMMA. Hmm, not the BLM. The contract is basically a fraud. I would get next to nothing, and NMMA would have a complete run of my land and be able to do anything, pollute anything, and bar me from going near the meteor, or the acreage around it. And they were not going to compensate me except for a hundred dollars and legal fees." Virginia looked up at Donna. "This is bull shit. I'd never sign this. What does a national marine agency care about in the desert? Why my desert? Have you ever heard of this NMMA?"

"No." Donna grabbed her laptop. "But while you're reading, I can look it up on the Internet. Hang on." She rapidly typed and paused to read. "Ah-ha." She pointed at the laptop's screen. "It's some sort of outfit that looks like a government agency but isn't. They let you *think* they're an official agency. They seem to be a private outfit that does government contracting of sorts. It doesn't say much about what it really does. Just a lot of words that don't mean anything. Looks official though. Talks about undersea exploration, sea mining, marine archeology and such stuff."

"I'll call the SCSS and see what they can find."

"Sounds like a plan." The phone rang. Donna answered it. She listened, then hung up. She hesitated, slowly turned, and then looked at Virginia with a shocked look on her face. "Houston, we have a problem."

Virginia swallowed. "What's up?"

"The men the park rangers and the sheriff's deputies arrested have escaped."

"Oh, shit. What happened?"

Donna plopped onto a chair. "They were ambushed on their way to the jail. Two rangers and a sheriff's deputy were injured. One of the men with Baker is dead. Whoever hit them used automatic weapons and smoke grenades."

"How did whoever attacked the officers know that Baker and his buddies were arrested?"

"Maybe they were watching."

"I'd better let Liana know. She needs to be on the lookout for trouble."

"Good idea. Maybe we should just bite the bullet on the costs and check out now and head to the ranch. The government is footing the bill anyway. Baker and company know where we are. They could try and get to us here, as well as try something at the ranch."

"Okay. Finish packing and let's go. I'll alert Liana." Virginia called Liana, then the SCSS. She finished packing and snapped her suitcase closed as Donna dragged her bags through the connecting door. Virginia yanked her bags off the bed. "Ready to roll?"

Donna nodded. "Did you call Liana?"

"Yes. She's expecting us and has the ranch on lockdown. I contacted the Smithsonian, too. They are checking into NMMA. I also checked us out of here using the TV check-out feature, so we can just load the car and head out."

"Good. The sooner we're at the ranch, the better I'll like it."

The women opened the door, peered out at the now dark parking lot, and hurried down to Donnas SUV. They loaded their bags, climbed in, and headed for the ranch. As Donna drove, Virginia kept an eye out for anyone following them as they headed into the desert.

Donna relaxed her grip on the steering wheel. "So far so good. No one following us, right?"

Virginia took another look out the rear window. "Not that I've seen."

Virginia sat at the desk in the ranch office. The desk clock said 10 pm. She looked at Donna sitting on an upholstered chair under the big oil painting of the ships of the desert. Liana was stretched out on the leather couch under the steel shuttered window. Virginia sighed, "Okay, what do we know?"

Donna took a breath. "We've got a boatload of people who want access to the ranch for similar, and some different, stated purposes. Then there's the National Marine Management Agency and the fake BLM agents.

Virginia ran her hands through her hair. "Someone murdered Carol. The meteor seems to be of high interest to a lot of people." She looked at the oil painting of the desert, above Donna that she had seen before. In the upper half of the painting, situated against the mountains, were two Spanish galleons seemingly floating on the desert floor. She remembered the date on it was seventeen seventy-five. Virginia rose and walked around the desk toward the painting. "I saw this when I was in here before. It shows the ships of the desert. But look more carefully." She pointed. "Look at that first ship. What's the name?"

Donna stood, bent closer, and looked. "Cordone."

Liana rose and stepped to the painting. "Look at the land near the ship. That little figure is Coyote, the Trickster God." Virginia went back to the desk and sat. "There are some features on that painting that are on the quilt in the workroom that glows. We need to compare them." She swung around and brought up the desk computer. "I've been meaning to do this. Let's see who this Cordone guy is, or was." She typed away. "Okay, look at this."

In 1610, King Phillip III of Spain ordered Alvarez de Cordone to search the Western coast of Mexico and recover the pearls residing there. Cordone hired two other captains, Juan de Iturbe and Pedro de Rosales. He also hired sixty pearl divers and began having three ships built. By July 1612 they set sail to plunder the west coast of its precious oysters. They sailed into the Gulf of California and up into Lake Cahuilla where they were attacked by Cahuilla Indians and killed. The ships floundered in a storm, then sunk carrying with them chests filled with pearls, silver, and gold. A couple of survivors returned to a mission and told of the slaughter...

Liana nodded. "What is left of Lake Cahuilla is now the Salton Sea. It was connected to the Gulf of California at that time."

"Okay." Virginia leaned back. "We know who this Cordone fellow was. I have a theory."

Donna glanced at Liana. "This'll be great, or she's off her meds."

"Off her meds?" Liana gave Donna a puzzled look. "Is she okay?"

Virginia looked up at the two women. "I'm right here, remember?"

"Yes." Donna grinned. "Okay, what's your grandiose theory?" She plopped down onto a chair.

"Liana, you said it was a home invasion that made Carol build this house-fort, right?"

"Yes."

Donna shrugged and gave her a perplexed look. "So, because of that, she overdid the building a little. I'd be inclined to do the same."

Virginia steepled her fingers in front of her and smiled. "Yes, anyone would build a place stronger. But she built this place as a fort and named it Fort Cordone. Why?"

Liana shook her head. "I do not know."

"Maybe this house is built either on the site of the actual treasure, or it's close by. Carol may have found the treasure, and this is the vault she built for it. This was probably paid for with things from the treasure she discreetly sold. That could be why people are so interested in the ranch. Someone identified something she sold. The meteor plays some role in this, too."

Liana nodded and smiled. "You said Mrs. Putman might have found the treasure. I think she may have found some of it at least." She pointed at the desk. "Look in the middle drawer toward the back."

Virginia opened the desk drawer and looked in the back. There was a small cloth bag tied with twine. She pulled it out, opened it. Two pearls rolled onto the desk followed by a small gold bar with a heart stamped on it. "Jackpot. Looks like she found some of the treasure anyway." Virginia searched the rest of the desk. "Nothing indicating where these things came from." She re-bagged the pearls and gold bar and put them back in the desk.

Donna looked up as Virginia put the bag back in the desk. "That gives some actual credence to there actually being a lost treasure and all this intrigue." She turned and studied the painting. "These pearls and gold bar, plus what we've learned so far and the picture and glowing quilt, explains a lot of what we're experiencing. I noticed a couple things in the painting that are similar to the glowing quilt. And I think this painting, and the quilt, needs a closer look. What else are we missing?"

Liana pointed at the painting. "Look at the sky and the area at the bottom right."

CHAPTER 14

On the ridgeline, a mile from the ranch house, two men sat in a jeep. One stared at the house through a night vision telescope. James Kincaid, sitting in the passenger seat lowered his scope. "They're all inside. Can't see anything, just some light leaking around the edges of those steel shutters. It's quiet."

Paul Blackman nodded. "We'll wait for them to go to bed, and then we can get close and try to locate a way in."

"Why? It's obvious they don't know what we're really after. And in case you didn't notice, they've got the metal shutters down. They've secured that place tighter than an ant's ass in a sandstorm. Let's let things settle down, then move. We have time."

"I'm not so sure." Blackman sighed. "They blew Baker's cover pretty fast. Ours may be at risk. And our employer wants to see results soon."

"What Baker did was damn stupid. He's a damn loose cannon. Now the women are on the alert. I don't know how they fingered Baker so fast. He was supposed to use the BLM agent cover as a last resort. The bastard jumped the gun to look like a hero. Then the escape turned messy too. He's drawn even more attention to the mission. That's why I think we should play it slow. The old lady wasn't cooperative, so why should those two women be either? Their guard is up. I think we should only push enough for them to do the legwork faster, so they find what we want. Then we swoop in and take the plunder. Anyway, we can stay close to them, nurse our cover story as company mining engineers and geologists looking for geothermal springs, energy generation, extracting lithium, and have a little fun with them." Kincaid grinned. "Who knows, we may get a little extra from them for our attentiveness."

"You just have a thing for the blonde. Good thing she liked you, as she's the new owner. But don't forget, they're both married."

"They went to dinner with us. They were going to go skinny dipping with us if someone hadn't blown the whistle." Kincaid rubbed his fingernails on his shirt. "I've always been good at seducing married women. It's the challenge."

"Yeah, yeah. I think they played us both. I have a feeling Virginia is not going to be an easy pushover for your charms. Your amorous maneuvering could get you shot." Blackman pulled a wool poncho over his head. "For being so damn hot during the day, it gets darn chilly at night." He looked back at the ranch house. "But you have a point. We may still be able to utilize our relationships with them. We need to find out what they know, and prod them in the right direction."

"So, why don't we just happen to be in the area tomorrow and drop in?" asked Kincaid.

"Without what they asked for? Are you nuts?"

"Call the office and tell them to hurry." Kincaid looked at the ranch house again. "We can offer information piecemeal, and string them along. If we see them tomorrow, we'll know what they're doing. They won't have to do anything stupid, or too dangerous."

"We could get closer and see if we can hear anything using the parabolic dish contraption of yours."

Kincaid nodded. "Good idea. What could it hurt?"

Virginia stepped closer to the painting. Liana and Donna stood staring at it.

Liana pointed. "Down at the lower right. If you look close, there seems to be some chests stacked up. They are near a sand dune. It's away from the water. There is a small heart on them."

Donna put her finger on the painting. "You're right. It is a heart. Why? And what does that have to do with the meteor that's pictured up there, over the ship?"

"*El Corazon* is Spanish for the heart. It also represents gold or treasure. It is like the little heart on the gold bar in the desk." Liana rubbed her chin. "Look at the shape on the thing that is flying over the ships. I don't think it's a meteor. It looks like Temayawet, ruler of the land of the dead. He's riding the celestial body." She frowned. "Maybe it *is* the meteor he is riding."

Virginia's face scrunched in concentration. "Another god depicted in the painting? Why? Maybe they're a warning. Through the ages, mankind has been fascinated with the heavens. For thousands of years we have been gazing upon the stars and marveling at rocks falling from the sky. In historic times, meteorites that were observed descending from the heavens were often regarded as messages from God. Depending upon the local culture and the current social environment, these objects were considered as either good or bad omens. Maybe that's why that god is riding it. The ships and their treasure are one puzzle we have, and whatever is going on with my meteor is another."

Whispering Threads

Liana turned and sat on the couch under the painting. "What do they have to do with the stuff that glows?"

Virginia shrugged. "Probably nothing. Carol used minerals from the ranch to make some special dyes. Maybe the glowing compounds were naturally out there, and the Indians thought they were from the gods. After all, the meteor crashed here. Maybe that's all there is to it. The real question is what is it that everyone else wants on the ranch? The meteor is valuable, but not worth killing over, unless there is more to it than we know. We've got an outfit that wants to do hydrothermal generation of power using my thermal vents and extract lithium. At least that's what they want us to think."

Donna nodded. "Don't forget the Indians and their mining request."

"At least we know the tribe is real," Virginia said.

Liana looked down at the floor and then up. "Mrs. Putman was most interested in the ghost ships and the treasure."

Virginia returned to the desk and drummed her fingers on the mouse pad in front of the computer. "Carol may have found the ships and some of the treasure, maybe all of it and that's what got her killed. I think we should make our finding the ships and the treasure our first priority. They may lead to Carol's killer. Maybe the quilt or this painting will yield a clue as to where to look."

Donna smiled. "I'm game."

Liana nodded. "Me too."

A buzzing sound interrupted them. Virginia looked at a panel on the side wall with a map of the compound. A small red diode light flashed. "Liana, what does that mean?"

"That's the outside alarm. It's a motion sensor system." Liana bolted out of her seat. "It means someone outside has come close to the side fence where that light indicates."

Donna stood, "Should we go see who it is?"

Liana looked at Virginia. "May I use the computer?"

Virginia slid the keyboard toward her. "Go for it."

Liana typed and then pointed at the computer screen. A CCTV picture of two figures appeared. They rested an apparatus with a parabolic dish on the end on a wooden fence rail and aimed it at the house. Liana glanced at Virginia. "Would you like me to get rid of them?"

"How?" Donna asked.

"Yes." Virginia nodded. "Go ahead."

"They have about a foot of that big thing near the dish resting on the fence. There is a large conductor embedded in the top rail. Watch." Liana used the mouse to move the cursor on the screen. Liana clicked on a file. When the file opened, she clicked on another icon and closed the file.

The screen showed the men jumping back and falling.

The smoking contraption dropped to the ground.

"Wow!" Donna's eyes widened. "You gave them a hell of a jolt. How many volts did you use?"

Liana smiled. "I sent a burst of about two thousand volts through the conductor. It works like a taser. That should discourage them, at least for a while. I probably broke that device they have." She looked at the monitor. The men climbed to their feet and hurried away into the dark. "It looks like they are leaving."

Virginia smiled. "Yeah, that was quite a show. They dropped their equipment and are running off. Nice for us, they left their toy behind. Let's wait a minute, and then go get it. Maybe we can trace it to whoever they are."

Liana turned off the blinking light. "What is that thing?"

"With a parabolic dish antenna on the end I think it's a listening device. We'll soon know for sure."

Donna took a breath. "Think they heard anything?"

Liana looked at the shuttered and thick windows. "No. The windows are thick composites with air spaces, and the shutters probably would not help them hear anything. I do not think they had time before I shocked them anyway."

They hurried to the kitchen door. Liana switched on the outside spotlights, raised the steel shutter, and opened the door. Virginia stepped out and dropped to her knee holding her gun out in front of her. Donna did the same on the other side. Seeing no one around, they rose and darted for the fence with Liana remaining by the door. Virginia reached the fence and turned toward Liana. "Is it safe for me to climb over it?"

"Yes," Liana responded.

Virginia climbed over the short wooden fence and picked up the instrument. She handed it to Donna and hopped back over the fence. They returned to the house and secured the door.

Donna set the long pole holding an electronics box and the dish on the kitchen table. She bent over and looked at it. "Yep. Looks like a listening device. Here is where the headphones plug in. Think we can trace it?"

Virginia examined the outside of the electronics package, then pried off the cover. "No label on the outside. Looks homemade. Funny this isn't screwed on." She looked inside at smoldering, blackened, circuit boards with some burnt components. Insulation on a few wires had bubbled. Solder had melted in a couple of spots shorting conductors. A couple of capacitors were fried, and the battery had exploded. She waved her hand over it. "It stinks. Looks like something for the scrap heap. It'll be hard to trace it from this mess."

Liana pointed at the dish. "There's a number on the back of this. Will it help?" She bent over and looked at the front of the dish. "This looks burnt, too."

Donna copied the number and handed it to Virginia. "I'll call Ferguson and see if the sheriff can trace it."

The phone on the counter rang. Liana answered it. "B bar P Ranch, this is Liana. How may I help you?" She listened then said, "Miss Virginia's right here, please hold." Liana handed the phone to Virginia. "It is a man from the Smithsonian."

Virginia took the phone and sat on a kitchen chair. "This is Virginia." After a few minutes of conversation, she gave them the number from the dish antenna, then hung up and leaned back. "That was the answer to our inquiries. First, Agua Caliente Mar Management is legit. It belongs to the Indians, and it does what we were told. Litio Products is real also, but here's the thing, it is owned by the National Marine Management Agency or NMMA. How convenient. The Smithsonian Central Security Service said it's somewhat shadowy. It isn't a federal agency. It's a private company of some type that's incorporated offshore. It has operations here and in other countries. Like you found on the Internet, Donna, they're into energy, undersea exploration, sea mining, and marine archeology. But the EPA, IRS, DOJ, Customs, the real BLM, and a few other alphabet soup agencies are interested in them. Interpol and Scotland Yard are investigating them, too. NMMA seems to be attracting a lot of attention for various reasons." She looked at the instrument on the table. "While I was talking to the Smithsonian, I asked them to trace that dish. They may be able to do it faster than the sheriff. We'll give this to Detective Ferguson tomorrow."

Liana sat across from Virginia. "Holy Mother, what has this NMMA been doing?"

"I don't know. The Smithsonian Central Security Service didn't say. But to attract that much attention, they're pretty shady."

Liana sat back. "What are your plans for tomorrow? Are you and Miss Donna still planning to look at the meteor and the mines tomorrow?"

Virginia paused to consider Liana's question. "Yes. I'd also like to look at the area where the ghost ships were seen and check out the meteor crater. I'll examine this painting and the quilt more before we go."

Donna hopped onto the granite countertop near the sink. "It's getting late." She looked at the kitchen clock. "Almost midnight. But I was curious about what Virginia said a while ago. If this place was built like a vault for part or all of the ghost ship's treasure, where would it be?"

Liana bit her lip and stared at the far wall. "I don't know. I have been in every room and didn't see anything out of the ordinary."

"But you weren't looking for anything either."

"You are right. Where would we start looking?"

Virginia tipped her head back and stared at the ceiling. "Did Carol keep a set of blueprints for the house and other buildings?"

Liana nodded. "They are all in a file cabinet in the office. She had a couple complete sets made."

"Good. Tomorrow, while Donna and I go exploring, I'd like you and Emilio to measure the outside of the buildings and the inside of each room. Write your measurement on the drawings for comparison. Maybe the marked-up blueprints will turn up a hidden space. Also, compare the drawings to each other to make sure they are alike. If there's a difference, maybe that's the vault." She patted the instrument on the table. "Tomorrow, please call Detective Ferguson and have him send a deputy to get this thing."

Liana grinned. "I will get Emilio right after breakfast. Are you sure you don't want him to go with you as a guide?"

Donna yawned. "I have the map he gave me. It's quite detailed and has his notations on it. If we need anything, we'll call or radio you. Virginia may find something of interest in the painting or on the quilt, too before we go."

"Okay. I hope we find something."

Virginia stretched. "I hope so, too. The stories say the ships move and the ships seem to be real. I wonder how they move and where they go undetected."

Liana smiled. "As the sun and the moon cross the sky, the shadows dance, the earth changes color and the landscape change as well. A person can get easily lost in the desert because of that. Everything looks different as the day progresses, even from day to day, especially during and after a storm, or when the wind blows. The ships don't move, the shadows, sand, and the earth moves. The desert around here is a dangerous place to be, especially in bad weather or at night. That's when the spirits walk. Very bad."

CHAPTER 15

At sunrise, Virginia and Donna, dressed in long-sleeved shirts, jeans, and hiking boots, drove a ranch jeep out of the compound into the desert. They followed Donna's map toward the southern section of the ranch to the meteor impact site. Stands of Joshua trees, Mojave yucca, and areas cloaked in creosote-bush scrub surrounded the winding path they traveled.

Virginia pointed at some California fan palms in the distance. "Must be water near there."

Donna consulted her map. "According to this map, that's a small oasis. Beyond that, it's sand and salt."

Virginia stopped where Donna told her to, raised her sunglasses, and looked around at the desolate hills. A dust devil crawled across the desert floor, stirring up a cyclone of dust. "Where's the meteor?"

Donna pointed at a ridge ahead of them. "That's the edge of the crater. Can't drive there, the thing is in a large bowl-shaped area with a dry arroyo running through it. We hike from here."

"Okay, let's grab our packs and slip on our gun belts. No telling what we'll find." After Virginia adjusted her backpack, she grabbed a camera. "Will you get the video camera?"

"Yeah." Donna hefted her pack and strapped on her leather gun belt. She attached her canteen like Virginia had done. "Don't forget the sunscreen."

Virginia held the plastic sun lotion bottle in the air. "Got it." She pulled on her University of Texas baseball cap and started up the incline toward the meteor crater with Donna, wearing a Green Bay Packers ball cap, following. At the top of the short ridge, they looked down at the impact crater.

Virginia sat on a boulder. "It's not as deep as the one in Arizona, but it's impressive. Looks like a dry stream runs through the crater. We need to gather some samples." She looked around. "Where are the mud volcanoes or whatever you called them that we saw before? They're around here someplace aren't they?

"Yes." She pointed southeast. "Over there about three miles." Donna slipped off her backpack and removed the map Emilio had given her. She looked at it. "After we pick up the samples, we should go up the arroyo toward the mountains."

"Why?"

"According to this map, Carol got some of the material she used in her dyes from a cave up there. The dyes that glow."

"The radioactive ones or the fluorescent ones?"

"Doesn't say. I guess we'll find out."

Virginia glanced at the streambed where it snaked out of the bowl toward the hills. The other end went toward the Salton Sea. "Okay. Let's get what we can here and then find the cave and pick up more samples. We can mark where we got them on your map."

"Sounds like a plan. I'll make a separate sketch of the crater, so we know exactly where the samples came from." Donna pulled her backpack on and followed Virginia in a zigzag route down the slope. At the bottom, Donna pulled out some plastic zip lock bags and two black Sharpie pens. She and Virginia spent the next half hour gathering rock and dirt samples and labeling the bags. Donna made the sketch of the meteor crater and indicated where the samples were collected. While Virginia finished putting the samples away, Donna pulled a small Geiger counter out of her pack. She turned it on, and it started to click softly. As she approached different locations in the crater, the needle read higher values, and the counter clicked faster. "We've got some radioactive stuff around. Is the, what did you call it... oh yeah... is an ataxite meteor radioactive?"

"No. Ataxite is not supposed to be. It's mainly iron, nickel, with a trace of iridium and a few other elements," Virginia said. "What areas are hot?"

"Mostly in and around the arroyo. Maybe the radioactive stuff is washed down the mountain by water when it rains."

Virginia stretched. "When we get back to the ranch, we can check each sample to see if any of them are hot. In the meantime, let's head up the arroyo and find that cave. Is there anything else around here we should see?"

"There's a silver mine about a hundred yards farther up the hill. A note on the map says that Carol got her fluorescent stuff there too. And few miles away is the turquoise mine and a played-out gold mine. Back toward the ranch house is where Carol was murdered. There's another silver mine, and a gold mine, in that area as well. According to the map, the turquoise mine is higher up on one of the mountains, and we can see the whole valley and the Salton sink from there. Maybe we'll see the ghost ships."

"Okay." Virginia pulled her backpack on. "Let's follow this arroyo and find the cave and then take a look at the silver mine. Then I want to see my turquoise mine. On the way back to the ranch, I want to stop again at the site where Carol was murdered. That was at the old played out uranium mine, wasn't it?"

"That's what everyone said. You saw the mine."

"Yeah, but I didn't own it then or go in it. Now it's different. And you said there were tracks off to the side made by someone other than the sheriff's folks."

"Yes. It's on the way back so we can stop there without going out of our way." Donna stopped and looked up the arroyo. "This is steeper than I thought." She wiped her forehead with a bandana.

Virginia looked over her shoulder. "Too many days behind a desk and too many power lunches takes a toll."

"I go to the gym religiously, for all the good it's done. This pack is heavier with the rocks in it," Donna grumbled. She started forward.

"Poor baby. You religious? You look great. I've seen men turn to watch you."

"Look who's talking about religion. Are we there yet?"

"You've got the map, what does it say?"

Donna stopped and pulled the map out of a side pouch on her backpack. She unfolded a section, looked at it, and then gazed around. "Okay, the cave is supposed to be about, and I'm guessing, fifty yards farther and on the right. It's just beyond a bend in the arroyo. This says there's a fault outcrop at the site."

"Let's get cracking." Virginia turned and continued to climb around some boulders and nasty vegetation with thorns up the slope. She heard Donna grumbling behind her.

Virginia stopped about where Donna told her, sipped some water from her canteen, and waited a minute for Donna to catch up. "Is this the spot?' She looked around. "The curve is back there, and that looks like a fault protrusion. Where's the cave?"

Donna sat on a flat rock and took a big swig of water. "According to this map, it should be over there in the side of the mountain near the... the... whatever those nasty plants are."

"Anything more specific?"

"Over there. Oh... watch for sidewinders."

"Watch for sidewinders is on the map?"

"Yep." Donna pulled her semiautomatic out, rested it on her lap, and put the map and canteen away.

Virginia pulled her gun. "Okay, let's head for those bushes and the cave, and watch for rattlers. Are they in the cave or outside?"

"Don't know."

They worked their way up the side of the arroyo to the area with some pale, scary, thorny plants. Just beyond the bushes under a rock overhang was a cave.

Virginia pointed. "That must be it. No snakes so far."

"Good," said Donna puffing. "I'd rather not make the acquaintance of a sidewinder. It's getting really hot, so maybe they're all in a snake bar having a cold beer or cactus wine."

"Snake bar? You've been in the sun too long. Get your Geiger counter out, and let's see what we've got." Virginia pulled her flashlight out, switched it on, and started into the cave. "Hey, come see this."

Donna switched on her flashlight and joined Virginia. On the wall of the cave were petroglyphs. They swung their lights around examining the figures. Donna stepped close to the left side and touched one of the images. "Looks like some desert varnish. These are very old."

"I didn't know the ancient people around here made cave drawings."

"You do now." Donna slowly worked her way down the tunnel looking at the petroglyphs and for snakes as Virginia snapped pictures of the petroglyphs. Donna abruptly stopped. "I think we may have an issue."

"What? Did you see a snake?"

"If I saw a rattlesnake you and everyone else within fifty miles would know, and my gun would be empty. No, these seem to be telling a story, and it says, now remember I'm not an archeologist, but I think they say the natives were extracting something magic, and over time it made them sick. They mixed whatever it was with something from another place, a cave or mine. Being ancient, my guess would be another cave. From this, I think it's close by. The result was used in some sort of rite or ritual. There is what may be a warning at the end of this."

"Turn on your Geiger counter."

Donna switched it on. The counter clicked rapidly. The meter needle swung to the right. "It's hot in here. I wonder what's radioactive in here. Uranium?"

"Maybe. Maybe this is where Carol got her radium. If it is, then this cave has uranium in it, and by the way that meter is behaving, there is a lot of it. Let's go a little farther and see what's here."

They moved cautiously for another fifty feet and then stopped. Donna held up the Geiger counter. "The clicking is really, really fast. I think it's time we blew this chicken coop."

"I agree. Let's grab some samples, then go up to the silver mine where Carol got her fluorescent materials for her dyes," Virginia said.

They picked up numerous dark rocks, some of which were yellow to greenish color with a luster. A few had greenish streaks. After the samples were bagged, Virginia and Donna went back to the dry streambed. Virginia turned and started up the incline with Donna followed and fussing about the temperature and the weight of the rock samples. They found the mine opening and rusting equipment scattered around in front of it. Pulling out their flashlights, they headed cautiously inside. In places, new timber or steel replaced old wooden supports. On the floor in the dust, old picks and tools were strewn around. Footprints could be seen in the dirt.

Virginia examined some of the rocks on the floor and examined the walls of the mine. "Looks like this mine has a lot of silver and some lead and zinc. They appear to be sulfates and sulfides. Let's bag some and see what we've got when we get to the ranch."

Donna stood with her mouth open, and then slowly spoke. "You know this how? Wait, don't tell me, you dated a geology student in college."

"Yes. He had a big—"

"I don't need to know how big his—"

"Boat. He had a big sailboat. Get your mind out of the gutter, girl. You've been away from your husband too long."

"Well... there's always our dinner dates."

"Donna!"

"Just kidding." She switched off her flashlight and looked farther down the cave. She pointed at the walls. "Oh boy. Take a look at that."

Virginia looked where Donna was pointing. Ahead was a faint greenish-blue glow. "We need to collect some of that, whatever it is. If it is the zinc sulfate and the radium mix, then this place is radioactive, too." She followed Donna to the fading glowing dust. "Turn on your Geiger counter and see what it says."

"Okay." Donna pulled out the instrument and turned it on. "Looks like this area is hot too. Not as bad as the last cave, but hot none the less."

"Let's grab the samples and get out of here."

They quickly bagged samples and exited the mine and returned to the crater. As they reached the top of the ridge above their jeep, Virginia's cell phone rang.

Virginia pulled her phone out of the pocket. "Hello?"

"Virginia, this is Liana. Mr. Frank Coombs, the man from the reservation, just called. He said you are being followed and to watch your six. Does watch your six mean anything to you?"

"Yes. Did he say how he knew we were being followed?"

"No. But he said there are two men, and they have rifles."

"Okay. We'll be on the lookout. How are you doing with the measurements?"

"We are still doing them, but we're almost finished. A couple of the other workers are helping by measuring some of the other buildings. I told them you are trying to determine exactly how big things are. How are you and Miss Donna doing?"

"Good. We've seen the meteor crater, we found a cave with petroglyphs in the hills above it, and we found the silver mine where Carol got fluorescent materials for her dyes. We're going to some more places, now."

"I know the cave, and the mine. They are... how do you say it... linked? I think that's the word. They are called *las cuevas de la muerte*. The caves of death."

CHAPTER 16

Virginia sat on a boulder and clicked her cell phone off. "That was Liana. She said Mr. Coombs just called and told her to tell us we're being watched by two men with rifles."

Donna looked around. "Where are they?"

"I don't know, but we need to be careful. Oh, she also said she knew about the cave and silver mine we were just in. They are connected somehow and are called the Caves of Death."

Donna sat on the boulder next to Virginia, pulled out her map, and studied it. "This shows the cave and mine, but doesn't have any names for them, especially Caves of Death. There is a small skull and crossbones near them though."

"Great. Now you mention that? Maybe they are called that because anyone who worked them died. You thought the cave drawings indicated something like that." Virginia took a drink from her canteen. "Let's dump these samples in the jeep and then go to the turquoise mine. We need to keep watch while we're out here."

Donna tucked the map away. "Okay. We may be able to hear them if they drive up here."

"I don't think they will, if they are watching us, they know we're armed. Now, about that mine."

"The turquoise mine we can drive to, I think. I've been dying to see it. I like turquoise. Can we collect some of it while we're there?"

Virginia rose and dusted off her jeans. "Yeah. I like turquoise, too, so let's get some nice specimens for both of us."

Donna got up and picked up her pack. "Good, let's go before it really gets hot." She glanced at her watch. "After we see the turquoise mine, how about lunch?"

Virginia waved her arm at the desert expanse. "You see a restaurant or fast food joint around here?"

"No, but Liana packed us some food."

Virginia's eyebrows shot up. "Oh. Okay. Let's go to the turquoise mine and eat there."

Virginia drove up the rutted, dirt, trail and parked the jeep in an open area at the entrance to the turquoise mine. Dust settled along the road behind them. "We're here. You're sure this is the turquoise mine?"

"Yep." Donna nodded. "Let's have a look. Bring the radio along; I think I spotted our watchers on the way here."

"I saw them too. They're about a mile and a half or so back, on one of those cinder cones."

"Right. I hope they stay there. You going to call the sheriff?"

"Not yet. Let's see what they do."

"Okay." Donna turned. "Take a look at the view. You can see the Salton Sea, the mud pots, and the steam vents over there."

Virginia rose, sat on the back of her seat and looked around. "Nice view. There are the sand dunes Liana mentioned where the ships are supposed to hide, and I think a couple oases. This looks like the view in the painting and the quilt."

"You're right. The dunes look a little different, but that painting was made a few hundred years ago, and the sand moves."

"This view is closer to the image in the quilt." Virginia pointed at them. "If you look carefully, you can see areas down there that are highlighted in the glowing areas on the quilt. That may be significant. I believe there are more dunes south and east of here."

"Yeah. They're owned by the Feds and the State of California. According to the map, those down there on the edge of the ranch are yours."

Virginia removed her hat and wiped her forehead. "It's getting hot. Let's have a look at the mine and then think about what we're going to do next, like eat lunch. At least in the mine, it'll be cooler. Let's get some samples first."

"Good idea." Donna hopped out of the jeep. "Don't forget the radio."

"Got it." Virginia followed Donna into the mine.

After an hour examining the mine and collecting various pieces of turquoise, they walked out of the mine and back to the jeep. Donna placed their bags with the turquoise in the back of the vehicle and tossed in her pack. "I noticed a good deal of copper in there as well as the turquoise."

"I noticed that too. Maybe they go together somehow."

"I see a dust cloud headed our way." Donna tucked her semiautomatic into her belt and pulled her shirttails over it. She watched Virginia do the same.

"I do, too. Probably whoever was by the cinder cones earlier." Virginia sat the radio on the front seat and picked up the rifle from behind the seat. "You move over by that rusted machine. That way we're not both in one spot and easy targets."

Donna stepped to the old piece of yellow mining equipment and leaned against it, her gun in her hand.

The white Ford Explorer slid to a stop about fifty feet behind the jeep. As the dust settled, Virginia stared at the two occupants through the sights of the rifle.

Virginia yelled. "Mr. Blackman, Mr. Kincaid, slowly exit the vehicle with your empty hands in plain sight." She watched Blackman and Kincaid open the doors and slowly climb out with their hands stretched out beside them. Virginia noticed a bandage on Kincaid's right hand.

Blackman cleared his throat. "Is this any way to treat friends?"

"You are trespassing, and you've been watching us. We don't appreciate that. You were warned about being here uninvited. It's a big desert, and you could easily have an accident."

"You mean you wouldn't just call the sheriff?"

Virginia smiled and motioned toward Donna with her head. "I would, but she said she needs target practice. Now, what do you want? I take it you don't have the information we requested, yet."

Kincaid gave her a nervous grin. "We have some of it coming this afternoon."

"Good. Call the house for an appointment."

Blackman wet his lips. "Can we put our hands down?"

Virginia nodded. "Yeah, but one fast move and you'll regret it."

"You don't trust us?"

"Now that I own eleven square miles of desert with all sorts of stuff on it that other people, like you, seem to covet, no," Virginia said. She gazed at his hand. "Just curious, James, what happened to your hand?"

Kincaid looked at his hand. "I had an accident last night."

"Burns can be painful."

"Yes, they can." His jaw tightened.

Holding her pistol, Donna stepped away from the machine. "What are you two doing up here anyway?"

Blackman turned slightly toward her. "We needed to take another look at the steam fields and saw what we hoped was you two driving up here."

Virginia stared. *Just happened to be in the area and on my ranch. Isn't that a coincidence? Yeah, right. And a burnt hand? I guess we know who visited us last night. They are rapidly moving up the list for suspects in Carol's death.* "Well, you're trespassing. So you can either get back in your car and leave the ranch, or you can get arrested, or you can take an accidental scenic tour down a mine shaft."

Donna frowned. "What'll it be, boys?"

Kincaid rubbed his hands together in front of him and smiled at Virginia. "We were just thinking about lunch. Would you ladies like to join us? Maybe we can discuss our future relationship."

Virginia raised an eyebrow. "How about you leave, and we'll take a rain check. Next time come with the information we asked for and call ahead for an appointment. Maybe a lunch could be arranged then. Showing up like this, especially armed, or late at night, is liable to get you shot, or electrocuted."

Kincaid covered his bandaged hand. "Okay. Next time, we'll call first." He glanced at Blackman. "Let's go so these ladies can get back to what they were doing." He climbed back into the car. As Blackman got in and clicked his seatbelt in place, Kincaid started the vehicle and turned the car around. It bounced down the rut-filled dirt road, leaving a large dust cloud behind.

Donna watched the dust behind the car as it grew smaller in the distance. "We could have had a nice cool lunch someplace with them."

"We could have. Mr. Kincaid thinks I'll be a pushover for his charms. This way we keep them interested but not too close. I don't trust them, and they may be involved with Carol's murder." Virginia leaned against the jeep, then jumped back. "Ouch! That's hot. Oh, did you notice James' bandaged hand? He said he had an accident. I think Liana's surprise jolt of electricity burned his hand last night."

"Yeah, you're probably right. Want to head someplace cooler for our picnic lunch?"

"How about the mine? It's cooler just inside the entrance. But there is one more thing we need to do first."

Coombs lay on the sand a hundred yards up hill from the turquoise mine watching through high-powered binoculars as Virginia and Donna handled the two men. He sat the field glasses down next to him and mumbled to himself. "Hmm. They made short work of those two. They've obviously been around the block, and I wouldn't want them upset with me. They can take care of themselves. Looks like they're going to eat inside. Good idea, it's cooler. I wonder where they're going next?"

"Why didn't you just come down and ask?" said Virginia, aiming her rifle at him.

Coombs tensed, then rolled over and reached for his sidearm. Virginia and Donna were behind him, guns aiming at him. He moved his hand away from his weapon. "What? How... how'd you get here? I saw you go into that mine? How'd you sneak up on me?"

"There is another entrance. As to sneaking up on you, we've had some experience in the wilderness before, so we're careful. Now, what are you doing here?"

Donna waved her gun. "How about you get on your knees and remove any weapons you might be carrying, besides the six-gun on your hip. Do it nice and slow."

"After spotting those men watching you, I thought you might need some protection. But it seems you didn't need help."

Donna smiled. "You catch on fast."

He un-holstered his revolver and set it on the ground. Then he pulled a black Ruger nine-millimeter semiautomatic from under his shirt and set it next to the other pistol. "That's it."

Virginia motioned with her rifle. "Stand up and move back."

He climbed to his feet and stepped back. "What are you going to do?"

She waved the gun. "Step over here by that little bush." He did what she told him.

Donna grabbed his guns and removed the bullets, and the magazine, then slid the slide back and caught the round that was in the chamber. She pocketed the bullets. "I'm sure you've got more, but this will slow you down."

He shrugged. "Look. I saw those two watching you and knew they had rifles in their car. I called your house."

Virginia lowered her rifle. "We know. Liana called us. Thanks for the warning. We caught sight of them right after your call. Now, why are you here?"

He hung his head and sighed. "I wanted to make sure you weren't harmed. I was also hoping you were going to look for the treasure and the ghost ships. I've heard the stories like I told you. I wanted to see if you could find the ships and maybe the treasure."

"So you could rob us?"

"No. Look, I'm not young anymore. Traipsing around out here looking for something that's been lost for hundreds of years wears on the bones. I'm getting too old for treasure hunting in the desert with tourists. I was hoping you'd find the ships. I'd love to actually see them."

"You just want to see the old ships of the desert, not the treasure?"

"Yes. Well... I would love to see the treasure if it's real, but the ships... that would be something. My tribe would like to do the mining I mentioned before, but I want to see the ships. You have been nice to me. When your people, like those men, see an Indian, especially one with a record, like me, they give me grief and look down at me. You have treated me with respect. I want to see you get the treasure. I'd like to see it, too. Ms. Putman searched for it for years. Maybe you'll let my tribe on your land and do the mining. Maybe you'll let me see the old ships." He gave her a hopeful look. "I'm almost done with the proposal I promised."

"Mr. Coombs. You aren't supposed to be here. But you did warn us of those other two, and I think you're being straight with us. Donna, give the gentleman back his weapons."

Donna stepped to Coombs and handed him his guns. He nodded. "Thank you."

Virginia pointed at the faint dust trail receding in the distance. "I take it you and your people watch this place."

"Well..."

"I hope you do. Because if you do, and you happen to see them, or anyone else who doesn't belong here, I would appreciate a call."

Coombs smiled. "I can see what we can do."

Virginia turned. "Mr. Coombs, where is the area your people want to mine?"

He pointed to the south. "Down there near those cinder cones. Should be gold and some other minerals."

"I see. Do you happen to know where we could mine some celestite, or sphalerite, or willemite?"

Donna frowned. "Where did you get that?"

"Andy told me about them. They are minerals that phosphoresce colors."

Coombs nodded. "Willemite is a zinc sulfate salt, and sphalerite is a zinc-iron sulfide. They both are common in zinc mines, and there is a lot of zinc, lead and some iron in your mines. You'll probably find some in one or more of the silver mines. May I ask why?"

"Just curious. How about a zinc sulfide and radium combination?"

Coombs shook his head. "I don't know. Maybe if a silver mine, with a lot of zinc sulfide, were near a uranium mine or deposit, you might get it. Usually, you have to obtain the materials separately then mix them. Ms. Putman did. They fluoresce. She got the idea from some minerals she got someplace around here, but never mentioned exactly where."

Donna tilted her head. "How do you know all this?"

He gave her a sheepish grin. "I have a degree in geochemistry from the Colorado School of Mines, compliments of the U.S. Army."

Virginia laughed. "Good for you and us. Mr. Coombs, we may need your services. You have my permission to wander around the ranch, but if you spot anyone else or anything out of the ordinary, I want a call. And if you don't mind, I may need to call upon your knowledge in the near future."

"Yes, ma'am. Thank you. You have my number. Call anytime. And I'll call you as soon as I have everything you asked for. It shouldn't be too long."

"Good." Virginia smiled. "You know it's damn hot. Would you care to join us in the mine for lunch and something cold to drink?"

"Yes, thank you."

They started to walk back to the turquoise mine when Virginia glanced at the sand dunes in the desert below them. "Mr. Coombs, just how far do those dunes actually move in the course of a year? Do you know?"

"They pretty much move about in the same general area. They shift size and shape some, but stay in the same basic location. In the old stories, they also say the treasure was taken from the ships and hidden in chests in a cave that can be located by the shadow of the moon."

"Interesting. Any chance there are undiscovered caves down there?"

He nodded. "Yes. There's a good chance."

"Mr. Coombs, I've been meaning to ask. Does, or did, your people ever make ceremonial tools, like knives, out of the meteor materials?"

"Yes. Our stories go back before the white man came. The ancient ones used the magic rock, that's the meteor, to make ceremonial items. There are stories about the shaman making some glow. Big magic at the time."

"Does anyone in the tribe still have any of them?"

"Yes. I believe Mrs. Putman also had one or two as well."

CHAPTER 17

After lunch, Virginia and Donna said goodbye to Coombs and drove down the mountain to the desert floor. They headed back in the direction of the ranch house, taking a detour to the old abandoned uranium mine where Carol Putman was found stabbed to death. Virginia pulled the Jeep up in front of the mine and stopped.

Leaning back in her seat, Virginia said, "That was interesting about the ceremonial knives made from the meteor."

"Yes. That explains where they came from. But over time I would think they made a number of them. We forgot to ask exactly how many the tribe still has and if anyone besides Carol has any."

"How many the tribe had or has may be unanswerable. We have one or maybe two at the ranch house. And how many were sold over the years. These are good questions, but there may not be a definitive answer."

Virginia climbed out of the Jeep and looked around the area directly in front of the mine opening. "I see a lot of tracks. Where was Carol's body found?"

Donna hopped out of the Jeep and stepped to a spot to the left of the mine entrance. "Over here."

Virginia walked to where Donna pointed. "This is where she was found? The ceremonial knife that had material on it that glowed was here too, right?"

"That's what Detective Ferguson said."

Virginia looked at the ground, and then at the surrounding desert. "If Mr. Coombs has been watching my ranch all along, maybe he saw something that he hasn't divulged yet."

"True. But maybe he's the murderer. Oh, we need to check on his education, too."

"I know. I think Carol's murder and those ships and treasure are somehow connected, and he's interested in both." Virginia turned and stared at the mine. "That's supposed to be played out, right?"

"Yes. That's what everyone said."

"Grab the Geiger counter, and let's have a look for ourselves."

"Okay." Donna dug the counter out of the back of the Jeep and joined Virginia just inside the mine entrance. "This is spooky. Look at the old timbers and beams holding the roof up. They look like desiccated driftwood. One good earthquake and this place could come down. That dirt on the floor to the side is still wet. Must be a small stream originating inside somewhere."

Virginia knelt, and looked at the ground. "I think you're right. And by the looks of these tracks, someone has been here rather recently. The sheriff's people, maybe?" She looked up at Donna. "What does the meter say?"

"I'll turn it on." Donna switched the Geiger counter on. It started a steady clicking sound as she read the dial. "We're standing, what, about ten feet inside the mine? This is registering a lot of radiation. Why?"

Virginia got to her feet and brushed off her jeans. "Maybe because of years of mining and dust settling on the ground as materials were taken out, or this place is still viable, and someone was still digging."

"Maybe." Donna turned and looked warily into the mine. "I'd love to go inside a little more, but this counter isn't giving me a warm feeling about my future health. Going farther could be dangerous from a radiation standpoint. And I don't like the looks of the wood holding the ceiling up."

"I agree, but I'd like to see if there is anything glowing in here. You stay here, and I'll go farther into the tunnel."

"I don't like it, but knowing you… be careful and watch for mine shafts." Donna wrinkled her brow and sighed. "Well, I can't very well let you go alone. I'll come too."

"You know, I'd rather you stayed here and kept watch. If you see anything suspicious yell."

Donna gave Virginia an exasperated look, then nodded. "Here, take the Geiger counter. Keep an eye on the radiation levels and get out if it gets much hotter."

"Okay." Virginia took the instrument and proceeded down the tunnel swinging her flashlight across the path in front of her. The Geiger counter continued to click at a steady but quick rate. She past some side tunnels and found the remains of old wiring and old light bulbs strung along the roof of the tunnel. *Where did they get the electricity, a generator? Doesn't seem to be much down here, and the counter hasn't increased its clicking.* She noticed a pile of rocks ahead. As she approached the counter went wild. *Oh boy. That's really hot.* Virginia slipped passed the rock pile and looked at the wall of stone in front of her. *By the looks of the cuts in the rock, that's been worked fairly recently. The wall is wet, and down there about a foot from the floor, water is slowly pouring out. Oh boy, this counter is still going bonkers. I'd better get out of here.*

Virginia turned and hurried out of the mine. She found Donna sitting on a rock just inside the entrance in the shade, talking on the radio.

Donna set the radio down as Virginia walked up. "How was it? Find anything useful?"

Virginia sat next to her. "I don't know. There are a number of side tunnels I didn't explore. A few hundred yards back, there's been some recent work done. At least I think it's recent. That's where the stream starts. The area is also very radioactive. For being played out, it was a lot hotter than I would have expected."

"Maybe we should have Mr. Coombs, if he really is a geochemist, look at it."

"Not a bad idea. It's only two o'clock. Want to take a run down to the sand dunes? Who were you talking to?"

Donna started to speak when they heard a low rumble from outside. Then the ground began to shake. She jumped to her feet and yanked Virginia up and out of the mine. The earth moved as they stumbled toward the gyrating Jeep. They leaned against it and watched as timbers cracked. A roar came from the mine as a dust cloud erupted out the entrance. They turned and watched the desert floor roll and patches of dirt spring upward. Rocks tumbled down the side of the mountain. The shaking stopped about a minute later.

"That was a beauty. Maybe a four... possibly a five." Virginia looked back at the mine and the rubble where the entrance once stood. "Looks like it's really closed now. I wonder how the other mines held up?"

Donna let out a breath. "I don't know. You know, a minute earlier and you would have been killed."

"Yeah. I know. Now if my heart will just slow down, I think I'll be okay. Thanks for dragging me out." Virginia said. "I wasn't paying attention like I should have been."

"Don't mention it. Oh, the radio message was from Liana. She's found something. I said we'd head back when you came out of the mine. I figured the sand dunes would be there tomorrow."

"I'm sure they will." Virginia nodded. "I could use a shower and a cold glass of—"

"Beer. A nice, cold, smooth, dark, beer." Donna had a dreamy look on her face.

"Beer? Dark beer? Here I thought you were a wine girl."

"I like wine, but right now a cold beer sounds real good."

"Okay then, beer it is. Let's mount up and head home." Virginia bent down and picked up the Geiger counter. "Take a look at this. It's registering radiation higher than the background it has indicated out here."

"Probably all the dust and dirt that blasted out of the mine when the earthquake collapsed it. And just think, we were breathing that stuff." Donna gave Virginia a hopeful look. "Does beer counter radiation?"

Virginia laughed. "I don't think that's one of its virtues."
Donna shrugged. "Me either."

Virginia and Donna, cleaned up and dressed in shorts and T-shirts, sat on a settee under the covered rear patio. The misters were on cooling the area. They drank cold beers and nibbled on some fruit and cheese Liana had set out for them.

Virginia finished a grape, then said, "I asked Detective Ferguson to run a background check on Mr. Coombs to see if he really went to the Colorado School of Mines and anything else of note that we don't know about." She looked around as she sipped her beer. "From what I've seen, it looks like the place held up well to that earthquake."

Liana sat facing them holding her notebook. "Yes. We had no damage. At first, the quake was reported to be a 4.5 on the Richter scale. Just a few minutes ago they upgraded the quake to a 5.5. It was on a side fault of the San Andreas, near the Salton Sea, not far from here. Ms. Putman had this place designed to take a big one. So far the aftershocks have been small."

"I noticed. I'm glad there was no damage, and everyone is okay."

Liana smiled. "Yes, everyone is safe. We finished the measurements as you requested,"

Virginia set her glass down. "Find anything interesting?"

"Yes and no. The measurements all matched the drawings within a few inches. But after we finished, when I was sitting in Ms. Putman's quilt room, I remembered how she was always the one who cleaned the room. She would not let me do it. So I looked around."

Virginia leaned forward. "Did you find anything?"

"Yes. I found a safe."

Donna set her beer on a coaster on the low table in front of her and leaned forward. "A safe? Where was it—in a wall hiding behind something?"

"No. It is in the floor under the big area rug. I could not open it. I do not know where the combination is. Maybe in her office."

Donna's eyes widened. "She kept something close to where she worked. How do we find the combination? If she kept the safe that close to where she spent time, maybe the combination is in her quilt room. Would the numbers be in a file or hidden under something?"

Liana shook her head. "The symbols on the combination lock are not numbers; they are… like I said… symbols."

Virginia stood. "Symbols? Symbols of what?"

"I do not know."

Virginia glanced at Donna. "Let's have a look." She rose and headed to the quilt room with Liana and Donna following.

Once they were in the room, Liana pulled the rug back and pointed. "See. There is the safe and the symbols."

Virginia knelt next to the floor safe and studied the dial. "These are alchemical symbols."

Donna, who still had her beer glass in her hand and frowned. "You know this how? Another boyfriend who was an alchemist?"

"No. We had an exhibit at my museum a while back about alchemy. The symbols were on display."

"Oh." Donna chuckled. "That would have been worth seeing."

"Yes, it was. Chemists today trace their history to the ancient alchemists."

"Good to know. What did they have symbols for, earth, air, fire, and water?"

"More than that. They even had a form of a periodic chart during the time of the alchemists."

"I didn't know that. Now, Ms. Alchemist, how do we open the safe? You going to conjure up the combination?"

Liana crossed herself. "Conjure up the combination? Conjuring is not good."

Virginia stood and looked at the quilt hanging on the wall.

She smiled. "No conjuring. The answer's in that quilt."

CHAPTER 18

Donna and Liana looked at the large quilt hanging on the wall. Donna frowned. "The combination is in that quilt?" She squinted. "I don't see it."

"Of course not. It's not there flashing 'look at me, I'm a combination,'" Virginia said. She stepped to the quilt, examined it, and then pointed. "Look here, around the binding. If we start at the top and go clockwise around the quilt, you'll see some of the alchemy symbols mixed with other designs. At the top is gold; it's the circle with a dot in the center. ☉ On the right is silver, the crescent. ☾ The bottom has the sign for tin, an oddly-shaped 4. ♃ And the left side is the symbol for copper, the sign of the female, or a circle with a cross on the bottom. ♀ If I recall, they are on the combination lock, along with other symbols. Try turning the dial three times to the right, and stop on gold—then to the left, stopping on silver, and then turn the knob to the right to tin. Finally, turn it left to copper, and see what happens."

"Okay." Liana knelt by the safe and spun the dial as directed. When she stopped, she turned the handle. The door swung up. She looked up at Virginia. "It worked!"

Donna moved to the safe, leaned over Liana's shoulder, and peered inside. "Looks like a cloth bag and a wooden box in there."

Liana pulled the bag out, untied the top, and looked inside. "My God! It's got pearls in it… good-sized pearls." She rose, went to the cutting table, and poured a few out on the green cutting board. "They sure look pretty… and expensive."

Donna tried pulling out the box. "This is heavy." She got on both knees and reached in. Using both hands, she slowly extracted the box and rested it on the floor. "It's nailed shut."

Virginia walked to the side of the cutting table, picked up her backpack and fished around inside. She removed a knife and handed it to Donna. "See if you can pry the top off with this."

Donna carefully pried the lid off the box. Inside were small gold bars. "These gold bars, and the pearls, are like the ones you found in the velvet bag in Carol's desk."

"Yes." Virginia looked at the gold. "Is there anything else in the safe?"

Donna leaned over the safe and looked inside. "Yes. There is a paper with writing on it." She reached in and got the document. "It is old." She handed it to Virginia.

Virginia moved to a white, wooden rocking chair in the corner of the room and sat. She carefully examined the paper. "It's written in Spanish. Here Liana, can you translate it for us?"

Liana took the paper and sat on the floor with her legs crossed in front of her. "*Sí*. I can read parts of it. This is old and some of the words are faded."

Donna set the pearl she was examining down and turned. "What does it say?"

Liana studied the paper. "It was written by Alvarez de Cordone. It tells of finding the pearls, silver, the gold, and of a bad storm. It is basically the same story that I told you before. Cordone sailed into the Gulf of California and up into Lake Cahuilla where they were attacked by Cahuilla Indians and killed. The crewless ships then floundered in a storm and sank carrying with them chests filled with pearls, silver, and gold. The story that we heard for generations about the treasure, was it is still in the ships. But this says a few of the survivors, which included Alvarez de Cordone, took the treasure to some caves in the nearby mountains and hid it. This states the treasure was hidden in a cave near steam from the earth, mud volcanoes, and heavy rocks. The cave faces the ships and has rock paintings, or… or…petroglyphs. There is something about seeing a ghost in the dark of night flying on a glowing body."

Donna chuckled. "Looks like Carol found the treasure. But according to that document, there must be more than this. Where is it?"

Virginia leaned back in the rocker. "I think that's what some nasty people want to know, too. The thing is, we know she found it, and we have some of it right here. That is probably what got her killed."

Liana looked at Virginia and Donna. "Do you want me to put it back in the safe?"

Virginia rose from the chair and knelt next to the open safe. "Why don't you get us some cold iced tea and we'll see about that."

"*Sí*." Liana jumped to her feet and headed for the kitchen. Virginia studied the safe's door and lock. After Liana left, Virginia looked at Donna. "I can change the combination from the inside. "I'll do it while you pick some samples of the pearls and take a couple gold bars. The rest we'll put back in the safe."

"You're the boss." Donna selected a handful of pearls and three gold bars. She returned the remainder to the safe as Virginia closed the door and spun the dial.

"That should do it. Now we begin our plan to find Carol's killer."

Donna frowned. "How do we do that?"

"We take the pearls you selected along with the gold bars into Palm Springs and get them appraised. That should start the gossip mill going. Then we locate the cave with the rest of the treasure and the ghost ships of the desert. That'll bring the bad guys out in droves. Then we have fun and find Carol's murderer."

Donna tilted her head. "That's your plan?"

"Yep."

"That's a little light on details. A gossip mill, and us just running into the desert locating stuff that's been lost for centuries?"

Virginia shrugged. "Pretty much."

"You know where the cave is don't you?"

Virginia nodded. "Yep. Well... possibly... mostly."

"You also know about where the ships are, too."

"Yep. I'm pretty sure anyway."

"How?"

Virginia pointed at the quilt. "It's all there. And we have some information from that document and the painting."

"We do?"

"Yep."

"If you say so. You'd better write down the new combination to the safe, just in case."

Virginia smiled. "Carol programed three different combinations into it. She also hid them in the quilt. I picked combination number three."

Donna glanced at the quilt. "All the combinations are in that quilt?"

"Yep."

"Will you stop with the 'yep' stuff? You're driving me crazy."

Virginia smiled. "Okay."

A minute later, Liana walked into the room with a tray and three cold drinks. She set the tray on the cutting table and looked at the floor. "You put everything back into the safe?"

"Yes. But we kept a couple pearls and a couple gold bars to get appraised in Palm Springs tomorrow." Virginia went to the table and picked up a glass of iced tea. "Let's drink to the successful day we just had."

Donna and Liana picked up their glasses and drank.

Liana set her glass down. "What are you going to do with all those dirty rocks you brought back that are sitting on the patio?"

Virginia cleared her throat. "When I changed, I called my husband, Andy, at the University of Texas. He called a couple of his old friends at the University of California at Irvine. A grad student, Todd Morrison, is

Whispering Threads

coming tomorrow morning to pick them up and take them back to UCI. Andy's friends are professors of geology and chemistry, and they'll do an analysis of the samples for me. I should have the reports in a couple days."

Donna finished her tea. "I also told Detective Ferguson about our two friends, Paul and James, who visited us in the desert today. He's doing a more in-depth background check on them."

Liana finished her drink. She picked up the tray. "If there is nothing else, I'll get back to my duties. There is much to do." She turned and left the room.

Donna rolled her neck from one side to the other to work out the kinks. "Who haven't we checked out?"

"I had the Smithsonian Central Security Service run a quick check again on everyone on the staff here. A couple of them are in the country illegally, but have been here for a number of years and have clean records. The SCSS isn't going to tell the immigration authorities about them. The rest were born here and also have clean records. No one has any outstanding or unusual debts either, and no large deposits have been made in any bank accounts. In other words, nothing new came up about them."

"So the staff is good to go."

"I hope so. I'm anxious to get the pearls and the gold bars appraised tomorrow."

After breakfast in a restaurant in Palm Springs, and dressed in expensive looking clothes, Donna drove Virginia and their treasures, in her Infiniti QX80, to a jewelry store to help establish their credentials as upper society women. The store handled top quality pearls and high-end gems and jewelry.

Virginia looked at the storefront. "Ferguson said this place is the perfect location to get our plan rolling. He said he thought the store was a front for stolen gems, but the local police and sheriff haven't been able to get enough on them to get a warrant."

Virginia and Donna walked in at ten in the morning, when it opened. They asked to see the owner.

A man about fifty-five with styled, salt and pepper hair, dressed in a gray suit, white shirt, and red and blue stripped regimental tie, came from the rear of the shop. He looked them over and smiled. "I am Mr. Jamison Brown. I'm the owner of this establishment. How may I be of service to you ladies?"

Virginia smiled and set the velvet bag she had made the night before and a small box on the counter. "We have some pearls and a couple samples of gold we'd like you to examine and give us an estimate of their value."

"How interesting. How soon do you need the results?"

"Now."

"I see." He slowly opened the bag and poured out the contents onto a black pad on the counter. He gasped. He picked up one of the pearls and looked at it. "Very nice. Let me get right on it." Then he moved some equipment to the counter and sat on a stool. "Can I get you ladies something to drink? Coffee, a soft drink, water maybe? This will take a while."

They shook their heads. Donna grinned. "No thank you. Just an estimate of the value of what we've got."

"Of course. Please feel free to browse around while I appraise these." He started to examine and measure the pearls while he made notes. Brown used a couple of instruments in the examination. He consulted a computer. Then, after twenty minutes, he motioned them to come to the counter. "These are natural pearls. These are extremely rare. They're perfectly round and have fine reflective luster. Luster is very sharp with a very high rate of reflection. They have easily recognized facial features. Reflected light sources have very crisp, defined edges. Blemish rate is between 0-5% on each pearl surface. Closer to 1 or 2 actually."

Virginia noticed him starting to perspire. His hands were a little unsteady.

"The sizes in this sample ranges from 10 to 15 millimeters. I would say, the value of these pieces ranges from eight hundred to over a thousand dollars per pearl. They are AAA quality. Do you have more? May I ask where you obtained them?"

Virginia bent over giving him a view of her cleavage as she scooped up the pearls and poured them back into the bag. "Yes. We have a lot more. The source is confidential at this point."

"I understand."

"About the gold bars?"

"Yes." Brown swallowed. "Let me take a look. I'll need to take one in the back for some quick tests."

Donna smiled. "I'll go with you."

"That's not…" he spotted the gun in her open purse. "Oh. Ahh… yes, that will be fine. This way."

A few minutes later, Donna followed Brown out into the showroom. They found Virginia, chatting with a sales clerk. Donna held the gold bar. "Mr. Brown thinks it's either 24 karat gold, or pretty darn close. With the price of gold today, these little guys are worth a couple grand each." She placed the bar back into the small box with the others. She smiled at Mr. Brown. "Thank you for the time and the estimates."

Brown cleared his throat. "Are you ladies looking to sell these items? Do you have more? I can arrange for you to get top dollar and… ahh…

confidential buyers."

Donna shook her head. "They're not for sale at this time, but maybe shortly. We do have more. If we do, you'll be on the top of our list as a possible buyer, or someone to arrange for a generous buyer."

Virginia closed the bag and started for the door. "Thank you again, Mr. Brown. You've been a big help." She strolled, with Donna at her side, toward the Infiniti. "That went well, and as Ferguson thought, Mr. Brown is on the telephone right now. Pretty soon all the interested parties will think we found the treasure."

Donna fingered her car's key fob. "Yeah, and they may try and kill us."

CHAPTER 19

Paul Blackman listened to the voice on the telephone in his hotel room, then hung up. He turned to James Kincaid. "That was Jamison Brown, the jeweler who owns Desert Jewelry. It seems our two favorite ladies found the treasure."

Kincaid looked up from a magazine he was reading. "They did?"

"That's what he thinks. They just brought him some AAA-rated pearls and a few gold bars with small hearts on them for appraisal."

Kincaid grinned. "Looks like it's time to revisit the women."

"I agree. But we should take them some of the proposals we promised. Otherwise we have no reason to be there."

"Good point. Maybe we can persuade them to dine with us again and tell us where the treasure is."

Blackman laughed. "Yeah, like that'll work. Virginia and Donna are sharp. They will have their guard up. I don't care how charming you think you are with the ladies, James, these two are different. Very different, and most assuredly very dangerous."

"I don't know. We almost got them naked into the pool with us. A few pictures for their husbands viewing would have made them very cooperative. Maybe we can try that again."

"Right. Did it ever occur to you that maybe they called the hotel security and not some old busybody?"

"No. They wouldn't have done that. They were infatuated with us. You saw them; they had their robes on and waved to us."

Blackman shook his head. "Your ego is bigger than Virginia's ranch. And you couldn't see what they had on, or didn't, under those robes. Let's try going to see them with what they asked for, and be nice. Maybe that way we can gain more of their confidence. You didn't do so well with Mrs. Putman the last time we were there. And don't forget, they held us at gunpoint the last time was saw them."

Kincaid stood and stretched. "Okay, let's get the proposal ready and call them for an appointment. We need to tell the boss about this new development, too."

Coombs drove his dilapidated Toyota north on Highway 111. He made a sharp turn on a side road and drove to what looked like an abandoned, wind-scoured gas station. Weeds and cacti sprouted from cracks in the pavement. Paint peeled from the sides. The windows were smudged with dirt and broken in places. He pulled in and stopped under a dilapidated gas pump island cover that tilted at a crazy angle. He hopped out. He pulled his nine-millimeter semiautomatic out of his belt and checked the magazine and the chamber to ensure it was loaded. He reached in the rear of the car, turned on a video camera, and waited.

A black Suburban SUV swung onto the street and drove up toward the gas station. It pulled under the island cover and stopped. The dark tinted rear window silently slid down as Coombs approached. A man in the rear seat spoke. "You have new information?"

"Yes. I just heard from Jamison Brown. He said the ladies approached him for appraisals for some high-quality pearls and a few gold bars. He thinks they are part of the old legend's treasure."

Cigar smoke wafted out the window. "Have you seen them locate the treasure?"

Coombs shifted his weight. "No. But I can't watch them all the time, and there are two of them."

"See if you can pinpoint the location. They got those samples somewhere."

"Maybe Ms. Putman had them."

"Frank," the man's voice rose, "I'm paying you to find the treasure. If these women have located it, then you must persuade them to disclose the exact location before anyone else gets it. Understand?"

Coombs took a breath. "Yes."

"Good. Call me when you have the exact location or the actual treasure. I don't care how you do it." The man motioned to the driver. The car drove off.

Coombs used his cell phone to photograph the license plate and turned off the recording function. He walked back to his car and leaned inside. He switched off the small video camera, climbed into the vehicle, and headed back south.

Jamison Brown made a third call. Finally, a man answered. Brown cleared his throat and spoke softly. "I wanted to tell you the two women from the

B bar P ranch came to see me. They had a few of the pearls and some gold you mentioned with them for an appraisal."

"You gave them what they asked for?"

"Yes. I even asked where the items came from, but they wouldn't say."

"Fine. You did well."

"Thank you." He wiped the perspiration from his brow.

"Who else have you told?" the voice asked.

"Ahh... no... no one."

"Good. Are you calling from your store?"

"Yes."

"Fine. After you hang up, go to the coffee shop three blocks north of you. You'll get your payment there."

"Who will I be meeting? You?"

"No. A friend. He'll have the payment and will buy you a cup of coffee."

"Okay." Brown hung up. *These professional types can be a pain. They try and put on the airs. They like playing spy and being mysterious.* He walked from his office into the store area. Seeing his salesman, he called to him. "John, I need to step out for a minute. Watch things for me."

"Okay, Mr. Brown."

Brown left the store and walked down the street to the coffee shop. He entered, went to a table near the rear of the shop, and waited.

After a few minutes a young man, with dark hair pulled back in a ponytail, entered, bought two cups of coffee, and joined Brown. "Mr. Brown?"

"Yes."

He handed Brown an envelope. "Count it."

Brown took the envelope, looked inside, and fingered through a number of fifty-dollar bills. He counted them, and then looked at the young man. "It's all here."

"Good." The man pushed a coffee cup toward Brown, then rose. "Enjoy the coffee and have a nice rest of your day." He turned and walked out.

Youth these days can be very rude. Brown tucked the envelope in his pocket and picked up his coffee. He drank it as he started to walk back toward the jewelry shop. A few yards from the coffee shop, he stopped, dropped the coffee, clenched his chest, staggered, and collapsed onto the sidewalk.

Virginia and Donna followed Brown up the street to the coffee shop in Donna's Infinity. They parked across the street and photographed the man Brown talked to.

"Looks like our Mr. Brown is on someone's payroll. That can be dangerous," said Donna.

"I got some good shots of the guy he's with." Virginia set the camera on her lap. "Looks like Brown is leaving, He's probably headed back to his store, so let's follow the other guy."

"Okay." Donna started the car. She gasped when she saw him totter and drop on the sidewalk. "That's not good."

Virginia tossed the camera in the rear seats. "Pull across the street quick. He's in trouble."

Donna turned and darted across the traffic lanes on Highway 111 causing other drivers to swerve and honk their horns. She stopped the car facing into the curb as Virginia jumped out. She glanced over her shoulder at Donna, "Call Ferguson and 911!"

Virginia sprinted to Brown and examined him. *He's dead.* She looked around for the coffee cup. She hopped to her feet and retrieved the cup with some remains of coffee still in it. She sniffed it and then put a couple of drops on her tongue and tasted it. *Poison. Tetrahydrozoline, eye drops.* She looked around. A small crowd had gathered. She pulled her badge out and displayed it. "Federal Officer. Please stay back; help is coming."

Donna joined her. "Ferguson has notified PSPD, and he's also coming. I called 911 and paramedics are on their way." She tilted her head. "I hear sirens, probably the medics. What did you find?"

"For starters, Mr. Brown is dead. It looks like a heart attack, but I think it's tetrahydrozoline poisoning. That's the main ingredient in eye drops."

Donna frowned. "Eye drops? You serious?"

"Yes. They're intended for use in your eyes. Ingestion can cause symptom similar to a heart attack. The bottles usually have about one to two milliliters in them. If you ingest more than about five to eight milliliters, it can be fatal. I smelled it in the remains of his coffee."

"Where did you learn that tidbit?"

"From a friend of Andy's. He's a retired pharmaceutical chemist and teaches biochemistry and organic chemistry at UT. The guy is a poison nut. He's got loads of information about common things that can be harmful, or deadly. He also has a poison garden."

Donna nodded toward the street. "The paramedics and a fire engine are here; you'd better tell them what you found."

"Right." Virginia handed the coffee cup to Donna, then approached the paramedics. They told her they were busy and to just stand aside. She moved back to Donna and crossed her arms. "I think I'll keep this poison stuff to myself. They were rude."

Donna chuckled. "How about we share it with Ferguson, He's coming toward us now."

Detective Ferguson walked up to Virginia and Donna. "Ms. Bolette here said you saw him collapse. Have the paramedics said anything yet?"

Virginia gave him a hurt look. "They don't like me."

Ferguson looked confused. "They don't? Why? What did you do?"

"I tried to tell them Mr. Brown was dead, and he was poisoned, but they shooed me away."

Ferguson's eyes widened. "Poisoned? With what?"

"Donna's holding his coffee cup. It's got coffee and tetrahydrozoline in it. Like I said, he was poisoned."

"What's that... tetrahydrozo... stuff?"

"Eye drops." Virginia smiled at Ferguson. "Trust me; he died of eye drop poisoning."

"If you say so. Wait right here." He stepped to the paramedic who had covered Brown's body. He displayed his badge. "I have reason to believe this man was poisoned."

The lead paramedic raised an eyebrow. "Poisoned? It looks like a heart attack."

Ferguson pointed. "You see that blonde lady over there. She tried to tell you, but you wouldn't listen."

The medic gave him an indignant look. "She's just a passerby, what would she know?"

Ferguson glared at him. "You idiot. Those two women over there are federal agents. This man was under their surveillance, and they witnessed what just happened. And she knows what poison was used. So, get on your radio, and call for the coroner. This is going to be a crime scene."

The paramedic stared at Ferguson for a second, shrugged, and called on his radio.

Ferguson walked up to the two uniformed Palm Springs Police officers who arrived and filled them in on what happened and then introduced them to Virginia and Donna.

Ferguson looked at Virginia and Donna. "Did either of you see where or how he got the poison?"

Donna pointed. "In that coffee shop. Virginia took pictures, and we have photographs of the guy who gave him the coffee and that envelope with money in it that is in his jacket pocket."

Virginia smiled. "I'll get the memory chip from the camera." She turned and went to the car. She returned and handed Ferguson the chip. "With this, and fingerprints from the envelope and cup, maybe you can ID the guy who murdered Mr. Brown." She pulled a notebook out of her backpack and wrote the name of the poison on it and gave it to Ferguson. "You can share this with the coroner and the Palm Springs cops."

He took the paper. "Thanks. The Palm Springs Police will need statements when their detectives arrive. Want me to stay and back you up?"

Donna nodded. "We'll take all the help we can get."

Whispering Threads

Virginia looked at the covered body of Mr. Brown. "He made some phone calls from his store. Can you get someone to track those calls? Maybe one of them is the murderer."

CHAPTER 20

Four hours after Jamison Brown's murder, Virginia and Donna sat at the kitchen table sipping iced tea. Virginia sat back and smiled. "At least the Palm Springs police were nice, and the coroners' officers were very receptive of our information."

Donna nodded. "Yeah. Being federal agents, and with Detective Ferguson's support, they finally listened. Once the coroner's guys agreed it was a crime scene, everything changed. I hope the cops get some useable fingerprints from the cup. Maybe the pictures you took will help them ID the killer."

"They were getting warrants for the phone search when we left."

"I'd like to know what that turns up." Donna took a drink. "I wonder why Brown was killed."

"Maybe because the person he was working for thought he might tell others, or he figured Brown betrayed him and killed Brown because of it."

Donna nodded. "Based on our outing to the jewelry store, I wonder how much the stuff we've got here in the house is worth?"

"Let's figure it out." Virginia stood and picked up a pad and pencil from a small kitchen desk and returned to the table. "How many pearls were in that bag?"

Donna's brow wrinkled in thought. "Eighty-one, I think."

"Okay, eighty-one times nine-hundred dollars per pearl equal…" She made a quick calculation. "That's $72,900."

"Where'd you get nine hundred dollars per pearl?"

"Brown said the pearls were worth eight hundred to a thousand dollars each depending on size. I took the average. Now, how many small gold bars were there in the bag?"

"Fifteen."

"So, fifteen that weigh 12 Troy ounces each, at $1,335 per ounce, according to Brown, equals…" She used the pad to calculate the total. "That is equal to $16,020 each. So, fifteen of them are equal to… $240,300."

Donna sat back, finished her drink, and said, "That's… over $300,000

Whispering Threads

worth of pearls and gold in that bag."

"Yes." Virginia eyed the calculator. "It's $313,200 to be exact. That's more than I thought."

"Me too." Donna set her glass down. "You said earlier you knew where the treasure and the ghost ships were. Care to share that information?"

"Well... I know about where they are. We'll need to do some more research here, then trek into the desert."

"When do you want to start?"

"Our hunt? Tomorrow. I think we should stick around here the rest of the day and see what our visit to the jewelry store brings us. I'm sure we'll start getting calls soon. And we can examine the quilt and picture more."

Donna smiled. "And it's almost dinner time. Think they'll be able to trace the source of the eye drops and who bought them?"

"Probably not. Eye drops are not controlled substances, and if the killer bought one or two bottles at a number of drug stores and discount stores around the county, you'd never trace him. Probably didn't use a credit card either." Virginia looked around the kitchen. "For being close to dinner time, where is Liana and why isn't she cooking?"

"I don't know," Donna said. "I didn't see her when we got here. Maybe she's outside with the men working around here someplace."

"Let's call her." Virginia pulled her cell phone out and dialed Liana's number. She waited. "Liana must be in a dead zone. The call couldn't go through."

"How about the radio. Maybe she took one of the mobile sets with her."

Virginia hopped off the seat and went to the radio base station and called Liana.

A second later Liana answered. "Ms. Virginia, I'm sorry about not being there with dinner. I am with Emilio and a couple of the men. We are bringing back turquoise, silver, copper and some of the meteor for some jewelry and other items the ranch has orders for. We make them and sell them to jewelry stores and outlets in the area. It took longer than planned."

"I vaguely remember that you said you made jewelry. I thought most of the ore was sold as just minerals."

"It is, but the jewelry brings in more money. I am sorry we are late. We should be back in about a half hour, and I will cook."

Virginia sighed with relief. "I'm just glad you are safe. Don't worry about dinner; we'll order pizza for everybody."

"That would be very generous, Ms. Virginia. Thank you. Oh, Ms. Virginia, that graduate student came by and picked up your mineral samples while you were gone. He left a receipt."

"Great. Thanks. Call if there is any trouble."

"Okay."

After dinner, while Liana busied herself in one of the studio buildings with Emilio and a couple of the men helping to get things ready to make the jewelry, Virginia and Donna sat in the quilting room. Virginia studied the large quilt hanging on the wall.

Donna watched the desk computer's printer spit out pictures of the painting in the office she took with her camera. She gathered them up and set them on the floor in front of the quilt. She stood with her hands on her hips. "Now we have everything in one spot, the quilt, the painting, the map Emilio gave me, and the note from the bag. Do we need anything else?"

Virginia shook her head. "This is what Carol had when she found the treasure and the ships, so we should be able to discern the exact locations from it."

"They've been lost for over three hundred years."

"So was the place in Mexico where I found the treasure and the lost city of gold."

"All right, I'll give you that one. So, Ms. Sherlock, where is it?"

Virginia started to speak when the phone rang. She picked up the phone on a small desk and answered. "Hello?"

"Virginia, this is Detective Ferguson. We got a warrant and found the numbers Mr. Brown called from his store prior to being killed."

"That was fast."

"The judge had no problem since it pertained to a murder."

"Good. Who did Brown call?" asked Virginia.

"One call was to Mr. Frank Coombs. Another was to your friends from Litio Products, and the last one was to a cell phone that was… well, a burner phone. Untraceable."

"So we've got a third party in the game."

"Maybe. Could be someone we know but isn't on our suspect list… yet. Be careful. We're still looking for the man in the photographs you provided. We've sent copies to the FBI and state. If we find anything else, I'll let you know. Oh, yeah, one more thing, according to the coroner, you were right about the poison."

"Good. Thanks for the update." Virginia hung up and looked at Donna. "That was Ferguson. I was right about the poison, and it seems Mr. Brown called Coombs, our friends, and a mystery person."

"By friends you mean our dinner dates?" Donna asked.

"Bingo."

"And a mystery person? A new player?"

"Maybe. But it could be someone who's been here all along, and we just didn't think of him as a suspect."

"We don't need another suspect."

"The police are using the pictures of the murderer, but no luck on his identification, yet. They've sent them to the FBI as well."

"Good." Donna sat on the floor with her legs crossed. "Now, we better find this treasure and get it someplace safe while we can. Someone out there plays for keeps. Now we have two murders."

"Yeah, the body count is going up." The phone rang again. Virginia glared at it. "I wonder who's calling now? One of the players, maybe?"

"Answer it and find out."

Virginia stuck out her tongue. "Okay, smarty pants." She plopped onto the desk chair, grabbed the receiver, and answered. "Hello?"

"Virginia, this is Tom Fargo from the Smithsonian Central Security Service in Washington. I've got the information you asked for about Mr. Frank Coombs."

"Hi, Tom. What did you find out?"

"He's part of the tribe he told you about, Agua Caliente Band of Cahuilla Indians. He has a B.S. degree in chemistry from Cal Poly in San Louis Obispo and an M.S. in geology from the Colorado School of Mines. He has a couple run-ins with the law for assault and battery and weapons charges. The A&B was a bar fight. The weapons charge was for unlicensed possession of a machine gun." She heard Tom chuckle. "Our friends at ATF have no sense of humor about such things. He served his time and has been clean since. Oh, there is one strange thing."

Virginia tilted her head. "Strange thing? What's that?"

"He's been working for an organization's called Agua Caliente Mar Management. It is owned by his band of Cahuilla Indians, and it's legit."

"I know. That's not strange, is it?"

"No, that's not, but the files indicate there's someone else, or some other organization, that he's dealing with. Who or what that happens to be is above my pay grade, and security clearance."

Virginia frowned. "What do you mean?"

"It's classified, Virginia. Restricted."

Virginia's eyes widened. "Classified? By who?"

"I don't know. I sent a request to the director for access. Virginia, you and Donna, be real careful. I'll let you know if I get anything else."

"We'll be careful, and thanks, Tom." She hung up. She looked at Donna. "It seems Coombs is a geochemist all right, but get this, he's also working for someone whose identity is classified by our government."

Donna sat staring at Virginia. "This is getting real scary. Now our own government is a player? I thought this was getting dangerous before... but now..." She leaned back and glanced at the quilt. "Could he be working for the man who killed Brown?"

CHAPTER 21

Virginia rose from the desk and walked to the front of the quilt. She stared at it, and then knelt to look at the photos of the old painting. She placed the map that Emilio made for Donna next to the pictures. "I don't know who Brown's killer is, who killed Carol, and we don't really know who else Coombs is working for, but I just thought of something."

Donna looked at Virginia. "I know that expression. I don't think I'm going to like what you just thought of. What's it going to cost?"

Virginia smiled. "You know me so well." She shuffled the papers around on the floor and pointed. "Look."

Donna examined the photographs, the map, and the quilt. "I give. What am I missing?"

Virginia sat on the floor. "Let's review what we've got, so far."

"Okay."

"Carol was murdered with an Indian ceremonial dagger made from ataxite, a very rare class of iron meteorites. Something on it glows in the dark. We have some minerals that glow due to radio luminescent powder and some materials that glow due to phosphorescence. We've got silver mines that have zinc and copper associated with them. Hell, there could be a copper mine out there too for all I know. There are gold and some old uranium mines that are still active and a few suspicious caves."

Donna nodded. "Don't forget the turquoise mine and the mud volcanoes."

"Yeah, and we've got the steam vents and a meteor crater, too." She motioned toward the map. "If you draw lines between the silver mine that's near that radioactive cave, the gold mine, the supposedly played out uranium mine, and the turquoise mine, what do you get?"

"A headache?"

Virginia pointed. "No, silly, look."

Donna glanced at the map. "The lines form a crescent around the meteor, a steam vent area, and the mud volcanoes."

"Right. And it's angled toward the sand dunes to the southeast."

"And the maps say the lower section of mountains has caves."

"The note written by Alvarez de Cordone said he and a few of the survivors took the treasure to some caves in the nearby mountains and hid it. These caves were *near* steam from the earth, mud volcanoes, and heavy rocks. The cave faces the ships and has rock paintings, or... or...petroglyphs. He mentioned something about seeing a ghost in the dark of night flying on a glowing body. A heavy rock probably means the meteor."

Donna studied the map, then the quilt, and then pictures of the painting. "That ghost that glows can't be the meteor, it landed many eons ago."

"True. But the natives had legends about flying gods. Something was flying, and it glowed. Maybe some of the radium and zinc salts got on something or other, and the wind tossed it around. Or, someone was using the glowing substances to intimidate the natives, or for religious purposes. At night it would seem miraculous to them. As we found out, the necessary materials are in the area."

"We haven't heard from the UCI professor about the analysis, yet."

"True. But I'll bet a steak dinner I'm right."

Donna stood and stretched. She bent over and looked at the map, then pointed. "So, the cave, or caves, with the treasure are down there."

Virginia smiled. "I think so. I got the idea from the quilt. Note which sections glow."

Donna looked at the quilt. "Turn off the lights." Virginia switched off the overhead light.

"By God, the areas that glow outline the area we pinpointed on the map. Over time, the mud volcanoes, the steam vents, and the meteor crater are the main landscape items that didn't change or move. And they are depicted on the quilt and map."

Virginia turned the light back on. "Exactly."

"So, we know about where to start. Want to go get the treasure?"

"No. For now, we put the pictures, the map, and the message from Alvarez de Cordone in the floor safe and go to bed. It's eleven o'clock. We've had a busy day, and tomorrow we'll plan our moves to get the treasure, find the ships, and maybe get closer to solving the murders."

Donna started to gather up the pictures while Virginia grabbed the map when she heard a scraping sound outside the quilt room door. She glanced at Virginia. "Sounds like we have a snoop."

Virginia hurried to the door and swung it open. A German Shepard puppy sat on the floor in front of the door. With his tail swiping across the floor, he looked up at her. She bent down and patted his head. "Aren't you cute puppy? I haven't seen you before. Where do you belong?"

Liana came rushing down the corridor. "So that's where you went, you silly dog. You aren't to bother the *Doña*." She stopped next to the puppy.

"I'm sorry. He got away. He's curious."

Virginia smiled. "What's his name, and who does he belong to?"

Liana glanced at the puppy. "The dog's name is Leonardo, and Emilio owns him. He is a rescue dog in training. Some bad people had him and mistreated him. He needed a good home. Leonardo lives in the men's house out back. He is no trouble. Can he stay? The men like him." She smiled. "I like him, too."

Virginia knelt next to Leonardo and looked at his collar and the tags attached. "Looks like he has an up-to-date dog license and has had all his shots, so I see no reason for him to leave. He's cute and needs a good home, so why not? Does he have a chip so if he strays, the authorities can find his home?"

"*Sí*. The vet gave Leonardo one when Emilio picked him up."

Leonardo licked Virginia's hand, then turned, and sniffed Donna's leg. She reached down and petted him. "*Gracias*. Emilio will be very happy." Liana attached a leash to the dog. "Come, Leonardo, time to go home and leave the *Doña* alone."

Donna smiled. "Liana, does Leonardo understand both English and Spanish?"

Liana nodded. "*Sí*." With the metal tags on his collar clinking, she led Leonardo away.

"Leonardo? An Italian named German Shepard, owned by a Hispanic man. Now that's quite a combination." Donna leaned against the doorframe and watched the dog follow Liana down the hall. "Cute little guy. I'm glad you let him stay."

"Why not? He looks like a good dog, and he needs a home. We aren't exactly running out of room, and he'll have a lot of space to romp. And the men like him, and obviously so does Liana." Virginia's eyes swept the quilt room. "Looks like everything is back in place, let's hit the hay."

The next morning, with the ranch Range Rover loaded with supplies, Virginia and Donna headed for the starting point they had indicated on Donna's map. They left the road through a gate about three miles south of the ranch house and drove to a ridge.

Donna keyed the radio. "B bar P mobile one to spy one." Emilio's voice responded. "Spy one."

"Got anything?"

"*Sí*. I see you. And about two miles southeast, off the ranch, there is another vehicle, a pickup truck, on a hill. Two men are watching you."

"Got it. Anything else?"

"No"

"Okay. Watch our six."

"Ahh… watch your six? I'm sorry… I—"

Donna smiled. "Sorry Emilio, it means watch our backs."

"Oh. Okay."

Virginia unfolded the map they had marked up and pointed. "Okay, we're here. Let's go to this spot. I think that will be the place that was used as a vantage point for the quilt and the old painting. From there we should be able to head in the right direction."

"Sounds like a plan," Donna said.

Virginia put the vehicle in four-wheel drive and slowly drove around scrub, boulders, and cacti toward the new site. Dust and increasing amounts of salt were kicked up behind them. The outside temperature was already in the high nineties by mid-morning when they reached the mountain. Virginia stopped, got out, and stretched. She stepped to the front of the Range Rover and leaned against it. Taking off her sunglasses she squinted at the vista below. "Looks like the right place." She pointed. "Over there are the steam vents. There are the mud volcanoes, and…" she turned slightly, "There is the meteor crater."

Donna consulted the pictures that she had taken of the painting and then looked where Virginia was pointing. "Yes, and down there are the sand dunes and the sort of end of these mountains—more like hills really."

"Did you bring that IR scope?"

"Yeah. It's in the car. I'll get it." Donna scurried to the back of the Rover and opened the tailgate. She rummaged through some boxes and pulled out the infrared scope. "Got it." She brought it around to the front, turned it on, and then slowly scanned the view in front of them. "Well, the desert is heating up. But there's some sort of shack toward the sand dunes. The steam vents are really hot. Seems like they're very active. There are cooler spots mixed into the hills. The mud pots are hotter than I thought they'd be." She handed the device to Virginia. "Take a look."

Virginia looked through the viewfinder. "Yeah, I see what you mean. Is that shack on the map?"

Donna put her sunglasses on. "No. Maybe it was an oversight. Or it's so old and not important that it was just left off."

Virginia turned her attention to the mud volcanoes. "Those mud pots are really going to town. More activity than when I saw them before. I think these mud pots and my steam vents are the only ones on this side of the Salton Sea." She turned off the IR scope. "Let's go down to the Salton Sea. There are some old deserted towns down there and probably a few desert rats who eke out their living from the area. Maybe, one of them could be informative. It's not that far out of the way."

Donna shrugged and climbed back in the car. "Okay. Could be interesting. Maybe we'd learn something before we go off-roading into hell and where sidewinders live."

As they approached the first turnoff to a once thriving vacation town on the shores of the Salton Sea, Donna looked out the window. "Did you know at one time the Salton Sea was bigger? People thought it would be a great desert vacation location with both desert climate and a lake for water sports and fishing. A number of resorts popped up. Hollywood celebs and others frequented the area. But when the waters receded and grew increasingly salty, the towns were left high and dry. The vacationers stopped coming, and the resorts and towns went bankrupt."

Virginia chuckled. "You know all this because?"

"I own and run a high-end travel agency in Newport Beach, remember?"

"Yeah."

"Anyway, when I was young my grandfather almost bought some land in Salton City. Thankfully, he didn't, but the place always intrigued me."

They drove toward what looked like a small city. As they got closer, they noticed the barren desert and salt-encrusted shores. The area was fringed with wrecked trailer parks and abandoned 1950s resorts. Rusted playground equipment sagged. Broken bicycles and salt-encrusted auto bodies littered windswept roads. Sand-blasted cinderblock structures with broken windows and skeletons of roof framing lined a few blocks. Faded sofas and chairs with springs protruding from their rotten fabric were scattered in places. Old houses were turning into driftwood. The area looked like the aftermath of a nuclear Armageddon. The land had been depopulated and sunburned to white.

The women found a sad-looking "antique" shop and stopped. The front window was covered with a hoarfrost of salt that made it almost opaque. They hopped out of the Rover and walked into the shop. With each step they took, blooms of finely powdered dust rose in small mushroom clouds as they climbed the few steps of desiccated wood to the veranda. There was a faint sound of movement within. She opened the sun-bleached door. "Pardon me," said Virginia. "Are you open for business?"

A man who could have been ninety stepped out of the back room. His skin was deep brown and wrinkled, resembling old leather. His hair was bushy and white. His scraggly beard was salt and pepper. He wore a faded, checkered, long-sleeved shirt and torn jeans. New looking hiking boots completed his outfit. "What do you want?"

CHAPTER 22

Donna frowned as she stepped into the shop. "This is an antique store, isn't it?" She looked around at the dusty items on display and noticed Virginia moving around to her left toward the display case by the unfriendly proprietor. Donna ran her finger over a dusty surface and looked at it. "I take it you don't get much business traffic."

"You figured that out by yourself, did you, missy?" the man said.

"With your attitude, I can see why this place looks so bad and obviously is devoid of customers." Donna picked up a bottle and blew dust off. "Real antique? What? Vintage 1956?"

"Yeah, about that. What do you want?"

Virginia tilted her head. "We came looking for antiques. What did you think? We aren't IRS agents." The man gave her a blank stare.

Donna hurried back to the counter from a table along the side wall. She held up an old, dusty, ship's lantern. "How much for this?" She rotated it. "There isn't any price on it."

The man's eyes widened. "How'd that get out here?"

Donna gave him a puzzled look. "I don't know. It was on that table behind an old typewriter. How much?"

He stiffened. "It ain't for sale." He reached for it. "Give it to me."

"No way." Donna yanked it away. "You had it on that table with a sign that says thirty-percent off. Thirty-percent off what? Now, how much?"

"I said it—"

Virginia stepped behind the display case and picked up a small box with turquoise stones in it. "Where did you get these?"

The man turned quickly. His eyes widened. "Them's turquoise. You interested in turquoise, lady?" He quickly eyed Donna and her lantern.

"Yes. Very. They're pretty and unusual. Got any other minerals?"

"Them turquoise is rare. Sure, I got more minerals." He moved closer to Virginia and pulled five more boxes from under the counter. He reached into one and pulled out a noticeably heavy rock. "Actual space rock this is. A meteor." He slid another box to her that held small rocks. "Real gold ore from them mountains west of here." He pointed to another. "Them there rocks glow in the dark under ultraviolet light." He pointed. "That one has some stuff that glows even without no ultraviolet light. And this one here has silver ore."

"Interesting, where'd you get them? From around here?"

"These parts are full of this stuff. Just got to know where to look." The man grinned, exposing straight, white, perfect teeth.

"I see." Virginia took a few samples from each box. "I like these. How much for them?"

He looked at the samples she had on the counter. "You all seem like nice ladies, how's twenty bucks?"

Virginia smiled. "How's ten?"

"I can't go that low. I got overhead you know."

Virginia looked around. "Yeah, right. Looks like your overhead is going to collapse soon." She pulled her badge out and showed it to him. *I hope he's as dumb as he sounds.* "I have reason to believe these ore samples were stolen from the B bar P ranch. I can seize them for evidence and take you into custody while we verify where these items came from." She smiled. "Labs can do that, you know. I'm also curious about that lantern and where it came from." *I hope he falls for it. I'm not sure I can really do this.*

The man stood stiffly. "Look lady... er, officer..."

Virginia glared at him. "Special Agent."

"Okay, Special Agent, I just sell this shit. The owner goes out and gets this stuff. I don't ask where he gets it and I don't care. You can take all this crap for all I care. I don't want any trouble."

Virginia pulled a twenty-dollar bill out and handed it to the man. "Here, that's for these rock samples and her lantern."

"Fine. Ha... have a nice day." He grabbed the money and hurried to the back room.

Virginia gathered up the rocks she purchased, put them in an empty cardboard box, and started for the car. Donna followed with her lantern. They set their purchases in the rear of the Range Rover.

"He was a piece of work." Donna stood next to Virginia studying the shop. "Did you notice how his backwoods sounding voice changed at the sight of your badge?"

"Yeah. And there was not a speck of dust on him. His boots were new, too."

"His clothes were supposed to look old and worn, but they weren't, and his hair and beard were clean. His teeth didn't look like that of a desert rat to me. Too nice," said Donna. She looked at the building. "The wood is old, but the nails are new. No rust, or pits, or salt encrustation. Looks like it's from a Hollywood back lot. He really got shook when I held up the lantern. Why?"

"You're right; he really did get nervous, and he didn't want to sell it. We can examine it in detail when we get back to the ranch."

Donna glanced in the back of the Range Rover. "It's old; maybe it's from one of our ghost ships."

Virginia nodded. "That's a possibility, I guess."

Donna turned and studied the shop. "Could be this is a place for someone to use as a headquarters for exploring the desert looking for the ships and the treasure. Or it's a front."

Virginia leaned against the car. "I agree. But it may be for the tourists. They also sell the stuff they find while looking for the treasure as a bonus."

"If you believe that I've got a nice, big, historic, bridge in New York City to sell you, cheap." Donna gave the shop another look. "What now?"

They heard a motorcycle engine rev up behind the shop. A second later it roared past them toward the street. The gray-haired man was driving it until it swerved out of control and crashed. The driver flew through the air and landed in a heap, unmoving, about three yards away from the bike, which was still kicking up dust.

A bullet landed in the salt and dirt about a foot in front of Virginia. She jumped behind the Rover with Donna on her heels. Virginia pulled her gun out and peered around the back of the car. "I don't see anyone."

"Let's wait a minute. Maybe it was a warning shot to tell us to stay put." Donna held her pistol with two hands. "I should be used to this when I'm with you, but it never gets easier."

"You could be right about that shot being a warning." Virginia frowned. "Something happened to that old man. If he was shot, then the shooter could have killed us, too. Why didn't he?"

"I don't know. If he had a rifle, we were easy targets. If he had a pistol... I didn't hear a gunshot... so a silencer?"

"Maybe. But why shoot the old guy and not us?"

"Maybe he didn't want to shoot us, just get us to duck so he could get away," offered Donna. "If the shooter used a silencer on a handgun, then he'd want us to take cover, so he could leave."

"You could be right. Makes sense."

Virginia and Donna cautiously ventured from behind the SUV and rushed to the man.

Donna knelt next to him and felt his neck. She looked at Virginia. "He's dead."

"I figured that. Look at his chest."

A red splotch stained the front of his shirt.

Donna slowly rose and looked around. "I don't see anyone, and like I said, I never heard the shot."

Virginia nodded. "Probably a rifle shot, and it was silenced. If the shooter thought the old guy might have told us something important or incriminating, then he should have shot us, too. He didn't. I think your idea about him making us take cover is correct. Why shoot the old guy?"

Donna shrugged. "I don't know." She quickly glanced around. "I'd better call 911."

They waited for the police and paramedics to arrive.

The paramedic's van arrived. A minute later a marked Imperial County Sheriff's unit pulled into the parking area and slid to a stop. Two deputies jumped out. One hurried to the paramedics with the man on the ground; the driver approached Virginia and Donna. "One of you called this in?"

Virginia nodded. "Yes, my friend did."

He pulled out a pad and pen. "I need to see some ID and ask a couple questions."

Virginia pulled out her SCSS badge and credentials and handed them to the deputy. Donna followed suit.

He looked at them and frowned. "Feds? Yeah, right. You don't look like a fed, and I've never heard of this agency. I'm going to have to detain you until we can check this out. You realize that impersonating a police officer is a felony, don't you?"

Virginia glared at him. "Yes. And just because you never heard of something doesn't make it not real."

He smirked. "Yeah, right. Are you so-called special agents armed?"

"Yes," said Virginia. "And I don't like the tone of voice you're using."

"Too damn bad, lady. I need your weapons."

Virginia gave him an icy gaze. "I'm afraid not."

The deputy reached for his gun, but he tried to get his sidearm and hold the notebook, pen, and the women's badges at the same time. That was a big mistake.

Virginia and Donna quickly pulled their pistols and aimed them at the two deputies. Virginia spoke in a slow, level, voice. "Don't move. We are federal agents. We have identified ourselves. Trying to disarm us was a mistake. Your attitude doesn't help any either. Now, get on your radio and call the Riverside Sheriff's office and ask for Detective Ferguson. He can vouch for us. That, or call our IDs into your agency and get confirmation. We were just shot at so we're not in real good moods. Reach for your guns and my partner and I will call for additional coroner's investigators, got it?"

The deputies stared at Virginia and Donna. The deputy next to the murdered man spoke. "You realize what you just did is another felony. You are in big trouble."

"That from a man looking down the barrels of guns held by women you two have royally pissed off? Not too smart. Get your shit together and call our IDs in, or call Ferguson, but do it quick. At this rate, the person who shot that man, and shot at us, is probably in San Diego."

The lead paramedic carefully approached. "Ma'am, ahh... the man is dead. He was shot in the upper chest. The bullet went through his heart. We've notified the coroner. Fire engines are on their way. Want us to call them off?"

Donna nodded. "I don't think the engines will be needed. Let them return to their station. You might want to stick around."

The medic looked at their pistols. "Yes, ma'am. We have to be here when the coroner arrives anyway."

Virginia nodded at the medic. "Okay. You two cops could take lessons from him. He's nice, polite, and he's professional."

The deputy that had examined the dead man clicked his radio and asked for verification of Virginia and Donna's credentials. Within a minute the dispatcher called back verifying the authenticity of their being real federal officers and said Detective Ferguson was also coming to the scene. The deputy gave them a sheepish smile. "Looks like you're for real."

Virginia lowered her weapon.

The deputy standing in front of her handed the badge cases back. "I'm sorry about this misunderstanding. We meet some real interesting people out here with some wild tales."

Donna lowered her gun. "I bet you do."

The deputy looked over his shoulder at the dead man, then back to Virginia. "Do you know him? Can you tell us what happened?"

Virginia and Donna told the deputies everything that had gone on from when they had gotten there to when the deputies arrived.

"We didn't hear any gunshots either," said Donna.

Virginia ran her fingers through her hair, and then looked at the deputy. "The question we had was: why shoot and kill the old guy and not us too? We thought maybe he just wanted us to take cover so he could vamoose."

"Good question, and you're probably right about the near miss," said the deputy. "An even better one is where did this antique shop come from? It looks old, but it wasn't here five days ago."

Virginia turned and looked at the building. "We thought it looked strange, you know, out of place. Parts of it don't fit the situation, like the nails and stuff."

"We'll need to look into this, too."

The deputies finished taking notes and obtained information on how to reach both Virginia and Donna in the future if the detectives had any further questions for them. The deputies said the detectives were busy responding from another part of the county so Virginia and Donna could go, and if the detectives needed anything else, they'd call them.

Virginia eyed the old antique shop then looked at the deputy. "Any reason we can't go into the shop and look around again?"

"Well, it is part of a crime scene, but seeing that you two are federal officers, I guess it'd be okay. Just be careful. We may have some CSU folks go in there. After we're done here, I'd like to take a look myself."

"Okay." She looked at Donna and motioned toward the building. "Let's go have a look at that back room."

Donna followed Virginia into the building. They slowly wove their way through the narrow aisles to the doorway to the back. They entered and looked around. Dust mites shimmered in the beams of light streaming into the room from two high windows. Dusty wooden boxes were piled in one corner. A battered, old, grey, metal desk sat against the far wall with two metal filing cabinets next to it. A long scarred wooden table, with odd artifacts from the desert on it, sat in the center of the room. On the walls were old maps with pins in them. Virginia took pictures of the maps with her cell phone and shook her head. "Hollywood couldn't have done a better job making this place look old."

Donna stepped into the area and picked a lantern similar to the one she bought off the table. "Check this out."

Virginia raised an eyebrow. "Looks like yours." She walked to the table. "Anything else of interest?"

Donna searched through the objects and then shook her head. "No. But did you notice there is no telephone in here?"

"Not until you pointed it out. Maybe he used his cell." Virginia went to the desk. On it was a photograph. She picked it up and stared at the image. "Well lookie here. This is strange."

CHAPTER 23

Donna worked her way around the table carrying a canvas bag with the lantern and glanced over Virginia's shoulder. "It's a picture of Emilio and a horse. What's it doing here?"

"I don't know, but look at the background."

Donna squinted. "Looks like dirt and some scrub bushes."

Virginia sighed. "Yes, it's dirt and bushes, but look again. Check out the background."

"Oh, it looks like some sort of cave or mine opening in the distance behind him. There's something hanging on the horse. What is it?"

"I don't know, but I think we need to take… no… borrow this photograph and get some answers at the ranch."

"We could be tampering with a crime scene."

Virginia gave her a sheepish look. "Yeah, but we're just borrowing it."

Donna sighed. "I didn't see any picture."

"Good. Let's go." Virginia stuck the picture in her backpack.

"Aren't we going to look around for the ships first?"

Virginia nodded. "Yeah. But we need to be careful. The shooter is still out there."

Virginia and Donna left the building and scurried to their car and climbed into the Range Rover. Donna tossed her cloth bag in the back. Virginia started the car and pulled out of the dusty parking area and left the scene as the coroner's and forensic vans arrived. Ahead of them, they could see another police car racing toward the scene. Donna fidgeted in her seat, then turned toward Virginia. "We didn't tell them about the rest of our case, at least not much."

Virginia briefly shook her head. "They didn't need to know, at least not right now. Ferguson may bring them up to speed. That's him coming. How'd he get here so fast?"

"I don't know. Now, what do we do?"

"We keep going. We also act normal with Emilio for now. We don't know why the picture of him was at the shop. It may well be innocent."

Donna frowned, then glanced at Virginia. "Wasn't there a magnifying glass next to that photo?"

Virginia wrinkled her forehead. "Hmm, come to think of it, yeah."

"Maybe the picture was taken a while ago by someone, and the old guy thought there was something of interest in the background and was studying it when we arrived."

"You could be right. Call Emilio and ask if he saw anything while we were there," said Virginia. "We haven't heard from him for a while. Maybe he saw something. He mentioned before that two people were watching us."

"If he saw the shooter, then why didn't he alert us?"

"I don't know. Call him."

Donna tried to raise Emilio on the radio. No response. "I can't get him."

"Maybe when we came down here, he went back to the ranch. Call Liana."

Donna called the ranch. Liana answered "B bar P ranch base. Is everything okay *Señora* Donna?"

"Yes and no. We witnessed another murder, and we can't reach Emilio. Where is he?"

"Another murder, *Señora* Donna? Are you and *Señora* Virginia okay?"

"Yes, to both questions. Where's Emilio?"

"I don't know. He was supposed to be backing you up. I'll try to reach him."

"Okay. Let us know when you find him."

"I will. B bar P base out."

Donna clicked off the radio. "Do we go to the caves?"

"I think we might as well. We're headed in the right direction. Maybe the death of that man back there will keep the killer busy avoiding the police, and he won't notice us missing."

"Yeah, but the shooter is either gone, or he's still out there watching. If he's still around, he'll probably not have any trouble following us."

Virginia pulled the Rover to the side of the road. "Why would anyone shoot and kill that poor man in the first place? He shot the guy on a moving motorcycle through the heart, so he's a darn good shot."

"I don't know. Maybe the shooter might have thought the guy trying to get away on that bike told us something he shouldn't have." Donna shrugged. "Like I said before, the shot near you may have been a warning to stay put so he could make a clean getaway."

"You could be right. But if the man was shot because the shooter thinks he told us something, then why not kill us too to keep whatever it is a secret?" Virginia let out a breath. "He didn't tell us anything of value. He may have gotten killed for nothing."

Whispering Threads

"You know that and so do I, but someone is worried that he did. That someone could still be watching us and with a big gun."

"This makes me think someone is waiting for us to find the treasure, then take it from us."

"They want us to do the legwork, and then take the spoils?"

"I think so. In that case, we sure as hell don't want to lead them directly to the treasure. We need a strategy." Virginia rubbed her forehead. "I'm getting a headache."

Donna handed Virginia a bottle of water, "Take a drink. You need to stay hydrated."

"Thanks." Virginia took a long drink.

Donna looked out the window at the shimmering heat rising from the road. "How about this. We go look for the ships of the desert and lead whoever may be out there all over the sand today. Then we figure out how to misdirect him, or them, from following us to the treasure later."

"Good idea. Pull out that map of yours and the photos of the old painting and the quilt. Let's see if we can pinpoint a general area to start looking for the ships." Virginia looked out the windows and smiled. "I'm sure if someone is following us they'll just love wandering all over the desert in this heat."

"Serves them right."

Virginia glanced toward the rear of the Rover. "You bought that ship's lantern. Why?"

"It's old and looked like one in the painting. It had some words on it in Spanish. Maybe it's from one of the ghost ships."

"Hmm. Good idea. We'll examine it tonight. Oh, what's in the bag you just brought from the shop?"

"The other lantern. That old guy won't need it, and it may be a clue."

"You stole it from a crime scene? The sheriff will love you. And weren't you the one worried about my borrowing that picture?"

"What he doesn't know won't hurt him, or me." Donna looked out the window. "While we're here, let's take a quick look at the remains of that deserted city over there by the Salton Sea, then head for the area the old Spanish ships may be."

"Okay. Our shooter may enjoy following us through a desiccated city." Virginia pulled out onto the highway.

The radio sounded. "B bar P ranch base to mobile one."

Donna clicked the microphone on the radio. "Mobile one, did you find Emilio, Liana?"

"Yes. He's in the hospital in Palm Desert."

Donna answered as Virginia pulled to the side of the road. "What happened? Is he going to be okay?"

"He was attacked. A man tried to stab him. He's in surgery."

Virginia's heart skipped a beat. She asked, "Any idea who assaulted him?"

"No. Emilio tried to fight him off. The sheriff thinks Emilio managed to wound his attacker with the man's stone knife. They are trying to find out who the man is from anything he may have left on the knife."

Virginia glanced over her shoulder as she pulled back onto the road. "Stone knife?"

"Yes. Similar to the one that killed Ms. Carol."

"Interesting. We are headed for the hospital. Would you like us to pick you up on the way?"

"No. I think I'd better stay here and lock the ranch down until you come back. Please let me know how Emilio does. If it is okay with you, I can go after you get back here."

Donna felt the acceleration as Virginia sped toward Palm Desert. "That sounds good. Liana, Virginia is breaking every traffic law possible to get us to the hospital as quick as possible. We'll let you know his condition as soon as we know."

"Thank you, *Señora* Donna. B bar P ranch out."

Donna noticed Virginia's extra tight grip on the steering wheel. "You thinking what I'm thinking?"

"I'm sure of it."

Donna sat back and grinned. "There's going to be hell to pay in the desert and soon."

CHAPTER 24

Virginia swung the Range Rover into the hospital driveway. Near the front entrance, she turned into an empty parking space, bumped the concrete curb at the end, and stopped. Donna flew out of the car just ahead of Virginia and rushed toward the hospital's main entrance. Virginia used the key fob to lock the vehicle as she hurried behind Donna. They entered the lobby and stopped at the front desk.

Virginia caught her breath and asked the volunteer, sitting behind the counter, where they could find Emilio.

The woman consulted a computer screen, then looked up at the two women. "The gentleman is out of surgery and is in the PACU. You can go to the surgical floor and wait there. There is a little waiting room available. The nurses will have more information, I'm sure." She pointed. "The elevators are just over there. Second floor, right."

Virginia nodded. "Thank you." They hurried to the elevators and took one to the second floor.

Virginia and Donna approached the nurse's station. A nurse in blue scrubs sitting at the counter looked up at them. "Can I help you?"

"Yes, we're looking for Emilio Montoya."

"Are you relatives?

"No. We're Special Agents Virginia Davies Clark and Donna Boletti of the Smithsonian Central Security Service." They displayed their badges and credentials. "Mr. Montoya also works on a ranch I own," said Virginia.

The nurse eyed their badges. "Okay. There is a policeman waiting in the visitor's lounge for Mr. Montoya as well." She pointed down the aisle. "I'll let you know when he's in his room and if he can see visitors."

Virginia nodded. "Thank you. Can you tell us anything about his condition?"

"I'm sorry, no. It says here he is out of surgery and the doctor will be up here shortly to speak to the officer, so I'm sure he'll talk to you, too."

"Thanks." Virginia and Donna walked to the waiting area. They stopped and stared. Virginia cleared her throat and spoke. "Mr. Coombs?

What are you doing here? The nurse said there was a police officer here, where is he?"

Frank Coombs, dressed in jeans, checkered shirt, and a photographer's vest, slowly rose from his chair and tossed a magazine onto a side table. "They need to update their subscriptions." He stepped to the women with a slight limp. "I owe you two an explanation. But it needs to be confidential."

Donna put her hands on her hips. "You could say that. Who the hell are you, really? Confidential? Why?"

"Yes, my identity was secret." He pointed to two chairs. "Have a seat, and I'll explain."

The women sat and fidgeted as Coombs slowly pulled a leather case from his vest pocket. He opened it and displayed a gold shield. "I'm a special agent with the BIA. I'm working with the FBI. I know you two are with the Smithsonian Central Security Service."

"You do?" asked Donna. "How? Who told you?"

"Your agency."

Virginia frowned. *This doesn't wash.* "Great. Our agency told you about us, but didn't bother to tell us about you. Wait 'till I get ahold of our boss and Ferguson. That sucks."

Coombs cleared his throat. "Detective Ferguson doesn't know."

Virginia's eyes widened. "He doesn't?"

"No."

"Why?"

"It's on a need to know basis."

"I guess it is. We tried to find out more about you, but the files were locked. We hit a brick wall. Now I get the idea. You're undercover." Virginia sighed. "Then, the whole thing about the tribe wanting to mine stuff on my land was just a cover?"

"No. The tribe really wants to do it, and they have agreed to have me pose as their agent for that purpose, and as a cover for my investigation."

Donna set her backpack on the floor next to her chair. "You're helping the FBI? Why aren't they doing the investigating themselves?"

"Manpower shortage, lack of knowledge about the area, the tribes, American antiquities, and the people involved. We're operating under Title 18, USC sections 668 and 1170, as I think you are."

Virginia nodded. "Yes. Now, what exactly are you investigating?"

"Theft and smuggling of native American artifacts, theft of minerals from Indian land and your land, and the threat of possible theft of some treasure that may be on government or tribal land. I was also looking into the murder of Carol Putman. That's when you showed up."

A male nurse entered carrying a tray with three cups of coffee. "Thought you would like a little something to drink while you wait." He set the tray down and left. Coombs took a cup and drank some of the coffee.

Virginia gave him a scowl. "Carol's murder and some treasure, huh? The treasure may be on my land."

Coombs nodded. "You're right. In that case, I have no jurisdiction unless *you* ask for my help."

"You're helping the FBI, anyone else we should know about?"

"The Department of Energy. They're kind of... well... interested in some of your mines."

"The radioactive ones."

"Yes. They're interested in some of the elements and isotopes in the ores from the mines. I haven't a clue as to why."

Virginia stiffened. "You're helping them, too?"

"No. They're just interested."

"Good to know. As to asking for your help, joining forces may be a good idea."

"Good. I'd hoped you'd say that. I'd like to work with you two. And to be frank, I can use the help."

"Okay, but why are you here? What's your interest in Emilio?"

Coombs eyed the two women. "Well, I saw the attack. Mr. Montoya fought the attacker off, but Mr. Montoya was severely injured. I tried to get to him and help, but it was over by the time I got there. I was the one who called for the paramedics and the sheriff."

"You know he may be—"

"Illegal? Yes, and I don't care. He's a nice man and a hard and loyal worker. And it isn't my jurisdiction."

Virginia smiled. "Thank you for coming to his aid and not turning him in. Have they said anything about his condition?"

"Not much. I was told the operation was successful, but nothing else. He's alive."

They turned and rose as a tall man in green scrubs entered the room. "I'm Dr. Adams. I'm looking for..." he consulted a clipboard. "Mrs. Virginia Clark."

Virginia stepped forward. "I'm Virginia. Is this about Emilio?"

"Yes." He motioned for them to take their seats. "I'm Dr. Mercer, the surgeon who treated Mr. Montoya. He's been in surgery for a little over five hours. He suffered severe and extensive stab wounds to the chest and abdomen. He had a broken rib, which caused a pneumothorax or collapsed lung. He's suffered wounds to his liver and his pancreas, and internal hemorrhaging. He was also slashed on his arms and torso by a stone knife that caused dirty, ragged cuts. It looked like he tried to defend himself.

"Based on information the paramedics brought to us, we cleaned a small amount of radioactive materials from his wounds as well. Fortunately, we were able to repair his injuries, but he's lost a lot of blood. Right now he's stable and should make a full recovery, but it will take time. He's in the PACU now, that is, the post-anesthesia care unit, and will be there for a few more hours. From there he will be moved to the intensive care unit, where he will be placed on a ventilator. You might want to go home and come back in two days or so."

Donna gave him a searching look. "If he'll be in his room in a few hours, why can't we see him?"

Dr. Mercer frowned. He looked tired. "He's on a lot of morphine and a number of other drugs for infection. Because of that, he'll be asleep for the next forty-eight hours, possibly more, so he won't know you're here. Furthermore, he will not be able to speak until he's off the ventilator, which may be another few days." The doctor looked at his clipboard. "I suggest you call the ICU in a few days to learn whether he's conscious and off the ventilator. If so, he'll be able to recognize you and talk to you then." Dr. Mercer looked at his clipboard. "He'll be in room 218 when he's brought up."

Virginia looked at the doctor. "I don't know if he has a private physician, will you be his doctor here?"

He nodded. "Yes, me and a hospitalist. We'll take good care of him. Oh, someone in the administrative office wants to talk to his... someone responsible for him."

Virginia laughed. "They want to know who's paying the bills."

"That's out of my hands. I'll do my best to get your friend back on his feet again. Nice to meet you, Mrs. Clark. I'm sure I'll see you during Mr. Montoya's stay with us."

"How long will he be in the hospital, Doctor?"

"At least two weeks, maybe a little longer. We'll know more when he wakes up."

Virginia shook his hand. "Thank you, Doctor. I'm sure we'll be speaking again." She watched the doctor leave, and then sat down. "I'll go see the Accounting Department. Donna, will you see what kind of cooperation we can arrange with Special Agent Coombs for this now joint investigation?"

Donna nodded. "I'll work with Mr. Coombs and call Liana. I'm sure she's a nervous wreck by now."

Virginia stood, grabbed her backpack, and headed for the door. "I'll be back shortly." She hurried down the hall toward the elevators.

Donna turned to Coombs. "Okay, looks like we're going to be working together."

He nodded. "I'd hoped you two would want to do that."

"You have to understand a couple things."

His eyebrow shot up. "Like what?"

"We operate, well, on our terms. We're not always well-behaved ladies, but we get the job done."

Coombs sat back and chuckled. "I heard you two could be unorthodox, but you're good at this stuff."

Donna smiled. "You could say that."

"I'd like to join you. I've been involved with this investigation for a year and haven't made a lot of progress. I've arranged it with the tribe, if you accepted my offer to work together, to allow you access to the reservation and to act officially within the reservation."

"Good. That may help. We can bring you up to speed later. Right now, I need to call Liana and tell her Emilio is going to be okay and when she should come visit him."

"While you do that, and we wait for Virginia, I'll arrange for a twenty-four-hour guard for Mr. Montoya. Someone wanted to kill him; I don't want them to succeed on our watch."

Donna reached over and patted Coombs' arm. "Thanks. That's a good idea." She rose and walked into the hall and stood near the door, within hearing distance of Coombs, and dialed Liana's number. After talking to Liana, she started to turn back to the waiting room when she saw Virginia step out of the elevator and frantically wave for Donna to join her. Donna hurried down the hall and stepped around the corner. "What's up?"

Virginia glanced back down the hall and then shook her head. "We were almost fooled. That could be dangerous for Emilio. I contacted the SCSS in Washington about Mr. Coombs. We have a problem."

Donna frowned. "What are you talking about?"

"We know that man in the waiting room as Frank Coombs, right?"

Donna shrugged. "Yeah."

"When we met him before he stated he was the tribe's representative, and now he's provided us with his badge and story about being undercover with the BIA, right?"

"Yeah. Where are you going with this? What's wrong? What did Washington say?"

Virginia turned her cell phone around. "This is the real Frank Coombs."

Donna's heart stopped. "If that's Mr. Coombs, who's the guy in the waiting room? Where is the real Mr. Coombs?"

"According to Washington, the real Frank Coombs disappeared somewhere in the desert around here a few weeks ago. As to who that man in the waiting area is, well, that's what we're going to find out."

"We'd better do it fast; he was calling someone about taking care of Emilio. I thought he meant guarding him."

Virginia started down the hall toward the waiting room, a 9mm pistol in her hand. "Let's go put a wrench in his plans."

CHAPTER 25

Virginia and Donna bolted into the waiting room and stopped. The room was empty. Virginia spun around. "Where did he go?"

Donna hustled out and went to the nurses' station. "Did you see the man who was waiting for Mr. Montoya leave?"

The nurse looked up. "The police detective?"

"Yeah."

"Yes, he seemed to be in a hurry."

"Did he say where he was going?"

The nurse nodded. "He asked where the PACU was, and then he used the stairs," she pointed, "over there."

"Where is the PACU?"

"On the first floor, near the surgery department. There are signs directing you."

"Thanks." Donna started for the door to the stairwell when Virginia caught up.

Virginia shoved her pistol back into her backpack as she raced toward the door. "Where are we going?"

"He's headed downstairs, probably to the PACU. I noticed he was limping when we met him in the waiting room."

"I did too. We'd better get down there fast." They bounded down the stairs two at a time. Entering the hallway, they found a sign pointing the way to the PACU. They dashed down the corridor, avoiding startled employees, and entered the PACU.

A nurse in blue scrubs stopped them. "You can't come in here."

Virginia flashed her badge. "Federal agents. We believe someone may try to kill Mr. Montoya."

The nurse stared at Virginia for a second. "You mean the man dressed in jeans, checkered shirt, and a photographer's vest?"

"Yes."

"He's on his way to the security office. The police stopped him when he bolted in here."

Whispering Threads

Virginia did a double take and gave the nurse a startled look. She glanced at Donna, who was frantically looking around. Virginia calmed, then asked, "What happened? Why were the police here? How did they grab him so fast?"

"Mr. Montoya has been under guard by the sheriff since he got here. The deputy in here guarding him stopped the man you mentioned when he stormed in. You can find the intruder in security. The deputy is still with the patient."

Virginia gave the nurse a puzzled look. "Emilio's being guarded by a sheriff's deputy?"

"Yes. It is unusual, but there's a deputy back there with Mr. Montoya."

Donna touched Virginia's arm. "You go see the deputy, and I'll go to security. We can meet up after."

Virginia nodded. "Okay." She followed the nurse to where Emilio was resting in a bed hooked to monitors and various IV lines.

A uniformed deputy sheriff sitting in a chair stood as she approached. Virginia provided her credentials to the deputy. She waited while he called for verification. "Nice to meet you, Mrs. Clark. I've heard about you from Detective Ferguson."

"I bet you did. I'm sure glad you are here, Deputy. What made you suspect something was wrong when that man came in?"

The deputy nodded toward the entrance. "He shot past the nurse and headed for Mr. Montoya with a firearm. He looked like he was hell-bent to kill someone."

"He was. He was going to kill Emilio."

"He didn't make it. That's why I'm here. The man is in custody. Detective Ferguson is on his way. You can meet him in the security office when he arrives. Oh, any idea why the man would want to harm, or kill, Mr. Montoya?"

"Yes." Virginia glanced at Emilio. "Emilio may have seen the man kill another person."

"I see. Then I'm glad I was here to protect him."

"I'm glad you were, too." She glanced at Emilio, who was sleeping. "I'll look in on Emilio later."

"Okay."

Virginia abruptly turned as she heard a call over the PA system. "Code Grey, security office. Code Grey." She stepped to the PACU nurse's station. "What's a Code Grey?"

The nurse looked at her. "Violence, security alert. Something happened at the security office, and they're calling for urgent medical assistance."

"Oh, shit." Virginia shot out of the door. She looked at the sign indicating the direction to security and raced down the corridor. She stopped at the entrance to the security office near the lobby, and waited as a team of doctors, nurses, and other hospital techs rushed in. A police officer stood outside. Virginia went to the officer and showed him her badge.

"I heard the Code Grey. What happened? My partner is here; is she okay?"

"The other federal agent from the Smithsonian? The pretty brunette?"

Virginia fidgeted. "Yes, that's her. Is she okay?"

"Oh, yeah. She's fine. It's the man we were holding that's in serious trouble."

"He is? What happened?"

"From the little I know, the suspect was being held for the sheriff and was handcuffed to a desk chair. When your partner came in, he yelled something, pulled a knife, and lunged toward her with it. He did it right in front of everyone. Everyone, that is, but me. I was just reporting for duty. It occurred so fast the officers with him didn't have a chance to react."

"And? What happened? What did she do?"

The officer chuckled. "She shot him."

Virginia took a deep breath and slowly let it out. "That sounds like her. What's the condition of the prisoner?"

"I don't know. They called for medical assistance at once. I heard she shot him six times. One shot right after the other at close range. My shift commander said she kept firing until he went down." The officer smiled. "He thinks she should work for us."

"Can I go in a see her?"

"Yes, but you'll have to wait for the medical team to leave and take him out." He turned his head and listened to his radio attached to his uniform. "Looks like they're calling for the coroner."

"He pulled a knife?" Virginia gave him a quizzical look. "Where did he get a knife?"

"He had it on him. When the officers searched him, they missed it somehow."

Virginia watched the medical staff leave. She stepped inside the office. Blood was on the floor and the far wall. An overturned desk chair still had a set of handcuffs attached to the armrest. Coombs body was on the floor in a pool of blood. Police officers stood around in a daze. She saw Donna talking to a police sergeant who was frantically taking notes.

Donna turned as Virginia scurried to her. "Hi. Before you ask, I'm fine, that jerk attacked me. Oh, just so you know, Detective Ferguson has Emilio in custody and under guard here at the hospital."

"In custody? I thought… why? What did he do?"

"Emilio didn't do anything. Ferguson heard ICE was coming to get Emilio, and by the sheriff holding him, ICE can't take custody of him."

"ICE? This is terrible." Virginia frowned. "So that's why the deputy is guarding him."

"Yep. He said, as SCSS agents, we could take custody of him when he's released. That'll keep ICE out of it. I figure we can make him invisible to ICE once he's back at the ranch."

"Sounds like a plan." Virginia smiled. "Remind me to put Ferguson on my Christmas card list."

Donna sat. "I think he'd settle for a nice bottle of wine, or better yet, a bottle of forty-year-old Scotch." She looked at her hands. "Now they start to shake. It's all over. My stomach doesn't feel too good either."

Virginia set her backpack down. "You realize you shot and killed one of our suspects, and it's the adrenaline coming down that's causing the shaking and your stomach issue."

"I know." Donna had a wounded look in her eyes. "He didn't give me much choice. Oh, the docs found, besides my six bullet holes, cuts on his arms and legs and a bad cut on his abdomen he had poorly bandaged. I think he was the one who attacked Emilio."

"I think you're right. Maybe the coroner will be able to identify him. That may give us a clue as to who's behind this."

"Want to bet?"

"No." Virginia glanced around the office, then back at Donna. "Why'd you shoot him six times?"

"He scared me. He wouldn't fall down, and my gun went click when I pulled the trigger the seventh time. Out of bullets. He finally went down."

Virginia's eyebrow shot up. "You were using my husband's snub-nosed .357 magnum?"

Donna gave her a sheepish grin. "You weren't using it. I had .38 special rounds in it. I figured a .357 bullet in it would kick too much for me. The gun isn't very big, but it's heavy." She patted her backpack. "He almost cut this, can you imagine him trying to cut this eighty-five-dollar, leather backpack? That's a crime in itself, or should be. And I like Andy's revolver because it doesn't jam, especially when I'm under stress like I was. I need to buy one of these."

Virginia chuckled and shook her head. "I guess you do. Why did he attack you? They had him prisoner. Hell, he was handcuffed to the chair."

"The police asked the same question." Donna sighed. "I don't know. When I came in, he just went berserk. He screamed, pulled a knife, and came at me, dragging that chair he was handcuffed to with him. Like I said, I was scared. I just defended myself. I don't have a taser." She glanced at the taser on a nearby police officers duty belt. "Maybe I should get one of those, too. You have one don't you?"

"Yes. It's at the ranch." Virginia looked at the police sergeant. "Can she go?"

He nodded. "Yes, ma'am. We have her statement, and we all saw what happened so she's free to go. If we need to talk to either of you again, we have your address. The crime scene unit is on the way as is the coroner and our detectives. A sheriff's detective is coming as well, so it'll be pretty busy around here. This would be the best time to leave before things really get hectic. We'll have some serious explaining to do to our chief because we missed that knife he had. And we'll have to explain why no officers used their Tasers on him before she shot him. He'll want to know why she reacted, and we didn't."

"Thanks for your help, Sergeant." Donna smiled at him. "Oh, tell your chief he tried to stab me, not you. That's why I got him before you guys could." She looked at the bloody mess and the fake Coombs on the floor, then back at Virginia. "I think he attacked Emilio because Emilio saw him shoot the old guy at the antique shop. And he used a stone ceremonial knife on Emilio like the one that killed Carol, so I'm thinking he also killed Carol."

"I was thinking the same thing." Virginia bit her lip. "He may well have killed the real Mr. Coombs, too. Let's go while we still can." Virginia led Donna out of the security office and toward their car. "Things are getting out of hand. We need to find those ships, the treasure, and figure out for sure if this fake Mr. Coombs murdered Carol alone, or if there were others involved. We'd better do it before more people are killed."

"That's what we've been trying to do."

"Yes, but I think we should go find those damn ships now and see what we can learn from them."

Donna slipped her backpack on. "Now? It's getting close to dinner time."

They walked out of the hospital to the Range Rover. Virginia slid into the driver's seat and looked at Donna sitting next to her. "This from the girl who a few minutes ago had a stomach ache and just shot someone? Besides eating, what else do you have to do tonight, Ms. Bolette?"

"My tummy feels better now, just hungry. Probably nerves. I eat when I'm nervous." Donna grinned. "And I think my schedule's clear. Do you know where we're going, exactly?"

"Close enough anyway. Then we go for a hike. But first, we'll get us some food."

"Okay. Sounds like a plan, I think. I like the eating part." Donna pulled the revolver out of her backpack and dumped the spent cartridges on the floor. She rummaged in her backpack that sat on the floor between her legs, fished out a box of ammunition, reloaded the pistol, and then snapped on her seatbelt. "Okay, that's done. Let's go. Oh, do you think anyone will be following us or may try to kill us while we're out there?"

Virginia started the car. "With our luck, probably."

CHAPTER 26

Virginia and Donna left the hospital and headed for the mountains on the ranch. Virginia turned off the main highway onto a dirt road and drove for a mile to a gate. Donna hopped out and went to the gate, unlocked it with a key from a set in the car. Virginia drove through the gate and waited as Donna closed it, relocked it, and climbed back into the Range Rover. They proceeded up the winding road to a wide spot and pulled over.

Virginia looked out the window at the desert, sand dunes, and the Salton Sea in the distance. She glanced at Donna, who was rummaging in her backpack. "Do you have the copies of the painting from the office and the pictures of the quilt?"

"Yeah, they're in here someplace." Donna yanked out a small tube. "Got it. They're in here." She handed the tube to Virginia. "They'll be easier to look at rolled instead of folded and creased."

Virginia took the tube. "Good idea." She opened the ends and pushed out the pictures. She studied the photographs of the painting in the office and then the view out the window. "Okay, this looks like the location the artist used as the basis of the painting."

Donna looked at the picture, then out the window. "I think you're right. The landscape looks similar. The buildings down there are about the only difference, those, and the flying gods in the painting, or whatever they were."

"If you look at the photograph of the quilt, you'll see that the ghost ships should be about…" She pointed. "…There."

"Agreed." Donna pulled out binoculars and scanned the indicated area. She picked up her map Emilio had given her and made some notations on it. "I've noted some landmarks so as we get closer we won't get lost or head in the wrong direction."

"Good idea." Virginia squinted against the glare. "Hand me the glasses, please."

Donna passed the binoculars to her. "See something else?"

"Possibly. There's a grey van parked just north of the turnoff to the ranch gate. It's been there for a while. It wasn't there when we took the side road to get here."

"We've been followed?"

"That, or they're just lost."

"Or we're paranoid."

"Just because you think someone is trying to kill you doesn't make you paranoid."

"Good point."

"Let's see what they do when we head toward the sand dunes." Virginia turned the car around and drove down the mountain. After they passed through the gate again and Donna locked it, Virginia said, "Oh, before you say anything, I propose we head to the Mexican restaurant that's on the way. That'll also give us a chance to see what that van does and get us some sustenance."

Donna feigned anguish. "Nourishment at last. My stomach thanks you. I think we'll need some libation, too."

"May want to wait on the alcohol until after our adventure. Alcohol and the desert are not a good combination, especially in the heat out there."

"All right, no excess. How about one, nice, cold, margarita?"

"Okay, one, but not the size of a swimming pool."

Donna gave her a wounded look. "Party pooper. Step on it lady; my stomach thinks my throat's been cut."

"Righto, Miss Drama Queen. Keep an eye out for that van, or anyone else looking suspicious."

They left the ranch and drove south for five miles to a Mexican restaurant. Virginia parked the car, and they walked into the air-conditioned establishment. A waitress, in a typical Mexican style uniform, seated them at a table by the front window. They ordered and sipped frozen margaritas while keeping an eye on the road. While eating, they noticed the grey van drive by and continue south.

Donna sighed. "Looks like they were just checking a map."

Virginia frowned. "Maybe, but we'll need to keep our guard up. Check in with Liana. See if things are still calm at the ranch."

"Okay." Donna pulled the radio out of her backpack and called the ranch.

"B bar P Ranch, hello *Señora* Donna," said Liana.

"Liana, everything in order there?"

"*Sí.* I'm finishing putting groceries away. I have the alarms on, and the men are out patrolling the ranch. They took their weapons."

"Good. Have you heard from the hospital?"

"*Sí.* I called. Emilio is doing well. They took him off the respirator. He'll be in his room tonight, but asleep."

"Virginia and I will take you to the hospital when he wakes up."

"*Gracias.* Where are you going now?"

"To find the ghost ships and see what we can learn."

"*Sea cuidadoso. Los barcos están atormentados.*"

"We'll be careful, and we love haunted things. We'll call you when we're on our way back. If anything happens there, call us right away."

"Okay. B bar P Ranch out."

Donna glanced at Virginia who was looking at her cell phone. "Someone send a text message?"

"Yeah. It's from our two friends from Litio Products. Our old dinner dates. They want a meeting to present their proposal. They'd like to go over it with us and talk about the National Marine Management Agency that owns Litio Products. They also want to show us the location on the ranch they'd like to use for their project."

"What are you going to tell them?"

"We'll meet them the day after tomorrow at the ranch. We still have some exploring to do." Virginia looked at the server who was bringing them their food. "When you said you were hungry, you meant it. That's a lot of food. You're not going to be able to eat dinner."

"Trust me; I'll be ready for dinner." Donna looked at her watch. "Well… we'd better have a late dinner."

After their afternoon 'snack,' they returned to the car. Virginia pulled out onto the highway and headed south. "Look at your map. When do we turn off this road and how do we get to our destination?"

Donna took her map out, consulted it, and then looked out the window. "It looks like we go another mile, then turn southwest. There's a dirt road for part of the way, about three miles, then it's off-roading."

"The dunes we are seeking are near the foothills to the mountains. Maybe that's also where the cave with the treasure is located."

"I would think so." Donna glanced at the sand dunes looming up and the mountains behind them. "It would have to be close because the treasure would be heavy. Probably up on the side of a hill because this area was under water."

"Okay. Here comes our turn." Virginia turned off the highway. "You're the navigator, now what?"

"Keep going 'til the road ends."

Virginia looked at the rutted dirt path in front of them. "This is a road?"

"You've driven on worse. At least you can see it. There is a little wind. How fast do the dunes move? If those dunes move, it could get iffy."

"I don't think they move too fast, so we're pretty safe." They drove on the dirt road until it ended. Virginia pulled herself up and looked over the steering wheel. "Now where?"

Donna pointed at sand dunes ahead and a little to the right. "That way." She looked at Virginia. "You do realize this is the hottest part of the day?"

"You want another margarita?" Virginia turned the car, and then slowly drove over the rocks, sand, and small bushes.

"That would be nice." Donna watched as Virginia maneuvered around larger bushes and rocks until they stopped at the edge of the sand dunes.

Virginia sat frowning.

Donna twisted in her seat and looked at Virginia. "What's wrong?"

"Should I put this thing in four-wheel drive and try going ahead, or should we walk?"

"Do you think AAA would venture out here to pull us out?"

"No." Virginia turned off the ignition. "Looks like we're hiking in the heat from here."

They climbed out and took their backpacks. From the rear of the Range Rover, they removed more gear. They strapped on belts with holsters for their guns, canteens, folded shovels, and rope, then put on floppy tan hats and sunglasses. Donna consulted her map and her compass and then pointed. "That way. We'll go along the edge of this dune for a while, then near that slight rise over there; we will need to do some climbing."

Virginia locked the Rover and followed Donna. After walking for thirty minutes, she stopped and looked around.

Donna turned. "What's wrong?"

"Probably nothing. It's just… well, we're easy targets out here."

"I've been watching and haven't seen anyone. You?"

"No. Just a feeling."

"Then let's get up this incline and see what we find." Donna led the way up the side of a large sand dune. At the top, she turned and started toward another dune when she suddenly stopped.

Virginia almost ran into her. She looked around. "Why'd you stop?"

"Look." Donna pointed. "Down there between the sand dunes and that foothill. That looks like part of an old sailing ship. That, or I've been out in the sun too long."

Virginia removed her sunglasses and peered in the direction Donna pointed. "You've got good eyes. Maybe that margarita was good for you. It does look like part of a ship. This is great!" Virginia scanned the hills around them. "Doesn't look like we were followed. Let's go take a look." She stepped out ahead of Donna and carefully descended the dune. At the bottom, she turned slightly and hurried toward a convergence of the rocky foothill and the sand dunes. She stopped and stared. Ahead of her were the bow, midsection and most of the stern of an Old Spanish galleon. She felt her heartbeat quicken. "Well, I'll be damned. It's really here."

Donna caught up with her and stopped. She examined her map. "Yep, right where we figured she'd be. Can you see her name?"

"It's on the stern."

"That's the back end of the boat, right?"

Virginia chuckled. "Not much of a sailor, are you?"

"If it's the size of a nice modern cruise ship or aircraft carrier, I'll go on it. Anything smaller should be played within the bathtub."

"This ship isn't the size of a cruise ship, but she was armed." Virginia pointed. "You can see a few cannons sticking out up there."

Donna studied the old ship. "Think it's safe to venture on board?"

"We came this far, looks like no one has followed us, so why not?"

"I can give you a few reasons, but knowing us, we're going anyway."

"Yeah, let's go. Watch your step. No telling what her condition is, or if there are any critters holed up in there." Virginia started for the ship. She walked around the bow to get a better look at it and to find a way to safely board the old ship. She bent down slightly and then pointed. "Looks like there are two of them. One is buried under more sand than this one. From what I can see, it's in worse condition." When she didn't hear anything from Donna, she turned to find her.

Donna was poking around in the sand at the side of the first ship. "I found some metal fittings. For being hundreds of years old, they're in pretty good shape. I guess iron doesn't rust too fast in the desert buried under sand."

"It's pretty dry out here, so I guess not. Find anything else?"

"Yep. Found a way to get on board. Maybe we'll find where my lanterns came from."

"That, and maybe some clues about the treasure, and if these ships had anything to do with Carol's murder."

Donna glanced at her watch. "Better move fast. By the time we explore these ships and get back to the car, it could be dark."

"Okay. Watch for snakes. Be careful; this wood is old and dry. But first, I'd like to take some photographs to document our find. Are we still on my ranch?"

"According to the maps, yes." Donna set her backpack on the sand and pulled out her camera. Virginia followed suit. They took pictures from different angles and distances. They hung their cameras from their necks, picked up their backpacks and climbed up the side of the sand dune. They hopped on a section of wooden rigging that had fallen and stuck out from the ship; its other end dug into the sand. They carefully walked across it to the deck of the ship. They stood listening for any sounds. The ship creaked with the slight wind blowing against the hull and moving sand across the deck.

Virginia pointed toward the stern. "That's probably the captain's cabin. Look up there. There's the wheel. It's still intact."

"I see it. The ship looks like something from an old pirate movie. It seems funny sitting in all this sand." Donna looked at the cannons. "The guns look somewhat pitted, but otherwise they're in pretty good shape. Tell you what; you look in the captain's cabin and up here. I'll check out below. We can take pictures as we go. Maybe we can do it fast and study them back at the ranch. I don't relish the idea of being out here in the dark."

"Good idea. Let's go. Turn your radio to channel 22. That way, if there is a problem, we can talk to each other."

"Okay. Donna switched channels on her radio. "I'll see you shortly. Don't get lost or in too much trouble."

CHAPTER 27

Virginia carefully stepped through sand and moved toward the stern, then tested each wooden step as she climbed the groaning stairs on the port side, past the mizzenmast, to the quarterdeck. She then moved up another set of stairs to the Stern Castle deck where the ship's wheel stood. Sinking ankle deep into the sand, Virginia finally reached the door at the rear of the deck. After scooping the sand away from the base of the door, she tugged on it. The door moved slightly. She gripped the handle and yanked. The door pushed sand around its base and creaked opened enough for her to slip through. *Funny, it didn't come apart, considering its age and being exposed to the elements.*

Turning on her flashlight, she scanned the large space filled with sand about a foot think on the floor. From the room's size, the large table in the middle, and a rack on one wall with cubby holes in it, she thought it must be the navigation room. Remains of old, faded, maps sticking out of the sand, littered a corner. *This place smells...stale... I think that's it. Strange anyway.* Virginia touched one of the maps. It crumbled into dust. *That didn't work.* She found a couple of bronze parallel dividers, a broken compass, and the vestiges of a sextant. She dusted them off and stuffed the dividers and sextant into her backpack. After taking pictures, she returned to the outside and moved back down to the quarterdeck. A gentle breeze scatted more sand across the deck.

Virginia forced open a door on the back bulkhead and stepped inside. A quick scan of the space with her light showed the room to be the captain's quarters. A layer of sand covered most everything. The remains of a bed sat attached to the port hull. In the back, where part of a window was broken, was a large, dilapidated desk. An armoire sat affixed to the starboard bulkhead. After yanking the doors open, she found a few cloth pieces of clothing. Brass buttons, medals, and other pieces of metal remained on shelves and the floor. She snapped a dozen pictures of the room's contents. She noticed the remains of a couple of well-faded paintings adorning the walls. She found two cutlasses on the floor. She took more pictures.

David Ciambrone

Virginia went back out and peered over the railing toward the bow. *That must be the forecastle.* Virginia went back down the stairs to the main deck and looked around. *"Okay, there's the main mast.* She looked up. *Looks like the wooden beam we came across to get on board came from up there. Part of that is broken. There are cannons, something that was tied down that is now unidentifiable, maybe a small boat from the looks of the remains, and up there, coming out the top of the forecastle, is another mast.* Virginia looked around the main deck. *Lots of cannons. What's in those small crates near the guns?* She took more pictures and climbed down onto the deck. *There's a part of a skeleton.* She looked at the base of the forecastle. *Another skeleton. It looks like most of it is still intact, at least for a bunch of bones.* When Virginia knelt next to the forecastle skeleton, she noticed what appeared to be an arrowhead stuck in the breastbone. *Okay, the natives did attack this ship like the story says.*

Donna cautiously descended a set of steep stairs into the bowels of the ship, hopped over a missing step to the deck, and turned on her flashlight. *I don't know what this deck is called, but there are a lot of big guns, boxes, and... large metal balls.* She touched one. *Iron. Must be cannon shot. Lots of sand, too. Smells musty.* Donna slowly walked around turned over cannons, dilapidated crates, and sections of brittle, old rope. She went to one of the cannons. On the deck next to it rested a small wooden box. She dusted the sand off. There had been something written on it, but the writing was too faded to read. She pulled the top off. Inside, she found cloth packages filled with dry gunpowder. *I guess this made for easier firing.* Further toward the stern, she found a capstan and a pitted iron chain with huge links, and finally the galley. Taking pictures as she went along toward the bow, Donna found what looked like the crew's quarters. *Still got remnants of some old hammocks.* Donna returned to the center of the deck and found another set of steep stairs. She carefully stepped down the creaking stairs to another deck, then slowly made her way around more cannons toward the stern. She found the infirmary and brig. *For being a few hundred years old, the iron bars are still pretty solid, and so are the shackles.* A number of lanterns still hung from the ceiling like the ones she took from the antique store. One was missing. *Maybe that's where mine came from.*

Donna gently descended more sand-covered stairs. The deck below held the magazine. *More gunpowder, but in kegs.* She glanced around. *There are the bags for it like the ones near the cannons.* In another area, she found casks. *They probably held water.* She noticed the remains of a couple of large pumps and the cargo hold. A beam of light from a broken section of the hull illuminated what was left of ship's stores. After snapping more photos, she started up the steps toward the main deck when she heard gunshots. Donna quickened her pace as she yanked the radio off her belt. "Donna to Virginia. What's going on?"

Virginia quickly responded. "We've got company, and they aren't too friendly."

"Someone followed us?"

"Yes, and they are definitely not part of a desert guided tour."

"Are you the one shooting, or your new friends? How many?"

"Both. I'm not sure how many there are exactly, maybe four or five, but they've got assault rifles. One of them took a shot at me after yelling something. I shot back. I think I hit one and they've taken cover in the sand. They're sniping at me. I've shot at them a few more times to keep them at bay, but they're persistent. Five-to-one are not good odds. Can you find another way off this tub? Our original route is blocked."

"Yeah. There are gun ports on the side down here. If we can force one open, we may be able to climb out."

"Okay. I'm working on leaving a little present for the people ruining the party and will join you. Where are you?"

"One deck down. I'll be on the right side trying to open a gun port."

"Starboard side, got it. Be there shortly."

Donna swung her light around and then stepped to a gun port where the cannon, resting on a broken caisson, set well back from the port. She held her penlight in her teeth and tried pushing on the wooden cover. It didn't move. *Shit!* She looked around and noticed a metal bar. It looked like an old pry bar. She picked it up. *This thing is heavy.* She stuck the curved end between the door cover and the hull and tried forcing the door open. It barely moved. She flashed the light around and noticed a chain coming through the hull near the gun port. *Maybe this opens the damn thing.* She grabbed it and tugged. Dust and a little rust fell from the hole, but nothing else happened. She started pounding on the chain and semi-plugged hole, and then she swerved around as she heard someone approach. "Who's...?"

Virginia hurried to Donna's side. "Can you get that thing open?"

"No. You try pulling on the chain, and I'll use the crowbar."

"Okay. We need to hurry." Virginia gripped the chain and pulled, while Donna leaned on the bar. The door creaked, then moved with a groan. They continued their efforts for another minute. The door finally opened enough for them to climb through. Virginia stuck her head out and looked around. "The dune's close to the right and the sandy bottom is about eight feet down. It's a steep slope. We'll hit it and slide, I hope. We don't want to break anything jumping."

"We have a choice?"

"Not really."

A loud explosion from above rocked the ship. Dust, splinters, and sand rained down. A rumbling sound rolled across the upper, creaking, deck. Screams were heard and thumping on the deck. Donna looked up. "What the hell was that?"

"I rigged a little surprise for our pursuers."

Donna gave Virginia a puzzled look. "What did you use?"

"I found some boxes near the cannons that had gunpowder packages and some pieces of metal. I stuffed a whole bunch of the gunpowder packs and some metal things that were around in a cannon. That gunpowder was old. It was dry though. There was some sand in it, so I hoped it would still explode. I made a makeshift fuse out of some twine and gunpowder. Trying to do that and take some shots to keep the men out there pinned down wasn't easy. They fired a few times, but the shots went high. Wasn't sure if it would work, or how long it would burn. I'm really surprised it worked at all."

"You're nasty. Sounds like it had some effect. We've got more gunpowder down here. Want to do it again?"

"No time. I don't know how much damage I did up there, but I bet they're not too happy with us right now. Anyway, we'd be stuck in the same room as the explosives."

"Not a good idea. Let's get our asses out that hole so we can vamoose."

Virginia slipped out the opening and jumped. She landed on the sand and slid down the slope of a dune. She rolled to the side as Donna skidded down beside her. They quickly glanced up at the ship and the opening. Donna brushed the sand from her black hair. "Okay, we're out, now to get the hell out of here alive."

Virginia pointed. "Let's get under the bowsprit. I don't think they can see under there. We can assess the situation and see if we can make it away safely."

"From the sound of your cannon and the screams, maybe they have more pressing concerns than us."

"I don't think so. If anything, I may have kicked the hornet's nest." Virginia led the way down the slope and hid under the ship's bow. Donna scrambled beside her. Virginia looked up at the sound of people on the main deck. "They appeared suddenly, but I think one of them was that Baker guy who impersonated a BLM agent we had arrested and then escaped. One of them shot at me, so I shot back. I think I wounded him. We don't know if my improvised cannon did any serious damage to them. Maybe I just pissed them off more."

"It sounded like you at least wounded a couple of them." Donna glanced around. "It's dusk, but there is still enough light for them to see us if we make a run for it. Any ideas?"

Virginia smiled. "I took a couple bags of gunpowder from the box next

Whispering Threads

to the cannon when I ran." She opened her backpack and pulled out four, leaking, cloth bags. "Maybe we can set off a bomb and…" she patted the hull, "burn this thing. The wood is dry enough."

Donna stared at the bags. "You should have mentioned that while we were on board. There was a lot of that stuff on the deck with the cannons."

"Too late now." Virginia leaned against the hull. "Maybe we can make a bomb, toss it through the gun port we just crawled through, and detonate the powder on that deck."

"I'm not sure we can do it in time, and not get killed trying. Anyway, it's eight feet above the sloping, loose, sand. Not exactly stable."

"Maybe just burning the ship would be enough. The gunpowder inside will blow up, or burn, when the flames get to it."

"May take too long, but we're running short of ideas and time, so go for it." Donna carefully leaned around the edge of the ship and looked up at the port they climbed out, and then quickly pulled back. "Thought I heard something. Someone stuck his head out the gun port we opened. He saw me. We're on borrowed time."

"This better work. They know where we are." Virginia tied the gunpowder bags together. Next, she pulled out her knife and cut a strip of cloth from her shirt. She poured some gunpowder along the length and rolled it up. She inserted the end of her fuse into the largest bag. "My improvised bomb. I hope it works."

Donna frowned. "Are we setting it off here, or are we going to try and throw it onto the main deck? Remember, we're still stuck here."

"I know. I was thinking about climbing back up there and tossing it through the gun port; the top deck is too high."

Donna looked at Virginia with wide eyes. "You nuts? I'm sure they figured out how we got off. That gun port is about eight feet above where we landed. If you remember, that gun port wasn't fully open. We had to squeeze through it. And you'd get one throw at best. That's if they don't shoot you first. By the way, when did you pitch for the Yankees?"

"You have a point. But we need to do something. They'll be coming down here looking for us pretty soon."

Donna looked around the side of the ship again. "I have an idea."

"I hope it's diabolical because we need a miracle."

CHAPTER 28

Donna peered around the ship, then back at Virginia. "It is probably not going to work, but… remember when we jumped from the ship how all the sand that poured down with us?"

"Yeah."

"That pile of sand behind the ship, and slowly engulfing it, is very steep. If we toss that bomb of yours at it, and it works, maybe we can cause an avalanche of sand."

"But if we throw it up there and it does work, it could bury both us, and the boat." Virginia peered around the bow and looked at the sand dune. "Okay, not the best idea." Virginia cocked her head. "What is that buzzing sound? You hear it?"

Donna tilted her head and listened. "Yes, and it's getting louder. It's not a plane or chopper, what is it, a huge bee?"

Gunfire erupted from above. They heard people running and swearing. More shots. Virginia felt her cell phone vibrate in her pocket. She pulled it out and looked at who was calling. The screen read Liana. Virginia tapped the open image on the screen and heard Liana's voice.

"*Señora* Virginia! I did not want to use the radio. It would make noise. You are clear to move to the southeast about fifty feet. You should reach a… a depression between the dunes and be out of sight of the ship. Get ready; I'll tell you when it's safe to move. Oh, light that fuse on your bomb when I tell you."

"How do you know where we were, and how did you—?"

"Light it now; press it against the hull, and move out *rápido*… fast. I'll direct you."

Virginia took a breath, tucked her bomb tight against the hull in a sand depression, and covered most of it. She pulled a lighter out of her backpack and lit the fuse. *I hope this works.* She motioned the direction they needed to run. Donna nodded and sprinted away the best she could in the sand. Virginia followed. As they neared the valley between the dunes someone on the deck above yelled at them. A volley of bullets dug a strip into the sand behind Donna. Virginia dove into the valley and scrambled up on the side of a dune next to Donna. They heard a commotion and then a muffled explosion from the direction of the ship. Shards of burnt wood, sand, and pieces of metal landed in the sand around them. A couple of seconds later, a resounding blast shook the earth and more sand, wood, and metal rained down. They covered their heads as another couple of rapid, louder, explosions caused larger pieces of burning wood, metal, debris, and sand to fall on them. The sand dunes started to shift, and a major sand avalanche poured down on the remains of the burning galleon. The side of the dune they hid behind shifted, causing a minor slide of sand to hit them. They brushed ankle deep dirt off and checked for injuries.

Donna looked at Virginia. "You okay? What just happened? You cause all that?"

"I'm fine." Virginia brushed sand from her blonde hair. "The first small explosion we just heard could have been the bomb we set next to the hull. I don't think I had anything to do with the rest. I wonder if any of the men on that ship survived."

"I'm seriously not in the mood to go look for survivors. We can send the sheriff later, assuming we get out of here safely."

Virginia moved to the edge of the dune and looked where the ship had been. What remained was broken apart, burning, and rapidly being engulfed with sand. "Don't see anyone. Looks like we can walk out." She looked at the phone still gripped in her fist. "Liana, you still there?"

"*Sí*. It is safe for you to return to the car. You are alone."

Virginia took a breath. "Okay, but just how do you know all this?"

"Look up."

Virginia and Donna looked at the top of the sand dunes they were resting on. A drone, about four feet long, circling slowly, descended, and came into view as it flew over them.

"You have a drone?" Virginia spoke into the phone. "Are you flying that thing?"

"No. One of the ranch hands is doing it. I'm telling him where to fly it and when to... to provide assistance to you."

"Okay. Thanks for the help. We were in quite a pickle. I think I winged one or more of the men, but what did you do to cause the explosions?"

"*Sí*. You are right. A couple of the men seemed to be injured. Your cannon fired and exploded and wounded two more. We did not cause the explosions. I could see the big gun you used. After it fired, it looked broken, and part of it was on fire. But your cannon rolled backward after it went off. When it stopped, it must have rested on some rotted wood. It slowly fell through the deck and probably set off some of the gun power below. I think that caused the fire that spread and blew up more powder down there, and then the fire quickly blew up the powder magazine. The ship, she's... not much left. Are you sure you and *Señora* Donna are unhurt?"

Virginia waved that the small plane. "Yes. We're fine, now. Maybe a little sore from some of the stuff that fell on us, but otherwise we're in good shape. How'd you know where we were?"

"Your cell phone has GPS. I tracked you. Did you find anything good on the ship?"

"You can track a cell phone's GPS? How?"

"*Señora* Putman's ranch is about eleven square miles of hot desert. When she would go out, we would keep track of her. In case she had trouble. If she didn't move for a while, we would go look for her. We did the same thing with the ranch hands. I got your and *Señora* Donna's GPS information off your phones. This is okay?"

"You did well. Thanks. We didn't get much from the ship, but we took a lot of pictures. We're going to head back to the ranch. You can call off your air force."

"Okay. Would you like dinner ready when you arrive?"

"Seriously?" Virginia laughed. "After all this? Food?"

Donna leaned close to the phone. "You bet, but we'll need to wash up first. We're covered in sand and dirt."

"We'll be ready. Be careful out there. It's getting cooler, and it's almost dark. This is when the really bad *critters* start to hunt."

Kincaid jumped to his feet from his hotel bed, padded across the room, and answered the telephone on the third ring. His grip tightened as he listened, and then hung up. He took a breath, turned, walked slowly to the connecting door to the next room, and knocked.

Blackman, dressed in shorts and a Spiderman T-shirt, opened it. "You look like you've seen a ghost. What's wrong?"

"I just heard from our guy from Litio Products and the National Marine Management Agency, who was informed by the leader, that things are rapidly going south."

Blackman waved his arm, motioning for Kincaid to enter the room. "They are? Why? What happened?"

"It seems your lady, Ms. Bolette, shot and killed Frank Coombs."

"She did?" Blackman plopped on the edge of the bed. "Why would she do that?"

"Well, for openers, it looked like Coombs shot the old guy who was fronting that fake antique shop. Then, he tried to kill the ranch hand of Virginia's who may have known approximately where the cave with the pearls is, and Coombs also attacked your friend, Donna."

"He attacked Donna? That was stupid. He went rogue?" Kincaid sighed. "I think he panicked."

"Panicked? That guy really was a little flakey."

"Coombs was a little too egocentric. He thought he should be doing the leading since he's the one that convinced the Indians to let him represent, them."

"Why did he go off the deep end and kill Graham? He was no threat. All the old guy had to do was run the antique shop like it was real, and sort out and catalog the stuff that was collected in the desert. It was just a staging area for our treks into the desert and a place for us to store and examine what was found. He didn't really know anything."

"Like I said, I think Coombs panicked. When Virginia and Donna went there, he probably thought they knew something and would get Graham to talk. According to the only message from Coombs, the women bought some stuff and seemed very curious."

Blackman shook his head. "I'm not sure I buy that. That was no reason to kill Graham. Why the hell did he attack the ranch hand? He could have been valuable."

"I don't know. Maybe Coombs was going to grab him and try and get information, and the guy fought back. We'll never know."

"At least Coombs is dead. He can't be traced back to us." Blackman leaned back on his arms.

"Don't bet on it. There's more."

Blackman flinched. "More?"

Kincaid pulled out the desk chair and dropped heavily into it. "Yes. The women found the old Spanish galleons. They went on board one."

"They did? Where?" Blackman leaned forward. "I guess that's good. Hell, we couldn't find the damn boats. Does the boss know where the ships are? How did he find out?"

"You mean where they were."

"I do? Where they were? Why? What happened?"

"Our colleague, Baker, another nut job, took some of the men and followed Virginia and Donna. He caught up with them on one of the old ships and tried to overpower them." Kincaid kneaded his forehead. "I think Baker figured if he could capture the galleon, and get any information about the treasure, he'd be forgiven for his last major screw up."

Blackman sat upright. "He caused another fiasco? Oh, God. He did that after what happened the last time he messed with those two women? That was stupid, real stupid."

"Yes, it was. He, and the men he took with him, are all dead and buried." Kincaid shook his head. "They're, now, under many feet and many tons of sand, lost somewhere in the desert."

"The women? How are they?"

"Oh, they're fine. They managed to take out Baker and all his men and just walk away."

Blackman grinned. "Just the two of them?"

"Yeah. But our leader, whoever he is, is fit to be tied. He's royally pissed. The two ladies have managed to decrease the manpower of our operation, cost us more money, blew the cover for our antique shop, may have destroyed the ships, or at best, reburied them, and we're no closer to the treasure than we were before. We don't even know exactly where the old ships were either. He said you and I are probably the only ones who can get the girls to freely divulge the location of the ships and treasure, or we'll be the ones to force them to tell us."

"He wants us to torture them?" Blackman stood and went to the small refrigerator, took out a small bottle of whiskey, and poured it into a glass. He took a swig, and then looked at Kincaid. "I'm not at all comfortable torturing them. I didn't sign up for that. No way."

"Too bad. It may come to that. You're comfortable with murder, but a little-applied pressure is against your principles?"

"Yes, I guess so. I like them." Blackman's back stiffened. "I'm not going to hurt them." He returned to the bottom edge of the bed and sat.

"But you will kill them if necessary, right?"

"I hope it doesn't come to either option. I'm not even sure I could kill them. Damn it; I won't hurt or kill them." Blackman frowned. "Wait! If Baker and company are all dead and buried under tons of sand, then just how does our leader know all this?"

"Like I said, Baker called him. Baker told him he was watching the ladies and was going to grab them and see what they knew." Kincaid glanced out the sliding glass door into the dark, then back at Blackman. "He said the ships were in the desert near the south end of Virginia's ranch. The boss went to look but found nothing. No ships, no treasure, and no Baker or his men. There were a couple of half-buried, wrecked, assault rifles, some burnt wood, and some odd metal scraps scattered across an extremely vast, and he emphasized vast, area of nothing but sand, salt, and dirt. There weren't even any tracks. It was almost dark when he went. Night closed in on him pretty fast so that seeing anything was impossible. Sand from the dunes was moving with the wind. He figured whatever the women did somehow caused the dunes to move faster. Tomorrow there won't be anything left to see. He did manage to get a glimpse of the girls driving north from the area on the main road toward their ranch, but nothing of Baker and company, except their rented SUV being towed away."

Blackman chuckled. "Virginia had it impounded?"

Kincaid shrugged. "Looks like it."

"We're still going to visit the girls in two days, aren't we?"

"Yes. And we'll do it like we have no clue as to what's been going on."

CHAPTER 29

After getting cleaned up and eating a light dinner, Virginia, Donna, and Liana sat, sipping wine, in the living room before a fire in the huge stone fireplace. Leonardo, the German Shepard puppy, rested in front of the fire.

Virginia sat back in the leather chair. "That drone was a surprise. I'm glad you thought of using it when you did."

Liana smiled. "I was concerned about you when I didn't hear from you for some time. I checked your location with the GPS on your phones and realized you were off-road. We flew the little plane to where you were to see if you were okay without disturbing you."

"Well, I'm glad you did. Why didn't you tell me about the drones and the GPS tracking before?"

Liana gave Virginia a sheepish grin. "We've had a lot going on, and they weren't important at the time. I was going to tell you, but with everything that has happened, I just forgot."

Donna swirled her wine and then took a sip. "Why do you have a drone around?"

Liana looked at the fire, then at Donna. "The ranch is very big. We use them to fly around and make sure things are okay. It is faster and safer than trying to ride all over it, and we can see more of the ranch faster, and respond if there is a need, like to trespassers, looters, and thieves or if someone is missing or gets hurt. There are places that are hard to get to, and this is easier to spot trouble or see if someone needs help. Ms. Putman came up with the idea and bought three."

"Three? Wow. It's a good idea. I'm glad you used it tonight." Donna set her glass on the coffee table. "Were you using the drone when we were at the antique shop, and Emilio was attacked?"

"No. You were mostly in public areas, and Emilio said he was watching you."

Donna glanced at the puppy, then back at Liana. "I can understand that. Now that everyone is safe and secure here at the ranch, we need to figure out what's going on and what we're going to do next."

Liana answered my unasked question. That's good, I think. Virginia nodded. "I agree. Based on what we now know, I think the late Mr. Coombs killed Carol. I'm not sure why though. Maybe he worked for whoever is behind all this. But he could have his own agenda. There are other players, and they all seem to want the treasure, too. People are dying over it. The body count is going up. Another question is, why now?"

Liana shifted to the edge of her chair. "What are you going to do?"

"We'll see the two guys from Litio Products in two days. I'm sure they'll have a good story. Let's see what they propose, and then decide on a course of action."

Donna picked up her wine and took a sip and looked at Virginia. "Maybe it's because I live and work near the ocean, but I'd like to know more about the National Marine Management Agency. They're involved somehow and have an interest in Litio Products. I know every alphabet soup agency in the government is investigating them, but I'd like to know what a marine company is doing poking around in the desert. They're reported to be involved with energy, undersea exploration, sea mining, and marine archeology. The desert isn't the ocean."

Liana jumped to her feet. "I forgot. A young man from the University of California came with a report on the samples you gave them. I'll get it for you." She scurried out of the room.

Donna's eyebrow went up. "I forgot about that. I wonder what it says?"

Virginia shrugged. "We'll know shortly."

Liana returned with a large, sealed, manila envelope with the University of California at Irvine logo on it, and handed it to Virginia. "This is what he left." She sat on the edge of her chair.

Virginia tore open the envelope and pulled out a sheaf of papers. She read them tossing a few on the coffee table as she went. Finally, she sat back. "That was interesting."

Donna finished her wine, moved to the edge of her seat and picked up the papers scanning through them. "Okay, these are out of order and make no sense. You've been mysterious enough, now what the hell does the report say?"

"To sum it up, the turquoise we have in our mine is rare and worth a fortune in the gem and jewelry world. The silver mine that we thought was somehow connected to the uranium mine actually is. The radium we found in the silver mine comes from the uranium mine. The silver mine has a lot of zinc sulfide, and there were some small samples of the radium-zinc sulfide mix that glowed. There's also some lead." She picked up the papers she dropped and put them back in order. "It also had willemite, or zinc silicate, which can glow green. Also, the ore from the gold mines indicates the mines are not played out, and there is some element called palladium in it. Interesting. There's more of it in the ground around that dry creek bed. I wonder where the creek comes from."

She continued reading. "The depleted uranium mine where Carol was murdered is not depleted either. It's very active. There is also a lot of silver, lead, and zinc in the samples from the mine, too. We've got calcite, celestite, fluorite, and some others that glow after exposure to light. Our meteor is confirmed to be a nickel-rich iron form with a number of other compounds and elements in some special crystal structure, but not ataxite. It has a trace of iridium, too. They said some of the meteors have the ability to form some sort of nanotubes that change it's properties somehow. Part of the meteor sample was contaminated with the radium-zinc sulfide that glowed in the dark. I think that's what we picked up at the crater. Coombs tried to use the same type of stone artifact knife on Emilio that killed Carol." Virginia looked at the two women. "That's my addition. The university doesn't know about Coombs attacking Emilio. The knives are the same, though. They are this new crystal nanothingie material with radium-zinc sulfide contamination and are very rare and valuable. They consulted an anthropologist, and he said our Native American neighbor's ancestors didn't make stone tools like this and didn't make cave wall paintings. That is, they didn't think so until now. And the materials we collected from the area of the steam vents show a good deal of lithium. Maybe that's the National Marine Management Agency interest in Litio Products and this area." Virginia set the papers on the table. "Liana, the university said the mines are active. Why did you tell me they were played out?"

Liana sat looking at the report on the table. "I was told the mines were not viable. I don't work in the mines. I help with the processes here. *Señora* Putman said the mines were old and not useful."

"Sounds like Carol was keeping something secret." Donna shook her head. "So, what we suspected was correct."

Virginia nodded. "Yep. Except for the meteor. I thought it was ataxite, and it isn't."

"So what's next... besides talking to Kincaid and Blackman?"

"In the morning, we'll examine what we brought back from the ship and look at the pictures. We need to update Detective Ferguson. We can call him sometime tomorrow."

"Probably a good idea. I'm surprised he hasn't contacted us. I hate to let anyone know where the ships are. You aren't going to tell him, are you?"

"No. We'll think of something to tell him. We'll check on Emilio, too." Virginia stretched. "Let's have another look at those two lanterns you obtained today."

"Okay, I'll go get them." Donna rose and hurried out of the room.

Virginia pulled her cell phone out and displayed the picture of Emilio in the desert she took at the fake antique shop. "Liana, do you know where this picture was taken? We found it in an antique shop south of here."

"In an antique shop?" Liana took the phone and examined the photograph. She shook her head. "No. I do not recognize it." She leaned back, closed her eyes, then abruptly straightened, and with a smile, looked at Virginia. "Wait. *Sí*, I do know. It was taken about six years ago. Just before Mrs. Putman rebuilt the B bar P Ranch house and the other buildings into forts, Cordone's Fort."

"Where was it taken?"

"Not too far from the meteor crater."

"Interesting. Someone was interested in the meteor, too." Virginia sat back. "I was thinking. If the sand dunes move, they must carry the ships with them, or do the ships remain and the sand moves around them?" She took a breath. "If they move with the dunes, then we may have a problem locating the caves."

Liana nodded. "*Sí*. The sand moves, but from what I know, the ships move only a little. The dunes move, but not very far."

"So, our ideas about the general location, and the information from the note we found in the safe with the small amount of treasure could still be valid."

"*Sí*. The problem with using landmarks is, as the time of day changes, the sun moves and changes the color of the desert and mountains and casts different shadows. You can get lost if you try and just use landmarks. The sand moves and changes shape, too."

"I didn't know that." Donna walked in carrying her two lanterns. She placed them on the coffee table and returned to her seat. "They're dusty, but in pretty good condition. One has some markings on it."

Virginia rose and stepped closer to the table. She picked up one of the lanterns and examined it. "It looks old, like some we saw on the ship." She returned it to the table and picked up the second one. After turning it around and upside down, she set it on the table. "This one with the markings is a copy... a fake. I can see fresh, well recent anyway, tool marks where the other one doesn't have any. And the wood finish is artificial. Chemically done."

Donna frowned. "You got all that from just looking?"

"Yes. I'm a curator of a museum, remember? We see a lot of fakes people try to pass as originals. This one isn't that good."

Donna bit her lip. "The fake one is the one that old guy at the antique store didn't want to sell me. The first one you picked up just now was the one I took when the guy was shot."

"Interesting. He didn't want to part with the fake, but you... borrowed... the real one. Nice."

"Glad you approve. Now what?"

"They don't tell us anything about the caves and treasure, but we are the only ones who know that."

"Where are you going with this?"

"We leave the new lantern along with the rock samples we took from the antique store on the table on the porch when our friends from Litio Products come. If they ask any questions, we can tell them we took it off the ships of the desert. I bet they copy or photograph the markings."

Liana tilted her head. "Would the marks tell them where the treasure is?"

Virginia smiled. "I don't think so, but we'll check our maps before we do it."

Donna refilled their wine glasses. "We need to close the loop with Ferguson, like you said. Are we going to tell him about the ships... and the bodies?"

"Yes. We can tell him about the ships and maybe about the men who attacked us. We'll be real vague about the exact location. I'm sure he knows about Coombs by now as well."

"The cops at the hospital said the Imperial County Sheriff and a detective from Riverside County were responding. I bet the Riverside detective was Ferguson. The hospital is in Riverside County."

"No bet." Virginia picked up her wine glass and took a sip. "He knows we had a sample of the treasure from when the jeweler was murdered. The cast of characters is getting smaller." She glanced at Liana. "Liana, I have a question. When did Emilio actually come to the ranch?"

A troubled expression filled Liana's eyes. She then looked at Leonardo, sleeping by the fire. "Emilio's dog is nice, don't you think? He's like Emilio. Quiet, but always there for you. Emilio came here not too long after I did. He's been here for about seven or eight years. He's a good man. Why do you ask?"

"I was wondering why Coombs attacked him."

"Maybe Emilio saw Mr. Coombs shoot the man at the antique shop and Coombs wanted to silence Emilio. Or, Coombs thought Emilio knew where the treasure caves were, and Emilio would not, or could not, tell him."

"Maybe Emilio tried to stop Coombs from shooting us," Donna added.

"Maybe." Virginia leaned back and thought. "Why would someone need a picture of him near the crater? What the hell is going on here?"

Liana shrugged. "I do not know. Most people are interested in the fabled treasure."

"Well, we'll know more when Emilio is able to talk," Virginia said.

Donna picked up her glass and finished her wine. "You said the university reported there nano... nanotube thingies and the meteor. What are they? What does that mean?"

"I'll call Andy and see what he thinks." Virginia looked at her watch. "It's now nine o'clock. Texas is two hours ahead of us, that makes it eleven there. I'll call him in the morning."

"So, we've got the report from UCI, and it confirms what we thought and added the tube stuff." Donna leaned back in her chair. "The meteor mineral is a new wrinkle. We are now positive about the meteor material being made into the knives, and why the knives, and the big quilt glow. We found the ghost ships, but that didn't help any. We managed to get a jeweler murdered. Coombs attacked Emilio, and I shot Coombs. Baker, and a few friends attacked us on the ship, and now he's dead along with his compatriots. We found some leads to the treasure caves because of the large painting in the office and a huge glow-in-the-dark quilt. We've got a sample of the treasure, too. What am I missing?"

"Where the treasure actually is and who's behind all this."

"Is there anything we can learn about Agua Caliente Mar Management? That's the company Coombs said he worked for as the representative of the Indians."

"Another good question and one we can ask Ferguson to run down. When our two friends from Litio Products come, we'll ask about the National Marine Management Agency, too."

Liana rubbed her hands together. "I have a question."

Virginia raised an eyebrow. "What is it?"

"The ships of the desert and the treasure have been here for centuries. The ranch has had the minerals, the meteor, the mud volcanoes, and mines all along, and again for millenniums. Why was *Señora* Putman murdered? Why is all this happening now?"

"Liana, Those are good questions. We're going to get to the bottom of this—and soon." Virginia glanced at the dog sleeping by the fire. "It has to do with the mines, the meteor, the treasure, or the lithium, or all of them."

Donna frowned. "What if there is something else that happens to be in the mix we don't know about?"

Virginia rose and stretched. "You could have something there. This new thing is complicating the picture." She walked to the fireplace and stared at the flames. "We're being played, and I think the person behind all this is someone we already know. Liana, lock our fort down tonight."

CHAPTER 30

The next morning, Donna walked into the kitchen and found Virginia on the telephone. Liana was by the stove dishing out plates of scrambled eggs and bacon and setting them on the table. Donna poured a glass of orange juice and drank it. "That was good. Gets my morning blood sugar level up before I fall to sleep again." She poured a cup of coffee, sat, and slipped two slices of homemade bread into the toaster. She looked up as Virginia hung up the phone and took the chair across from her.

Virginia spoke as she started to eat her breakfast. "That was Detective Ferguson. I brought him up to speed on what we know, minus the actual location of the ships."

"Did you happen to mention the guys who attacked us on them?" Donna took a bite of her food.

"No. I was afraid if I did, he'd want the exact location to retrieve the bodies and investigate. As it is, they are just missing and wanted by the police."

"You do know that's illegal, don't you?"

"Yeah, but it's not going to make any difference. They are wanted men, and they're still missing. Since they won't be committing any more crimes, I'm sure the cops won't lose sleep over them. Anyway, they are buried under tons of shifting sand."

"Devious, but still…" Donna munched on some toast. "Did the good detective have anything new about Coombs or his attacking Emilio?"

"Yes. It seems Coombs is only part Indian. He got the tribe to agree to let him represent them to us. The tribe wants to use part of the ranch, and of course have access to some of the, ahh, natural resources they think they're entitled to. They want to do some mining."

"That's what Coombs said. Anything on Agua Caliente Mar Management?" Donna finished her eggs. "You asked, didn't you?"

"Yes, I asked." Virginia ate some eggs and a strip of bacon. "He said the Agua Caliente Mar Management Company was formed to prospect for minerals and steam vents in the desert with extractable quantities of lithium, like ours, and then obtain the rights. The company would then either sell the rights to someone or form a joint venture."

"Did it have any success?"

"According to Ferguson, the firm did actually do what it advertised." Virginia ate some eggs. "Coombs was a principal in the company. He and some tribal elders own it. They're profitable, but there is talk about some lawsuits on the horizon. Ferguson said he's getting warrants to search the company's offices for reasons unrelated to our situation. It'll take a little longer than usual because the offices are on a reservation, hence a federal judge. Maybe federal officers will have to go along and actually serve the warrant."

"Did Ferguson, or the Imperial County Sheriff, have any idea why Coombs attacked Emilio?"

"No. But they think it may have to do with Carol's murder. Same type of weapon was used. We'll know more when we talk to Emilio. Oh, the bullet that killed the old guy at the antique store came from Coombs' rifle." Virginia sipped some coffee.

"If that's the case, then either Coombs, or his company, is working for the same people that Baker and his band of thugs were."

"Possibly. But I wouldn't be surprised if Coombs was acting on his own with that bunch. I don't think the Agua Caliente Mar Management Company was involved. The tribe has nothing to gain from Carol's murder and all the other problems."

"Have you called Andy yet?" Donna asked.

"Yeah. First thing this morning before he went to the university. He'll call back tonight. Now, want to go find some treasure today?" Virginia finished her eggs, toast, and bacon. She glanced at Donna sitting across from her with a slice of toast halfway to her mouth. "What? You don't want to go?"

Donna ate the toast and then replied. "You bet I want to go. We've got a pretty good idea where the cave is. All we need to do now is find it."

Virginia chuckled. "People have been trying to find it for centuries."

"Yeah, but they don't have the quilt that glows, the letter from the safe, the old painting, or my map."

"I know. When we're done eating, let's gather our gear, load up the Range Rover, and head out before it becomes a furnace out there."

Donna drained her coffee cup. "Think anyone will be watching for us? Maybe try to kill us again?"

"Probably."

"Then we'd better go prepared. Let's take bigger guns with us."

Liana stepped to the table wiping her hands on an apron and sat near Virginia. "Do you need anything from the ranch? Shovels, picks, Geiger counter, generator?"

Whispering Threads

Donna grinned. "Yeah. I'd like you flying that drone of yours, keeping an eye on us, and keeping the radio on, just in case."

Liana nodded. "Where do you want me to fly it?"

Virginia finished her coffee. "You can probably start by looking near the sand dunes we were at last night. You'll be able to spot us and track us from there. How high can that thing go?"

"The larger drones we have can fly up to about a kilometer. We try to stay below that, because of airplanes and the law. The cameras are still able to see the ground well. I can zoom in."

Donna frowned. "A kilometer?"

"About three thousand feet," Virginia said.

"Oh. So pretty high. It should be hard to hear from that altitude."

Virginia nodded. "That's the idea. If we need help, Liana can get it and watch us at the same time. She could direct the cops, or whomever, to our location without anyone knowing they were being watched."

Donna scooted her chair back. "Give me a little time to get dressed and ready. I'll meet you back here." She rose and hurried out of the room.

Liana cleared her throat. "*Señora* Virginia. I'm sorry… I do not trust the *Policía*. They threatened Emilio when they came to talk to us about Mrs. Putman's murder. The detective… he… seems… strange."

Virginia smiled and patted Liana's arm. "It hasn't gone unnoticed, Liana. Detective Ferguson's protecting Emilio right now, but as soon as he can be moved back here, we'll protect him. As for the rest of what's going on, we will have to just be ready for it and take action as required. The one thing we have going for us is Donna and I are federal special agents."

Liana gave her a small smile and nodded. "I will watch you and *Señora* Donna from the air and help."

Virginia and Donna climbed into the Range Rover and headed in the direction of the sand dunes. At the ranch road they had used the day before, Virginia turned and drove up to the gate. Donna hopped out, unlocked it, and held it open as Virginia drove through. After closing and relocking it, Donna jumped back into the car. Virginia looked at the navigation system screen on the Rover's dashboard. "We're in the ether. Just blank space."

Donna put on her sunglasses. "What did you expect? That's why we have my map."

"I know. But I like the idea of a GPS knowing where I am."

"We're in the middle of nowhere. Your phone is letting Liana know our location."

"Funny, she asked where we were going. She could just look at my GPS signal." Virginia chuckled. "Oh well. Let's have a look at your map.

You did mark where the ships were, didn't you?"

Donna unfolded the map and stared at it. "Yes." She pointed at the map. "The ships are here, or they were. So, according to the note written by Alvarez de Cordone, he and a few of the survivors took the treasure to some caves in the nearby mountains and hid it. These caves were *near* steam from the earth, mud volcanoes, and heavy rocks. The cave faces the ships and has rock paintings, or petroglyphs. The heavy rocks probably mean the meteor. She motioned toward the map. "If you draw lines between the silver mine that's near that radioactive cave, the gold mine, the uranium mine, and the turquoise mine, like we did before, what do you get?"

Virginia wrinkled her brow in thought. "If I remember correctly, the lines form a crescent around the meteor, a steam vent area, and the mud volcanoes."

"Right. And it's angled toward the sand dunes to the southeast near the old ships that we found. So far so good."

"The map says the lower section of the mountain has caves."

"The information we gleaned from the glowing quilt and the triangulation you just mentioned confirms that." Donna pointed out the windshield at the edge of the mountains near the sand dunes. "So, the cave, or caves, should be up there someplace. We'll get a better location when we get closer."

Virginia looked in the direction Donna pointed. "Let's head that way. We can see how far we can drive before we have to hoof it."

"I hope we can get close. It's still early, but the temperature is racing up. It'll be hotter than hell out there later. Glad we brought a lot of water."

Virginia put the car in gear and drove into the desert. She plowed over small bushes, Mojave yucca, a couple of creosote bushes, rocks, and around larger obstacles. They stopped a few times to survey the area in order to find ways to drive cross some dry arroyos with steep banks. After an hour of slow going around arroyos, Joshua trees, mesquite, and other desert plants, and huge boulders, they found the bare desert floor. They were able to drive in a relatively straight line kicking up sand and salt. Further into the desert and uphill from the main road, they drove past some Fremont cottonwood and willows that shouldered a fault-line creek in a defile or small valley. At a deep arroyo, they stopped. Virginia climbed out of the vehicle, stretched, and walked to the edge of the arroyo. "Feels good to move around and get the kinks out." She looked at the arroyo. Looks like this is as far as we can drive."

Donna hopped out and joined Virginia at the edge of the incline. "Looks like it. Any ideas on how we get across this? The sides are steep and don't look all that sturdy. Kind of crumbly."

Virginia pushed her sunglasses up on top her head. "What does your map say?"

"Deep arroyo and aguas mortales. I think that means deadly waters." Donna looked at the bottom of the arroyo. "No water. Lots of brush though."

"From the number and size of the plants down there, the water is probably underground and not too far below the surface."

"If it's aguas mortales, then why are those plants growing?"

Virginia shrugged. "Maybe they can tolerate what's in the water, but people can't."

"Oh. The map also mentions quicksand. That's not good."

"Quicksand in the middle of the desert. Talk about an oxymoron. But probably true." Virginia put her sunglasses back on. "Let's gather our gear and figure out how to get across this small canyon."

"Oh, remember that dry creek with the palladium in it? Well, it is a tributary of this arroyo." Donna pointed at the bottom of the arroyo and shivered. "Look, there's a sidewinder. I don't like snakes, especially rattlesnakes. Can we go home now?"

"After all we've been through, one rattlesnake has you unnerved?"

"Well, as long as I don't have to get close to one and make his acquaintance, I guess I'll be okay." Donna sighed. "But keep an eye out for them; they have no sense of humor." She patted the .357 revolver in a holster on her hip. "A little insurance."

Virginia eyed the gun. "You still got .38s in it?"

"No. I went for the big stuff. .357. I just hope the recoil doesn't knock it out of my hands."

"Me too." Virginia turned and started back toward the car. She stopped. Her hand shielded her eyes as she stared down the slope. "That isn't a mirage. At least I don't think so. There's someone down there."

Donna turned. "Where? I don't see anything."

Virginia pointed. "By that dark reddish rock outcropping. It's quite a distance away, but someone is there."

Donna shielded her eyes with her hand. "I still don't see anything. What makes you think someone is down there?"

"I saw a quick flash of light, like the sun reflection of a mirror or glass."

Donna strained her eyes looking. "Maybe it was a broken bottle an animal disturbed."

Virginia kept looking. "Give me your binoculars."

Donna retrieved her field glasses from the car and handed them to Virginia.

Virginia took them and looked in the direction the flash came from. "You may be right. I don't see anything now. I guess I'm just jumpy out here. After all, we're standing by deadly waters, and you saw a rattlesnake. Then there was last night on the ship when Baker and his pals attacked us."

Donna took the binoculars. "Okay, we need to head out. Let's get our stuff and find a way around this canyon. We can keep an eye out for anyone following us."

Virginia stopped and unhooked her radio. "Virginia to B bar P ranch."

Liana answered. "B bar P. Go ahead."

"Do you have our eye in the sky up and flying yet?"

"No. We're fueling it now. We had to change the radio control module. It should be flying in about ten minutes."

"Good. I'll feel better with it watching us." Virginia glanced at the tops of the mountains. "Dark clouds. It's raining up there. Things may get exciting down here, especially in that arroyo."

CHAPTER 31

Virginia and Donna started their climb up the foothill's incline alongside the arroyo. They marched around plants and huge rocks. Donna stopped to take some water and soil samples in plastic bottles. After walking for a half hour, they stopped, sat on some small boulders, and drank some water.

Virginia turned and looked at the desert below. She pointed. "Over there is the meteor. Down that way are the steam vents, and to the right of them you can make out the mud volcanoes."

Donna watched where Virginia pointed. "I see them. The mud pots look more active than the last time I saw them, and the steam vents look like they're shooting off faster and higher."

"You're right. What does that mean?"

"Maybe we're due for an earthquake. A geologist would love being out here."

Virginia gave Donna a conspiring look. "Your friend Paul Blackman has a degree in geology."

"I didn't want to invite him along today for obvious reasons. Anyway, we're seeing the boys tomorrow. Maybe by then, we'll have the treasure."

"I hope so." Virginia glanced in the direction of the red rock outcropping and squinted. "I guess I was just seeing things before. I don't see anyone or anything threatening from where I saw the flash of light earlier."

"Well, we still need to keep our guard up."

Virginia rose. "Ready to continue our trek? I think I see a way across the damn arroyo."

They hiked for another half mile then carefully descended into the arroyo via an old wildlife trail. They stepped across an area where a small spring had emerged from the earth and then started for the path up the bank on the opposite side.

Donna stopped. "Do you feel anything? I think I hear something."

Virginia looked up at the mountaintop. Her eyes widened. "Oh shit! Move! Move! We need to get out of here fast!"

"What's wrong?"

"We're going to get about a twelve-foot wall of water coming through here at about thirty miles an hour and real soon! Move it!"

They hurried across the stream bed and clambered up the narrow trail. About three feet from the top the sound was becoming a roar. It sounded like a train coming at them. The ground vibrated. Small rocks tumbled around them into the arroyo. Donna scampered over the top with Virginia following. They lay on the ground watching as a huge wall of brownish-black water boiled and thundered past them, carrying dead trees, plants, rocks, refuse, and dirt.

Donna sighed. "That was close. If we were caught in that, we'd be killed in seconds. How'd you know what was happening?"

"It's been raining in the mountains since well before we got here." Virginia sat up. "I saw the clouds earlier, but now you can also see lightening up there. The water drains down here. The creeks and streams come together and form the arroyos. This one is huge. I saw the storm had gotten worse when you mentioned the vibration and sound. I knew that was the water coming down toward us. Andy and I have been desert rats for years, and you get to know the signs of trouble in the desert."

"I'm glad I'm with you. I'd be dead if I had been here alone." Donna sat up.

"Between things like this, and the dry heat out here, the desert claims a lot of lives every year. That's especially true of city folks who think they're outdoorsy, he-man types. They drink beer and party and play out in the direct, hot, desert sun. The drinking of alcohol and the desert heat don't work well together. Beer is a diuretic. They urinate a lot, get dehydrated, hallucinate, get lost, and die. They drive ATVs or dune buggies drunk and break an axle, get a flat tire, or get hurt, then try to hike back to their camp or hotel in the hot sun. The ground temperature usually goes well over one hundred and sixty degrees. The combination of the sun and the hot desert floor can dry you out really fast. They get caught in arroyos like this one with a flash flood coming and die. Fail to observe and respect the desert environment and be dumb, you die."

"I'll stick to the city and the beach. They have lifeguards. If someone was following us and was in there, they're toast." Donna looked at the water rushing by. "How long will this thing go on?"

"Could be for hours or days." Virginia climbed to her feet. "Depends on how long it rains and how much water is coming down the mountain. It will slow down later, but it will still be dangerous." She looked around. "Take a look at your map. How much farther do we have to go? That mountain is close."

Donna studied the map. "We've had to go around things, like that arroyo we just came through, so we've got another couple miles until we can start exploring caves. Let's start climbing up the hill. A couple hundred

Whispering Threads

yards up and we should find the trail up the side of the mountain."

Virginia's radio vibrated. Liana's voice came through. "B bar P ranch, Liana to Virginia."

Virginia pulled it off her belt and pressed talk. "Virginia here."

"We have our drone in the air and over where the old ships were. Where are you?"

She doesn't know? What happened to the GPS on my phone? "We're about three miles southeast of there, on a foothill, almost to the base of a mountain. We're next to a wild arroyo."

"Is the arroyo you were in big and deep?"

"Yes. It's got a lot of water in it right now."

"Oh. Be careful. It will eat the sides near turns and widen. I know about where you are. We're sending the drone there now. I'll call you when I spot you. Oh, turn your cell phone on. I couldn't get a GPS fix."

So that's why. "Okay. Virginia out." She looked at Donna. "Now we'll have some eyes in the sky to watch over us." Virginia turned her phone on.

"Liana won't be the only one," Donna pointed at the sky. "That's a plane. From here you can see it flying in a circle down there. It's looking for something, maybe us."

"Let's move; maybe we can get closer to the mountain and the scrub brush at the base before it spots us."

They hiked up the slope to the base of the mountain and stopped. Virginia wiped the sweat off her brow. "Okay, where are we?"

Donna pulled out her map and looked at it. She glanced around at the terrain, then back at the map. "Okay, I put us about here." She turned the map so Virginia could see it.

"Where are the caves relative to us?"

Donna pointed. "Here and here. We're close. Where is that plane?"

Virginia motioned for them to move near a large bush in the shade of an outcropping. She looked at the sky and horizon. "It's still over there. The plane has moved closer to where the dunes buried the ships. Maybe it's the police looking for Baker and his merry band. All they'll see is sand." Virginia's radio buzzed. She answered it. "Virginia."

"Liana here. We can see the arroyo. It is not happy. You are fine?"

"Yes, we're safe."

"Good. We are now flying near the base of the mountain. I think we are near you, but we can't see you."

"Hang on a second." Virginia stepped from the shadows and waved.

"I see you. There are caves in the mountain next to you. I will keep watch. I hope one of them is the treasure cave."

"Liana, there's a plane circling where we were last night in the dunes. Can you safely see who it is?"

"I'll try and call you back."

Virginia returned the radio to her belt and stepped back into the shade with Donna. "Liana thinks we're close to some caves, and she's going to try and identify that plane from her drone."

Donna sat on the ground and took a drink of water. "When this is over I'm going to have a very large—no, a number of very large strawberry-coconut daiquiris."

"If we find the treasure, you can buy your own bartender."

"Oh. Good. He'll be a hunk. Strong, gentle, smart, makes a great drink, have a…" Donna squinted as she peered through the brush. "Why is that plane coming our way? It doesn't look like the one near the dunes. Oh shit!" Donna grabbed Virginia and pulled her down as bullets riddled the area. Plants were shredded. Rock chips flew from the side of the mountain behind them. The plane flew past about thirty feet away from the cliff. Virginia and Donna crawled behind a rock. "Damn. I saw that side door on the plane was open, and a guy was leaning out holding something long."

"Good thing you did." Virginia unclamped her radio. "Liana, who the hell is shooting at us?"

"*Señora* Virginia. The plane you asked me to look for is headed north toward Palm Springs. I can see another plane, but it is away from where my drone is. I'm turning now. The zoom image is fuzzy, but the plane is a high wing single engine propeller craft and doesn't seem to have any markings. It's a green and gold color. Is that it?"

"Yes. That's it. Someone on it just shot at us. It's turning and will make another pass soon."

"Do you want me to call the police?"

"They won't be able to do anything quick enough. Head your drone this way, and we'll see what we can do."

"Okay. B bar P out."

Virginia put the radio away and looked at Donna. She had pulled her black hair back into a ponytail and lay on the ground holding her .357 revolver with both hands. Donna aimed at the plane and waited for it to complete its turn and start back toward them. Virginia crawled to another bush, unholstered her 9mm semiautomatic, and watched.

The plane flew toward them and then turned parallel to them. The side door was open and a man holding an assault rifle aimed in their direction. Virginia started to aim her pistol, then flinched as Donna's gun roared. Donna fired twice. The man jerked, fell back, and dropped his gun. As the plane started to turn away Donna fired twice more. Smoke erupted from the engine on the front. The engine sputtered as the pilot tried to gain altitude. It rose about five hundred feet before the engine quit. It banked and started a steep, sideways slip toward the desert floor. Virginia chuckled. "That won't be a soft landing." She glanced at Donna. "Nice shooting."

Donna sat up holding her gun. "God, this thing kicks like a mule. Kicks

Whispering Threads

a lot more with the .357s in it than with the .38s. My hand hurts." She looked at the plane. "I think I hit the shooter with both shots. He'll need medical attention real soon, that is, if he's still alive when they crash. If they send out a MAYDAY, the police will come. This could get interesting. They'll probably want to talk to us."

"Trust me; those guys won't call the police. But they know where we are and have probably already told someone. We should expect company soon. Let's find those caves while we figure out how to keep the treasure, and us, safe."

Virginia's radio buzzed. "B bar P ranch to *Señora* Virginia."

"Virginia grabbed her radio. "Virginia here, go ahead, Liana."

"The plane that was near you has no markings. I saw them shoot at you and it looked like you or *Señora* Donna shot them. They are going to crash about eight miles from you. They must have called someone because there is a large green Humvee driving toward where they may crash. What do you want me to do?"

"Secure the ranch. And keep watch on the Humvee and anyone inside. Let us know if anyone heads our way. We're going to see if we can find the treasure."

"Okay. We can stay up about three hours. Then we can refuel and return."

"Great. Watch our backs."

"Oh, Detective Ferguson called. I told him you were out on the ranch and would call him later. It was a strange call."

"Why?"

"It was noisy and sounded like he was in a small airplane."

CHAPTER 32

Donna turned toward Virginia. "Ferguson is in an airplane? I hope that wasn't his plane I just shot down."

"Liana didn't say he was in distress. I'm guessing he's in the other one that was near the sand dunes. Probably following up on someone calling about the explosion and fires last night. I'll have to call him when we get back to the ranch."

"We already told him about last night. Well, minus a few details."

"Yeah, the details are probably what he was looking for." Virginia stood and holstered her gun.

Donna rose and slipped her revolver into the holster on her hip. "We'd better get a move on before we get more company."

Virginia pointed north and up the side of the mountain. "You said the caves are that way?"

"Yeah." Donna nodded. "The map says caves. We could be in for a long exploration."

They hiked for a half mile and stopped when they heard an explosion. They looked back toward where the plane had crashed about seven or eight miles across the desert below. Virginia shaded her eyes and squinted as she looked down toward the desert floor. "Looks like the plane didn't survive the crash, at least not for long. Look at the smoke. I wonder if the people in the green Humvee were able to pull anyone out before the explosion?"

"Since they shot at us, I'm not sure I care. Is the Humvee still there?"

"I don't see it."

Donna looked at the map. "We've got a couple miles to go. Then we'll be above the sand dunes where the caves are. It's getting hot."

Virginia unhooked her canteen and took a swig of water. "I had a thought."

"Does it involve getting shot at again, or someone trying to kill us?"

"I don't think so."

"Good." Donna put the map back in her pack. "I know I'm going to regret this, but okay, what is it?"

Whispering Threads

"The treasure has been here for about three hundred years, and no one has found it."

"Maybe your friend Carol did."

"Yes. And if she did would she leave it in the cave and just take a sample?"

"I don't know. I wouldn't. I'd move it to someplace where it would be safe, and only I knew where it was."

Virginia smiled. "Precisely. I would, too. So why have all these people suddenly gone hunting for it?"

"Good question. Probably because they don't know Carol found it and moved it. For that matter, we know Carol found it, so if she moved it, why are we traipsing all over the desert in this heat looking for it?"

"They don't know Carol found it. Maybe each of the groups heard another group was looking for it and wanted to be first. That could explain why so many want to get on my ranch. "We're out here to insure the treasure was found and moved. If it wasn't, then we'll have it relocated someplace safe. But why all the murders?"

Donna tightened her ponytail. "It does seem strange. And why shoot at us?"

"Because they don't know Carol found it and moved it, like you said, and they think it's still out here and don't want us to find it first. Let's find the caves. Maybe there is something there that will help us figure this out."

Donna turned and pointed north and uphill. "This way. Looks like a game trail going our way. Might make the going easier and faster. Let's follow it."

The game trail was easy to follow. An hour later they stopped on a wide ledge approximately six hundred feet above the sand dunes. "Down there are the sand dunes where the ships are." Virginia pointed down the slope. "Over there is the shoreline of an ancient lake or sea. The caves must be nearby."

Donna consulted the map. "You're right. The caves are around here." She walked to a dead bush and yanked off two long limbs. "Let's use these for poking around. We can use them to make sure we don't unexpectedly meet a snake."

They hiked up and down the slope finding two, small, empty caves. Donna used her stick to move some brush and stopped. "I found one. Looks bigger than the other two."

Virginia moved to Donna's side and looked. "You're right. Let's take a look."

Donna hesitated. "Let's shine some light in first and see if it is owner-occupied."

"Good idea. Virginia pulled a Maglite from here backpack and moved closer to the opening. Bending, she illuminated the cave. "Looks like some sort of nest."

"For a small animal?"

"No." Virginia swung the light beam around. "Maybe a mountain lion, or something else that's large. But that cave definitely has an owner who probably doesn't have a big sense of humor about trespassers. Lots of bones scattered around."

Donna shivered in the heat. "Okay, not our cave. Let's leave before the owner returns. There must be more."

They searched the area for another half hour before Virginia found a cave in a side canyon behind some scrub brush about five hundred feet above the old shoreline. "Got a good size cave over here," she yelled to Donna.

Donna hurried to her side and looked around. "How'd you find this? It's not facing the old lake below and higher up than the caves around the bend in the mountain. It's somewhat hidden from where the old sea was."

"Just luck I guess. I heard some noise, like a faint wind."

Donna stepped closer to the cave. "I can feel a little air movement. It must have another opening."

"Feel like exploring it?"

"Let's see if it has a resident first."

Virginia shined her light inside the entrance. The entrance to the cave was through a short tunnel. The floor of the tunnel was unmarked, smooth sand. The walls were smooth as well. It seemed undisturbed. "Looks like no one's home." She pulled out her nine-millimeter and stepped inside the entrance. "Leave your gun in its holster. Shooting that thing in here will deafen us both."

"Okay. I'll use this big canister of bear-strength pepper spray."

"Good. Let's go."

They stooped and proceeded into the tunnel. Using the light, they followed the passageway a short distance to a larger cavern where they could stand straight up. Virginia swung the light around. Bands of color streaked the walls. She walked around the expanse to a low-ceilinged section toward the left side and pointed the light at the ground near the sidewall. "Look! There are rectangular depressions in the sand. Looks like a few footprints and the marks of something smooth used for dragging that weren't covered up. Maybe that's where the treasure chests were." Virginia moved closer to the sand imprints and played her light over the cavern wall. "Petroglyphs. Matches the stories." She swung her light around the cave floor. "Well, lookie here." She bent down and picked a pearl out of the sand near the wall. "Right place."

Donna moved to the back of the cavern. "Looks like this was used for more than storing treasure."

"What do you mean? What did you find?" Virginia hurried to Donna's

Whispering Threads

side and looked at where Donna's light illuminated an area of the cave floor, exposing a couple of plastic bags containing something white and a couple of bottles filled with a tan liquid.

Virginia walked around. "I don't see any more. Let's collect them for testing when we get out of here."

Donna pointed to the side of the cave near the back. "Over there are some small piles of what looks like mining tailings. Someone's been digging and testing this cave for minerals, and recently. The chips in the walls look fairly fresh." She went to the cave wall that had been dug into. "There is something scratched down there."

"You're right." Virginia moved to the wall and bent over. "It looks like pd46. What does that mean?"

"I don't know. Someone's initials and age?"

"I doubt it. Grab some of the tailing for tests." Virginia straightened and walked toward a side notch in the wall. "I see a broken machine in there." She stepped closer and pulled it out. "It's a broken sealing machine." She held her light up and looked where the machine had been. Farther back she spotted a coiled power cord and a cardboard box on its side containing broken bottles and what appeared to be discarded, stained, laboratory glassware. "I think we're in trouble."

Donna frowned "Why?"

"More broken equipment: laboratory equipment to be exact. And the entrance was smooth sand. There were no animal or human tracks."

Donna glanced back toward the entrance, then rubbed her hands together. "You're right. Why does that mean we're in trouble?"

Virginia shined her light around "If Carol moved the treasure out of here, there'd be tracks."

"I see what you mean. Maybe it has been used for something else since then."

"Yes. A lab. I bet they were making drugs in here."

"Who are *they*? And if they were making drugs in here, why take rock samples?"

"*They* may actually be one of the three groups. Maybe more, but I'm betting on three. And I don't know why they would take rocks."

Donna looked puzzled. "Three?"

"Yes. One is looking for the treasure. And one is a drug manufacturer who doesn't want us to nose around out here and discover what they've been doing. They moved out recently. And the last one wants to mine something of great value like the meteor, or some materials from one or more of my mines. I don't know."

Donna picked up the bags of materials and the bottles and stuck them in her pack. She marked where the cave was on her map and turned. "Now you're getting scary. Let's get out of here while we still can." Donna tilted her head. "I hear something. Not more water I hope."

Virginia listened. "You're right, and it's not water. Someone is near the entrance to the cave. Maybe it's the people in that Humvee we saw where the plane crashed."

"Oh, great, just what we need. Let's get out before we're trapped."

They turned and made their way toward the entrance. Entering the tunnel, they moved to the right side and slinked toward the light. Both Virginia and Donna pulled out their pistols. Near the opening, they heard sounds of footfalls on the hardened dirt outside. Virginia whispered. "We're sitting ducks in here, and whoever is out there is close. We'd better backtrack."

"Inside we're trapped. What if they have explosives?" Virginia sighed. "Right now we're the fish in the barrel."

"I still feel a slight breeze on my back. Think there is another way out?"

"No idea, but we're not safe here." They dropped to their knees as gunfire erupted and bullets flew past them pinging off the tunnel walls on their left side. "That proves it. Let's move back."

They scurried back into the cavern and knelt on both sides of the tunnel, guns aiming toward the light.

Donna reloaded her gun. "Need more bullets. I didn't reload after I shot at the plane. Think we should fire to let them know we're here and armed?"

"I think they already know. You have the cannon, keep watch while I look for another way out of here. Try not to fire unless absolutely necessary. The .357 going off in here will be deafening."

"Okay."

Virginia stood and leaned against the side of the cavern shielded from the tunnel. "How many rounds do you have?"

Donna thought for a minute, and then said. "About a hundred. All .357."

"Good lord. You brought a hundred rounds?"

Donna grinned. "A girl needs to be prepared."

"Okay, you keep watch and be careful." Virginia turned, wet her finger and held it up. "There is a slight breeze, and it's coming from that direction." Virginia carefully crept in the direction of the air movement, keeping herself clear of a direct line of sight from the tunnel. She dropped and spun around aiming her gun at the tunnel as Donna fired three rounds. Virginia's ears rung. "What the... someone is coming?"

Donna shook her head. "Not anymore. One down and not moving; one fled with an injured wing." She reloaded.

"Good, keep them at bay for a while. I'll be right back, I hope." Virginia maneuvered around a boulder to a notch in the side of the cave wall. Air moved out of the notch into the cavern. She moved her light along the crevice and looked. *Hmm. Looks clear. The air is coming from someplace. It smells fresh. Let's see how far I can go.* She slid into the opening sideways and navigated along the smooth walls around curves. The floor started to slope down as she shuffled along. *At least there haven't been any snakes.* She continued until the roof of the passage started to lower. *It's getting too small for us to use as an escape route.* Virginia inched her way back to the cavern, stopped, and listened. *Shit! That sounds like gunfire. I hope Donna is okay.* As she hurriedly exited the shaft there were two very loud gunshots, then a small explosion. *Donna!* Fear gripped Virginia. Her heart pounded. She peered out of the opening and looked toward the tunnel. Fog and dust were settling. She heard screams. Men were swearing. There were sounds of people running into each other and the sides of the tunnel and falling. Virginia ducked as a series of wild gunshots came from the tunnel. A bullet screamed by Virginia's head and slammed into the wall behind her. Donna had her back to the wall, her hands over her ears and grinned. She picked up her pistol, swung around and fired into the haze. In the tunnel there was more screaming and noise, then nothing.

Virginia sprinted to the tunnel and dropped next to her friend. "Are you okay? What the hell happened? Did they use explosives?"

Donna shook her head. "No. Well, I kinda did."

"Huh? What do you mean?"

"I figured they'd try and rush us. You know, open up with a large volley of bullets to make us take cover, rush in, guns blazing and screaming at the top of their lungs to scare us like the macho jerks in the movies." Donna wiped a tear from her eyes. "The little pepper spray that drifted in here stings. Find another way out?"

Pepper spray? She was shooting. Virginia shook her head. "This looks like the only way in or out for us. The opening where the air is coming from is too small for us to navigate."

Donna quickly peered down the tunnel. "Okay, I may have overdone it a little."

Virginia looked down the tunnel. Three mangled bodies were either not moving or were bleeding and writhing in pain. "What the hell did you do? That mist is pepper spray, isn't it?"

"Yes." Donna lowered her weapon, wiped a wisp of dark hair from her eyes, and took a breath. "When they started shooting like crazy and yelling, I waited a few seconds for them to get part way into the tunnel. Then I tossed my large canister of bear-strength pepper spray and mace into it. I shot at it. After a couple shots I hit it. I wasn't too sure if my plan would actually work. It did. I figured the extra strong pepper spray would be concentrated in a confined space with little air movement, and if I managed to shoot the pressurized canister, it would explode. It did. No one has shot since. The slight breeze helped move most of it down the tunnel toward the entrance and the men."

Virginia shook her head and laughed. "It sure did. Couldn't have done better if I tried. You are one dangerous lady."

"We make a great team. Let's move before any of their friends outside come to get revenge."

"Right." Virginia climbed to her feet and started down the tunnel with Donna behind her. Three men were dead, and two were writhing on the ground seriously wounded. As Virginia and Donna moved into the tunnel, they kicked the men's weapons away. One of the injured men stopped moving. The other one died as they checked him. They did a quick examination to make sure all the men were actually dead.

As they approached the entrance, they dropped to their knees and pressed against the right side. High caliber rounds screamed above them hitting the left side of the tunnel wall. They slid back, relieved the dead men of their weapons, and crawled down the right side of the entrance. Donna touched Virginia's arm. "Okay, we've got more weapons, but what do we do now?"

"I don't know. Wait. I have an idea." Virginia pulled her radio out. "Virginia to B bar P ranch."

"B bar P, go ahead."

"Liana, we are pinned down in a cave entrance above where the ships were. There are people out there shooting at us. Is your bird still up?"

"Yes. I tried calling you, but got no response. I lost your GPS signal from your phone."

"We were inside the cave. Is your drone close?" Virginia's mouth was dry. Perspiration beaded on her brow. "Can you see where the people who are shooting at us are, and how many there are?"

"Wait a minute."

"Liana, we may not have a minute."

"Are you in the area where there was smoke and dust a few minutes ago?"

Virginia gripped the radio tighter. "Yes. Yes. Can you get a fix on us?"

"*Sí.* I see where you are. There is a cave there?"

"Yes. We're in it." Virginia took a breath to slow her heart pounding in her chest. "Now, how many people are out there and where are they?"

"I see two men with rifles. They are on your right, level with you. They are hiding behind some bushes and a big rock. They have a clear shot at the cave entrance. Another man is lugging something up the slope from the dunes toward your location."

Virginia's voice cracked. "Is there any way for us to get into a position to stop them, or escape?"

There was a slight pause, then Liana answered. "No."

CHAPTER 33

Virginia tensed. "Liana, call the sheriff. Maybe we can hold them off long enough for help to arrive."

Liana's voice cracked. *"La policía?"*

"Yes. Call the sheriff."

"*La policía* are too far. I can see the men with the rifles are moving closer and getting ready to shoot again. They have that crate the other man pulled up there. I will make a pass with the drone and see what is in the box and if I can help you."

"Liana, what are you going to do? Don't risk the drone. You are our only eyes."

Donna touched Virginia's arm. "What's she going to do, crash the drone into them?"

"I think so. It may not be enough."

Liana called back. "You, and *Señora* Donna, take cover and stay in the tunnel. I'm going to clear a path for you."

"What are…?"

Virginia dropped the radio, flattened against the sidewall, and covered her head. Donna did the same as a loud explosion, followed a second later by a second detonation, rocked the mountain. Dirt and small stones fell on them from the tunnel roof. Virginia looked up. Dust, remains of plants, and rubble flew past the tunnel opening. Some debris blew into the tunnel. Rocks rained down outside near the entrance. They waited.

Virginia's radio buzzed. She picked it up, coughed, and then and pressed the talk button. "Virginia here."

"*Señora* Virginia," said Liana. "You can come out of the cave now. It is safe."

"Are you sure?"

"*Sí*. There is a now large hole in the ground where the men and their box were."

Oh, my God. Virginia sat up. "Liana, what did you do, crash the drone?"

"No. I hope this is all right. When you went into the cave, we brought the drone back. There was a battery problem. When we changed the power pack, I put a medium size explosive on it. We have different size explosive packages. We have license. We use them to clear big rocks and in the mines. I used a remote fuse like we used in the mines and had it on board when you called. I tried to drop it on the side of the mountain a little above the men to make them take cover, or run. I missed."

"You missed? What did you hit?"

"*Sí*. I am sorry. Trying to hit a small target from a high and moving drone was *dificil*... difficult. This was the first time I tried to drop an explosive. There is a slight uphill wind next to the mountain I forgot about until too late. I accidentally dropped it on the men. Whatever was in the crate exploded, too."

"Why did you put the explosives on the drone if you didn't know where we were?"

"Because I had to bring the drone back, and then find you again, I was afraid you might be in trouble and thought this might help. I didn't know what else to do."

"You sure did, Liana. Don't be sorry. Tonight, Donna and I are taking you out to dinner."

"That is not necessary. I just want to be of help. I can make dinner."

"No. Liana, get ready for a night out. That's an order."

"*Sí. Gracias, Doña* Virginia.*"*

Virginia and Donna brushed off the dust and slowly exited the tunnel into the light. They looked around and found a small crater, a few smoldering bushes, displaced boulders, the burnt remains of a crate, and a few bloody body parts scattered over the area. Part of the trail was gone. What looked like the burnt and bent remains of an assault rifle and pieces of charred wood rested twelve feet up the side of the mountain on their right. Down slope, among some sparse brush, were what appeared to be the twisted remnants of a rocket launcher and other unidentifiable objects.

Donna took a few steps toward the black hole in the ground. "Think anyone survived?"

Virginia shook her head. "No."

"We're going to have a hell of a time explaining all this and what happened to Baker and his cronies to the sheriff."

"I have an idea." Virginia pulled out her cell phone and dialed the Smithsonian Central Security Service. When someone answered, she asked for the special operations department. After a detailed discussion, she disconnected, and looked at Donna. "Not to worry. We can go to the ranch now. The SCSS will take care of everything. This never happened, at least not here."

Donna glanced around, then gave a Virginia a quizzical look. "You're kidding?"

"No. A clean-up crew is on the way."

"Clean-up crew? What's a clean-up crew?"

"They sort of mop up after a special operation and either make it look like nothing happened, or it happened differently someplace else. This way any families will find out there was an accident or something, and there won't be anything relating to us."

Donna sighed. "That's good."

"Let's grab our gear and hightail it out of here. There's nothing more here to see."

"I couldn't agree more." Donna followed Virginia back into the cave to retrieve their packs. They started hiking back in the direction they had just come from.

Two hours later they arrived at the Range Rover. They dumped their equipment in the back and tossed their backpacks in the rear seat.

Donna slipped into the front passenger seat and attached her seatbelt. She took off her hat, shook out her dark-brown hair, and watched Virginia get in and buckle up. "Okay, start this thing up and get the air on. I think I've been broiled."

"Broiled? With your nice olive complexion, how would you know? You can take the sun."

"You're just jealous, pale face. That light complexion you have will burn easily."

Virginia removed her ball cap, tossed it in the rear seat, and ran her fingers through her blonde hair. "Damn gritty. I think I have more dust in my hair than on the ranch. And you've managed to drink most of our water." Virginia started the car and the air conditioning. "When we get back to the ranch, I'm going to take a nice long shower to get this dust off me, then have a cool libation. Maybe a pitcher. Let's stop at UC Riverside first and drop off your rock samples. I'm sure we can get one of the chemistry professors to do a quick analysis for us. The Smithsonian will pay for it."

Donna looked out the window at three desert-camouflaged helicopters flying low toward where they had been. "Looks like your cleaning crew is arriving." Donna settled back. "Oh, that cool air feels great. We're taking Liana out for dinner later, so we'd better hurry if we're going to the university, then go back to the ranch, clean up, and detox before we go."

Virginia drove to the ranch road gate. The chain had been cut. "I see how that Hummer got in." She continued through the gate to the state highway and turned north toward the ranch headquarters. As they sped along the four-lane highway, slightly above the speed limit, Virginia's cell phone rang. She pulled it from her pocket and tossed it to Donna. "Answer it for me, please."

Donna took the phone and pressed the talk symbol. "Virginia Davies

Clark's phone. Donna Bolette speaking. How can we help you?"

"Donna, it's Andy. Is my wife around?"

"Yes, but she's driving. Can I take a message?"

"Can you put me on speaker? You both should hear what I have to tell you."

Donna hit the speaker icon. "Okay, Andy, you've got our attention. What is it?"

"Did you guys get the report from UCI about the materials you sent there?"

Virginia glanced at the phone. "Yes. Why?"

"I just got some more information. It's about your meteor."

"My meteor?" Virginia frowned. "What about it?"

"The report mentioned that the meteor had some special crystal structures, right?"

"Yeah. They form nanothingies or something."

"Right, the... ahh, nanothingies as you called them, combined with the other unique compounds and elements in the meteor, under a medium strength electromagnetic field, create a superconductor at room temperature. It also becomes extremely hard, but not brittle."

"Is that good?"

Andy chuckled. "Yes. And very valuable. So far there are just a few compounds that are superconductors near room temperature, but not at room temperature. It would be extremely valuable to the electronics and computer industries, power companies, to the U.S. Department of Energy, NASA, NSA, and the Department of Defense. The only other sample in existence was found about two years ago in the Mediterranean off Southern France."

Virginia took a deep breath and let it out in a loud sigh. "That explains a few things. What should I do?"

"Guard it and watch yourselves. I'll make some inquiries."

"Make them discreet. I've got enough problems out here."

"More than a murder?" Andy asked.

"Yes. I think someone was using part of the ranch to make drugs. We found what we think was a drug lab in a cave. Some... ahh... people tried to prevent us from leaving a while ago. We're also taking some ore and water samples to UC Riverside. Can you make some calls to grease the skids for us?"

"Good lord, Virginia. Are you two okay? What happened? Did you call the police?"

"We're fine, Andy. It's all over. The men who interfered with us are all, well... vaporized. We haven't told the cops, yet. We're driving to UCR and then back to the ranch now."

"Did you say vaporized?" Andy's voice cracked. "What the hell did you two do?"

"Yeah, vaporized. Poof. Liana dropped a pack of explosives on them. She was aiming for the side of the cliff above them, but she missed."

"Oh. Oh, good God. What have you gotten into out there? She dropped the explosives? From a plane?"

"No, she bombed them from a drone. I have some drones at the ranch. We were treasure hunting. We're putting the pieces of this puzzle together, and we should be wrapping things up soon, I hope."

"I hope so, too. You two be careful. You know, whoever those men worked for isn't going to be pleased."

"We know."

"Be careful, and I'll make some calls to UCR."

"We will. Thanks. Love you. Bye." She nodded at Donna, who hit the disconnect icon.

Donna set the phone on the console between them. "That may explain the National Marine Management Agency. They know about the meteor in the Mediterranean off France. But how did they find out about your meteor?"

"Litio Products. It's owned by the National Marine Management Agency. They were probably looking at my steam vents and found the meteor and did an analysis of it along with the stuff from the steam vents. Not sure if they know anything about the drug lab. We'd better get your samples analyzed."

"I agree." Donna fidgeted in her seat. "It's funny. As the day progresses and the sun moves, the ground changes color; the shadows cause the desert to change. Things look different. I can see how someone could easily get lost." She turned on the radio and found a country music station. "Well, tomorrow will be interesting. I wonder if our two old dinner date friends from Litio will happen to mention your meteor or hint about the drugs."

"We'll find out. But we better be prepared for trouble. And since when do you listen to country music?"

CHAPTER 34

The next day Virginia and Donna sat on the covered back patio sipping their morning coffee and staring out over the colorful desert expanse before them. Virginia set her cup on the small iron table between them. "Dinner with Liana at that steak place was fun, and no one tried to kill us."

"Yeah," Donna agreed. "I think Liana had a good time. I'm glad we took her out. The floor show at that club was enjoyable."

"It was entertaining. This morning I gave the samples from the cave to a DEA agent to transport to their lab in L.A. I was surprised he came so early. And now that we know the treasure is not in the caves. We need to figure out where it is."

Donna finished her coffee. "Yeah, but we've got the guys from Litio Products coming here later today." She glanced at Virginia. "What time are they arriving?"

"At two." Virginia slowly rose. "Let's go find Liana and see if she knows anything about a rented storage space somewhere, or if there is another bank with a safe deposit box we don't know about holding the treasure."

"Okay." Donna stood and followed Virginia into the house.

After searching the house, they walked to the largest barn. They found Liana in a room at the back, sitting on a chair next to a drone with a wide wingspan and a propeller on the rear. A small hatch near the nose was open, and she was doing something inside it.

Liana looked up as Virginia and Donna approached. "*Buenos días.* Thank you for last night."

"Good morning, Liana," said Virginia. "It was our pleasure. What are you doing?"

"Taking the flash drive from the camera on the drone. This is the one I used when you were on the ship and at the cave."

Virginia's eyes widened. "You mean everything that you saw in the last couple days is recorded on that drive?"

"*Sí.*"

Whispering Threads

"And we can play it back on the computer in the office?"

"*Sí.*" Liana smiled. "I thought you might want to see it or save it."

"Yes, we most certainly do. But I have another question."

Liana's face brightened. "How can I help?"

"Did Carol have another place where she kept things?"

Liana frowned. "Another place, like another ranch? A building? I do not understand."

Virginia shook her head. "No. Not another ranch. Like a rented storage building or a bank safety deposit box?"

Liana thought. "No. No storage buildings or bank safety boxes that I know of, but she owns a condo in Orange County. It is on the beach."

Donna looked startled. "She does? On the beach?"

"*Sí.*"

"Do you know where exactly?" asked Virginia.

"*Sí.* It is in Newport Beach. I went there with her a couple times. She went there about two months before she died." Liana set the memory chip on a small table, inserted another memory card, closed the cover on the drone, and then screwed it in place. She picked up the chip from the table, stood, and motioned for Virginia and Donna to follow her. "The address and legal papers, like the deed and HOA rules, are in a file in the office. I'll get them for you."

As they walked, Virginia asked, "Liana, why didn't you tell me about this before?"

"There is a lot going on here. *Señora* Putman's murder. The people trying to come on the *rancho*. Emilio being almost killed. And the ships, you and *Señora Donna* coming, people trying to hurt you, and things, *no pienso*... I didn't think it was important. Not yet. I have copies of the legal papers he sent over in the office."

Virginia frowned. "It could be."

They entered the house, and while Virginia and Donna went to the living room, Liana retrieved the keys, the address, a map, an entrance code, and the name of the management company for the condo development, and gave them to Virginia. "You are now the owner of the condo, too."

"I am? Have a seat, Liana. I don't remember anyone saying anything about a condo."

Liana sat in a wing chair across from Virginia. "*Sí.* You are the owner. When you signed all the papers with the lawyer and bank a while ago, this was included. There were a lot of papers. I filed it for you."

"I see. Just how big is it?"

Liana furrowed her brow in thought. "It is about two hundred square meters, plus a three-car garage. Mrs. Putman enlarged the garage a while back. The condo has a nice balcony that overlooks the beach and the ocean."

Donna looked puzzled. "Two hundred square meters? What's that in square feet?"

Virginia thought for a second. "A little over three thousand square feet."

"Wow. That's a good size for the beach area. Expensive as hell. Is it furnished?"

Liana nodded. "*Sí.*"

Donna leaned on the side of the desk. "Is the garage attached?"

"*Sí.* It is attached to the condo."

"Is there a vehicle in the garage?" Virginia asked. Liana laughed. "No. It's full of crates."

"Crates?"

"*Sí.* More like chests, or trunks, actually. They are like the travel trunks you see in old movies. There are some boxes and crates, too."

"Who else besides us knows about it?"

"*Señora* Putman's lawyer knows about the condo, me, and Emilio. You and *Señora* Donna know about it now. Only you two, Emilio, and me know about the boxes. He told me about the boxes; I haven't seen them. I don't know what's in them. Maybe things from her travels over the years."

"Good. We need to keep it that way. Don't tell anyone else."

Liana nodded.

Donna's face brightened. "Looks like another road trip's in store."

Virginia sat back on the sofa. "Because of all that has happened, Donna, I think you should take Liana and go to the condo. Check it out, and call me. Once we know what's there, we'll be able to handle anything that may come up."

"Okay, but what about the boys from Litio Products coming this afternoon?"

"I'll handle them."

"You sure? Alone?"

"Yes." Virginia had a mischievous look on her face. "I'll be ready. They won't be prepared for what I have in mind."

Donna sighed and shook her head. "God help them."

The phone rang. Liana jumped up and answered it on the extension in the kitchen. After a couple of minutes, she returned with a big smile. "That was the hospital. Emilio is awake and is doing well. He asked for food, and… ahh… me."

Virginia grinned. "That's wonderful." She turned toward Donna. "Take Liana to the hospital first, then head to Newport Beach. I need to call Washington about something else, but I'll get some protection for him from the SCSS while I'm at it."

"Right." Donna rose. "Grab your stuff, Liana, we're off to the hospital, and then a long drive to the beach."

Liana nodded. "I'll get my things and meet you at the back door. What vehicle do you want to take?"

"We could take my car."

"*Sí, Señora* Donna. But the black Toyota SUV is... is bigger and bulletproof."

"Bulletproof? Okay, we take the black Toyota. Let's get a move on." Donna headed for her room. "I'll get my stuff and see you here in a few minutes."

At a little after two, Virginia remotely opened the gate and watched the CCTV monitor as James Kincaid and Paul Blackman drove up the driveway and parked their white Chevy Tahoe in front of the house. Virginia, dressed in tight, white, shorts and a thin, tight, light-red tank top, braless, walked out onto the covered front porch. She watched as the two men exited the vehicle carrying some rolled drawings, folders, and a tan, leather briefcase. She smiled. "Hello, boys. I see you've got something for me."

They stopped and stared at her for an instant. James swallowed, then grinned. "Hello, Virginia, and yes, we came with what you asked for."

She looked at Paul. "Nice to see you too, Paul."

He took a quick breath. "Ye... yes. Nice to see you... as well."

She turned, unfazed. "Follow me." With a pert wiggle, she led them into the house and the living room. On the way, she glanced over her shoulder and saw the two men glance at the old lantern on the patio table. "Take a seat. I have some iced tea on the coffee table if you'd like some."

She sat on the couch and leaned forward. "You said you had what I asked for. Let's start with exactly what you want to do on my ranch, how, and how much space you want to use? Also, I'd like to see your proposal to compensate me for whatever it is you want to do." She watched them look at her chest and fidget in their seats. *Good, acting like teenage boys. They weren't expecting me dressed like this. They're nervous.*

James took a sip of tea. "Okay, let me show you the areas we are interested in." He rolled out an aerial view of her ranch with an area outlined in red. He pointed. "This is the principal expanse we are requesting. There are maps here, too."

Virginia scooted forward and bent over the aerial picture. "I see you want to make an access road."

"Yes."

She ran her finger around the area indicated. "This shows an area surrounding my steam vents and extends to my meteor. The new road also goes to a mine? The note on the picture says uranium mine." *That's not the uranium mine. It's the cave we were just in.* "What do you want with my meteor and the mine? They don't have any lithium in them."

James wiped his palms on his pant legs. "Let's discuss the steam vents and the extraction of the lithium, first."

"Okay. But you do realize I'm going to have my engineers and lawyers go over everything later."

James nodded. "We figured as much." Paul looked around. "Where is Donna?"

"She had to make a quick trip back to L.A. Something for her business. She'll be back this evening."

"Oh. That's too bad. I would have liked to see her again."

"I'm sure you will. She wants to see you, too." She turned back to the aerial picture. "This looks like you want to run power lines and build buildings near the vents."

James nodded. "Yes."

"The lithium extraction takes place there?"

"Yes"

"What is the process you'll use?"

"The details are proprietary. But the basic schematic looks like this." James pulled out a notebook, thumbed through a few pages then handed the open document to Virginia. She looked at the block diagram flow chart with terms like Boron solvent extraction, thickeners and clarifiers, calcium and magnesium purification, vacuum belt filters, lithium carbonate precipitators, and flotation units on it. She studied it for a minute and then looked at James. "I'll need some more detail."

"Like I just said, the details are proprietary."

Virginia straightened. "You expect me to let some Johnny-come-lately just waltz onto my land with who knows what, and possibly pollute the hell out of it? How are you going to protect my land?"

"That's detailed in this other folder." He handed her a red binder. "We have the details of how we handle wastes and by-products safely for the employees and the environment."

Virginia took the folder and flipped through it. She sat back. "Okay. I'll look at the details later. Where is the compensation section?"

Paul handed Virginia another black folder. "This is what our management gave us to give to you. We haven't been party to it, so we don't know all the details. But I can tell you they will pay you some upfront monies, then scheduled installment payments. Later you will get a percentage of the profits of the enterprise out here. The details are spelled out in here."

"I'll look at it, and have my accountant and lawyer look at it." She placed all the documents and maps on the table. "Now, about my meteor."

Paul cleared his throat. "The meteor is of interest to our parent company, the National Marine Management Agency. James and I don't know what they are thinking about. In the materials we just gave you, there is a section about the meteor. If I remember from glancing at it, they are saying they want an option to do some mining of it. I don't know what they are after exactly. And the uranium mine is covered in this section as well."

"I see." She noticed James take quick glances at his briefcase as he closed it. *Is there a gun in there? What's he need it for?* She slid her right hand slowly into the space between the cushions on the couch and felt the nine-millimeter semiautomatic she had hidden there. "I'll take these documents to my engineer, lawyer, and accountant, and get back to you as soon as I can."

Paul swallowed. "Can we tell our management you're considering their proposal?"

Virginia took a deep breath and smiled. "I don't see why not."

"I noticed what looked like an old ship's lantern on your front porch. May we take a look at it?"

"Sure." Virginia stood and followed James and Paul out the front door. They moved to the table.

James picked up the lantern and examined it. "There is some worn writing on it. Could it be from one of the old lost ships of the desert?"

Virginia nodded. "I think so."

"May I ask where you got it?"

"I could tease you and say from one of the old ships, but we actually got it from an antique store down near the Salton Sea."

"An antique store?"

"Yep."

"Have you seen the ships since you've been here?" Paul looked around the front yard and driveway. "We heard that the ships were sighted the other day."

"I heard that, too." Virginia turned. "It's hot out here. Let's go back inside where it's cooler." Before they could speak, Virginia entered the house and listened to the men as she walked.

James leaned close to Paul. "Let's ask about the treasure and then decide what action we need to take. She's here alone."

"You have your gun?"

"Yes. In the briefcase."

CHAPTER 35

Virginia turned when she heard James call her. "Yes?"

James pointed at the lantern. "Would you mind if we took some pictures of your lantern?"

She shook her head. "No, not at all. But why?"

"It's interesting. I'd like to study the marking."

She shrugged. "Knock yourself out." She leaned against the doorframe and watched as James and Paul used their cell phones to take pictures of the lantern and the markings on it. James looked speculatively at Virginia. He wet his lips.

"Would you mind holding it for some pictures?"

I was wondering how long it would be before he asked me to pose with something. She gave him a warm smile. "Sure. I'd love to, James." She took the lantern and held it in numerous positions, looking as provocative as she could while they both took pictures with their phones.

When the men finished, they followed Virginia back into the living room and sat in their respective seats.

Virginia leaned back into the couch and stretched her arms across the back, causing the thin fabric of her top to stretch tighter over her breasts. "So, what's next?"

James wiped his sweaty hands on his pant legs. "We… we have reason to believe you actually found and boarded the old ships. We understand you may have had someone try and take the ship from you. We were wondering if you've had any luck finding the treasure."

Virginia smiled. "You two have been looking for the ships for some time, haven't you?"

Paul nodded. "Yes, and I might add we haven't had any luck. How'd you do it?"

She smiled. "I had a map." She shifted in her seat.

"No shit?" Paul's eyes stared at her chest.

"Like I said, I had a map. And yes, Donna and I were on the ships."

Paul glanced at James. "I told you these two were good." James leaned forward. "Did you meet anyone out there?"

Virginia folded her legs under her and rested her arms on her lap. "Meet anyone?"

"Did someone else board the ship, too? Did someone try and take the ships from you?"

She tilted her head. "Why?"

"Ahh… just interested."

Interesting question. I wonder where they got this information. "I bet. We didn't find the treasure on the ship if that was your next question."

Virginia unfolded her legs, leaned forward, dropped more ice from a silver ice chest on the table into her glass, and poured herself some iced tea. "More tea, gentlemen?"

James moved his glass toward her. "Yes, please."

She poured his tea and handed him a small packet of sugar like he'd used earlier and watched him open it and pour it into his tea.

James took a drink and set the glass down. His left hand rested on the unlatched briefcase on the table between the two chairs. "You have a map to the treasure, don't you?"

"Map? Not really. The treasure was supposed to be on the ship."

"You and I both know the treasure was removed from the ship in the seventeen hundreds. Now…" James shook his head as if to clear cobwebs from his brain. "You have a… a…" His eyes fluttered. "You…" He fell back into the chair, unconscious.

A spasm crossed Paul's face as he watched James collapse. He jerked his head toward Virginia and looked at her with wide eyes. He said, in a strained voice, "What happened? What did you do?"

Virginia pointed at James's tea glass. "I drugged him. He'll be okay in about an hour or so. Well, maybe two or three."

Paul looked at his glass, then expectantly at Virginia.

Virginia chuckled. "If you're wondering, no, I didn't drug you."

He sighed. "Good. I mean… thank you. I… Why didn't you? Why'd you knock him out?"

"He has a gun in that briefcase. He was reaching for it. James was a threat. I either had to drug him, tase him, or shoot him." She gave Paul and innocent smile. "Shooting him would make such a mess, and a taser is painful."

"I guess so." Paul's eyes took on a hunted look. His voice broke. "Are you going to shoot, tase, or drug me?"

"Are you going to do something stupid?"

"No. And to be quite frank, we were told by a person who… who is calling the shots for our organization now, that we were to get the information about the treasure and the ships from you peaceably, or force you to tell us. I told James I couldn't do anything to harm you or Donna."

"Good. I'm glad to hear that you wouldn't harm us, Paul." Virginia looked at James's limp form in the chair. "Was he actually going to try and torture me?"

"To be candid, I don't think so. I like you and Donna, and I wouldn't harm you. James likes you. He was like a high school boy that had a chance with a cheerleader when he thought about you, especially today when we got here and saw you. Dressed like you are, I'm sure he was seriously fantasizing about you."

"I'm sure he was." She smiled. "Were you?"

Paul swallowed. "Oh yeah. And about Donna, too."

"I'm sure she'll be glad to hear that. But was he going to try and force me to talk about the treasure?"

"He was caught between liking you and his orders. Deep down, I know he liked you, and I don't think he would do anything to harm you or Donna."

"Why are you telling me this?"

"Because we started out coming to the desert looking for promising lithium streams. That was our job. Nothing more. But somehow, when we sent samples back to the lab, someone at Litio Products told NMMA about something in your meteorite. That's when things went south. I don't know what's going on. Maybe James knows more, but if he does, I don't think he knows much more than I do."

"What do the meteorite and the mine have to do with the treasure?"

Paul shook his head. "I haven't a clue. Probably nothing."

"Would the person they told at NMMA be at NMMA headquarters?"

"Maybe. But they're in Barbados. It takes time to get information to them and back. These orders came too quick."

Virginia reached into the space between the cushions and pulled out her gun.

Paul flinched.

Virginia tucked it in her waistband. "I'm not going to shoot you. Help me get James back to your car. Later when he wakes up, you can tell him I must have caused him to get high blood pressure and he passed out, or the heat got to him. He'll have a terrible headache."

Paul stood and then peered at Virginia. "May I ask a question?"

"Of course."

"Will you still consider the offer from Litio Products for the lithium rights?"

"Because you've been straight with me, yes, I'll consider it, but tell them the meteor and the mine are off the table. And I make no promises. My lawyer, engineer, and accountant get a crack at the materials you gave me before I do anything. But the ultimate decision is mine."

"Okay. I understand. I'll tell them, and James, when he wakes up." Paul looked down at James. "I'll get him, will you please bring his briefcase? I'll carry him to the car." Paul carried James over his shoulder to the car.

Virginia followed Paul to the car and waited for him to dump James in the passenger seat and buckle him in. She handed Paul the briefcase and watched him place it on the rear seat. "Paul, be careful. The people behind your company work for the National Marine Management Agency. They want the meteor."

Paul frowned. "I know they are the biggest shareholder in Litio Products. Anyway, they're a marine company. Why would they want your meteor or the mine?"

"I don't know, yet." She leaned against the side of the vehicle. "I don't know if they are involved with Carol's death or anything else going on around here. Maybe they just want the meteor. But why would they be interested in the mine indicated on your map is strange? Do you have any ideas who in Litio or NMMA that might want the treasure or that specific mine, and want it bad enough to kill for it? Who is the mysterious person you mentioned before?"

Paul thought for a second. "I have no idea why either company wants the mine. From looking at the map and the aerial shots, it's not the easiest thing to get to. I don't know if it really has uranium in it or not. I've never been to it. Everyone knows the stories about the lost treasure. James and I looked for it while we were here, too. Hell, it made the trip fun. Who wouldn't want to go treasure hunting? This entire other thing about the meteor, the mine, and formally going after the treasure started after they did the analysis on the meteor and other samples we sent to our lab. Then, they didn't want us to venture into the mountains. I told them there could be more minerals up there, but they said we were to convince you to let them gain access to the lithium, the meteor, and that mine. Who at either company would want the treasure is beyond me. I don't see how they'd think they could keep it. It is supposed to be on your land."

"Is there a local agent for the NMMA that you know about?"

"No. I'm a senior engineer type at Litio Products, and not in management. I was sent to do a job. I don't know about any offices around here for Litio Products or NMMA. We're from the Litio Products office in San Diego."

"Okay. Sniff around and see if you can come up with a name for me. Get back with me."

Paul looked at Virginia's chest. "Get back with you?" He smiled. "Like... in person?"

Virginia gave him a demure smile. "You and James do want to come back, don't you? Donna will be here, too."

Paul's eyes dilated. He cracked a smile. "Of course. Okay. I'll do some digging."

"Be discreet." She continued in a sultry voice. "I don't want to endanger either of you."

He took a deep breath. "Any connection between the lithium, the meteor, the mine, and the old Spanish treasure escapes me. I wouldn't mind finding out why they clamped a lid on our field study so fast, and what's going on. Oh, I forgot about the knife."

Virginia straightened and stepped away from the car. "Knife? What knife? What about it?"

"One of the things we sent to the lab was an old Indian stone knife. It had a carved wood and bone handle with some gold and a pearl in it. Most of the wood is still intact. The dang thing would glow in the dark."

"I see. So you stole an ancient knife? From where?"

"We, James really, found it buried in a stream bed between the steam vents and the meteor crater."

"Oh. That made it mine. You two had no right to take it." She glanced at James asleep in the car. "We'll talk about that later. You better take sleeping beauty back to your hotel. He'll be miserable when he wakes up."

"And mad." Paul looked hopeful. "Maybe we'll see more of you and possibly more of Donna, again."

Virginia shrugged. "I'm sure you will, Paul. Much more." Virginia watched Paul drive the Chevy Tahoe down the driveway toward the highway. *Poor guy is completely clueless.*

After she returned to the house and cleaned up the glasses, the phone rang. She answered it. "This is Virginia."

"Virginia, Hailey Jameson from the SCSS in Washington. I'm calling to tell you we borrowed three deputy U.S. marshals, and they just arrived at the hospital where your man Emilio is. They just took over the security of him from the sheriff. But—"

Virginia tightened her grip on the phone receiver. "But what?"

"But I just got a call from the lead marshal. He said ICE had been there. They want Emilio. I told our guys that they were not to release him to ICE unless they get the specific authorization from you personally. I may have fibbed a little. I told them he is needed in an ongoing federal investigation, and you are the lead investigator."

"Thank you, and he is. No fib."

"Oh, That's good. The doctors said if things continue to go as well as they have, he'd be able to go home in three days. You might want to make your friend disappear then."

"It's a big desert out here, and I own a hell of a lot of it."

"ICE can get federal warrants you know."

"Like I said, this is a huge ranch with a lot of places to vanish. And I

Whispering Threads

have an active investigation underway. I need him."

"Well, good luck. Oh, thanks for helping my nephew last year. I still owe you."

"Not anymore. Thanks, Hailey." *Emilio can come back to the ranch shortly. Liana will like that. Speaking about Liana, I wonder how she and Donna are doing? I'll give Donna a call.*

The phone rang just as Virginia was going to dial. "Virginia Davies Clark."

"This is Special Agent Dan Solomon from the L.A. office of the DEA, Agent Clark. I have the results of the tests we did on the samples you sent this morning."

"Already?" Virginia sat on a kitchen chair. "That was fast."

"Yes. You put a rush on it. I had them move your stuff to the top of the heap. Our chemists have a lot of new equipment that makes the analysis faster and more accurate."

"Thanks. What did you find?"

"The full report will be sent to you tomorrow, but I thought you should know, we found high-grade oxycodone. This stuff is better than Big Pharma makes. And the other substance was ultra-pure Fentanyl. There was a little residue in one of the bottles that had the Fentanyl cut with carfentanil."

She scribbled the names of the drugs on a piece of paper. "I know what fentanyl is. What is carfentanil?"

"Carfentanil is an elephant tranquilizer," said Solomon. "It's a hundred times more powerful than fentanyl and ten thousand times as potent as morphine. It's a killer. Less than a milligram can kill an adult human. It's popping up in a lot of the bigger cities."

"Is it controlled?"

"It's a schedule II drug. Vets use it on very large animals, like elephants, rhinos, and hippos."

"So our samples were of high-quality drugs that can be used by drug pushers."

"Yes. And unscrupulous pushers who cut it with the poison. Why they would poison their customers is not clear to me. Where'd you get it?"

"In a cave. I'm investigating it because it has to do with another case."

"Okay. Keep me in the loop. I'm your contact here at the DEA on this. This stuff is the best street drugs I've seen in years. But carfentanil on the street is a killer. We need to stop it."

Virginia chuckled. "I may have put a hitch in their gitty-up."

"What? Hitch in their gitty-up?"

Virginia smirked. "You never watched old western movies when you grew up, did you?"

"Not really. I was more into science fiction."

"I thought so. I'll keep you posted, Agent Solomon." Virginia bit her lip. "I have a small request. The SCSS is working on it too, but you may have more luck and be able to work faster."

"What do you need?"

Virginia told him what she wanted. She heard Agent Solomon type on a keyboard.

After a few seconds, he said, "Got it rolling. I'll see what we can do and get back with you."

"Great. Thanks for the quick testing, the update, and for doing my little search."

"No problem. The written report will be sent later today. Let me know if you need anything else. Bye."

Virginia hung up and stared at her note. "Oxycodone, fentanyl, and carfentanil? All high grade and manufactured in a cave on my ranch. Who's behind this? From what Paul said, I don't think NMMA or Litio Products are into this crap. NMMA wants the nanothingies in my meteor. And maybe uranium. Why the uranium? The proposal says uranium mine, but the map shows the cave we were just in. Did the pd46 scratched into the wall of the cave have something to do with it?" She tapped her pencil on the table as she stared at the note. *Will the SCSS or DEA find anything from the search I asked for?* She jumped when the phone rang. "Virginia Davies Clark."

Donna's voice boomed over the phone. "Virginia. We found it!"

"Found what?"

"The treasure, silly. Virginia, the heat must be getting to you. There are six steamer trunks packed to the hilt with the most perfect pearls I've ever seen. And there are twelve very large, heavy crates full of gold."

"That's a lot. It's at the condo?"

"It's in the garage like we thought." Donna's excited voice cracked. "There's more."

Virginia's heart rate picked up. "More?"

"Yeah. There are an additional nine large containers of silver and twenty big crates of turquoise. Then there are six huge boxes of some stuff that is radioactive. Most of it glows in the dark. And I'm guessing on this next one, but what must be at least a ton of pebble size pieces of meteor in here. The rocks look like the meteor samples we collected ourselves. Remember the pd46 from the cave? Well, there are other rocks in fifteen or so boxes that have pd46, whatever that means, on them. We're still counting."

"That's a lot." Virginia frowned. "How big is the garage?"

"It's an oversized three car garage I'm guessing about twelve to fifteen hundred square feet or so. I think Carol added on to the garage that came with the condo. It's an end unit. But it's full of this stuff. Oh, there're boxes of artifacts and things from the ships in here, too."

"Okay. Close it up, and lock it. Then get back here."

Donna's voice softened. "Shouldn't we move this stuff to a more secure location first?"

"Did anyone follow you?"

"I don't think so."

Virginia chuckled. "How are the two of you going to move it discreetly? You said it weights a whole hell of a lot."

"You're right. This stuff is heavy. We'd be pretty obvious moving any of it."

"Can you do something to ensure its safety?"

Donna's voice took on a conspiratorial tone. "Oh, yeah. You bet. Hell, the garage is lined with steel. The doors look more like they belong at Fort Knox. We'll be back later tonight after we totally secure this place. I'll run my ideas past Andy if that's okay with you."

"Definitely."

"Good. Trust me; when we're done, no one will get in."

"Don't do anything *too* illegal."

"Don't limit my creativity, girlfriend. See you this evening. Oh, how'd it go with the boys?"

"Good. I should say enlightening. I heard from the DEA about our samples, too. I'll fill you in tonight."

"Okay. Got work to do. See you later."

Virginia hung up the phone. *I've got someone using the ranch for the manufacture of high-grade drugs, the National Marine Management Agency wanting my meteor and a uranium mine that's actually the old drug cave, and Litio Products wanting the lithium in my steam vents. And they all want my treasure too. Someone is just greedy.*

She jumped when the alarm system sounded. She ran to the study and looked at the ranch map indicating where the security system detected someone. *The main gate?* She switched the CCTV on and looked at the monitor. A large green Humvee mangled the iron gate and sped toward the house. *Shit. Another damn Humvee. What did GM do, give them away? Maybe the bad guys got a quantity discount. Now what? It looks like the one from the mountain.* She reached over and hit the red panic button locking down Cordone's Fort.

CHAPTER 36

Virginia typed on the keyboard and looked at the large TV screen on the wall. All the security camera feeds were displayed at once. She watched the Hummer come to a stop in front of the house. Six large, armed men emerged. They stood together talking to the driver. One man had raised the tailgate and was doing something she couldn't see. *I'd better see if the workers here are okay.* She pressed the call button on the hardwired intercom for the bunkhouse.

A man answered. "Juan here. What's going on *Señora* Clark?"

"There are a bunch of armed men out front. They crashed the gate. Are you okay?"

"*Sí*. All the ranch buildings are now secure. When you pressed the red button, everything locked and the steel shutters came down."

"Good. Are the other men with you?"

"No. They are out on the ranch. But when you locked the ranch down a signal was sent. They will be coming back, but carefully. *Señora* Putman set it up that way."

"Are they armed?"

"*Sí*. Oh, *Señora* Clark, the strangers are jamming the radios and cell phones now and have stopped the phone lines. I think maybe I should come and help you."

"No. You won't make it from there to the main house."

"Okay. Let me know when you need me."

"I will, Juan. Thanks."

Virginia sat and watched the monitors. *That guy behind the Humvee must be the one doing the jamming. He's got a headset on. What are they up to? Why now? Better get ready for an assault.* She hurried to the bedroom and pulled her guns out. *Two nine-millimeters, a .38, two hundred rounds of ammo for each. Better see what Carol had for protection.* She scurried down the hall to a locked storage room. Using the keys she had grabbed in the bedroom, she opened it and stepped in.

On a sidewall rested a gun case. Virginia unlocked it, opened it, and looked at the weapons. *Carol was serious about protection. We've got what looks like an old, but well kept, thirty caliber M-1 rifle, like my grandfather had from World War II. We've got two 30-06 hunting rifles, three semiautomatic shotguns—a street sweeper? Where the hell did she get that? Are they legal for a civilian to have in California? Maybe Texas. There are six revolvers and six semiautomatic pistols.* She pulled open drawers. *Holy shit! There's enough ammo to start a small war.* She listened. *Awful quiet. Too quiet.* She yanked a semiautomatic twelve-gage shotgun, a box of ammunition and a set of ear protectors from their cases. She locked the gun case and scurried to the office, loading ten rounds into the gun as she went and pocketed a few more. She looked at the monitors. The men outside held assault rifles and had bandoleers strung across their chests. Tactical holsters now held their side arms. *Looks like they're going to make their needs known. Wait, what happened to two of them?*

Virginia looked at the small pictures from the various CCTV security cameras on the wall screen. "There you are." She watched one man approach the barn. He stood staring at the steel shutters over the doors. He grabbed what looked like a handle. She pressed a key on the computer. He stiffened, quivered, and collapsed to the ground. He didn't move. "One down. High voltage will do that. Shocking." She looked at the next screen. Another big man marched up to the bunkhouse and pounded on the metal shutter. He then stepped back and fired at the wall next to the door. His body jerked, he stumbled around as he turned, and fell facedown in the dirt. She called Juan on the intercom. "I take it you just shot that guy outside who fired at the building."

"*Sí. Señora* Clark. I used a big tranquilizer. He will cause you no more trouble."

"Good for you, Juan. Thanks. Are you okay? Any damage to your building?"

"I am fine, thank you. No damage to the structure. We are secure."

"Good. I'll handle the rest of them." *Two down, four to go.*

Virginia watched as two men slowly and cautiously approached the front porch. They carefully examined the steel shutters over the door and the windows, and then returned to the Humvee. One pulled a microphone out and spoke into a public address system. "Mrs. Clark. We know you're in there. We won't hurt you if you open up and talk to us... now."

Virginia pressed the button on the door speaker. "What do you want?"

"We want to talk."

"So talk."

The huge man stiffened and then swung his assault weapon up toward the house. "I demand on a face to face meeting."

"You demand? Who the hell do you think you are?" *Better get to the door fast.* Virginia jumped to her feet and hurried to the front door. She switched on the monitor at the side of the door. One of the men was yelling, but she couldn't hear him. Virginia saw the speaker indicator was red. She turned it on and heard him speaking. "Mrs. Clark. Open up, or we'll force our way in."

Virginia pressed the talk button. "Hello out there. Did you say something? Sorry. I had to make a pit stop."

With a tense voice, the man responded. "You did what?"

"I had to pee, stupid." Virginia stifled a giggle.

"Look, lady, I'm serious. This is no time for jokes. Now open up before I get mad."

"No."

"You open up, missy, or we'll force our way in. You've got two minutes."

"Missy? That's not my name. And I don't need two minutes. The answer is still no. Now, what the hell do you want? Oh, and another thing, where do I send the bill for my mangled gate?"

"Your... your gate?"

"Yes. You broke my gate, damn it." She watched him turn to another man and say something. The fellow went to the back of the Humvee and returned with what she thought looked like a rocket launcher. *Where the hell did he get that?* She watched as he moved to a point in the driveway directly in front of the front door, hoisted it to his shoulder, and started to aim. Virginia put her ear protectors on, opened a small port next to the door, stuck the barrel of the shotgun out, aimed, and fired. The man with the launcher trembled as he dropped the weapon, grabbed his chest, and then fell forward onto the driveway. Blood spread out around him. Virginia pressed the talk button on the communication system. "Trying to shoot at my house isn't very nice. If you value your lives, you'd better leave."

The man who appeared to be the leader looked around. He and two other men were all that were left. He moved to the side of the man Virginia shot, and examined him, then stood. He used his vehicle's PA system again. "Okay, Mrs. Clark, we'll do it your way. We can do this in a friendly manner."

Yeah, right. Like I'd trust them. Virginia watched him for a second. "Okay. Put your weapons on the ground and step a few feet toward the house."

The three men slowly made a show of removing their pistols and dropping them followed by the assault weapons. The man spoke, "See? No weapons."

"Knives, mace, or pepper spray, too."

They took some nasty looking knives out of their scabbards and placed them on the ground. One of the men with a blonde crew-cut set a canister of some chemical on the ground as well.

Whispering Threads

"Step forward, then kneel. Put your hand on your heads." They followed her orders.

Careful, Virginia. Virginia turned a knob, and the steel shutter covering the front door slid up. She opened the door and stepped out on the porch, holding the shotgun. "Which one of you is the leader of this farce?"

The biggest and most menacing looking of the men spoke through gritted teeth. "I am. You think this is a farce?"

"I thought so, and yes, this is a farce."

He slowly started to lower his hand and stand when she pointed the shotgun at him. "I didn't tell you to move."

He stood facing her. "I'm not armed. You shoot me now, and it's murder."

"So you figure you can just physically attack me and get away with it?"

He snarled as he stood. "Looks like it. There is no one around to help you."

"What do you want?"

"Before yesterday, we were going to warn you to stay away from the mountain. But now that you and your nosey friend discovered our operation and killed our associates, we have to take more drastic action. Nothing personal you understand."

"Funny. I take it very personally. Drastic action? Who do you work for?" Virginia watched him shuffle a few steps closer. She brushed a blonde strand of hair from her face. *Where does he think he's going?*

He stopped. His eyes ranged freely up and down her body. "You always answer the door dressed like that, honey?"

"Sometimes. Sometimes with less on."

His eyes widened. "Really?"

"And I'm not your honey or missy. Now, answer my questions. Who do you work for, and what are your intentions? Don't let it go unnoticed that I've reduced the size of your group by half in just a few minutes."

He looked around. "I noticed. You'll pay for that, bitch." He wrenched a large knife from behind his back and lunged forward when Virginia's shotgun roared. Blood, tissue, and bone sprayed out from his upper right thigh, striking the other two kneeling men behind him. The big man dropped the wicked blade and tumbled to the dirt as he grabbed his mutilated leg, writhing in pain. "You bitch!"

"Your mother never told you not to take a knife to a gunfight? She should have also taught you not to insult a lady, especially one holding a gun. Not real bright. You must have a single digit IQ. If you're nice, I'll call the paramedics. If you keep insulting me, I'll wait for you to bleed out. Your choice asshole." She noticed the blood pulsing through his fingers. *Looks like that decision has already been made. Not enough room for a tourniquet. Paramedics won't make it here in time, even if I call them now.*

Virginia stepped closer to him and bent over. "You've got maybe ninety seconds left to tell me who you work for." He looked confused. "You're bleeding to death, moron. Getting cold?"

He nodded.

"You macho types usually believe your own press releases. You're a badass, and the rest of us are supposed to cower in fear and bow to your wishes. Didn't work this time did it?" The man's hands fell from his leg. His body stopped moving. She straightened and moved to the two remaining men kneeling in the dirt. "One of you boys want to start talking?" She pointed at their leader. "He won't be talking anymore."

They looked at each other, and then a Hispanic looking man with a shiny, bald head, and a tattoo on his bare, left, muscled, arm, spoke. "We were hired to find out what you know, and stop you from interfering with our... err... his employer's activities."

"Strong arm stuff and intimidation?"

He nodded. "Yeah. Things sort of got out of hand. Our leader is the guy you just shot. He was from Fresno. He worked part-time on oilrigs, fixes trucks, and runs some drugs and girls. He is... was ex-military and a small-time mercenary type. He said to come on strong, and you'd scare real easy. He said you would be a pushover."

"I see." Virginia chuckled. "How'd that work for you?"

The Hispanic guy shook his head. "Not too well, obviously."

"Okay, your leader was a dumb ass and is now dead. He ran drugs and girls? He was a pusher and a pimp?"

The man nodded. "Pretty much."

"How about you two?"

"I'm from East L.A. Never been in the service, and I'm not a drug dealer or user. Do some ahh... security type work and... some other stuff."

"Name?"

"Galeno."

Virginia glanced at the solidly built man next to him and noticed his crotch was wet. *Macho with a shy bladder. A blonde made him pee himself? Oh, that's funny.* "I think you missed your potty break. Where are you from?"

"Southcentral L.A." He just gave her a pained look. "We're the only two left out of the six of us?"

Virginia glanced around and then shrugged. "Looks like it."

He eyed her body with a confused look. "*You* took everyone out? You did it all by yourself?"

"Pretty much. You want to be next?"

"No." He bit his lip. A tear ran down his cheek.

"Okay." She glanced at the ground as her foot made a circle on the driveway and then back at them. "Now why don't you boys tell me what I want to know so we can all be friends and get on with life?"

Galeno tensed. "You've murdered four men. I'll wait for the cops."

Still trying to be tough? Virginia stepped directly in front of him, bent down, aimed the shotgun at his chest, and said, "Listen, chrome dome. You're trespassing on private land. You broke my gate. You and your tough friends attacked me with big, nasty, weapons. I defended myself. How's this going to look to the sheriff? Six burly, mean, armed, men verses one ditzy little blonde? And in case you didn't notice, this is a huge ranch. Over eleven square miles of hot, dry, desert. I've got plenty of places to lose a body or two, or six, without anyone noticing. You can become food for the local fauna." She straightened and smiled. "The police won't come unless I call them. And guess what? I'm not calling them."

The men stared at her with wide eyes, trembling.

She gave Galeno a mischievous grin. "I just took down four of your armed friends without much trouble." She looked at the fingers of her right hand. "Didn't even break a fingernail. I can *make* you talk, and trust me, my methods are far worse than anything you, or your stupid leader, could dream up. Waterboarding will seem like a pleasant day at the beach when I'm done. Just so you know, I'm not opposed to attaching jumper cables from a tractor to sensitive parts of your anatomy, and seeing how much juice you can tolerate. I'm sure your screams will hit octaves higher than you ever thought possible. I've got equipment that can grind you into confetti, a little at a time. If you scream for mercy, no one can hear you. Don't think for a minute I won't do it. You are the only two left out of the six that came here. I'm still pissed."

The man with the wet pants looked around her at their leader on the ground, then at Galeno. He glanced at Virginia, and sighed. "I believe you. Can we please lower our arms?"

Virginia stepped back and aimed the shotgun at them. "In case you're wondering, this is a semiautomatic. All I need to do is pull the trigger." *Did he say please?* "Lower your hands and sit, but don't make any other moves without my permission first."

They carefully lowered their arms and sat on the ground. Galeno looked at her with a stricken expression. "We were hired to do what we said. The guy over there on the ground hired us. He said this would be a simple job that paid very well."

Virginia frowned. "Who hired him?"

"Some guy in Palm Springs. Seemed to know a lot about you. Obviously not as much as he thought he did. We were told you were some pretty, sexy, SoCal beach type blonde. A girl who was a buttoned-up museum type. A pretty egghead. He said you would be a pushover. Easy to scare. Obviously, he was dead wrong."

"Does all this involve illegal drugs?" Virginia asked.

"From what he's paying us, I think so. We never saw any drugs, and we're not selling any." He motioned toward the man next to him. "This was a one-time gig for the two of us. It looked like quick and easy cash. I'm not so sure about the guy with the rocket launcher you blew away. We hadn't met him before, same for the other two who went out back. We were the new guys to the crew."

Virginia eyed them skeptically. "So, this guy who hired you is from Palm Springs?"

The second man nodded. "Yes. He operates out of there. Has some sort of office or something there."

"Hmm. Now that your leader is dead, can you still communicate with this mystery man?"

"Yes. We can take our boss's cell phone. The big man will call from a burner phone for a status at five tonight."

"Thank you. How does this sound to you boys?" Virginia lowered her shotgun. She spoke in a low, steady voice. "I take the phone. I make sure the bodies of your friends are taken care of. You two just disappear into the bowels of east, or south central L.A. and never, ever, return here. You ask no questions, and you forget you were ever here. You forget about me. I never existed. The only other alternative is… you never leave here and become food for the local wildlife."

"Can we take the Humvee?" Galeno asked.

Virginia tilted her head. "You want the vehicle?"

"Yes. There is a safe in it with the money we were all to be paid and water. And it beats walking in this heat."

Virginia smiled. "You boys just got a raise. You get the nice car and get to split the money two ways instead of six."

Galeno nodded. "Okay. We'll disappear, just like you said. No problem. We were never here. We don't know you. Never saw you before. We don't even know where this ranch is. We'll never come back. The Humvee, money, and our lives will be more than enough compensation and to ensure our silence, trust me."

"Good. Remember, if you fellas ever come back, I promise you, none of you will survive."

Galeno looked at Virginia with wide eyes. "I believe you.

May I ask, what are you going to tell the big boss?"

Virginia shouldered the shotgun and smiled. "His days are numbered."

CHAPTER 37

Virginia watched the men get into the Humvee and drive off the ranch, and then returned to the house. She turned off the lockdown system and called Juan on the intercom. "The problem has been taken care of. It's safe to come out. I'll unlock the ranch."

"Okay. The men just called. They are close. I will tell them we are now not locked down anymore."

Virginia called the SCSS with her cell phone and requested a second clean-up crew. The woman on the phone coughed. "Again? You just had one."

"Do I get a quantity discount?"

"No discount. You're not paying anyway. What are you doing out there?"

"I had some more armed nasty, folks visit who wanted me dead. They weren't very nice. I take issue with people like that."

"I guess so. How many bodies this time?"

"Four."

"Four for clean-up; got it." Virginia heard the woman type on a keyboard. "How's the investigation coming?"

"I found out who killed Carol Putman."

"Good."

"Problem is, there is more crazy and illegal stuff going on besides the murder."

"Oh."

"We have a complex investigation out here, but the bad guy's numbers are rapidly dwindling."

"Yeah, you could say that. Okay, I'm activating the closest clean-up team. They'll be there in about an hour."

"Thanks." Virginia hung up. Next, she called the lawyer, Brian Wilson, who handled the estate transfer for her.

His secretary answered, "Mr. Wilson's Office."

"This is Virginia Davies Clark. Is Mr. Wilson in?"

"Yes, Mrs. Clark. Please hold."

Wilson quickly answered. "Hello, Mrs. Clark. How can I help you?"

"Mr. Wilson, I was wondering, if something happened to me, who inherits the ranch?"

"Well, now that it's yours, it would be your husband or whoever you leave it to in a will or trust."

"So, there are no other interests who would gain from my demise?"

"No. Like I said, only your husband, or those in any will or trust you may have."

"Okay. Good to know. Thanks."

Virginia hung up and sat, staring at the phone. "So, if something happens to me, no one but Andy will benefit. Good."

Virginia went to her bedroom, changed, and returned to the office. She stepped to the whiteboard, picked up a purple marker, and made notes. "Okay," she said to herself, "the Agua Caliente Band of Cahuilla Indians and the Agua Caliente Mar Management are just interested in the mining. They're legit. Litio Products wants the lithium in the steam vents. They seem legit, too. The National Marine Management Agency or NMMA wants my meteor, and a uranium mine that is actually the drug cave with pd46 scribbled on the wall. Problem one: Litio and NMMA are connected and are not immune to violence, but at least they may not be involved with the drugs. Problem two: the drugs issue is most likely someone else. The leader of the drug operation operates out of Palm Springs and thinks he knows me and how I operate. Wrong. Possible problem three: Are the drug guys and NMMA connected? If so, how? How does this all tie into Carol's murder? I think I know who did it, but what does all the rest have to do with it?"

She plopped into her desk chair when she heard someone at the front door. "Now what?" She jumped to her feet, grabbed the shotgun, and bolted for the door. She looked at the monitor. Two armed men in desert camouflage uniforms and boots stood there. Behind them were three unmarked, desert camouflaged, military type trucks. More people in similar clothes were pulling out equipment and body bags. She opened the door.

The shorter man eyed her shotgun and then spoke. "Special Agent Virginia Davies Clark?"

"Yes?" She noticed there were no name labels or other markings on their clothes except a patch with Wile E. Coyote on it.

"We are from the Acme Rehabilitation Company. Your friend in Washington sent us. We should be finished in about an hour and a half. Is that acceptable, ma'am?"

Wile E. Coyote from the Acme Rehabilitation Company? Cute. He's polite, too. Virginia nodded. "Yes, sir."

"We will take care of everything."

Whispering Threads

Virginia pointed. "There are two more bodies out back."

"Yes, ma'am. We know. Thank you." The men saluted her, turned, and marched toward the trucks.

Marines? Army? CIA? Virginia watched them for a second, then stepped back and closed the door. *In about an hour and a half, no one will be able to tell the dead guys were ever here. Spooky.* She returned to the office, sat at the desk and looked at the cell phone she took from the dead leader. *The boss will call at five. I can't trace this call. How do I play it?* Virginia jerked when the desk phone rang. She answered it. "Hello?"

"Hi. We're on the way back." Donna said with enthusiasm. "The condo and garage are locked up as tight as Fort Knox."

Virginia leaned her elbows on the desk. "You absolutely sure?"

"Positive. It would take an army M1 tank to even get close to the treasure."

Virginia thought for a minute. "Where exactly are you?"

"On the 405 freeway heading north toward Interstate 10. The traffic's getting a lot heavier."

Virginia's heart rate rose. "Do you remember the old case we worked on in Long Beach near the ocean?" *I hope she remembers this distress code.*

"Huh?" After a couple heartbeats, Donna responded. "Long Beach? Oh, yeah. I remember. When we rescued Andy, right?"

Virginia took a long breath and slowly let it out. "Yes. Could you and Liana do me a huge favor and move Fort Knox?"

"To the building you have in Long Beach on Elm, near where we first worked together? The one near the pier, right?"

"Yes, that's it."

Donna chuckled. "Oh sure. We can do that. If I recall, the address is 5508 Elm."

"Yes. Thanks. I'll see you later tonight." Virginia hung up. *I'm glad she did remember the distress code and played along. We rescued Andy in Newport Beach.* She went to the kitchen and made herself some tea, returned to the office and sat staring at the whiteboard. "Hmm. The big drug guy has someone here on the ranch to inform on me. He slipped up. I know who the bastard is." She rubbed her chin. "I'm now pretty sure I know who the drug kingpin is, too. Now I need to use the snitch to help me nail the drug lord. Virginia rose and went to the kitchen. She picked up a bag of potato chips and returned to the office.

She sat back sipping her tea and munching on the chips when her cell phone rang. "This is Virginia."

"Hello, Virginia. This is Senior Special Agent Tom Mason, SCSS in Washington. I got word you just had another clean-up."

Virginia swallowed. *Oh boy.* "Yes."

"Are you and your partner okay? Any present danger?"

Virginia's heart rate increased. "Not at the moment, but things have been changing pretty fast, sir."

"Is there anything I can do from here to assist?"

Virginia frowned. "Why do you ask?"

Agent Mason's voice deepened. "You and Agent Donna Bolette are outstanding agents and a great team. If I may say so, you two have a better track record than most of our regular, full-time agents, even if you leave a trail of bodies behind. You two finding the petroglyphs in that area are an example. And because they are on your land. I hope the Smithsonian will be the first to investigate and study them."

"That can be arranged, sir."

"Good. But my job right now is to support your field activities by mobilizing resources and assets for you when necessary. You've had some rather strange things happen, so we've been monitoring the local police communications. Oh, I received your request for any aerial surveillance we could muster. So, I had our friends at the NSA take pictures of your ranch as their satellite flew over you for every day. I noticed you two manage to get into a hell of a lot of pickles, and then when the dust settles, literally, you two manage to walk out, and your much bigger and better-armed opponents don't. I'm very impressed. I'm sending you the images we took from the satellite. They'll be in your e-mail shortly. I think you'll see some enlightening things. I learned from Hailey Johnson, you requested agents to guard one of your people in a hospital, too. We had to borrow some federal marshals to do it. They've been told to take orders strictly from you or Agent Bolette. I'm also forwarding an audio file of some of the things your man Emilio said over the phone at the hospital and to the marshals guarding him. You will find it most interesting. The detailed email you sent requesting monitoring Emilio's phone calls was enough to get a federal warrant to tap his phone."

They actually bugged the hospital phone? Virginia let out a sigh of relief. "Wow. Thank you. I'll take a look and listen to the files."

"Good. I have also repositioned agents from our San Francisco office to L.A., should you need backup."

"How do I reach the other agents if I need help?"

"You have the emergency phone number we gave you when you started with us, right?"

"Yes, sir. I keep it with me all the time. I was told to use it if I needed emergency help."

"Good. That number is answered 24 hours a day every day of the year. They will send whatever you need, when you want it, and where you want it."

"The Smithsonian can do that?" She drank some tea.

"Yes." Agent Mason chuckled. "But sometimes we use some help from other agencies, so we get authorization from a little higher up."

Virginia folded her legs under her in the chair. "Oh. May I ask who?"

"Virginia, the number rings into the White House situation desk."

She jerked upright, her legs slipped out from under her, and she caught herself before falling to the floor. "Oh, my God."

Agent Mason's voice sounded serious. "No, Virginia, not God, the President of the United States."

"Oh. Wow. I have a need for those repositioned agents, sir."

"What do you need, where do you want them, and when?"

"Donna… err Agent Bolette, my housekeeper, staff person, and go-to-lady around here, Liana, are in Long Beach near an old warehouse. They are watching it to see who shows up to steal my treasure. I think my regular phone line here is tapped."

"We know."

"You do?"

"That's why I called on your cell phone."

"Okay, I guess." *Big brother really is watching.* "I'm glad you used my cell. Anyway, we're sending the suspects on a wild goose chase to see who they are. Can you dispatch the repositioned agents to back up Donna?"

"Yes. Where are they?"

"5508 Elm in Long Beach. They are in a black Toyota SUV." She gave him the license number.

She heard him type on a keyboard. "The agents are on their way. Anything else?"

She thought for a second, took a breath, then said, "Agent Mason, I do have a situation I could use some help on."

"Name it."

"Sir, I have a cell phone I took from a mercenary type who attacked me. He's now dead." Virginia picked up the cell phone she got from the dead man who attacked her. She hit the button to activate it and looked at the phone number. "The leader of the group behind a major drug operation, and part of my investigation, is going to call it at five, Pacific Time, for a sitrep. It's also tied to some special stuff in my meteor and maybe something else."

"The meteor's nanotubes, superconductivity, and hardness?"

Virginia gave a startled gasp. "You know about that?"

"Yes. The NSA, at Fort Meade, monitors signals for keywords, phrases, and things, and makes note of them if they pertain to national interests. This does. It also pertains to a couple very special agents of ours, specifically you, and Mrs. Bolette. They informed on you. By the way, DARPA knows, too. They would like to talk to you about your meteor after all this has been settled."

The Defense Advanced Research Project Agency? News travels fast. "Well, tell the folks at the NSA I think they're tattle tails. Is there any way you, or the NSA, can backtrack this cell phone and find out where the call will come from? You know it's physical location. The call will most likely be from a burner phone, but if I can find out where it's being used, it will probably help me a whole lot."

"Give me the number. I'll see what our friends from Fort Meade can do to help."

Virginia gave him the phone number and other information the phone had in its 'about me' file. "Anything you can do will help, sir."

"Okay. I'm sending the information and request to Fort Meade right now. Anything else?" asked Agent Mason.

"I don't think so."

"How about the snitch that's listening to your house phone?" Agent Mason asked. "Want us to pick him up?"

"No. I'll take care of him."

"In that case, should I have another clean-up team standing by?"

"Nooo." Virginia laughed. "Well, I hope not. Maybe. Might be a good idea."

"Oh, Agent Clark, I just got the information you requested earlier. It looks like the DEA, for some reason, just gave us some additional data. I'm sending it to you now."

Virginia looked at her computer. "It's coming in now along with the pictures. Thanks."

"Okay, Agent Clark. Good luck."

"Thank you, sir." She hung up and stared at the whiteboard. *I'd better call Donna and tell her the other agents will be backing her up. Can't have her shoot them.* She punched Donna's cell phone number in her cell phone.

Donna answered. "Hi, Virginia. We're near the warehouse. It's getting dark, so I hope we can identify anyone that shows up."

"I've got backup coming. You may not see them, but in case of trouble, you will have some friends around."

"Where'd you get them, recruit a street gang?"

"No. Washington sent them. I asked that they back you up."

"Thanks for the heads up and the help. I'll call you if we get any action."

"Okay. Stay safe."

Virginia rose, holding her cup of tea, and examined the large quilt that glows in the dark. *I don't see anything else on here that may be helpful. This thing has been important to the case. I probably should take it down and hide it to be on the safe side.* She stood on a step stool and removed the quilt from the wall hanger and started to fold it. Her hand ran over a slight bump in the bottom binding. She felt it again. *I didn't see this before.*

Whispering Threads

Something is rolled up in there. She went to the quilt room and picked up some tools and a needle and thread that matched the quilt. She returned to the office and carefully opened the quilt binding and pulled out a tiny rolled up paper. She unrolled it and read it. *"Oh shit! Now I find Carol's message! How do I safely tell Donna? Maybe it's better to not tell her... yet.*

CHAPTER 38

Donna and Liana sat in the SUV finishing their food and watching the old warehouse down the street. A little after eight, a dark van drove slowly down the road and stopped in front of the warehouse under a broken streetlamp. Some refuse blew along the gutter driven by a breeze off the ocean. A man stepped from the shadows and talked to the driver. He pointed toward Donna and Liana's SUV.

Donna's stomach knotted. "Oh shit! We've been made. Let's get out of here." She started the car, but the van accelerated forward and blocked her. As she pulled her revolver out, there was a loud roar of motorcycles. She looked around. "Now what?"

Six large motorcycles rolled into view and stopped around the van. Tough looking bikers with long, scraggly hair and beards, wore dark, leather jackets with *Banditos* stitched on the back, sat on their rumbling bikes. One of the bikes raced down the street and caught the man who had pointed them out and forced him back toward the van. The biker climbed off his motorcycle.

Donna leaned forward. "Who the hell are they?" *Virginia's friends?*

"Maybe they work for the people who want the treasure," said Liana. "Or, maybe they are the drug guys."

Donna and Liana watched as the bikers dismounted, drew handguns, and moved to the van. The van doors opened, and three men climbed out. The three men stepped away from the vehicle and dropped to their knees, placing their hands on their heads.

Liana's voice trembled. "What do we do?"

"Nothing." Donna's hands became clammy. "We're blocked. We can't drive, and they've got more firepower than we do. Guess we wait and see what they want. I hope you're right about this SUV being bulletproof." She watched the motorcycle gang search the van. After searching the van, the bikers put plastic ties on the men's wrists, and push them back inside the van.

A biker who seemed to be in charge walked toward Donna. He stood next to the car and motioned for her to lower her window. She slid it part way down. He smiled, leaned close, and said in a whisper, "Special Agent Bolette and Miss Liana, I presume." He looked at Donna's lap and the silver revolver. "You can put the gun away."

Donna's grip tightened on the pistol. Her eyes narrowed. "Who the hell are you?"

"I'm special Agent McCutcheon, SCSS. We were sent to backstop you. It looked like you could use a little help."

Donna raised an eyebrow. "Can I see your badge?"

He reached into his vest pocket and pulled out his gold SCSS badge and credentials. "Agent Clark requested backup for you, and Washington sent us."

"So you're the guys she sent." Donna sighed. "Glad to see you. You scared us to death. What now?"

"The gentlemen we just intercepted will be held incognito for a while." He glanced at his men and the van. "They'll think they're the prisoners of an outlaw motorcycle gang. We'll make them think we're angry because we believe they want to muscle in on our territory. We can be quite convincing. Would you like us to interrogate them and find out what they were doing, and who they work for?"

"Yes. That would be great. How long can you hold them?"

He leaned against the SUV and glanced at the men on their knees. "If we identify ourselves as police, we've got seventy-two hours before we have to either charge them or release them." He grinned. "But since we're an outlaw motorcycle gang and not cops, at least in their eyes, who knows?"

Donna smiled. "Talk to them first. Then we can figure out if they should get lost in the hot desert, take a long one-way boat ride in the Catalina Channel, or go to jail."

Agent McCutcheon nodded. "I was told you were pretty spunky, like your partner. We can threaten them with the desert, or a boat ride, but actually doing it is another matter."

Donna raised an eyebrow. "They don't know that."

"I like how you think. We'll take them away now. Want us to guard the building?"

"No. There's nothing in it."

"Huh?" He gave her a quizzical look and then nodded. "I understand. Good job. I'll call the ranch when we get something out of them."

"Don't you mean if you get anything out of them?"

"If you were a bunch of hired, stupid street thugs, and were captured by a bunch of pissed off, tough, armed, motorcycle gang types who just overpowered you and could inflict serious bodily harm or kill you, would you put up much of a fight if there was a way to get free? They probably aren't paid enough to endure much pain."

"I see what you mean," Donna smirked. "I can't wait to hear from you. Thanks." Donna watched as the van and the motorcycles were moved so she could drive away. As they drove Donna noticed Liana was thumbing her cell phone in her lap. "You sending a text?"

Liana's head jerked around. "Ahh... yes. To Juan at the ranch, I wanted to tell him we are okay and coming back. With Emilio in the hospital, he is the acting foreman, and he worries about all of us."

"Okay. Sit back and relax. At this time of day we've got at least a three-hour drive."

Liana sat back. *"Señora* Donna. When I was getting our food, you did something at the condo to secure the treasure. You said it was *estupendo*... super safe. What did you do?"

"Sorry, Liana, but the only other person who knows is Virginia. It's safer that way. But be assured. If someone is stupid enough to try and open or get into the garage by any means, they will be extremely sorry. It'll be the last thing they ever try."

Liana's eyes widened. "They will die?"

"Painfully."

"Oh." Liana sat staring out the window, wringing her hands as they drove.

After about a half hour of driving, Donna turned to Liana. "Call Virginia and tell her mission accomplished. The bad, good guys, like with the 1933 quilt case, have been found."

"Sí, Señora Donna." She called Virginia and relayed the message. After hanging up, she looked at Donna. "The bad, good guys? 1933 quilt case? I do not understand."

"You will."

Virginia hung up and then dialed Andy on her landline. She heard a slight click as the phone rang. She grinned.

On the fourth ring, Andy answered. "Hi, beautiful. How are things going?"

"Good. We got Carol's murderer. I found the treasure. And I know who's behind all this. I've got it all written down and scribbled the locations on a map. I'm waiting for Donna to return, then we'll end this investigation."

"Good. How soon will you be done? I miss you."

"Not sure, but soon. I miss you, too. I'll call you as soon as things are wrapped up."

"Okay. Be careful."

Whispering Threads

"Don't worry." She hung up. *That should finish putting the wheels in motion.* Virginia started to turn when her cell phone rang. She answered it. "Hello?"

"Agent Clark, this is Agent McCutcheon, SCCS. We were backing up your friend, Agent Boletti, and intercepted some local muscle. She said to call you when we got something interesting out of them."

"Great. What did you get?"

"The name of the person who hired them. And some men tried to break into your condo in Newport Beach and set off the alarm. Two of my agents got there before the police. We removed them from the scene. They didn't get in but suffered greatly from trying. I think they'll live. If they do, they'll be in constant pain for the rest of their lives. I'd sure hate to have your diabolical partner mad at me. The cops think they got a false alarm call. Please tell her booby traps are illegal as security measures. Firefighters and police officers could get hurt responding to an emergency. I had my guys make some tweaks so real emergency people won't be killed or maimed if they responded to an alarm."

"Thanks. I'll caution her. Who is the person who hired them?" Virginia grinned when he told her. She thanked him and hung up. Virginia opened her computer and downloaded the images taken from the spy satellite the SCSS had focused on her ranch and the report she asked for. Next, she opened the audio files and listened. *Oh shit. That explains part of the dilemma.* She then read the information from the SCSS and DEA. This, the note in the binding of the quilt, and the info from the NSA about the burner phone's location pretty well solves it.

Virginia went to the living room and waited. She jumped when her cell phone rang. "Hello?"

"Mrs. Clark?"

"Yes."

"This is Dr. Richardson at UCR. I'm a professor of geochemistry. Your samples were given to me to examine. I know it's late, but I was told this analysis is very important for a government investigation, and I was to call you when we were finished."

"Thank you, professor, it is. Did you get it done already?"

"Yes. The rock samples contain high levels of palladium. It has an atomic number of 46. Wherever you got them, they assay the highest of any samples in the U.S. The bottles with the water and dirt contain it, too. The water is toxic to some plants. When ingested, humans poorly absorb it. A person might get sick. Animal toxicity varies. It runs about $1100 per ounce, right up there with gold. It's used in almost all electronics and as a catalyst, like in car exhaust systems."

"Great. Thanks for the information. Be sure to send a bill to the Smithsonian and use the reference number that came with the samples."

"I will. Have a good rest of the day." He hung up.

Virginia put her phone away. *Palladium? Andy mentioned it before. That explains the discrepancy in Litio Products proposal. Now I know why the cave had Pd46 scratched on the wall. The arroyo is labeled aguas mortals because the water had palladium salts in it. I have to remember to tell Donna. The proposal from Litio Products mentioned palladium but didn't elaborate. They also wanted that cave.*

When she saw headlights approaching in the monitor, Virginia used the intercom and told Juan to come to the main house.

Juan arrived and knocked on the front door. When she opened it, he gave her a nervous look. "You wanted me, *Señora* Clark?"

"Yes. Come in and have a seat. Donna and Liana will be here shortly." She glanced out the window. The Toyota SUV stopped in the circle driveway. Donna and Liana climbed out and entered the house.

"Liana's eyes narrowed when she saw Juan. "What are you doing here?"

"I don't know. *Señora* Clark asked me to come."

"Have a seat next to him, Liana. There are a few more people I'm expecting."

Liana looked puzzled. "Who?"

"You will see." Virginia motioned for Donna to join her in the hallway. "The boss of the men who attacked me here at the ranch called. I told him things didn't go well for his team. He hung up. The NSA backtracked the location of the call."

"Any word on our samples?"

"Yes. They contained palladium, atomic number 46. Great stuff and valuable." Virginia handed a piece of paper to Donna. "Take a look at this. I found it in the binding of the quilt. We've got them. Now for the cherry on the cake. We will try and wheedle a confession from the various parties."

"Let's hope it works."

"We're going to have more company. Sit to the side and keep your gun ready."

"You got it. Thanks for the backup in Long Beach."

"No problem. This is going to get interesting."

Donna walked to the side of the fireplace and sat in a wingback chair. She set her backpack on the floor next to her right leg. She looked at Liana and Juan. "Isn't this nice. The only person missing is Emilio. He'll be home soon."

A car's lights followed the driveway and stopped behind the SUV. Detective Ferguson got out, climbed onto the porch, and was about to knock when Virginia opened the door. "Come in, Detective. We've been expecting you."

He stepped into the front room. "You have?"

"Yes. Have a seat."

"You have a development in the case?"

Virginia grinned. "Yep."

Ferguson sat next to Liana. He gave Virginia a quizzical look. "What is it? Did you find the treasure? The ships?"

Virginia grinned. "Oh, yeah. Donna and I found both of them and more."

Ferguson fidgeted in his chair. "You really did? More?"

"Yes." She peered out the window. "Good. More guests."

After a short wait, James and Paul entered.

Donna smiled. "Hi boys. You're just in time for the finale."

Paul looked at Ferguson. "What's going on?" He and James sat down.

Ferguson shook his head. "I think Mrs. Clark is going to wrap up this case."

James gave Virginia a confused expression. "Why'd you drug me the other day?"

"You were reaching for a gun in your briefcase. The choices I had were shoot you, tase you, or drug you. The drug was the less painful and deadly of the choices, and a lot less messy."

James slouched in his chair. "Oh. Yeah, I guess it was." Virginia looked at the group. "Shall we start? First is Carol Putman's murder. We now know Mr. Coombs did *not* kill Mrs. Putman."

Ferguson frowned. "How did you figure that out? Coombs confessed, didn't he? If Coombs didn't do it, who did?"

"Let me paint the picture of what happened. Coombs, more about him a little later, used a stone knife similar to one that killed Carol to defend himself from Emilio. He didn't have a gun, especially a rifle."

"How do you know that? Emilio couldn't say anything." Ferguson fidgeted in his chair. "Last I heard, he's still unconscious."

"No, he isn't. Emilio recovered and is awake. I had deputy U.S. Marshals relieve your deputies guarding him." Virginia started to pace.

Ferguson stiffened. "No one told me that. But if Coombs didn't kill Mrs. Putman, who did, and why did Emilio attack him?"

"Emilio told the marshals about what happened and why he was stabbed. He said Coombs attacked him because Emilio saw Mr. Coombs shoot the clerk from the fake antique shop. Emilio said Coombs tried to bribe Emilio in joining the… organization for a cut. But Coombs didn't have a handgun or a rifle. He couldn't have shot the clerk at the antique shop. And he had nothing to gain from killing Carol.

"He told Emilio there would be mining claims for the land filed by Litio Products, the NMMA, and the Indians. Coombs knew the mines were not played out. Emilio knew that too, Emilio knew the treasure was hidden in Carol's Condo garage in Newport Beach. That's because Emilio helped Carol move it after she found it. He and Carol knew about the palladium as well."

Virginia continued to pace. "Coombs saw Emilio kill Carol. Emilio threatened to kill him if he said anything. Later, Coombs saw Emilio shoot the clerk outside the antique shop. Coombs tried to stop Emilio, but just had the stone knife. Those things are extremely sharp. Emilio shot him during the struggle."

James leaned forward. "Why would Emilio kill Mrs. Putman?"

"She found the treasure where the Spaniards hid it in the cave. Carol didn't know where the ships were. She was looking for them like everyone else. But she had spotted strange lights some nights in the desert where we now know the ships were located. Only the lights were vehicles coming and going from the drug lab in the cave above the ships' location. She knew about the cave, but couldn't figure out why someone was now going to it. The treasure had been relocated by then. She was going to investigate. Emilio couldn't let her do that."

Ferguson knitted his brow. "How do you know this? Emilio wouldn't have told you."

"I'll explain how I know this in a few minutes."

Paul cleared his throat. "So, what does all that have to do with James and me?"

CHAPTER 39

Virginia glanced at Paul as she walked in front of the group. "You two represented Litio Products. Like you told me, you were initially exploring for possible steam vents with extractable quantities of lithium and other minerals. You're acting under orders from your company. You stumbled onto my meteor, the other mines, and the caves. After you sent the samples to your lab, the company wanted the rights not just to the lithium rich steam vents, but the meteor, and the cave marked as a uranium mine as well. In case you really didn't know, that cave doesn't have any uranium in it. But the meteor has some rather unique properties. A lot of people want to exploit it."

Virginia stopped pacing and faced the group. "Then there are the gold and uranium mines that are still very viable. Like Mr. Coombs and Emilio, you, Paul, and James knew that."

Paul and James sat stone-faced.

"Don't worry boys; we've got this figured out."

James looked around. "Yes, we did know. But how did you figure it out?"

"Paul said when you stumbled on the meteor and sent in samples to your lab, the company changed your mission. You were to secure the rights for the lithium, the cave your proposal stated was a uranium mine, *and* the meteor from the cute, ditzy blonde. You two were to work your manly charms on an attractive egghead and her pretty friend who were new on the scene and didn't know anything. You thought some smooth talk, wine, dinner, dancing, and some romancing would get you what you wanted... with the ranch that is. It might have worked. Donna and I liked you two. Your proposal was straightforward. But by then, I knew about the special nanothingies in the meteor. If you had said you knew, too, and wanted to help develop the resource, we might have gone along with it."

Paul slowly nodded as he looked at James. "I told you they were sharp."

Virginia looked at James and Paul. "You came to see me with the proposal from Litio Products. I think the proposal from the company was the real deal, except for the cave… mine thing. Paul, I think you were honest about what you said. But something didn't add up. Litio Products is partially owned by NMMA. You know more than a field engineer would about the location of NMMA's headquarters."

Paul bolted to his feet. "That's a lie!"

Virginia smiled. "Is it? You said NMMA headquarters is in Barbados. None of us knew that, not even the police. The IRS, Homeland Security, and the Customs people didn't either, but they do now. How did you come across that information?"

Paul plopped into his seat and glared at James. "James told me. Why would we want the meteor? It doesn't have any lithium in it, does it?"

"No. The meteor doesn't have lithium in it. Your company lab found the special properties of my meteor. Part of it has superconductivity capability at room temperature. Carol got suspicious and nosed around. She found out about the cave and the meteor's properties. She was killed to silence her. By the way, she was afraid of what was going on, so she documented her suspicions in a note that was sown in the big glow-in-the-dark quilt that's in the office here."

"Huh?" Paul looked around. "What glow-in-the-dark quilt?"

"You wouldn't know about that because it didn't concern you. But she was aware of the overt interest in the meteor, and she wanted to understand why. Your lab figured it out, and I had samples analyzed and found the secret too. The things in it that were superconductors."

Paul slumped to his seat. "Oh. I guess we would want the meteor. You said Emilio killed Carol. Wouldn't it make more sense that Coombs killed her? He had a stone knife like the one used to murder Mrs. Putman."

"On the surface, it would. But he didn't do it. Coombs worked for the Indians, but he was freelancing as well. He was a desert guide. He knew more about this area than any outsider and most local ranchers and real estate people. So he was paid to help some people find the ships and other unique things in the desert. He also knew about the treasure, and knew Carol and Emilio found it."

"I still don't get it." Paul shook his head. "We were just after the minerals like you said."

Virginia nodded. "Paul, this gets even more convoluted. Let's settle the part about the meteor and the mines first. You, Paul, and you, James, work for Litio Products and are midlevel employees. At least you are Paul. NMMA is a partial owner of your company and found out about the meteor from your laboratory. They wanted the lithium, the meteor, and the mine. One specific mine, that in reality, is a cave.

"The thing about the proposal is, the uranium mine that was discussed was not the actual uranium mine on my ranch. The location in the proposal is at the exact latitude and longitude of the cave where the drugs were made. That cave happens to have a boatload of palladium in it. It will be the richest palladium mine in the U.S. or North America for that matter, if I let someone mine the thing. Paul, you knew about the palladium, but didn't tell me. That's what NMMA wanted. By mentioning a uranium mine instead of the cave, your management figured I would go along with the proposal and not notice the discrepancy. After all, I'm just a beach type, dumb blonde."

Virginia fished a pearl from her pocket and showed it to Paul and James. "But you also wanted the treasure for yourselves. Looking for lost treasure would be a natural thing to do. There's really no law against it except trespassing. Hiring Baker and the others to do your dirty work was your mistake. Baker had an ego problem and kept trying to be the big man on campus, if you will. That didn't bode well for him."

Paul looked down and sighed. "Yes. Litio Products is part of NMMA. That's not a secret or a crime. We didn't hire Baker. The owner of NMMA did that. After the report came back about the lithium, the palladium, and the meteor, the head honcho, who I don't know personally, gave the orders to get the rights and to secure the treasure any way possible. Baker was to be used if we couldn't get the rights. He got way out of hand. Paul glanced at James. "James, do you know who the head man is who's been calling the shots?"

James sat stone-faced.

Virginia stuck her hands in her jeans pockets. "Paul, *you* didn't hire Baker. James did. James is the top banana... one of the big guys at NMMA. He's part of a consortium that runs it. How long have you two actually known each other, or worked together?"

Paul sighed, then pursed his lips and thought. "Well... a little before we were sent out here. James was to be the senior man. I was sent here on assignment to support him." He glared at James. "You've been behind this all along? You're the mysterious head guy? Why? Are you behind Mrs. Putman's death, too?"

James looked at the rug. "What Virginia said is true. But I had nothing to do with Mrs. Putman's murder. I found out Baker was a loose cannon too late. He had his own agenda. Before I could stop him, he got arrested. Then he escaped. He disappeared. I didn't know where the hell he went. I didn't hire the other thugs who were with him, though. They were his addition to the group. I heard Baker went after the treasure the other night. I never told him to do that. I got a call from someone who was in the desert when things went wrong for Baker. Someone else knew he worked for us. But they knew Baker was out there, and I didn't. They reported Baker's vehicle being towed. As to the treasure, you are right, Virginia. Paul and I were looking for it and the ships as a lark. We heard about it and figured, while we were out here, we'd go treasure hunting."

"That confirms part of what's been going on." Virginia cracked a smile. "It gets better. Someone's been making drugs on my ranch. They tried to kill Donna and me when we found the cave where their lab was located."

Paul tensed. "Drugs?" He looked at James. "You know anything about this? Were drugs involved?" He wiped his palms on his pant legs and gave Virginia a pleading look. "I didn't know anything about a drug lab."

James had a blank expression. "Drug lab? I don't know anything about drugs being involved either."

Virginia took a breath. "I thought everything had to do with the treasure, my meteor, and the mines, maybe even the palladium. I was wrong. Somehow a drug lab was involved, too. Which means, someone else involved," Virginia said. "I have to admit, the drug lab was a surprise."

Virginia continued, "Someone was making drugs in a deep cave on a mountain in the southern part of my ranch. They made top-notch drugs, including high-grade oxycodone and ultrapure fentanyl. They also sold some of the fentanyl cut with carfentanil."

Paul looked confused. "What's carfentanil?"

"It's a powerful animal tranquilizer that is used on huge mammals such as elephants, and hippos. Even a small amount is fatal to humans." Virginia turned and looked at Juan. "It's what you used on the guy who attacked us when you shot him with a tranquilizer."

Juan jumped to his feet and started to pull a knife, then stopped. He stared at Donna, sitting across from him, aiming her pistol at him.

Virginia spoke in a soft, even tone. "Put the knife down, Juan, and sit. I won't tell you again. I'd hate to have Donna mess up the décor with your blood."

He glanced at Liana. She motioned for him to obey Donna. He laid the knife on the floor and sat.

Ferguson started to stand, and then noticing Donna's gun swing toward him, sat. "Don't point that thing at me, young lady. That could be considered a felony."

Donna smiled. "I'll chance it. Stay put." She glanced at Virginia. "Please continue."

The phone rang. Donna answered the extension on the table next to her chair. "Hello, B Bar P Ranch. This is Donna." She listened, thanked the caller and hung up. She motioned for Virginia to come to her and whispered in Virginia's ear.

"Thanks." Virginia turned back to the group. "That was the SCSS. The NSA traced an incoming call to a phone belonging to a man who attacked my house. The cell originated from a cell phone moving between Riverside and Palm Springs."

Virginia looked around the room. "Where was I? Oh, yes, the thing was, someone knew what Donna and I were doing as we did it. So, we had a mole. Juan was part of that. I know the ranch telephone landline is tapped, and he was listening in on the calls. Also, I had no idea we had drones until a little while ago. Liana, you've been watching us out there all the time. I looked at the memory chips and found a section that wasn't erased and some more of them stored in the barn. Also, what kind of ranch has a sophisticated GPS tracking system like the government? None."

Ferguson's furrowed his brow. "How do you explain the jeweler being murdered?"

"The people behind the drug lab had him killed, then killed the murderer."

"The jeweler was looking at pearls." Ferguson knitted his brow. "But the jeweler called Coombs. It was about the treasure."

"Poor Mr. Coombs was a go-between. But this gets interesting. The Mr. Frank Coombs we all knew was not the real guy. The real Mr. Coombs died of a heroin overdose in LA a few years ago. The fake Mr. Coombs is… was Gordon Longfellow. He was Coombs's cellmate in prison and looked a lot like him. He was from 29 Palms and knew the area. He knew about the treasure and the ships from stories Coombs told him in prison and from living not too far away. Once the real Coombs was dead, Longfellow took his place. He posed as Coombs with us, and the Indians. He was caught between being killed or cooperating with the bad guys. Like I said earlier, he was a freelance desert guide. Besides working for the Indians, he did other work for a variety of folks. Only this time, as a paid informant of the Bureau of Indian Affairs and DEA, he got into deeper water than he planned. The DEA didn't know he wasn't the real Mr. Coombs either until after he died. The treasure was located where the drug people set up their lab. Only they didn't know it because the treasure was moved before they got there. His ID as an informant got to the wrong people. This is when things got messy. When Longfellow was at the hospital waiting to find out about Emilio, he was drugged. According to the autopsy Longfellow was given a cocktail of synthetic amphetamines and hallucinogens, commonly known as "bath salts. That caused his sudden change in behavior, his wanting to attack Emilio, and consequently his violent outburst when he saw Donna and tried to stab her. He really didn't know what he was doing. But I found out about this after the coroner gave the autopsy report to the Sheriff's office and Detective Ferguson. The coroner also gave a copy to me. It was the coroner who finally identified him." She turned toward Ferguson. "You were going to tell me about that, weren't you, since you found out before the coroner?"

He stared at her.

Virginia continued. "The poison was in the coffee a fake male nurse delivered to the waiting room at the hospital. I found out there were no male nurses assigned to that floor on that shift. Good thing Donna and I didn't drink it. Longfellow's job was three-fold. To secure certain mineral rights for the Indians, be a DEA snitch, and keep me from investigating the area where the drug lab was. He was murdered to prevent him from talking. Longfellow was considered a loose end by the drug people."

Virginia faced the group. "The drug lab is serious business. And I know who is behind the lab." Virginia let the statement hang in the air.

Finally, James frowned and looked around. "The drug leader is here?"

"Yes."

"Who is it?"

Virginia pointed. "It's Liana and Juan."

Liana jumped to her feet. "You said Emilio was behind the treasure and drugs."

"Emilio wanted the treasure. He couldn't get it because Carol had secured it extremely well. He'd been selling antiquities, gold, silver, copper, and turquoise he stole from the ranch and saved a lot of money in various bank accounts. I had the SCSS look into his banking activities. The treasure, which is worth a fortune, was out of his reach. He heard about the value of the meteor and about the NMMA after he learned about a meteor in the Mediterranean that is similar to mine. They were both parts of the same big meteor that broke apart when it hit the earth's atmosphere. They both had the nanothingies. They are worth a lot of money. He knew about the palladium too, but not what it was worth. But while trying to figure out how to capitalize on the value of the meteor, Emilio was approached to make drugs by a person who was the leader of the drug lab, along with a crooked drug chemist. Emilio knew of a large cave with a freshwater stream that was well hidden they could use. He partnered with the drug people and made a lot of quick cash without having to know how to actually make the drugs. He tried to hide it in multiple bank accounts. Hiding money isn't in his skill set. Emilio recruited and paid Liana and Juan to help him with the drug operation. They used the drones to keep watch on the ranch for anyone getting close to the lab. They also used them to fly product out if it looked like there were too many cops in the area. When Carol was about to find the drug lab, Emilio panicked and killed her. He used an ancient stone knife. He had a few around here and knew Coombs… Longfellow had one or more, too. Using the knife made Coombs look suspicious and threw the spotlight off him, and anyone on the ranch."

Ferguson looked confused. "So, Emilio killed Mrs. Putman and Mr. Coombs, or Longfellow as you stated, and was part of the drug lab operation. Emilio also took minerals off the ranch without permission and had people try and steal the treasure."

Virginia nodded.

"But Liana protected you by blowing up some men who were going to kill you at the cave."

Ferguson knows about that? Good. More confirmation. "Yes, she did. Thank you for that, Liana. She couldn't let them kill us. That would be bad for business and cause for another investigation, probably by the FBI or DEA. Maybe the men she blew up were acting on their own. We'll probably never know. She said she tried to drop her bomb to scare them and missed. Trying to drop an explosive package from a moving drone at an altitude of about a thousand feet, near the side of a mountain, and make a direct hit without an expensive bombsight is almost impossible. I think she really did mean to scare them away. But she did miss her target and hit them. Personally, I was happy with the outcome."

"So, what does the NMMA have to do with all this besides wanting the mineral rights?" Ferguson asked. "What did they want with the ships and the treasure?"

CHAPTER 40

Virginia glanced around the living room and took a breath. "Emilio invested in Litio Products when he learned they were interested in the steam vents and extracting lithium. That was just before he learned about the value of the meteor and NMMA. Emilio didn't know a lot about the palladium though. He knew James and Paul worked for Litio Products. James and Paul were looking for the ships and the treasure as well, but for themselves. There's nothing wrong with that. They had nothing to do with the actual murders. In reality, NMMA didn't have anything to do with Carol's murder, either."

"What happened to Baker and his group?" Ferguson asked. "Baker has disappeared."

"When Donna and I found the ships, we went on board. Baker and his gang of thugs thought they'd follow us. Then, when we found the ships and the treasure they'd move in and take it and kill us. The treasure wasn't there. They attacked us with guns. We defended ourselves and blew up the whole shebang. The ships, and Baker, and his friends are out there somewhere in the desert in multiple small pieces, buried under many, many tons of sand. You went looking for them in an airplane, Detective."

Ferguson shifted uncomfortably in his seat. "Yes, I did. I couldn't find them. You were going to also tell me about that little incident sometime, weren't you?"

"Of course."

Ferguson shifted in his seat. "So, Emilio, an illegal immigrant, invested in Litio Products. He also was selling stolen minerals on the black market under Mrs. Putman's nose and helped build a drug lab on the ranch. He masterminded the whole thing? That's hard to believe."

"You are correct. He couldn't have done it all by himself. Liana and Juan helped. Liana had the inside track on what was going on with Carol and the ranch on a daily basis. Liana could keep an eye on Carol's activities, and the mines with the drones. She had a sophisticated GPS tracking system, too. Liana could watch Carol's movement, even off the ranch. Those are things most ranches don't have. Like I said, the drones were really for watching the ranch for possible drug raids by police or other crooks. I saw some footage from a memory chip showing the surveillance. Oh, the SCSS found that Liana has a B.S. degree in physics from a university in Morelia, Michoacán, Mexico." She looked around the room. "Emilio and Juan could and did make sure none of the other hired ranch hands got in the way."

Virginia grinned. "I failed to mention that the SCSS had a government satellite from another agency make some flights over the ranch for a while. It's used mostly for border security and catching drug runners. They flew it over the ranch just a few times. It's expensive so it wasn't overhead much. The satellite spotted some strange activity in the area of the cave where the drug lab was when the equipment was being removed. That was not long before Donna, and I stumbled onto it. They also got pictures of the fake Coombs and Emilio's fight. That's how I knew the fake Coombs didn't have a gun. The satellite captured some photos I couldn't quite figure out until just a while ago."

Ferguson stood, pulled out handcuffs and told Liana to turn around. He handcuffed her. He motioned for Juan to stay in his seat. Ferguson looked at Virginia. "You guys have any plastic ties?"

Donna jumped up. "Yes, in the kitchen. I'll get some." She rushed into the kitchen.

Virginia smiled at Ferguson. "Thanks for coming, Detective."

"No problem. I have to admit, you two are good."

"Thank you, Detective," Donna said when she returned with the plastic ties. "But you should step aside and put your hands behind your back, too."

Ferguson swung around starting to draw his sidearm. "What is the meaning—" He stared at Donna's gun, then let out a breath. "When did you know?"

Virginia motioned for him to put his gun down. He laid it on the floor and sat.

Virginia eyed Liana and Juan. "Don't even think of trying to escape. Either Donna or I will shoot you if you do." Virginia picked up the detective's gun and stuck it in her waistband. "When the jeweler was killed, you were on the scene faster than the Palm Springs police. It was their problem, not the sheriff's. You were in the plane looking for the ships and Baker when he and his crew disappeared after they attacked us. You knew about where to go look for Baker. I never told you. You responded to the hospital when Donna shot Coombs, really Longfellow, even though it's not in your normal prevue. The hospital is in a city with its own police department. You just mentioned the men trying to kill us at the cave. Donna and I didn't tell you. Someone else had to. When Carol was murdered, you were seen talking in the shadows with someone who was never mentioned in your report. I finally figured out who was you were talking to in the corner by the mine. It was Emilio. The drone Liana was flying had a picture of the two of you. She didn't erase all the video memory. You made a deal with Emilio. Emilio wasn't the drug leader. You were, Detective Ferguson."

Ferguson sat back. "That's all supposition and easily explained. No court will buy that."

Virginia shrugged. "We'll see. But let me continue. You wouldn't and couldn't arrest Emilio because he was part of your drug operation. If things weren't going your way, you were going to kill him and blame others like you did with the jeweler. The Palm Springs coroner discovered that the jeweler was killed with a cocktail of fentanyl cut with carfentanil. You also commented on the played out mines. As you know, they aren't played out. Baker had assistance when he escaped custody. No one knew the route the officers transporting him were taking except the U.S. Park Service Rangers, and you. Also, you were the person who told James about Baker's vehicle being impounded. I called the sheriff to have it towed. You knew that."

Virginia looked at James, then back at Ferguson. "James may have hired Baker, but you, Detective, bought his loyalty. You knew Baker's record and that he was in it for the quick buck and part of the treasure. He'd easily and quickly trade sides for more money. That's how you knew about where to look with the plane. The sitrep call to the thug that attacked me here at the ranch came from a cell phone moving between Riverside and here. I answered it, but it was quickly turned off, and couldn't be traced after that. But you were driving down here when the call was made. I bet we find the phone when we search your police vehicle. The GPS in your county car will show where you were when that phone as used. Won't take much to compare your location with the phone's pinging off towers or however the NSA found it. It turns out that Carol did have some suspicions about what was going on and wrote them down. She also named who she suspected and why. It was on a note I found rolled up in the binding of the big glowing quilt here.

"I asked the SCSS and DEA to look into your banking records and the movement of large sums of money in Riverside County, especially Palm Springs, and Imperial County areas, and L.A." Virginia leaned against a bookcase. "After eliminating legitimate organizations, and banks, they looked at suspicious transfers. The SCSS, DEA asked the IRS for assistance. The IRS found you, Detective. You were behind the drug lab operation. You tried to hide it with multiple wire transfers, fake businesses, personal bank accounts, and rapid movement of money to offshore banks. You weren't as smart as you thought. The IRS forensic accountants found it all pretty quickly. You were in it for the drug money. You had little interest in the meteor, the palladium, or the lithium. I guess you figured your county pension either wouldn't be enough to live on in the style you wanted or figured it might not be there at all when it came time for you to retire. Investments on your eighty-five grand salary are hard with your living expenses here in California. Being divorced and paying child support payments cuts into it. And your new, pretty, younger, trophy wife has very expensive tastes."

Virginia shook her head. "Men. You should have gone after the palladium. Emilio knew it was in the drug cave but didn't grasp the significance. It's extremely valuable and stealing it doesn't carry the same sentence as making and distributing illegal and dangerous drugs. Especially drugs laced with poison. Why would you poison your customers? Crazy. The DEA will be filing charges soon. Oh, yeah, this is the best one, the IRS is formulating tax fraud and other tax-related charges against you as well. If I were you, I'd be afraid of them most of all." Virginia smiled. "Detective Ferguson, Liana, and Juan, you are all under arrest. Federal Marshals have taken Emilio into custody at the hospital. He has been talking to them. He's naming people involved in the drug operation and other crimes and telling them where to find evidence. Even after the deputy marshals advised him of his rights and to get a lawyer, the marshals can't shut him up. Emilio figured the first person to turn state's evidence had the best shot at leniency. He's probably right."

Paul looked shell-shocked. "I can't believe it. This was all going on around me, and I had no idea." He looked at Virginia and Donna. "What are you going to do with the ranch?"

Virginia heard Donna on the phone calling for back up and prisoner transport. *The next few days will be nothing but paperwork and meetings with all kinds of lawyers. Oh, joy.* Virginia shrugged. "Well... I thought I'd negotiate with the Indians about mining the copper, silver, gold, and turquoise. If everything checks out with my lawyer, accountant, and engineer, Litio products might be doing the lithium extraction. The Smithsonian, UCR, and the University of Texas will get to investigate the meteor. My museum in Texas, UCI, and the Smithsonian will get to study the petroglyphs. I'll think about doing something with the palladium later."

She plopped onto a chair, keeping a watch on the prisoners. Virginia continued, "I need to find someone, or a reliable property management company, to run the ranch for me until I figure out what to do with the rest of it. The artifacts stored with the treasure will be split between my museum in Texas, the one in Palm Springs, and the Smithsonian. But a large part of the artifacts will go to the local Indians as well. Getting all that done will take some time."

Virginia glanced out the window, and then looked back at the group. "The money I make from the Indians and Litio Products will go toward the upkeep of the ranch and the medical bills for the tribe members who worked here and helped Carol with her glowing dyes. They were exposed to, and ingested radioactive materials and developed cancer like Carol did. They have about a year left to live. The proceeds will then be used to set up a trust fund to take care of their families after they die and provide college scholarships for their children if they want to go to college. The sad thing is Carol had about six months left to live because of the radiation. Her murder caused all this crime to be exposed. Because of her murder, Donna and I investigated. If she were left alone with just her suspicions and cancer, nothing probably would have happened."

"That sounds great." James gave her a sheepish grin. "What are you going to do with Paul and me?"

She smiled. "We're considering charges under Title 18, USC Sections 6 and 8 and section 1170. And criminal trespass."

Paul furrowed his brow. "What are those statues?"

"Art theft and transferring of Native American artifacts and cultural and physical remains without a permit. All federal felonies. Trespassing is a state offense."

James looked deflated. "Oh. But... but... never mind."

Donna smiled and spoke. "You were primarily looking for the ships of the desert, and treasure, and not deliberately trying to steal any Indian artifacts or remains. The fake antique shop was yours, but unknown to you, it had been taken over by the drug guys. You guys used it as a staging area. The drug folks used it as a transfer site. Sorry about that. The old guy who worked there for you was also doing the shipping for the drug people. He was being paid twice for being there. When we showed up, he panicked. You know what happened to him. Oh, the county wants to fine you for operating an antique store without a license. But... you two didn't actually do anything *too* wrong or *too* illegal, and you had nothing to do with the drugs, and... well, Virginia and I like you, we've asked the U.S. Attorney to not charge you with anything. He agreed."

"He did? Wonderful. Thank you." James looked curious. "Got more cases to investigate? Anything you're looking forward to?"

Virginia's face brightened. "Yes. My husband and I are going to attend an estate auction where an old ship's log or captain's diary and very old quilt are up for sale. That should be fun and harmless.

ABOUT THE AUTHOR

Dr. David Ciambrone is a retired aerospace and defense company executive, scientist, professor of engineering, and a business and environmental consultant and is now a best-selling, award-winning author living in Georgetown, Texas with his wife Kathy. He has published twenty-five (25) books: four (4) non-fiction, two (2) textbooks for a California university, and nineteen (19) mysteries and has two (2) new mysteries in work. He is the author of the Virginia Davies Quilt Mysteries.

Dave has been a speaker at writer's groups, schools, colleges, libraries, quilt guilds, writer's conferences, and business/scientific conferences internationally.

Dr. Ciambrone also wrote three newspaper columns and wrote a column for a business journal.

Dave is a member of Sisters in Crime, the San Gabriel Writer's League, the Writer's League of Texas, Mystery Writers of America, the International Thriller Writers Association, The Beacon Society, and DFW Sherlock Homes Society.

Dave was appointed a U.S. Treasury Commissioner and to the management board of the Resolution Trust Corporation (RTC) by President Clinton.

He is a Fellow of the International Oceanographic Foundation.

Visit David at

Author's Website:davidciambrone.com

Facebook:facebook.com/david.ciambrone?fref=ts

Twitter: twitter.com/mysterywriter5

LinkedIn: linkedin.com/pub/david-ciambrone-sc-d-fiof/11/ab5/bb3

Amazon: amazon.com/author/davidciambrone

Progressive Rising Phoenix Press is an independent publisher. We offer wholesale pricing and multiple binding options with no minimum purchases for schools, libraries, book clubs, and retail vendors. We offer substantial discounts on bulk orders and discounts on individual sales through our online store. Please visit our website at:
www.ProgressiveRisingPhoenix.com

If you enjoyed reading this book, please review it on Amazon, B & N, or Goodreads.
Thank you in advance!

www.ingramcontent.com/pod-product-compliance
Lightning Source LLC
LaVergne TN
LVHW010256260326
834688LV00044B/1312